AIR RAID

Eileen Enwright Hodgetts

978-0-9982154-8-8

CHAPTER ONE

February 1952
Brighton, England
Anthea Clark

Anthea Clark was shocked. If her gray hair had not been constrained by a quantity of hairpins, she was quite certain it would have stood on end. So great was her shock that she forgot herself entirely and actually questioned her employer's plans.

"Surely not, Mr. Champion; you could not possibly be thinking of sending Mr. Whitby. He's so young and he has only just qualified and …"

"And what?"

"He's rather shy; he's not very good at conversation."

Mr. Champion considered his secretary through ancient rheumy eyes. "He will not be required to engage in conversation. This is not a social event and we have no one else, Miss Clark. Mr. Whitby will have to rise to the occasion."

Anthea expressed her disapproval of the decision by turning away from Mr. Champion and staring down at the body on the floor. Robert Alderton, Mr. Champion's junior partner in the firm of Champion and Company, Solicitors at Law, had bled profusely from a head wound. The blood had pooled on the oriental rug, and the police had tracked carelessly through the blood. She could see the imprint of their heavy boots on the various legal papers scattered around the floor.

Anthea shivered in the cold wind that blew in through the open windows, carrying the scent of the ocean and the calling of seagulls. The police would not allow her to close the windows until they had finished their assessment of the scene of the crime.

Mr. Champion maneuvered carefully around the windblown papers on the floor and examined the files on his late partner's desk.

"It's not there," Anthea blurted out. "I've already looked."

"I see."

Mr. Champion seemed momentarily nonplussed. He stared hopefully at the bloodstained papers on the floor, but Anthea shook her head. "I've looked everywhere. The Southwold file isn't here."

She took a deep breath and made a second attempt to sway her employer's opinion. "I don't see how Mr. Whitby can be of any use if he doesn't have the file."

Mr. Champion straightened his frail frame and assumed an expression of stubborn determination. "We have never let the Southwold family down, and we will not do so now. Mr. Whitby will go to Southwold Hall."

A policeman entered without knocking. Anthea resisted the temptation to rebuke him. This was a legal office; highly confidential papers were scattered around the room and should not be disturbed by flat-footed men in blue. On the other hand, and she had to be reasonable about this, Mr. Alderton was quite obviously the victim of a murder. She attributed her ability to remain calm in the face of such violence to her recent years in London. She had lived through the Blitz. She had seen bodies lying in the street, and many of them had not died as tidily or easily as Mr. Alderton. She had walked to work some mornings past shattered houses and stepped over body parts, a hand, a leg, a torso.

It was not the sight of Mr. Alderton's dead body that shocked her, or even the fact that he was so obviously the victim of foul play; she would think about all of that later, when she was alone. What shocked her now was Mr. Champion's decision to send young Toby Whitby to keep Mr. Alderton's appointment with the Earl of Southwold.

She blamed Mr. Champion's lack of judgment on the fact that he, unlike Anthea, had been very upset at finding his junior partner dead on the floor. She placed a tentative hand under her employer's elbow and felt him lean his weight against her. Yes, he was far more shocked than he was willing to admit. She would lead him back to his office and give him a cup of sweet tea, and in a few minutes, she would return alone to look for the missing file.

Toby Whitby was in his office; a small cramped room suited to his position as a junior associate. He had left his door open and was obviously watching the comings and goings of the men in blue. When he saw Anthea leading Mr. Champion away from the scene of the crime, he hurried forward.

"What's happened? What's going on? The police say it's murder."

Anthea sniffed her disapproval. "You should know better than to talk to the police."

Toby's eyes were bright and challenging behind the thick lenses of his spectacles. "I'm not talking to them, Miss Clark, they're talking to me."

He'd be a good-looking young man, Anthea thought, if he took off those glasses. She dismissed the thought immediately. She was old enough to be Toby Whitby's mother, and she had no business even noticing the way his brown hair curled or the length of his legs or the strength in his hands as he helped her keep Edwin Champion upright.

"Whitby!" Mr. Champion's voice was no more than a croak, but it was a determined croak. "You will keep Mr. Alderton's appointment with the Earl of Southwold. Leave immediately or you will be late. The Earl doesn't like to be kept waiting."

Anthea saw desperation in Toby's look as he protested. "Surely, in the circumstances, we could postpone it."

Mr. Champion shook his head. "Champion and Company never postpones. We serve at our client's convenience."

"But in the circumstances—"

"The circumstances do not concern our client."

"But I need time to read the file."

Mr. Champion sighed impatiently. "There is no file."

Anthea locked eyes with Toby and shook her head. "We don't know where it is. It should have been in his office or in his briefcase, but it's not there."

Toby glanced toward Alderton's office, where the victim's feet were visible through the open door. "Was that why he was murdered? Did someone want the file?"

Mr. Champion shook his head. "Stuff and nonsense!"

Anthea thought that her employer's declaration lacked conviction, but she resisted the urge to ask questions.

"Come and sit down, Mr. Champion. I'll make you a nice cup of tea."

Mr. Champion shook off Toby's supporting arm. "Get on with it, Whitby, and don't be late."

Toby Whitby

Toby drove along the coast road from Brighton to Southwold Hall with his mind reeling from the shock of Alderton's death. Someone had entered through a window, or so the police believed, and delivered a blow to Alderton's head; a blow that had killed him. The motive was not the theft of Mr. Alderton's valuables. The only thing missing from the office was the Southwold file. He had no idea what that file had contained, although he suspected that Mr. Champion knew more than he was telling. Now he was making his way toward Southwold Hall for a meeting with the Earl on a matter that seemed to have cost Mr. Alderton his life.

He rebuked himself for being dramatic. This was nothing to do with the Southwold file. Alderton had a reputation as a lady-killer. His end had probably come at the hands of a jealous husband. The police would soon get to the bottom of it, and the missing file would turn up in someone else's filing cabinet.

The day was clear and sunny with a cold wind blowing in from the Channel. The chill wind cut through the thin fabric of Toby's overcoat as he stood on the doorstep of Southwold Hall. He took off his glasses and wiped them clean before pulling on the rope that he assumed would ring a bell somewhere within the cavernous interior of the Hall.

The great oak door opened slowly, revealing a plump smiling girl in a gray dress and white apron. He had expected a butler, but perhaps butlers were in short supply along with everything else in postwar Britain. Apparently, even the Earl of Southwold with all of his royal connections had been unable to find a suitable retainer.

"Hello," said the girl. Her smile was warm and welcoming, and she was very young, perhaps no more than fifteen, making her only half the age of Toby.

"Toby Whitby, Champion and Company, to see the Earl," said Toby.

A thin woman in a similar gray dress but minus the apron elbowed the smiling girl aside.

"I'll take care of this."

The woman was old enough to have been the girl's mother, but there was nothing maternal about her pinched face and disapproving frown. She looked Toby up and down noting, Toby was sure, his inexpensive and ill-fitting suit, and the thickness of his glasses betraying the extreme shortsightedness that had kept him out of the war.

"I have an appointment with the Earl," Toby said.

"Really?"

The housekeeper, if that was what she was, seemed not only suspicious but also somewhat affronted. Toby wondered if he should have gone to the tradesman's entrance. No, he reassured himself, he was a fully qualified solicitor, albeit very newly qualified, and he had every right to use the front door.

"Where is Mr. Alderton? We usually see Mr. Alderton."

Toby knew he would have to tell someone what had happened to Robert Alderton, but telling the housekeeper would be inappropriate. He would tell the Earl and only the Earl.

"Mr. Alderton was not available, so I'm here." He took a step forward and crossed the imposing threshold. "Mr. Champion has asked me personally to take care of the Earl's affairs for the time being."

He took another step and established a foothold in the marble-tiled entryway.

The housekeeper, forced into a retreat by Toby's determination, rounded on the young maid.

"Go about your business, Maisie, and don't be listening to your betters."

The rebuke was like water off a duck's back to the cheerful child, who maintained her breezy smile as she curtsied and disappeared from sight.

Having established that both she and Toby were higher in the pecking order than a mere maid, the housekeeper ducked behind Toby and closed the front door.

Toby looked up and saw an imposing stairway leading to a wide landing lit by stained-glass panels that had somehow survived the bombing raids. He squinted to bring the panels into better focus and made out the crest and shield of the Southwold family, an honor awarded for service to some long-dead monarch.

He reined in his wandering thoughts of monarchs and war damage, handed his hat and coat to the housekeeper, and smoothed his unruly brown hair.

"If you could tell the Earl that I'm here …"

A voice floated down to him from somewhere above. "It's all right, Mrs. Pearson, I'll take care of this."

She was tall and dark haired, dressed entirely in black apart from a small string of pearls around her neck. With a sinking heart, Toby realized his mistake. He should have worn a black tie or a mourning band. The whole nation was mourning the death of George VI, the king who led them through the war. This woman was an aristocrat; she probably knew the King personally, and no doubt she knew Princess Elizabeth, who was now queen, and here he was wearing a red tie. Why hadn't Mr. Champion warned him? He could have purchased a black tie in Brighton before he set out.

Mrs. Pearson looked at Toby's tie as though it was an object beneath her contempt, but she took a step backward and acknowledged the woman in black with a respectful gesture.

"Lady Sylvia."

Lady Sylvia paused on the bottom step of the grand staircase and looked at Toby with a mixture of suspicion and condescension.

"We were expecting Mr. Alderton."

"Mr. Alderton was … unwell. My name is Whitby, Toby Whitby. I am a fully qualified solicitor."

Lady Sylvia offered him a tight smile. "Newly qualified?"

"Yes, but—"

Lady Sylvia descended the last step and held out a slim white hand.

"I'm sorry to hear that Mr. Alderton is … unwell."

Toby thought that Lady Sylvia had hesitated over her use of words. Did she know something? Did she already know that Alderton was dead;

and not just dead, murdered? Had it been on the radio?

Her Ladyship was still speaking, still holding out her hand. "I'm glad that Mr. Alderton has sent me a young person. Mr. Champion and Mr. Alderton seem so set in their ways. Perhaps you will be more flexible than they are."

Toby's studies under the tutelage of Edwin Champion had not covered the possibility of any flexibility in the law. Mr. Champion had, however, emphasized the importance of the patronage of the widowed Earl of Southwold and his only child, his daughter, Lady Sylvia. Toby took Lady Sylvia's extended hand and gave her a noncommittal smile.

Lady Sylvia freed her hand. "Tea," she said. It was not a question, simply an instruction to Mrs. Pearson.

The housekeeper, who had not yet managed even a hint of a smile, nodded sullenly and turned on her heel. Toby followed Lady Sylvia into a book-lined room that she identified as her father's library. She seated herself on a chintz-covered sofa and indicated that Toby should make himself comfortable on a battered leather wing chair drawn up close to the glowing coal fire.

"Unfortunately," said Lady Sylvia, "my father is unwell and will not be able to see you today."

She could have phoned, Toby thought. She could have given us time to find the file; maybe go to Alderton's flat to see if he had left it there. He tried to suppress his irritation. He had no prior experience of the aristocracy, and he was not sure whether it was reasonable to expect an aristocrat to make phone calls purely for the convenience of insignificant, newly qualified solicitors.

"I'm sorry," Toby said, struggling to keep his irritation from showing. "Perhaps I could return another day."

Lady Sylvia's voice was firm and determined. "Oh no. We must do this today. Enough time has been wasted already."

She leaned forward fixing him with a wide-eyed gaze. Her eyes were bright blue in contrast to her pale skin and midnight-black hair. He thought that she could have been pretty, maybe even beautiful, but there was a quality of aloof coldness in her eyes and a determined set to her mouth that created a zone of hostility around her.

"Cigarettes," said Lady Sylvia.

Toby anxiously considered the contents of his pockets. He had left home with half a packet of Woodbines, and he'd smoked a couple in the office and one in the car on the way to Southwold Hall. How many were left? If there was only one left in the packet, should he offer it to her? Would a lady of her breeding even smoke a Woodbine, the cheapest cigarette on the market?

"They're killing him," said Lady Sylvia. "That's what killed His

Majesty."

"Cigarettes?"

"Yes, cigarettes. No one is going to actually say it; no one will say the C word, but that's what it was; lung cancer. His Majesty was a smoker, always had a cigarette in his mouth, not in public, of course, but on social occasions."

She sighed. "It's too late for the King, and it's too late for my father. He's going downhill fast and still puffing away on the cigarettes. I doubt if he will be around for the coronation."

She closed her eyes for a moment, her face assembled into an expression of sorrow, although Toby saw no softening of her features. He reminded himself that her ancestors would have led the troops at Waterloo and Gallipoli, maybe even at Agincourt. Lady Sylvia was made of strong stuff.

She sighed again. "It will all fall on my shoulders; I'm the only heir. Fortunately, the estate has no ridiculous stipulations about the title only descending to the men of the family."

"So you will be ..." Toby hesitated, his mind suddenly blank. She wouldn't be the Earl, so what would she be?

Lady Sylvia supplied the answer without Toby asking the question. "I will be Countess of Southwold. It will be my responsibility to hold Southwold in trust for future generations."

Her eyelids closed briefly, the dark lashes fanning out across her pale cheeks, her expression unreadable.

The door of the study banged open, and Mrs. Pearson entered followed by the young maid who was pushing a laden tea trolley. Lady Sylvia, the future countess, opened her eyes and regarded Mrs. Pearson and her offerings.

"I'll pour," she said. "Perhaps you could take a cup of tea to Daddy. Please do it personally, Mrs. Pearson, you know how much he likes your company."

Mrs. Pearson's smile was small, tight, and spiteful as she brushed her helper aside.

"You can go back into the kitchen, Maisie. You're not needed here."

The girl bobbed a curtsey and abandoned her post beside the tea trolley. Lady Sylvia poured milk into a bone china cup, added tea from the silver teapot, and handed it to Mrs. Pearson.

"Tell him I'll be up shortly," she said, and Mrs. Pearson removed herself from the room, closing the door behind her.

"So," said Lady Sylvia, her hand steady as she poured Toby's tea from the heavy silver pot, "we come to the delicate part of our discussion."

Toby took the proffered teacup and decided to remain silent. Perhaps she would tell him what he needed to know, and he would not have to reveal the loss of the file or the unfortunate fate of his predecessor.

"It's a question of the future succession," Lady Sylvia said, "of what will happen when I am gone."

"Oh, but you're young," Toby protested.

Lady Sylvia's voice was cold. "If you consult your files, you will see that I am thirty years old. You will also see that I have no husband."

With no file to consult, Toby found himself blustering inappropriately. "There's plenty of time. You'll find a husband."

He could hardly believe that the words had come from his mouth; that he had implied that Lady Sylvia would go out like some pagan huntress to find a husband.

Lady Sylvia threw him a chilling glance. "Please do not presume to know my future. You're here in a professional capacity, and I have no need of comforting or consoling words."

Toby felt the blood rise in his cheeks as he stammered an apology.

"Allow me to continue," said Lady Sylvia.

"Of course."

Toby sipped his tea and kept his eyes fixed on the carpet, a faded oriental, no doubt the spoils of some empire-building endeavor by one of Lady Sylvia's ancestors.

"I will not produce children to inherit the estate," said Lady Sylvia. "I am not able."

Toby shifted uncomfortably in his seat, and the tea spilled into his saucer.

Lady Sylvia sighed. "Does this embarrass you? I had hoped you would be able to be professional about this."

Toby fought down a desire to stalk out of the room and leave Lady Sylvia to her own devices. However, he was not here on his own account, he was here to represent Champion and Company. He would swallow his pride and stay.

He lifted his eyes from the teacup and looked her full in the face. "I am not embarrassed."

"Are you married, Mr. Whitby?"

"No," said Toby, thinking about how little success he had achieved in his relationship with women.

Lady Sylvia raised her delicate eyebrows. "I would prefer to discuss this with a more experienced man. Mr. Alderton was not married, but he was a man of the world."

Toby caught his breath. She was referring to Alderton in the past tense. She knew something. Maybe it had been on the radio.

"Mr. Alderton has …" He could not think of the polite way to express what had happened to Robert Alderton. Passed away? Met his maker? Kicked the bucket? Shuffled off this mortal coil?

Lady Sylvia raised inquiring eyebrows.

Toby abandoned euphemisms. "Mr. Alderton is dead, and I'm the only solicitor in the office apart from Mr. Champion."

He waited for her to question him. How had Mr. Alderton died? Had he been sick? Was it an accident?

Lady Sylvia showed no emotion beyond mild irritation. "In the circumstances, I suppose you will have to do. I am willing to set aside the unfortunate fact that you are so very inexperienced. Let us continue with our discussion."

She paused and sipped her tea.

"I had already discussed the inheritance with Mr. Alderton, and we had already made some preliminary inquiries."

"I see," said Toby, although he would be hard put to say exactly what he could see. He reached into his pocket for his notebook. "What kind of inquiries?"

"Mr. Alderton prepared a file."

Toby thought of Miss Clark's hurried search of the bloodstained papers on the floor of Alderton's office. "I … we … were unable to locate the file. It was not in his office."

"I would hope not. This is a private and confidential matter requiring the utmost discretion. Are you capable of discretion, Mr. Whitby?"

"Of course."

Toby set the teacup down on the filigree side table and uncapped his fountain pen, determined to appear professional, discreet, and well informed.

"So in the event of your … demise, the title would pass to …?"

"The title will pass to my daughter."

Toby stared at her. "Your daughter, but …"

"I was not always infertile; it is a new occurrence and one that cannot be reversed."

Toby felt an unwelcome blush rising up from his collar.

"Oh really," said Lady Sylvia. "Are you able to treat this in an adult fashion, or will you have to ask your mother for an explanation?"

"No, of course not," said Toby, stung into a sharp response. "Whatever you say to me is confidential. I give you my word."

"Are you certain? I know that the activities of high society are always of interest to the lower classes.

Toby's rapidly growing dislike of his client allowed him to look her in the face, no longer embarrassed by her references to her reproductive organs.

"I have given you my word. Now, if we could continue ..."

Lady Sylvia raised her eyebrows, apparently unused to anyone standing up to her.

"So," Toby said, "you say that you have a daughter?"

"Yes, I do," she confirmed. "You may have noticed, Mr. Whitby, that I said that I can no longer have children; I did not say that I have never had a child."

Well, Toby thought, if you could just have told me that when I first sat down, we could have avoided this whole embarrassing conversation. It occurred to him that Lady Sylvia enjoyed embarrassing people and that the conversation was planned ahead of time to make him feel inadequate and inferior. He returned the notebook to his pocket and started to rise.

"Well, I can't see that there will be a problem. If the title can be passed through the female line, and you have a daughter—"

"I don't know where my daughter is," said Lady Sylvia, "and that is why you are here."

Toby sat down again. "You don't know where she is?"

"No."

"But ..."

"If I knew where she was, I wouldn't need your services."

"Your husband, her father—"

Lady Sylvia was outraged.

"Of course my husband was her father. Do you imagine that the child is a bastard?"

"Oh no, of course not."

Toby was amazed at the way Lady Sylvia could keep him off balance and unable to do anything but stammer questions and apologies.

"My husband was Jack Harrigan," said Lady Sylvia, "an officer in the U.S. Army. He died in Normandy."

"Oh, I'm sorry."

"So am I," said Lady Sylvia, with a hint of bitterness breaking through her aloof exterior. "Such a waste. He was so looking forward to coming back here and helping us to rebuild."

She doesn't sound sorry, Toby thought. She sounds angry, as though her husband had let her down by having the misfortune of dying in the invasion of France.

"So many of them died," said Lady Sylvia. "Were you in Normandy, Mr. Whitby?"

The question was familiar and always unwelcome. Toby shook his head, flooded with an old shame. No, he wasn't in Normandy. He hadn't crossed the Rhine. He hadn't even crossed the Channel. He and his pathetically shortsighted eyes had spent the entire war behind a desk in Whitehall with no rank, no uniform, and no possibility of making an overt contribution to the war effort.

"Well, no doubt you did your part," said Lady Sylvia in what Toby chose to believe was a tone of disbelief.

"If we could return to the subject of your child, I don't understand how—"

Lady Sylvia set her teacup on the trolley and rose abruptly. As Toby struggled to stand, she waved her hand dismissively. "No, no, stay there. I'm going to get the file from Daddy's desk. I can't bear to keep repeating things."

She had the file! That was why it was not in Alderton's office. The explanation was simple. But if Lady Sylvia had the file, why was Robert Alderton lying on the floor of his office in a pool of blood?

Toby set the question aside. It was up to the police to look into Alderton's life and find out who wanted him dead. He was just glad to know that the file still existed.

He sat back and looked around the room. He found himself reassessing it in the light of Lady Sylvia's remarks about Jack Harrigan, her American husband, helping her to rebuild the estate. The weak afternoon sunlight filtering through the windows showed a layer of dust shrouding the spines of the leather-bound books. The red velvet drapes at either side of the tall windows were faded to rusty brown along the edges, and the leather chair on which he was seated was not just old and comfortable, it was also ripped, with horsehair stuffing peeking through the padded armrests. Even the teacup that sat beside him on the table was chipped along the gold rim. The war had been hard on everyone, even the Earl of Southwold.

Lady Sylvia swept back into the room, carrying a stiff red cardboard binder of the kind reserved for the use of Mr. Alderton. Mr. Champion's files were blue, while Toby kept his papers in plain brown binders.

"These are the documents you'll need," said Lady Sylvia, "marriage license, birth certificate, and so on."

Toby hesitated. "I'm sorry, but you said that you don't know where your daughter is …?"

Lady Sylvia tossed her black curls impatiently. "No, I don't, Mr. Whitby, and that is why you're here."

Toby struggled to make sense of what he was hearing. Lady Sylvia's husband, Jack, had been killed in the Normandy landings. That was six years ago, which meant that the child of the marriage was no more than five years old, or maybe even six if the marriage had been a rushed affair to cover up a pregnancy. Whatever the case, this daughter was a little child, certainly not capable of running away and disappearing. There had been nothing in the newspapers, nothing said in the office, not even a hint of gossip about a missing child.

"You don't know where she is?" Toby repeated.

"No, I do not. She's been missing since the day she was born. I entrusted her to someone; someone who stole her."

Lady Sylvia thrust the folder into Toby's hands. "It's all in there. I gave Mr. Alderton a full statement. Daddy was with me; he heard everything. We have to find her, Mr. Whitby. We need to make certain that the succession is secure."

Toby was at a loss for words. This woman's child had been kidnapped on the day of her birth, and it had taken six years for her to mention this fact.

"What about the police?" Toby asked.

"We will not involve the police. I am not accusing anyone of a crime."

How could it not be a crime? Toby asked himself.

"I thought she died," said Lady Sylvia, as if to answer the questions swarming in Toby's brain. "There was an air raid, flying bombs, the first of the V-2s."

Toby nodded his understanding. How could he forget; how could anyone who had been in London forget the horror of the V-2s? Launched from the French coast, silent and unmanned, they had rained devastation indiscriminately across the south of England.

"The maternity clinic was destroyed," said Lady Sylvia. "Total confusion, of course, smoke, flames, people screaming. They told me she'd died, but she didn't die, and now I know it for a fact. Mrs. Pearson was with me, of course. She knows what happened, and now we know who took her."

Toby untied the red bindings on Robert Alderton's folder and found only a few legal documents; a marriage certificate, a birth certificate, some papers that seemed to have originated with the U.S. Army. He flicked through the papers, looking for Alderton's notes. Nothing. Alderton was a taker of copious notes; his files were usually stuffed full of notes written in Alderton's distinctive turquoise ink. Office rules required that all notes be hole punched and secured in the file by metal prongs. Mr. Champion did not permit loose papers. Everything was kept in chronological order. So where were Alderton's notes? They could not have fallen out of the file.

"Celeste," said Lady Sylvia

Toby dragged his mind away from the missing notes. "Is that the name of the person who took her?"

"No, Celeste is my daughter's name, Celeste Victoria Blanchard Harrigan. It's on the birth certificate."

"And the person who took her?""

"Vera Chapman."

Toby opened his mouth to ask another question, but Lady Sylvia rose abruptly.

"The documents are all in the file. You have no need of any other proof. You are not required to find the child, I have made other arrangements, you are only required to verify the facts as I have stated them and to draw up the appropriate documents. Now, if you'll excuse me, I have to see to my father."

Toby hastily gathered the papers back into the file folder. "Yes, of course, I'm sorry."

He felt as though he had been in a constant state of apology since he first entered the room. Lady Sylvia had an uncanny ability to throw him off his stride and leave him feeling as though he had done something wrong; as though he was too gauche and uneducated to approach her with the hundreds of questions that he was longing to ask. He had no idea how he was going to get to the crux of this situation if he could not even frame a question without also adding an apology for his impertinence in asking.

"Mrs. Pearson will see you out," said Lady Sylvia.

Toby pulled himself together. "I'll need another appointment, after I've read the file. There are obviously a number of questions—"

"Obviously."

"So …"

"You may telephone for an appointment when you have something to tell me. Good day, Mr. Whitby."

She swept from the room, leaving Toby to gather up the scattered papers and his equally scattered thoughts.

Dennis Blanchard, Earl of Southwold

The Earl shifted restlessly, unable to get comfortable in the wide four-poster bed. He reached for his cigarettes.

His daughter put out a hand to stop him. "No, please, Daddy. They're not good for you."

"Stuff and nonsense," said Dennis. "I'll be the judge of what's good for me."

He pulled a cigarette from the silver cigarette case, struck a match against the built-in striker, and took a long draw on the cigarette. He knew that at any moment he would start coughing again and he would feel as though his lungs were going to burst out through his mouth, but it would be worth it for this moment of pleasure.

"So," he said to his daughter, "I heard voices downstairs. Why did Champion send a different solicitor? Where was Mr. Alderton?"

Sylvia sat on the edge of the bed. "He's dead, Daddy."

Sylvia's voice betrayed no emotion. Perhaps he had misheard her. His hearing was not what it used to be.

"Did you say that Alderton is dead?"

"Yes, I did."

"How?"

"I don't know, Daddy. Does it matter?"

Of course it matters, Dennis thought. Every death matters, but there had been so many that perhaps his daughter had hardened her heart against regret and compassion.

Sylvia patted his hand. "Don't worry about Mr. Alderton; this young man is far more suitable. His name is Whitby; he's very recently qualified and not very bright."

"Are you sure?" Dennis asked. "It takes a certain amount of intelligence to pass the bar."

"Well, maybe he's bright, but he's not experienced and he's very easily embarrassed, which makes him just the man we want. He didn't hesitate at all. I even asked him if he could be more flexible than Mr. Alderton, and he didn't say no."

"Did he say yes?"

"Not exactly, but he can be persuaded."

Dennis released the cough that had been building in his chest. Through watering eyes he saw worry on his daughter's face.

"Don't worry," he croaked. "I'm not going to die just yet."

"Of course not."

Dennis hesitated, and wished that Sylvia's mother was still alive to take the burden of intimate conversations away from him.

"My dear—"

"Yes, Daddy?"

"Are you absolutely certain about this? It's not too late to find you a husband."

"Another husband," Sylvia corrected him.

"Yes, of course. It's not too late to find you another husband, and you're not too old to have a child. It would be so much easier."

Sylvia's dark eyebrows came together in a scowl. "Do we have to talk about this again? I told you. I can't have children."

"But maybe a specialist?"

"No."

"How can you be sure? Doctors are so much better than they used to be, and perhaps we could find someone who could help you."

Sylvia glared at her father. "No one can help me."

"But—"

Sylvia rose angrily. "Why won't you believe me? Do you think I would go to all this trouble if there were some other way?" She walked away from her father and looked out of the window for a moment. "Do you really want me to tell you? Wouldn't you prefer to be spared the gruesome details?"

Dennis stared at the back of her head. "I think you should tell me, because I don't understand how you can be so certain."

She turned to face him with an expression of grim determination. “Two years ago I was pregnant.”

“Two years ago?” Dennis queried. “You said your child was six years old. All the documents you showed me give her birth as 1946. This is important, Sylvia. You … we … have to be consistent.”

“I’m speaking of a different baby.”

Dennis tried to control a shocked exclamation. He reached for the water glass and swallowed hastily.

“Two years ago,” said Sylvia, “I met a man who was in every way suitable to be my husband, except that he was already married.”

“Sylvia!”

“Yes, Daddy, a married man.”

Dennis could hardly breathe. “You had his baby?”

“No, of course I didn’t. I have more sense than that. Cecil was a lot of fun, but he wasn’t going to get a divorce—”

Dennis was scandalized. “A divorce!”

“Oh, don’t worry, it would never happen. His wife has all the money. So, unfortunately, I couldn’t have his baby.”

“I should think not. So you had the baby adopted?”

“No, Daddy, I had an abortion.”

Dennis stared into his daughter’s eyes. They had grown cold and hard.

“I’m sure you understand, Daddy, that I did what needed to be done, not just for my own sake, but for the sake of the family name. It was not like it was in the war, when the papers had real news to report. The gossip columnists were already sniffing around.”

Dennis took another sip of water.

“So you had an … operation,” he said, hesitating over his choice of words. “I understand that such an operation is illegal.”

Sylvia gave a harsh laugh. “It’s just a matter of knowing the right people. Cecil found someone for me. It wasn’t his first time. I wasn’t the first woman who was afraid to have his baby.”

Dennis felt momentarily sad for his daughter, wondering where she could have gone for such an operation. He imagined it would be a grimy, back-alley kind of place somewhere in London, maybe Soho. Who had been with her? Who had helped her to recover?

Sylvia’s hand crept down to cover her stomach, an almost defensive gesture. “It didn’t go well,” she said. “I had an infection.”

Dennis waited.

“I was forced to tell Mrs. Pearson.”

“You could have told me.”

Sylvia laughed scornfully. “No, I could not have told you. The first thing you would have done is ship me off out of the country and bury me in some colonial outpost where I couldn’t shame the family name by having fun. I like to have fun, Daddy."

"Are you having fun now?" Dennis asked angrily. He took a calming breath. What was done was done, and no point in getting himself upset. "So what did Mrs. Pearson do?"

"She booked me into a private clinic and I had another surgery. That is why I can't have any more children."

"You're sure?"

"Absolutely sure."

Dennis patted the side of the bed, inviting his daughter to sit down again. In the course of two world wars, he had learned to make the best of things. What could not be changed must be endured.

"So," he said, "do you think this young Mr. Whitby will be able to find Vera?"

"It's not his job to find her," Sylvia replied. "I have other people who will do that. Mr. Whitby's job is to make everything legal. He seems capable of doing that."

"I hope so." Dennis took another sip of water. "I liked Vera Chapman. I invited her to tea, you know."

Sylvia patted her father's cheek. "Don't get sentimental, Daddy. She's probably got a whole houseful of children by now, and she won't miss this one."

Sam Ruddle

Sam watched the new young solicitor climb into his car and drive away into the gathering twilight of the short winter day.

"Morris Oxford," he said to his granddaughter. "That will have cost him a pretty penny. What's a young fellow doing with a car like that, and all I have is my old bike? I don't know what the world's coming to, Maisie, I really don't."

"He's not married," Maisie commented, "so he can spend his money on himself, I suppose."

"You been listening at keyholes again?" Sam asked.

Maisie smiled at him, her cheeks glowing red in the sharp cold wind and her eyes dancing with mischief. "Of course I have."

Sam patted her on the shoulder, leaving a muddy handprint on her gray dress.

"Grandad," Maisie protested, swiping at the stain on her dress. "Mrs. Pearson will have me for that, miserable old trout."

"Don't you worry about Mrs. Pearson," Sam said. He looked across the lawn, where a muscular young man was pushing a heavy roller haphazardly around the muddy grass. "I know a thing or two about what that nephew of hers has been up to. She wouldn't want me to tell anyone what I know."

"Oh, Grandad, Robbie's just slow and a bit daft; he's not dangerous. He wouldn't hurt a fly."

"He would if his aunt told him to. He'd do anything she told him. He can't tell right from wrong. Just does what she says."

"But he's strong."

"Too strong for his own good." Sam raised his voice and shouted across the lawn. "Straight lines, Robbie. Straight lines."

The boy nodded his head enthusiastically and continued to make his wavering way around the soggy grass.

"Daft as a brush," said Sam. "But like I say, I know a thing or two about what he gets up to."

Maisie smiled. "You know a thing or two about everyone."

Sam sniffed. "Well," he said, "it was part of my duties, wasn't it? Air-raid warden, making sure we kept the blackout, getting everyone into the shelters, carrying my little light and shining it in corners. Oh yes, I saw things, not being nosy, just doing my duty, and I don't talk about what I saw."

"Yes, you do."

Sam patted Maisie on the shoulder, leaving another muddy stain. "Only to you, love. I only talk to you; don't talk to no one else. They all have their war stories, Italy, Germany, France. Who wants to hear about the Home Front? No, no one wants to listen to me; but I know things. Oh yes, I know things."

"And so do I," said Maisie.

"Well …?"

"The new solicitor, Mr. Whitby, he came because Mr. Alderton, who used to come, is dead."

"Really? How did that happen?"

"Lady Sylvia didn't even ask. The new solicitor said that the old one was dead, and Lady Sylvia just went right on talking as though it didn't matter to her."

"It doesn't matter to her," Sam muttered. "She's cold as stone."

"Lady Sylvia gave him the file, you know, the red one with all the documents—"

"Did you see the documents?"

"No, but I thought the file was thinner than it used to be; as though someone had taken something out."

Sam cocked his head sideways and waited for a suggestion from his granddaughter as to what papers could have been removed. Maisie, however, had more important news to deliver.

"I heard her telling the new man all about what she wanted him to do, and it's like you said; there is a baby."

"I knew it!"

"Stolen," said Maisie.

"Stolen!" Sam exclaimed with satisfaction.

"And …" Maisie let the word hang in the air.

"Get on with it, girl."

"And she said the name. She said who stole her."

Sam watched his granddaughter's face light up with the anticipation of giving him the information he wanted. This, he thought, was the power of the peasantry; the power to dig out the secrets of the aristocracy in much the same way that they were expected to dig out the weeds from the flowerbeds and the vermin from the attics and cellars.

"Vera Chapman," said Maisie.

"You sure?"

"That's the name she gave him."

"Vera had her own baby; a little girl. Why would she be stealing Her Ladyship's baby?"

"I don't know. It's a mystery, Grandad."

"And not one that we'll ever solve," Sam declared.

"Why not?"

"Vera went to America. No one's heard from her since. Big country, America. If she's stolen Lady Sylvia's baby and she don't want to be found, no one's going to find her."

"But why would she steal Lady Sylvia's baby," Maisie asked, "and take it so far away?"

"I don't know," said Sam. "She was a strange girl, but plucky. Very plucky." He winked at Maisie. "She knew what she wanted and she knew how to get it, even if it meant taking off her knickers."

Maisie's face flushed red and she burst into giggles. "Grandad!"

"She reckoned that was the best way to get their attention. Oh, she was determined."

February 1944

Sam thought that being on blackout duty was like reading the gossip column in the newspaper. Better really because, with the war raging into its fifth year, there was precious little society gossip left to report.

Blackout inspection took Sam from one familiar cottage to another, with permission to peek into windows and knock on back doors if he saw so much as a spark of light showing.

"What are you trying to do?" he'd ask. "Why don't you light a big bonfire so Hitler's bombers can really see where they're going? Did you think they were never coming back? Well, you were wrong. Took them three years, but they're

back. Wouldn't want them to miss London, would you? Wouldn't want them to give poor old London a night off?"

The homeowner, suitably chastened and fearing that Sam might report them as possible German spies, would hasten to drop the blackout curtains and plunge the village into darkness.

He was on his way to carry out his duties when he saw the indistinct shapes of two girls crossing the village green, arm in arm and giggling. The village was blanketed in winter darkness, but the two girls seemed to know where they going despite the blackout and the lack of light.

"Who goes there?" he called, his breath misting in the cold air.

The girls giggled. "It's just us, Mr. Ruddle. We're not German spies."

"Don't be making jokes about German spies."

"Sorry, Mr. Ruddle."

"Approach and be recognized."

They laughed again. Not a serious thought in their empty little heads.

"Where are you going at this hour of night?"

"To the dance at the village hall."

He lifted his shuttered flashlight and shone it briefly on their faces. Yes, he knew this one. He recognized the spray of freckles across her nose. This was Carol Elliot, whose mother ran the village shop. They grow up so fast, he thought. He remembered her being just a little kiddie, toddling around among the newspapers and penny candy.

And the other one? Yes, that was Vera Chapman, whose mother had once been quite a looker. The girl was growing up to be just like her. Dark hair tortured into curls, and a skimpy winter coat, probably cut down from something bought before the war, before rationing made new clothes impossible.

"It's my birthday," Vera said.

Lipstick, Sam thought, she's wearing lipstick. Little hussy.

"I'm seventeen today."

Seventeen. Oh, to be seventeen again with all the world ahead, and him knowing nothing about the two world wars just over the horizon. "Happy birthday," he said. "Don't do anything I wouldn't do."

"I'm going to dance with a Yank," Vera declared.

"And that's something you wouldn't do," Carol chimed in.

"No, I wouldn't," Sam agreed. "Too little and too late, that's what I say. Didn't do a darned thing, did they, until the Japs hit them? Well, we held our own in 1940 and we'll hold our own now. We don't need them."

The girls giggled.

"We need them, Mr. Ruddle."

"Oh, go on with you. But you be careful. They're only after one thing."

They ran from him and his stern warning, tripping lightly across the green toward the dark shape of the village hall. As they opened the door, music and light spilled out for just a moment, and then the night returned to darkness.

Sam looked around at the huddled cottages and up into the unfriendly skies. This new war, he thought, was stealing their youth, just as the old war had stolen his.

"Happy birthday," he said under his breath. "Keep dancing while you can."

CHAPTER TWO

March 1952 Toby Whitby

Toby drove the Morris Oxford along the Brighton seafront. The day was cold but bright and clear, and the sun reflected from the tops of the waves as they curled lazily onto the shore. The tide was out, and the remains of anti-tank barriers and rusting coils of barbed wire were fully exposed. The war was over. It had been over for almost six years, but the damage remained, and rebuilding seemed to be an impossible dream.

The great hotels lining the seafront of the once fashionable resort looked abandoned. Those that still had windows or facades were closed and shuttered, but many of the elegant buildings were open to the elements and the cold wind from the Channel. Toby had never become accustomed to the sight of bomb-damaged buildings sliced open to reveal rain-soaked wallpaper, doors that led to nowhere, and shreds of fabric that had once been curtains or bedspreads. He thought they looked like the ruined dollhouses of giant children.

For the first time in years, Toby was able to assess his surroundings without a paralyzing sadness for the destruction of his homeland; for the historic buildings that had been reduced to dust, for the ruined beaches, and the shattered dreams of a generation. Let someone else rebuild it, Toby thought, and someday in the future, I'll come back and visit and say what a good job they've done.

He slipped his hand into the pocket of his suit coat and felt the reassuring shape of the official brown envelope that had arrived yesterday in the post. He had opened the envelope with trembling fingers and whooped with joy in his solitary bedsitter when he saw the contents. He'd been accepted by the colonial government of Rhodesia. His paperwork was being processed, and he would be told of his departure date. In the meantime, he should set his affairs in order because he had a five-year contract to work as a Crown Court prosecutor in the faraway city of Bulawayo. He was going to the heart of Africa, where the sun was always shining and the bombs had never fallen.

He parked on the street outside the offices of Champion and Company. He was already making a list of what he would have to do, including selling the little car. His new position would come with a driver and a Land Rover or something equally rugged. He would have to resign his position at Champion and Company, but not yet. He would say nothing yet. It might be months before he could be booked on a ship to Africa because so many passenger liners had been converted into troop ships and they had to be refitted and put back into luxury service, with transatlantic trade as a priority.

He pushed his way through the heavy oak front door with his mind on the pleasures of a long ocean voyage down the west coast of Africa. He entered the outer office forgetting to offer his usual deferential morning greeting to Anthea Clark, the reigning queen of the office. He was surprised to see that she had not only failed to notice his arrival, she was even ignoring the buzzing of her telephone as she perused a brightly colored magazine.

"Miss Clark."

The magazine was Woman's Own, the cover promising knitting patterns, recipes, and romance stories.

Miss Clark looked up from her reading, scowled, and thrust the magazine into the drawer of her desk.

"Where have you been?" she hissed. "Mr. Champion's been waiting for you."

Toby consulted his watch; just past 9:00. "Why is he so early?"

"He can be early if he wants to be," Miss Clark sniffed, "and you're late. I phoned him and told him about the telegram, and, of course, he insisted on coming in."

"What telegram?"

"From America."

Toby's mind lurched from the imagined beauties of Rhodesia to the reality of Lady Sylvia Blanchard and her missing baby. Three weeks of research had brought him no nearer to the truth of what could have happened to the Harrigan baby, or even if the baby had ever existed. Now a telegram had arrived from America, and whatever it said, Mr. Champion would want answers; answers he didn't have.

"What did the telegram say?" he asked.

"Mr. Champion will have to tell you himself," said Miss Clark primly. "I never discuss his affairs with the junior staff."

She looked away from him, and her eyes strayed to her desk drawer where she had thrust the magazine. Apparently, she was anxious to continue reading. Toby smiled to himself at the thought of Miss Clark secretly reading romance stories. There was more to Miss Clark than met the eye.

He left her to her surreptitious reading and knocked on the senior partner's door. A faint voice told him to enter.

Edwin Champion was a shriveled figure behind a huge mahogany desk. He wore the formal clothes of a prewar solicitor; a morning coat, a gray waistcoat, and a striped cravat. His thin white hair was parted in the center and rigidly controlled with brilliantine. Toby could see that Alderton's death and the burden of extra work had aged him. His frustration at the lack of progress in finding the murderer was reflected in his general air of impatience.

"You're late."

"Yes, sir, I am most sorry for that."

"And so you should be. Punctuality is the politeness of princes, and I don't pay you to be late."

"No, sir."

Mr. Champion's hand trembled slightly as he extended it across the desk, holding out a yellow telegram form.

"Sit down," he said.

Toby sat and took the paper from Mr. Champion's hand.

HAVE LOCATED MALLOY FAMILY STOP WILL TAKE CUSTODY PDQ AND BRING CHILD TO ENGLAND STOP WILL CABLE DETAILS STOP HARRIGAN STOP.

"Rash, impetuous, totally unacceptable," said Mr. Champion.

Toby, with the news about Rhodesia still bubbling at the back of his mind, thought that his secret had been uncovered and that Mr. Champion knew of his plans to go to Africa.

"Americans," Mr. Champion said, and then broke into a fit of coughing.

While his employer reached for a glass of water, Toby dragged his mind back from the contemplation of his escape plans and reassessed the situation. America; nothing to do with Africa.

"Presumably, Harrigan is the father of the deceased husband," Toby said, reading the name from the telegram.

"Be careful about presuming," Mr. Champion barked. "We are not certain about anything. I was not aware that anyone in America had been told of this matter. Perhaps Alderton made a note of it, but how are we to know, since his notes are still missing? However, you are probably correct in your assumption. This is no doubt a telegram from the child's supposed grandfather. I'm sure that he's anxious to find his granddaughter. She may be all that he has left to connect him to his son and his son's wife."

"It must have come as a shock to him to find that she existed," Toby said. "I wonder how much he really knows about Lady Sylvia."

"Very little, I should think," said Mr. Champion in a rare burst of candor. "Lady Sylvia has been very secretive about this American husband of hers, if he was in fact her husband."

"She has documents—"

"They are copies, are they not? They are not the originals."

"Lady Sylvia says the originals no longer exist."

Mr. Champion sniffed his disapproval. "And why should we take her word for that? I expect better from you, Mr. Whitby. What, if anything, have you done to find the truth for yourself?"

"I have done what I can, sir. I have confirmed that the church where Her Ladyship was married and the facility where the child was born have both been destroyed."

"And what else have you done?"

"I've written letters to the mother of Vera Chapman, the young woman who stole the baby—"

"Allegedly stole the baby!"

"Yes, of course, allegedly. I have written to the mother of that young woman, but I have not received a reply."

"I'm not surprised," said Mr. Champion. "What else?"

"I have attempted to trace the vicar who married Lady Sylvia and Captain Harrigan."

"Allegedly, allegedly," said Mr. Champion. "None of these facts are proven, none of them. Have you found the said vicar?"

"Not yet, sir." Toby paused. "It's very difficult, Mr. Champion, the war—"

"The war was over six years ago, and it is no longer an acceptable excuse. People have been moved, buildings have been destroyed, records are missing, but you are an intelligent young man, and you should be able to do better."

Toby nodded his head in agreement. "Yes, sir."

Mr. Champion was not finished. "Before I agreed to bring you into the firm, I looked into your war record. It seems that your work at the Home Office required some investigative skills. Is that correct?"

"Well, yes, but this isn't the same."

Mr. Champion was not interested in excuses. "I am disappointed in you, Whitby, I really am."

Toby stared down at the telegram in his hand. He was disappointed in himself. He should have made more progress. He should have had something definite to tell his employer. The truth was that he had been so concentrated on the possibility of leaving the gray, damaged country of his birth, that he had allowed the recovered Southwold file to sit on his desk and gather dust.

He shook his head. No point in saying any of this to Mr. Champion. He had to free himself from the grim memory of war and get on with the task in hand. He had to earn his paycheck.

Mr. Champion retrieved the telegram from Toby's hand. "PDQ, what does that mean?"

"I don't know, sir."

Mr. Champion continued to study the telegram. "Perhaps PDQ is some kind of American legal term giving him the right to claim her."

"I don't know, sir."

"Of course you don't know. I don't expect you to know, but I expect you to find out. I believe that even in America it is not possible just to take a child without some kind of legal process."

"According to Lady Sylvia, Mr. Harrigan is a very wealthy man—"

Mr. Champion dismissed the importance of wealth. "Perhaps wealth takes the place of law in America, but not here," he said. "We still have work to do, and you won't find any answers by standing here looking sheepish. Pay another visit to Rose Hill and get to the bottom of things. Writing letters will get you nowhere; you need to speak to the people face to face. Find the girl's mother, find her friends, put yourself about a bit, Mr. Whitby. You have an everyman kind of face, and you don't yet look like a solicitor; you will find someone who is willing to speak to you. You may take money from petty cash for your expenses. I understand that petrol is no longer rationed, so you may take that automobile you so recently and rashly purchased."

Does he know everything about me? Toby thought. Does he know about Africa?

"Before you go …" said Mr. Champion.

"Yes, sir."

"I fear that my years of service to the Southwold family may have clouded my judgement."

"Sir?"

"Perhaps I don't see things as they really are. Perhaps I see them as I wish them to be. I am unwell, Mr. Whitby."

"I know, sir."

"Mr. Alderton's death came as a very great shock, and I don't have the energy left to devote myself to this issue in the way that I should. Therefore, I am relying on your good judgement."

"Yes, sir. Of course."

"So, Mr. Whitby, is it your judgement that Lady Sylvia is telling the truth? Is she in fact the mother of this missing child?"

Toby turned the question over in his mind. "Well," he said at length, "if Lady Sylvia needed to find a baby to claim, a baby who is not hers, why would she insist on this particular child when orphanages in London are full of unclaimed children? Why insist on a child from America?"

Mr. Champion nodded his head in agreement.

"But, on the other hand," said Toby, wondering if he should risk upsetting his employer, "Lady Sylvia did tell me that she hoped I would be more flexible than Mr. Alderton."

"Flexible?" snapped Mr. Champion.

"Flexible about the law. More accommodating."

"And will you be … flexible?"

"No, sir."

"Good!" Mr. Champion waved a pale hand in dismissal. "You can go. Close the door behind you. I can hear that policeman outside, and I have no wish to see him."

Toby had been unaware of the conversation taking place in the outer office, but now he heard Miss Clark stoutly refusing to allow Mr. Champion to be disturbed. He closed the door behind him and faced Detective Sergeant Slater, a stocky, red-faced man with a London accent and an empty sleeve held out of the way with a safety pin.

"Miss Clark says I've no need to look for your missing file," Slater declared. "She says you've found it."

"Yes, we have."

"And you didn't think to tell me? Do you think I've all the time in the world to go looking for missing files that are no longer missing?"

"I'm sorry, I didn't think—"

"Nobody thinks, that's the trouble these days. We're short staffed, a lot of our men didn't make it back, and you think we have time for a wild goose chase."

Toby repeated his apology.

"So where is it?" Slater barked. "Hand it over."

Toby took a step backward. "I can't do that. It's a client file. It's highly confidential."

Slater shook his head. "It's evidence."

He fumbled in his pocket with his left hand and then withdrew the hand. An expression of embarrassment crossed his face.

He's used to writing in a notebook, Toby thought, but he can't do it one-handed; he has to rely on his memory. Where had he been when he sacrificed that arm to the war effort? Germany? Italy? North Africa?

"So," said Slater, "according to what your boss told me, the victim had the file in his possession on the day he was murdered, but when we came to search his office, it wasn't there. Now you say you've found it, and I want to know where you found it."

"The client had it," Toby replied.

"The client had it, I see. So who is this client?"

"The Earl of Southwold."

He heard Miss Clark's sharp intake of breath. Perhaps he should not have named the client, but what harm could it possibly do?

"Is it normal for the client to retain his own file?"

Toby looked over Slater's head and saw Miss Clark's pursed lips. "Perfectly normal," he said.

Miss Clark nodded her approval, but he knew his answer had been a lie. There was nothing normal about a client keeping his or her own file. All files were kept in the office. What would be the point of a file being kept elsewhere?

Toby took his hat and overcoat from the coat rack and tried to push past Slater. The policeman planted himself firmly in Toby's path.

"I get the impression you don't want to talk about this, Mr. Whitby."

Toby shrugged his shoulders. "There's nothing to talk about. The file isn't missing; never was."

"And what about Alderton's other files?"

Miss Clark provided the answer. "All present and correct."

"All present and correct," Slater repeated. "So no one else keeps their own file, only the Earl."

"We make allowances for the aristocracy," Miss Clark replied.

Slater sniffed. "Well, I don't. Things aren't what they used to be. Those days will never come again."

"More's the pity," Miss Clark muttered.

Slater shook his head and turned toward the door. "Not so far as I'm concerned," he said. He took his hat from the coatrack and jammed it on his head. "We'll talk again, Mr. Whitby."

Toby waited until the door had closed behind the detective before he spoke.

"Miss Clark, I have some questions about the Southwold file."

She raised her thin gray eyebrows. "So do I!"

"Well—"

Miss Clark interrupted impatiently. "I saw the file on your desk. There's nothing in it, Mr. Whitby, nothing at all."

"Copies of the legal documents," Toby said.

Miss Clark sniffed. "Copies! What good are copies? But that's not the end of it. Mr. Alderton had pages of notes in that file. I filed them for him myself. Where are they now?"

Toby perched himself on the edge of Miss Clark's desk, and for once she made no objection.

"Do you know what was in the notes?"

She nodded. "Names and phone numbers; dozens of them."

"Perhaps he was planning to investigate American military records."

"No, nothing like that." Miss Clark leaned forward and spoke in a confidential whisper. "I'm sure you know that Mr. Alderton enjoyed a busy social life, and he had many friends in London society."

Toby thought of Robert Alderton with his Old Etonian ties and his frequent attendance at house parties and opening nights in London. Yes, he was quite sure that Alderton had friends in high places.

"So," said Miss Clark, "Mr. Alderton was quite sure that some of the people he knew would also move in the same circles as Lady Sylvia. He began to collect names, people who knew people. He was trying to find someone who had seen Lady Sylvia with the man she claims to be her husband. He was hoping, for our sake, that he could find someone who had attended the wedding."

She paused and looked sideways at the closed door of Mr. Champion's office. "Mr. Alderton didn't like to work too hard. He liked to find the easiest way of accomplishing tasks, and finding someone who witnessed the wedding would certainly be a step in the right direction."

Toby felt a sense of relief. If Alderton had found a witness to the wedding and if Miss Clark knew the name of the witness …

Miss Clark shook her head. "I don't know if he found anyone; I only know that he was making phone calls to acquaintances. If he had obtained any information, he certainly did not share it with me."

Toby obeyed her impatient gesture that he should remove himself from his perch on the corner of her desk. He waited as she unlocked her desk drawer and took out the black metal petty-cash box.

He signed for his petrol money and smiled to himself as he saw her gaze drift to the center drawer, where she kept her magazines. He knew what she would be doing while Mr. Champion dozed and he drove to Rose Hill.

CHAPTER THREE

By the time Toby had filled the petrol tank of the Morris, the morning sun had given way to a cold February drizzle. As he drove inland from the coast, he resolved to stop dreaming of Africa and to start thinking about the telegram from America.

He wondered how Mr. Harrigan had managed to find the stolen child and how he planned to take custody of her. Would he snatch her illegally from her supposed mother and father, or had he found some kind of proof that the long-vanished Vera Chapman and her soldier husband were not the parents of the little girl? He wondered how one could even prove such a thing. His own research had told him that a blood test was not definitive and would not stand up in court. A blood test might prove that someone was not the parent, but could not prove the opposite.

Toby had never visited the village of Rose Hill. His previous visit had been to Southwold Hall, and on that occasion, he had ignored the one-track road that led into the village itself. This time, he bypassed the Hall with its newly restored wrought iron gates and drove on through the cold winter rain, past muddy fields and leafless trees, until he came to the village green.

He parked the car outside the Rose Hill Post Office. The building apparently doubled as a general store and newsagent, advertising the availability of newspapers, sausages, and George VI commemorative postage stamps on rain-drenched posters.

Despite his best intentions, Toby let his mind wander from the huddled village and bare windblown gardens to the letter in his pocket that would take him to Africa and endless sunshine. He touched the envelope just to reassure himself, and then he climbed out of the car and ran into the post office to make his enquiries.

The bell above the door rattled as he entered the cluttered gloom of the one-room shop. His eyes, as always, were slow to adjust, and he stumbled as he tried to negotiate his way toward the dimly perceived wire cage protecting the actual post office portion of the premises. "Sorry," he called out as a stack of children's comics tumbled onto the floor.

"Oh, don't worry about it," said a cheerful female voice from somewhere behind the counter. "Can't see a thing in here myself."

Toby looked up and found himself face to face with a young woman whose red hair seemed to light up the space around her. Flustered by the girl's bright smile and mesmerized by the spray of freckles across her delightful nose, he gathered up a pile of School Friend and Boy's Own comics and thrust them toward her.

"Sorry," he said again.

"No problem," said the girl. "They'll be soaking wet anyway by the time they're delivered. The boy doesn't come in until after school, and he's really careless about keeping the papers dry." She laughed. "Now look what I've done. I suppose you've come to ask for newspaper delivery, and now I've gone and spoiled it. You won't want your papers delivered by us now that you know what a mess we make."

Toby was overcome by the effect of her freckles and her smile and could barely stammer, "Oh no, I'd love to have my papers delivered by you … by your newspaper boy … only, well, I don't live here."

"Sorry, I thought you might have come from the new houses they're building out where the American barracks used to be. Oh well, never mind. What can I get you, stamps, newspaper, packet of crisps?

"I wasn't going to buy anything …"

"Really?" She arched her eyebrows and stared at him quizzically. "We are a shop, you know."

"Yes, yes, I know."

"Then what can I do for you Mr. …?"

"Whitby, Toby Whitby."

"Carol Elliot," she said.

"Well, Mrs. Elliot—"

"Miss Elliot."

He was strangely pleased to find that she was unmarried.

"You can call me Carol," she said.

"Well, Carol," said Toby, "I need some information."

"Oh yes, what kind of information?"

"I thought that as this is the post office, you might be able to supply me with directions. I'm trying to find 14 Rose Hill Lane."

She was suddenly wary. Her smile faded. "Who are you looking for?"

"Mrs. Chapman. Mildred Chapman."

Carol hesitated.

Toby shrugged his shoulders. "If you don't want to tell me, I'll go and ask someone else." He looked out across the rain-swept village green. "I'm sure someone will tell me."

"Why do you want to find her?"

"It's a legal matter. I'm a solicitor."

Toby waited. This was the post office. He was asking for directions. He couldn't imagine why this could be a problem.

Carol seemed to be involved in an internal struggle. Finally she burst out with a question. "Is it bad news?"

"No," said Toby, although he suspected that the suggestion that her daughter had stolen a baby might be very bad news indeed for Mrs. Chapman.

"That poor woman has had enough bad news." Carol's eyes were wide with sympathy. "There was the telegram, you know, when her husband died. Of course, that was at the beginning of the war. I was just a kid then. I wasn't working here, but my mother was."

"It's not about her husband," Toby assured her.

"And then her son, Terry. Well, we were all quite sure he wouldn't come back. They died by the thousands, didn't they, on the Burma Railway?"

"He was in Burma?"

"He was captured in Singapore and sent to Burma. We heard such dreadful things about how the POWs were treated. Everyone thought he was dead, and then the Red Cross found him, although sometimes you have to wonder if it wouldn't have been better if they'd never found him."

Toby made a quick calculation. He had already told the girl that the news was not about Vera's deceased father, but if he also told her that it was not about her prisoner of war son, she would know that it must be about Vera, and he was not at liberty to talk about Vera, not yet. Unfortunately, Carol was already ahead of him. She drew in a sudden sharp breath. "It's not Vera, is it? Has something happened to Vera? We all thought she was so lucky, marrying her Yank and going to America. Has something happened to her?"

"I'm not at liberty to say." Toby knew that by not saying, he had given Carol all the information she needed.

"What? You have to tell me. We were friends, you know, not real close, but friends, only she never wrote."

"Ah," said Toby. "I was going to ask you if you had any idea where she is in America."

Carol shook her head, and the dim light bounced off her red curls. "No, I don't know. She went on the boat to New York, but I don't know where she went after that. She said Nick was from California. I suppose that's where she went. I don't know anything else."

Toby hesitated, wondering what he could do to keep her talking, and tossing her curls.

"I don't know anything," she repeated. She drew a deep breath as if afraid to ask the next question. "Did something happen to her little girl?"

"Not that I know of," said Toby cautiously. "I really can't discuss it with you; my work requires absolute confidentiality."

Carol stared at him with wide worried brown eyes. Red hair and brown eyes! He had no idea the combination would be so attractive. He didn't know that he could be so drawn to a spray of freckles across a small upturned nose. Her skin was pale and creamy. He found himself wondering what would happen to such pale skin under the heat of African skies. Would the freckles spread? Would she be able to stand the sun?

Her question brought him back to reality. For heaven's sake, he had just met the girl. They'd never had a date. They'd never really had a conversation. All he had done was upset her by asking for information. Why was she so easily upset? Was she really upset, or just very defensive? What was she defending?

"You're sure nothing happened to the little girl?" Carol asked.

She looked so worried that Toby felt compelled to reassure her. "I'm quite sure."

"Vera's well out of it," Carol said. "It would break her heart to see the way her brother is. He came back, but not really, if you know what I mean. Won't talk to anyone, just sits there. When the weather is nice, he sits outside in the garden, but he might as well be one of the rosebushes for all he knows about what's going on around him. I don't know what they did to him, but it was something awful."

"I'm sorry." It was all he could think to say.

"She promised she'd write," Carol said wistfully, "but she didn't. I never heard a word. I suppose it's better this way."

"Why do you say that?"

"So she doesn't know about her brother. She can't do anything about it, so why upset her?"

"I see what you mean."

Toby could think of no way to continue the conversation on a more personal level and returned to his original question. "If you could direct me to Mrs. Chapman's house; number 14 Rose Hill Lane."

"Yes. Yes. Sorry I was a bit hesitant. We all worry about Mrs. Chapman. I wouldn't want to see anything else happen to her."

"You can't prevent it by refusing to tell people where she lives," Toby said mildly.

"I know. I know. It's just that you took me by surprise."

And you took me by surprise, Toby thought, still reeling from the sudden shock of realizing that this was the girl he wanted to take to Africa.

"You can see the house from here," Carol said. "Let me show you."

He observed her as she walked ahead of him to the door, revealing a curved figure with a small waist, generous hips, and ample breasts, a perfect hourglass. She opened the door and stood beside him in the shelter of the doorway, looking out through the misty drizzle.

"You can walk from here. There's nowhere to park a car on the lane. Nice car by the way …"

"Thank you," said Toby. "Perhaps you might ..."

She stared at him.

"I mean, if you're interested in cars, I could take you for a ride sometime?"

She was silent. Of course she wasn't interested in cars. What girl was interested in cars? What girl would be interested in a secondhand Morris Minor?

"It doesn't have to be a ride," he amended. "Perhaps we could go for a drink."

"A drink?"

"Yes."

Again he observed the internal conflict. She seemed to be two girls rolled into one. One was the bright, smiling, open-faced girl who had greeted him when he entered the shop. The other was suspicious and withdrawn, defending some hidden part of herself.

She smiled, and apparently the happy girl had won the contest. "Come back when you've finished talking to Vera's mum. I'll be ready to close by then, and you'll be in need of a drink."

"Is she difficult to talk to?"

"Impossible," said Carol with a shrug of her shoulders.

Toby felt a small thrill of pleasure as she took hold of his arm and pointed him in the right direction.

"Just go across the village green. Mind you don't fall into the bomb crater, don't know when they are ever going to fill it in, and then you'll be on the lane."

Toby squinted to see where she was pointing and perceived the edge of the green dimly through the curtain of rain.

"It's full of water now," said Carol.

"What is?"

"The bomb crater."

Carol's voice held a hint of impatience. Perhaps he should have known about the bomb crater, but in a country pockmarked with bomb craters, the existence of one particular crater was easily overlooked.

"Right in the middle of the cricket pitch," Carol explained.

"Well, the Germans weren't planning to play cricket," Toby said. It wasn't much of a joke, but it made Carol laugh. He added a sense of humor to her growing list of attributes.

He took off his glasses and wiped them with his handkerchief. “I’ll be careful,” he said.

“See you later,” Carol replied cheerfully. She went back inside the shop, the doorbell clanging as she closed the door behind her.

CHAPTER FOUR

Toby followed a muddy path across the village green and arrived at the entrance to Rose Hill Lane. The cottages huddled together against the rain, with water dripping from their thatched roofs, and sulfur-laden coal smoke rising from their redbrick chimneys. Toby located Mrs. Chapman's cottage hidden behind a garden of tangled weeds and spindly rosebushes. He was not surprised that Vera had chosen to leave this life behind and sail away to California. He wondered why Carol had not also left with an American.

The garden gate was hanging by one rusted hinge. He pushed his way past and knocked on the door. Vera's mother had failed to answer his letter, but maybe she would answer him in person. Maybe she could tell him why her daughter had stolen a baby. As he waited for the door to open, he thought of Mr. Champion hunched behind his mahogany desk and was reminded that his job was to find the truth, whatever the truth might be. So perhaps Vera Chapman had not stolen a baby, perhaps Lady Sylvia's story was a pack of lies. He heard footsteps shuffling toward the door and prepared himself to keep an open mind.

The front door, heavy old oak, opened slowly.

"Good afternoon," said Toby. "I'm—"

The man who had opened the door took no notice of Toby. His rehearsed greeting faded away as the man walked past him and out into the rain, his eyes sliding past, staring into nothingness.

Toby had heard people speak of the blank-eyed stare of the returning POWs, but this was the first time had had seen it for himself. He assumed that the man was Terry, the brother who had returned from Burma. He was a small man, thin to the point of emaciation. What little remained of his hair was a dull brown interspersed with gray. His face and the whites of his eyes were both a sickly yellow. He seemed unaware of Toby's presence, as though he had no memory of opening the door.

Toby remembered Carol's words. "It might have been better if they'd never found him."

He hesitated, wondering what he should do. Surely he shouldn't leave the man standing out there in the pouring rain.

"Mr. Chapman," he said. "Terry …"

The man turned slowly.

"You should go back into the house," Toby said.

He reached out to touch the other man's arm, thinking he might need to lead him inside, but Terry Chapman would not be touched. He cowered away from Toby and crouched low to the ground, wrapping his arms around his head.

"Now look what you've done," said an irritated voice from the doorway.

Toby looked behind him and saw a short, heavyset woman. Her dark hair was enclosed in a hairnet, and her meaty body was encased in a floral wraparound apron. Her face was set in what looked like a permanent scowl.

"I'm sorry," said Toby.

The woman snorted. "I'd have expected you to understand, a man of your age. You know what it was like."

She hesitated, a terrible sadness settling over her unhappy features.

"I don't suppose anyone really understands," she said, "if they weren't there. Starved, beaten, worked like a mule, I don't know how he survived. We didn't even know. We thought he was dead." She sighed. "Maybe he should have been."

She reached out a hand, not touching the crouching man, just offering, not insisting. The maternal gesture and the pain on her face told him that this was Mrs. Chapman, Terry's mother. Vera's mother!

"Come on, Terry love, time to come inside." Mrs. Chapman looked at Toby. "How was your war?" she asked.

"Well …"

He decided not to answer her. He could not expose the truth of his bad eyesight as a comparison to the suffering of the tortured man who had now staggered to his feet and was making his way back along the path. He changed the subject.

"Mrs. Chapman, I wrote to you. I'm with Champion and Company, and I asked about your daughter, Vera."

"What about her?"

"My client is trying to find her."

"Good luck. I've no idea where she is."

"But I thought she went to America."

"Oh yes," said Mrs. Chapman, "she went to America all right, and that's the last I heard from her. Took the little kiddie and off she went, and then not a word, a postcard from New York and then nothing."

"I'm sorry."

"She made a fool of herself over that American," said Mrs. Chapman, "and now she's too ashamed to even write to me. She could be dead for all I know."

She's not dead, Toby thought, because Mr. Harrigan has found her. Well, he had found the child; he said nothing about the mother. Toby wondered if he had a duty to inform Vera's mother about the telegram, but Mrs. Chapman gave him no chance to interrupt.

"April 1946," she said. "Off she went on the Queen Mary. There were thousands of them, women and kiddies. I went to Southampton and waved goodbye. I thought it was the least I could do. The way she behaved, she didn't even deserve that, but at least she married him before the kiddie was born."

"So she did have a baby?" Toby did not intend to ask the question aloud.

"Of course she did. What kind of question is that? She had a little girl. Anita, she called her. I don't know where she got that from; Anita Mary Malloy."

"Is it possible," Toby asked hesitantly, realizing how ridiculous it would sound, "that the little girl was not actually your daughter's baby?"

Mrs. Chapman looked at him in amazement. "Don't be daft! If she hadn't had the baby, she would never have gone to America. That soldier only married her because of the baby and because of the Earl. Of course it was her baby. Not that it matters now, I'll never see Vera again. All I have is him." She jerked her thumb at the shambling figure of Terry Chapman making his way into the house. "It's wicked what they did, downright wicked. Japs! What did we ever do to them?"

"I'm sorry," said Toby, knowing that sorry was hardly an adequate description for how he felt about Terry Chapman's fate.

"Well, sorry won't get anyone anywhere," Mrs. Chapman declared. "If you want to do something for me, you can stop writing me letters and you can stop asking daft questions. Do I think the baby belonged to Vera? What kind of question is that?"

"Were you with her when the baby was born?"

"None of your business!"

She turned away and followed her son into the house, slamming the front door behind her. Moments later she appeared at an upstairs window, standing still and staring over his head to the village green and the crater that had once been a bomb shelter.

February 1944
Mildred Chapman

Mildred stood in front of the mirror, putting her hair up in rags. She'd go to bed in a minute, but she wouldn't sleep, not until Vera came home. She should never have let her go out, but it was the girl's birthday. She looked down at the cut glass dish on the dressing table. Her one remaining stub of red lipstick was gone. She knew who had it. Well, what was so wrong in a girl wanting to put on a bit of lipstick? She was seventeen now. She could wear lipstick. It didn't mean she was loose or easy. Vera just liked to have fun.

With the last rag tied in place, Mildred went into the kitchen to fill the kettle for the hot-water bottles; one for herself and one for Vera. When Walter had been alive, Mildred hadn't needed a hot-water bottle, but he was gone now, torpedoed in the North Atlantic.

When the air-raid siren sounded, Mildred sighed in exasperation. Another night without sleep; another night with the forced companionship of her neighbors. She took the kettle off the stove, wrapped herself in Walter's old dressing gown, and picked up her knitting bag. She turned off the lights, slipped out the back door, and made her way to the shelter, guided by the sound of voices. The village green was in darkness but she knew the way. Everyone knew the way.

Once inside she sat down on her usual bench and pulled out her patriotic knitting. She was knitting socks for soldiers. The yarn was coarse gray wool, and she imagined the poor boy who was destined to receive her gift would soon have blisters.

Her hands worked the needles automatically, the gray lumpy mass growing beneath her fingers. The shelter was beginning to fill with people. Mrs. Rollins came down the steps with her newborn baby. Mrs. Evans had brought her cat, a defiance of regulations, but she knew that Sam Ruddle would not insist on evicting the creature. Mrs. Shenton, breathing heavily as though she had been running, sat down beside Mildred and pulled out her own patriotic knitting.

No sign of Vera. She would come soon. She wouldn't be able to stay at the dance. No one would be allowed to stay at the dance.

Mrs. Elliot came down the steps with a thermos of tea. She looked inquiringly at Mildred. Mildred shook her head. Carol and Vera hadn't yet arrived. Mrs. Elliot's face set in a worried frown.

Sam Ruddle arrived in his tin hat and warden's uniform, and stood by the door counting heads and looking for stragglers. Carol hurried in alone. Mrs. Elliot smiled contentedly. Mildred began to worry.

The door was still open, but Mr. Ruddle had now taken up a position at the head of the steps, alternately looking at the sky and looking across the green. He was only waiting for one person: Vera.

Mildred tried to concentrate on her increasingly misshapen knitting. Wild thoughts of her absent daughter ran through her mind. Suppose Vera had tripped and fallen in the dark, or suppose she was still in the village hall, locked in the ladies room. The door used to stick and no one had oiled it. Maybe the door was stuck. She should tell Sam. She should ask him to go and look.

Elsie Shenton, knitting smoothly, looked sideways at Mildred's knitting. "Do you want me to help you with that?"

Mildred looked down at the work of her hands.

"You haven't turned that heel properly," her neighbor said. "Let me do it."

Mildred slapped away the helping hand. "No, thank you. I'll do it myself."

"You're wasting good wool. Who do you think is going to wear those socks?"

Mrs. Evans, still clasping her cat, slid along the bench to inspect Mildred's knitting. "You've dropped a stitch," she announced.

"Mind your own business," Mildred snapped back.

Elsie Shenton changed the subject. "So, where's your Vera, then? Are we all going to wait with the door open until your Vera decides to put in an appearance?"

Mrs. Evans chose to address her next remark to her cat. "She's out with a Yank, isn't she? Everyone knows she's running after the Yanks." The cat yawned.

Mildred shoved her knitting back into its bag and stood up. "Don't you talk about my daughter that way!"

Sam's voice interrupted their squabble. "Ladies, ladies, behave yourselves. We're all a bit on edge. None of us expected to be bombed all over again, not after three years, but it's no use having a go at each other. We've got enough trouble with Hitler; we don't need no argy-bargy from you. Just sit down and we'll have a song. How about it, Mrs. Rollins? How about you start us off with 'There'll Always Be an England?'"

"But you haven't closed the door," Mrs. Shenton complained.

"And I'm not going to," Sam told her. "We're going to wait for Vera for as long as we possibly can. We're not helping the war effort by arguing among ourselves. Now, you start singing, Mrs. Rollins, and you, Elsie Shenton, you keep on knitting and mind your own business." He looked at Mrs. Evans. "Don't bring that cat down here again."

Mrs. Rollins and the ragged chorus of women had already reached the end of the first verse when Vera tumbled breathlessly down the steps and sat down next to her mother. She slid a brown paper packet onto Mildred's lap.

"Tea," she whispered.

Sam closed the door.

March 1952
Toby Whitby

Toby stood still and allowed the rain to pour down on him. Where should he go now? Who should he talk to? Obviously, Vera's mother was going to be no help. He couldn't face the idea of going up to the Hall and asking Lady Sylvia any more questions. She had told him pretty clearly not to come back until he had something to say.

Ignoring the path, he chose the shortest route across the green, thinking only of the warmth and comfort of his car. Perhaps he could just wait there and kill time until his date with Carol, if it was really a date. There was no time to go back to the office, and what could he do at his desk that he couldn't do here? Mr. Harrigan had found the child and he was bringing her to England, so what was really left to do?

Well, said a nagging voice at the back of his mind, Mr. Harrigan found a child, but who's to say it's Lady Sylvia's child? You only have her word for it.

And a file folder full of papers to prove it.

Really? Do they prove anything? Papers can be forged. Doesn't it strike you as strange that everything's been destroyed; the church where she was married, the clinic where the baby was born, the records office? Isn't that strange?

No, it's not. We had six years of war.

But where are Robert Alderton's notes, and why is Alderton dead?

"Be careful, mister."

Toby spun around to see who was calling out to him. A woman was hurrying toward him, dragging a small boy in a school cap and raincoat.

"That's the bomb crater," she called.

Toby looked down at his feet. He was standing at the edge of what looked like a small pond. Another couple of steps and he would have fallen in.

"You'll get soaked," the woman called. "It's deep. They put up barriers but people take them away. They need the wood, you know."

She was alongside him now. She was a young woman, probably younger than he was. Her slight figure was swamped by a man's gabardine raincoat, and her hair was covered by a floral headscarf tied under her chin. Her face was dominated by a small mouth with protruding teeth, a feature she shared with the small rabbit-featured boy.

She looked Toby up and down. "So, you're not from here."

"No, I'm from Brighton. I came on legal business." He extended his hand. "Toby Whitby."

"Pleased to meet you, I'm sure." The woman released her son's hand and offered him a limp, damp handshake. "Beth Rollins, and this is my son, Ted."

Mrs. Rollins was silent for a moment, staring down into the muddy depths of the bomb crater and then back at Toby.

"This happened on the day after I got the telegram; I remember sitting down there in the shelter. I didn't care, not if they dropped a bomb right on top of us, not after I got the news that Frank, that's my husband … that was my husband ... killed in North Africa. What a world it was where a young man like my Frank could get himself shot in North Africa. He'd never left Rose Hill before, not in his whole life, and now he's not even buried here. I don't know where he's buried."

She took hold of her son's hand again. "He never even saw our Teddy. Never set eyes on him."

"I'm sorry," Toby repeated helplessly.

Now she's going to ask me about my war, he thought. He would offer his stammering explanation about his eyesight and his work in Whitehall, and she would give him that look, the one that said, "You don't deserve to be here."

"It must have been a big one," he said, pointing to the bomb crater and hoping to head off any more questions about the war.

Mrs. Rollins shrugged her shoulders.

"Big enough. London was getting a real beating that night, not as bad as the Blitz, but bad."

"Yes," said Toby, involuntarily agreeing with her. "I was in London. Fire watch."

"Oh." She looked at him sideways. "Was you on leave?"

"War work."

He'd given himself away.

Mrs. Rollins sniffed disapprovingly. "Something essential, I'm sure."

"Mum." The little boy was pulling on his mother's arm. "I'm all wet."

Mrs. Rollins looked down at her offspring. Water streamed from his school cap and down across his hunched shoulders. "I have to go," she said. "It's time for his tea."

"Just a moment, Mrs. Rollins, I wonder if I could ask you a couple of questions."

She looked at him suspiciously. "What about?"

"Did you know a girl named Vera Chapman?"

"Yes."

"Do you know what happened to her?"

The little boy pulled on his mother's arm again, whining softly under his breath. "Mum, I'm hungry."

"Vera Chapman?" Toby asked again.

"One of the lucky ones," said Mrs. Rollins. "She got herself pregnant, and off to America she went. She said he came from California, but they all said that, didn't they? California or New York. I don't think he did, but what does it matter? It has to be better than here."

Teddy's voice rose to a determined screech. "Mum, I'm hungry." The screech was accompanied by a determined tugging of his mother's arm. She turned away from Toby and allowed her son to bring their conversation to an abrupt end as he dragged her away.

"Take that path over there," she called over her shoulder, "and you won't get wet."

Toby watched her until she had disappeared through the curtain of rain. So now he had confirmation from three different sources; Vera's mother, Carol Elliot, and Mrs. Rollins. They all agreed that Vera had been pregnant, given birth, and gone to America. So why, he wondered, was Lady Sylvia laying claim to Vera's child? Why was the wealthy Mr. Harrigan, even now, threatening to drag Vera's child back across the Atlantic?

As he walked back to his car, all he could think of was Lady Sylvia's question. "Are you more flexible than Mr. Champion?"

Sam Ruddle

Sam had supervised Robbie Pearson's clumsy attempts at cleaning and oiling the Earl's meagre horde of antiquated gardening implements and returned them to the potting shed. The war was over, it had been over for six years, but he despaired of ever being given new tools to replace those donated to the war effort. If he had a nice sharp pair of secateurs, he could do a proper job of pruning the roses instead of hacking at them with a warped and blunted handsaw. With a few decent tools, he wouldn't have to put up with Nell Pearson sniffing in disapproval at his handiwork and telling him that her slow-witted nephew could do a better job. He knew that was what she was hoping for. Any little slip up, and his job would be taken away and given to Robbie, who wouldn't know a rose from a turnip. That's what she was waiting for.

He surveyed the windblown rose garden and the recently truncated rosebushes. Robbie Pearson had already sloped off to wherever it was he spent his evenings. Sam decided that he'd done all he could do for one day, and he didn't owe it to the Earl to spend any more time kneeling in the mud with cramp in his bad leg and his sciatica screaming for relief. In fact, he thought, he didn't owe the Earl anything; not a thing. It was people like the Earl who had sent peasants like Sam "over the top" in that terrible war while they stayed behind the lines in comfort.

As for the last war, what had the Earl suffered? Nothing! He'd been safe and warm in his own home, and when the night raids came, he'd only to go down the stairs to his own cellar and sit them out in comfort; him and Nell Pearson and that cold witch of a daughter. It hadn't been that way for Sam; not when they made him air-raid warden; not on the night the bomb fell.

February 1944

"There'll always be an England."

Sam listened to the villagers singing defiantly as they huddled in the bomb shelter on the village green. He was glad they could still sing after so many years and so many air raids. Singing patriotic songs would keep their spirits up. Singing would take their minds off the damp discomfort of the underground shelter and drown out the sound of German planes droning overhead on their way to bomb London yet again.

He kept his eye on the two teenaged girls. When the air-raid siren had interrupted the dance in the village hall, Carol Elliot had hurried obediently into the shelter, but not Vera. Oh no, not Vera! Vera had tumbled into the shelter at the very last minute, flushed and giggling, and now he saw her slide a packet of tea onto her mother's lap. He knew that the brown paper packet could only have come from an American soldier she had met at the dance. He was of the opinion that there was only one way for a girl to get gifts from American soldiers.

He knew about soldiers. He'd been a soldier thirty years ago, fighting the "war to end all wars," and he had the battle scars to prove it. He'd fought alongside Americans, and he'd seen how they were with the girls. French, English, Belgian, it didn't matter. The British Tommies didn't stand a chance when the Americans turned on the charm.

He was too old to fight now, but he could still do his bit. His eyes were not as good as they used to be, but his hearing was still sharp. He watched Carol slide along the rough wooden bench until she could whisper in her friend's ear. Their heads were close together, Carol's red curls intermingled with Vera's long dark tresses.

He moved closer. He wasn't nosy, no one could call him nosy, but it was his duty to know what was going on in the village, and Carol's whispered questions were very easy to overhear.

"What did you do?" she asked.

"Enough," Vera replied.

Sam could see the shock on Carol's face.

"How much is enough?" she asked.

"I would have gone all the way," Vera replied, "but the siren went off. Mr. Ruddle started shining his light into the bushes and telling the Americans to go back to their barrack, and I couldn't find my knickers." She giggled. "Soldier boy

had them in his pocket. He said he wanted a souvenir."

"But you'd only just met him," Carol protested.

"So what?" Vera asked. "He's from California. He has a house with a swimming pool, and orange trees, and—"

"But Vera ..."

"Don't 'But Vera' me. Listen to them all singing away. There'll always be an England. I don't think so. It won't be the same ever again and I'm not staying here. I already told you, I'm going to get myself an American soldier."

"Do you even know his name?"

"Of course I do. His name is Nick. All I have to do is get pregnant, and he'll have to marry me and I can go to California."

"But what if he gets killed?"

"Then I'll be a war widow, and I can still go to America if I want to."

Sam looked at Vera's happy flushed face. Hitler's bombers were on their way to destroy what was left of London, and all she could see was opportunity. He'd heard it all before in the last war. He'd seen what happened to the women. There would be no happy ending for Vera.

Vera was still whispering excitedly. "I don't think I can get pregnant from what we did tonight. It was too cold to lie down on the ground, and I think you have to be lying down. He says he has a pass tomorrow. I'm going to meet him in the bicycle sheds. I think we can do it there."

Sam shook his head and wondered if he should tell Vera's mother what he had heard.

Before he could come to a decision, the patriotic singing ended abruptly. Mrs. Rollins, who had been leading them in a strong contralto, stopped singing and began to sob, and everyone fell silent.

Sam looked away from the two girls.

"Keep singing, Mrs. Rollins. We all need to keep our spirits up."

He was surprised when Elsie Shenton, not known for her kindness, glared at him and wrapped a bony arm around the crying woman.

"She got a telegram," she said, "today."

"Oh."

Sam nodded at Mrs. Rollins. "Sorry to hear that."

Mrs. Rollins clasped her baby, causing it to give a muffled wail of disapproval. "Poor little mite," she said. "He'll never see his father."

"Taken prisoner?" Sam asked.

Elsie Shenton glared at him again. "No," she said flatly.

With the singing at an end, Carol's mother pulled her daughter away from Vera. "I don't know what you girls are whispering about," she said, "but you need to be quiet. Try to get some sleep."

Sam rose stiffly to his feet and decided to risk cracking the door open just a little to let in some fresh air. The shelter was perpetually damp, and ventilated by one small shaft. Several of the now-sleeping babies were adding their own unfortunate deposits to the dank, overcrowded space, not that the mothers could be expected to do anything about it. Sleeping babies, however odorous, were preferable to screaming babies.

Sam breathed in the draft of fresh air and listened for the sound of Hitler's planes. He could see a flickering glow in the northern sky. The bombers had reached London. It would be a few minutes before they began their return journey. He would be safe in leaving the door open a crack and letting in some air. He extinguished his kerosene lantern and allowed moonlight to filter in through the doorway.

"Blackout won't help tonight," he muttered. "London's a sitting duck in the moonlight."

"Poor old London," said a voice from the corner.

"Poor old London," Sam agreed.

Vera rose to her feet. "I have to get some air," she said in a panicked voice.

Her mother pulled her back down. "Don't be daft. Mr. Ruddle can have you arrested for interfering with his duties."

"I'd like to see him try," Vera muttered.

Sam kept his ear to the crack in the door. Soon he heard the sound of the German bombers droning through the night sky on their way back from London. He slammed the door and relit the lantern.

He looked around at the people under his charge. All of the children were sleeping, but the adults were awake and staring upward at the corrugated sheeting of the roof. They knew the danger. They knew how vulnerable they were. This was the time when a pilot who had somehow failed to drop his bombs on target would drop them over the south coast before he headed back across the Channel. The pilot would not see the village itself, nestled in a fold of the South Downs, but he would see the open waters of the Channel ahead, and he would jettison his bombs over this last sliver of coastline and hope to damage something, anything, while he still had the chance.

He heard it and felt it; a muffled explosion and a light tremor. A bomb had been dropped some distance away. He saw fear in every face at the first impact. He wanted to say something to relieve the tension, but what could he say? They all knew the score. Four bombs in a stick; how many were left?

The second explosion was still to the north, but closer. A shower of dust fell from the roof and woke Mrs. Rollins's baby. The baby's cries were the only sound in the tense silence.

The third impact came in the form of a shuddering blow that shook the shelter. The brick walls bowed inward, overturning the benches and throwing the occupants onto the floor. The roof creaked and sagged, and Sam's kerosene lantern flickered and died, leaving them in sudden suffocating darkness. No one screamed; not even the baby. Sam held his breath. No explosion!

In the fleeting moment of silence, he heard the fourth explosion somewhere to the south.

His heart was racing. These were his people. He was in charge. Where were the matches? He had to light the lantern. He had to let them see his face and know that he was not afraid. He groped around on the floor and made contact with someone's leg. A woman, or a girl.

"Matches," he muttered, continuing to scrabble around on the floor. He realized that everyone was on the floor. The impact had hurled them all from their seats, and they were tangled in a heap in the darkness and damp.

"I have matches."

He recognized Vera's voice and inappropriately wondered if she had American matches, not that it would make any difference so long as they worked. He heard a sharp scraping sound and smelt sulfur. The match light flickered for a moment, and he saw Vera beside him. He thrust the lantern toward her.

"Shit," she muttered as she dropped the match. The scraping sound came again, and this time she was ready. The flare of the kerosene lamp rose from a guttering flame to a fierce orange light, illuminating the terrified faces of the villagers.

"Don't no one move," Sam said. It was all he could think to say. He had no other command to give.

The villagers stayed where they were. They were breathing now, in ragged terrified gasps.

Mrs. Rollins was wide-eyed, grasping her baby with fierce desperation. "It hit us," she whispered.

Murmurs of agreement greeted her statement.

"Four in a stick," said Sam. "Two to the north, heard them clear as anything."

"And one to the south," said Mrs. Shenton.

"And one right on top of us," whispered Vera.

Sam bit back a curse. In the trenches of his own war, he had been very free with his curses, but cursing had made no difference then, as it would make no difference now.

"Don't no one move," he said again.

Of course, it was Vera who challenged him. "Why the hell not?" she asked.

"Ooh, the mouth on that one!" exclaimed Mrs. Shenton.

Vera freed herself from the tangle of arms and legs, and rose shakily to her feet. She stared around with the look of a trapped animal.

Sam's brain finally began to fit the pieces together. It's a dud, he thought. It didn't explode. If it had exploded, we'd all be dead. It's a dud. It was known to happen. Every now and then, a bomb would fail to explode on impact.

The thought brought no relief. The bomb had failed to explode on impact, but that didn't mean it was never going to explode. Anything could set it off. Any slight shifting or settling of the earth could bring the detonator contacts together, and there was nothing they could do about it. They were like rats in a trap.

Vera's voice was steady and, for once, respectful. "Where is it, Mr. Ruddle?"

Ruddle raised his eyebrows and looked toward the door. "Right outside, I think."

Vera's mother reached out to grasp her daughter's arm. The villagers were slowly untangling themselves, moving as a group to huddle against the far wall. Vera was the only one standing, meeting Mr. Ruddle eye to eye. "Open the door, Mr. Ruddle, and take a look."

Mrs. Shenton's cracked voice was close to a scream. "No."

Vera rounded on the older woman. "You can stay here and get blown up if you want to, but I'm not going to stay here with you. We've only got Mr. Ruddle's word for it that it's right outside. It might not be. It might be farther away. We won't know if we don't look."

"You don't give the orders around here," Mrs. Shenton grumbled. "I say we all sit still and wait for help. Don't let her do it, Sam. She'll be the death of all of us."

Mr. Ruddle retrieved the courage of his youth and settled his tin hat firmly on his head. "She's right," he said. "We have to know. Now, you all stay back out of the way, and don't no one make any noise."

He reached into his pocket for his flashlight. No use worrying about using up the battery; he had to know. His hand shook as he placed it on the door handle, and he winced as the door creaked.

"You be careful," said Mrs. Shenton.

"You be quiet," Sam rejoined, as he cracked the door open and shone the wavering beam of the flashlight through the gap.

"Oh my God," he whispered. "Don't no one start screaming, you understand. No one make a sound."

His trembling grasp offered no resistance as Vera pulled the flashlight from his hand and held it steady.

"Let me," she said softly, and he thought that there was kindness in her young voice. Together they looked along the beam of light and saw where it reflected on a large metal object at the top of the steps. He saw where the nose cone was buried in the ground and where the fins reached up into the night sky.

"Is it …?" she asked.

"Aye," said Sam, "it's a bomb."

"Shit," said Vera, and no one corrected her.

The all-clear siren blared through the quiet air. Sam looked around in surprise as people began to gather their belongings. Foolishness, sheer foolishness; all except for Vera Chapman. She might have a headful of foolish notions about American soldiers, but she was the only one with the sense to stand still.

Sam raised his voice. "Don't be so blooming daft. No one's leaving. We can't go outside. Move back, everyone, back into the corner."

Mrs. Shenton was the first to point out the obvious. "Fat lot of good that will do. If that there thing goes off, it won't make no difference where we're sitting."

"Just move back out of the way and let me think," Sam said.

The children were awake now, staring wide-eyed at the adults.

"So what are you going to do?" asked Mrs. Rollins, cradling her baby. "How long are you going to keep us cooped up in here?"

Mrs. Shenton's voice was cracked and spiteful. "He don't know what to do. Look at him; he's white as a sheet. He don't have no idea what to do."

"We'll just wait here," said Sam, "until someone comes."

Mrs. Shenton was not to be silenced. "How long do you think that will be? You heard the explosions. There's other people been hit, or leastways some cows or pigs or something. They'll all be out there putting that right. No one knows we're in here."

"Oh, they'll realize it soon enough; soon as I don't report in," Sam replied, trying to sound confident and hoping that the expression on his face would not betray his words.

"Meantime we just sit here with a bloody great bomb on our doorstep; is that what you want us to do?" Mrs. Shenton snapped.

Sam was not one to approve of ladies using swear words, but he knew that Elsie Shenton had said aloud what no one else wanted to say; there was a bloody great bomb on their doorstep, and no one, including Sam, knew what to do about it.

He felt a hand on his arm. Vera was still standing beside him holding the flashlight. Her calm voice was a welcome reprieve from Elsie Shenton's panicked complaints.

"Mr. Ruddle," said Vera, "I think I can get past it."

"Don't be daft."

"Look for yourself."

Vera, her hand steady as a rock, shone the flashlight through the crack in the door.

"There's enough room for me to squeeze past it."

"If you touch it, it will—"

"I'm not going to touch it. I can get past without touching it."

Vera's mother rose to her feet. "No, I absolutely forbid it. You are not to go out there, Vera. Come and sit down. We have to wait. Give that light back to Mr. Ruddle. He's in charge, not you."

"You're like a bunch of sheep," Vera said, her gaze sweeping around the cluttered space. "I'm not going to sit here and wait just because he says I have to. If I'm going to die, I'm going to die trying."

"What about us?" Mrs. Rollins asked. "Don't you care what happens to us?"

"Not really!"

Vera flashed a quick smile at Sam and pulled the door open another couple of inches. "Close the door behind me," she said as she slipped through the crack.

March 1952

Sam thought a brisk walk would do him good and take his mind off the past. He'd go home by way of the cliff path. It would add a mile or so to his route, but he wanted to stretch his cramped muscles and fill his lungs with sea air. He'd been fortunate to come away from the Great War without a lungful of mustard gas, but, gas or no gas, he'd been coughing lately. There were those folks who said it was the cigarettes that made you cough. They said it was the cigarettes that had killed the King. Didn't seem very likely to him, but nonetheless, it would do him good to breathe some good clean sea air.

The rain had reduced to a fine drizzle, although storm clouds were building again on the southern horizon. If he kept up a steady pace and gave his legs a good stretch, he could be back in his cottage before the next downpour. He made his way out through the back gate to the place where the Earl's property ended abruptly at the cliff path and he could look down on the waves crashing onto the beach at Rose Hill Bay. The tide was high and the bay was deserted. He saw no boats on the horizon. Food was still in short supply, but no one needed it so desperately that they would take a fishing boat out on a day like this with whitecaps on the waves and a storm looming.

He lifted his eyes to the horizon, thinking of the night the invasion fleet had set sail for Normandy. He shivered inside his threadbare old raincoat. It had been June when the fleet had set sail, but the sea had been just as dark and rough as it was now. He stared out across the heaving waves, imagining that he could see the French coast, so close and now so accessible, but in those dark days, it had bristled with guns.

The sun made an unexpected appearance, sending a beam of watery light through a break in the clouds. The light played on the water, turning it from gray to green. Sam squinted and tried to focus on a dark object that rode the waves, rolling and tossing, occasionally disappearing and then reappearing. He reached into his pocket and pulled out his glasses. He could see better now. The object was large and round, a metal ball with … yes, spikes.

"Oh my God," Sam said aloud.

He looked around. He needed someone to confirm his opinion. He needed someone to agree with him that he had seen what he had seen. A mine! A German mine, or maybe even a British mine, broken loose from the rusted chain that had once anchored it to the seabed. He stood for a moment staring at the distant object; five hundred pounds of explosives drifting at the whim of the tide and the waves.

The tide was high and on the turn. When it began to ebb, the mine would be carried out away from the beach, but when it turned again, the mine would be carried back inshore. The game might continue for several days, but eventually the mine would collide with something, a beach, a harbor wall, a boat, a pier, and the result would be deadly.

"Right," said Sam, and he was speaking aloud again. "You know what it is and you need to report this, Sammy my boy. Let's get a move on."

He would have to phone the police, and the nearest telephone would be the one at Southwold Hall. He sighed and began to retrace his footsteps along the cliff path. The sun had disappeared again and the rain was increasing in intensity. He pulled his cap down low over his eyes and lowered his head as he battled the wind.

He entered the Hall by the back door and hurried through the kitchen and pantry. Normally he would stop to remove his boots before entering the main hall, but not today. He slammed open the green baize door separating the servant's domain from the rest of the house and called out for help.

"I need to use the Earl's phone," he shouted.

No one answered him. No one came to remonstrate with him for sullying the marble floors with his muddy boots or for keeping his hat on indoors.

"Nell. Nell Pearson," he called.

Women's voices rose angrily from the drawing room. He took a step closer. He recognized Lady Sylvia's voice, loud but still carefully controlled. He hesitated and then he heard Nell Pearson. Nell's voice was pitched in a high scolding tone, and her ugly words spewed across the echoing cavern of the main hall.

"Nosy little bitch. Thieving little slut."

Surely she wasn't talking to Lady Sylvia. Not in his wildest dreams could Sam imagine Nell Pearson using such words to Her Ladyship. Perhaps he should just go into the Earl's study and leave them alone. He turned away and then he heard another voice.

"I'm not. I'm not. I didn't do nothing. I was dusting."

Maisie!

Sam forgot about his urgent need to use the telephone. Nell Pearson was calling Maisie, his granddaughter, disgusting names. Maisie, who was just turning fifteen years old and as innocent as a newborn lamb, was being called a bitch and a slut by Nell Pearson, and Lady Sylvia seemed to be joining in.

He flung open the door of the dining room and stepped inside, careless of his muddy boots on the Persian rug. Maisie, in her gray maid's dress and white apron, was standing between the two angry women with tears running down her face, and a feather duster grasped in her hand.

"What do you think you're doing?" Sam bellowed.

Nell Pearson turned toward him, her face twisted in rage. "You'll stay out of this if you know what's good for you!"

As Sam watched, Lady Sylvia seemed to recall who she was and where she was, and she looked away from the crying child as though the matter was of no interest to her.

Her voice was cold and impersonal. "The girl has been dismissed, Mr. Ruddle. You can take her home."

"Dismissed! Why?"

"Theft."

"I didn't steal nothing," Maisie protested.

"You were going to," said Lady Sylvia. "She was going to steal money from my desk."

"I wasn't. I wasn't. I was dusting."

Lady Sylvia raised her elegant eyebrows. "Enough. She's dismissed without a reference. Take her away."

"Now, wait a minute," Sam protested.

"Boots!" said Nell Pearson suddenly. "What are you doing in here with your boots on? And take off your hat when you address Her Ladyship."

Sam looked down at his boots and the great clods of mud clinging to them, and then he looked at his granddaughter. He looked Lady Sylvia in the eye.

"She's no thief."

"And I say that she is and I don't want her in my house. If you're not careful, Mr. Ruddle, I shall be forced to dismiss you as well."

Sam stamped his feet, watching with satisfaction as a several large clumps of mud fell to the carpet.

"That's what I think of you and your job," he said. "That's what I think of your whole family. Come on, Maisie."

He put an arm around Maisie and led her to the door.

"She can't take the uniform," Nell Pearson said. "She has to take off the uniform."

Sam could not think of an appropriate response. He had no words to express his outrage, so he stamped his feet again, depositing another clod of mud on the carpet. He took Maisie's hand and led her out into the hallway. Instead of turning toward the kitchen, he steered her toward the carved oak front door.

"Grandad!"

"We're going out the front door," he said, "and we're walking away with our heads held high."

"I didn't do it, Grandad. I heard them talking. I didn't mean to. I was just doing the dusting."

Sam accompanied his granddaughter down the front steps and turned to look back at the imposing portico and ivy-clad walls of the Hall.

"Secrets are valuable," he said. "Now, why don't you come home with me and tell me what you heard, then we'll see what we can do with what we know."

CHAPTER FIVE

Toby Whitby

Toby was surprised to find that his date was a beer drinker. He couldn't imagine how Carol could find room in her small body for her first pint of ale, let alone the second one that she was consuming with alacrity, but he was happy with the effect.

When he had picked her up in the village, she had been very quiet, with hardly a word to say and a wary expression on her face. After the first pint, she had begun to relax and lose her anxious expression. Now, well into her second pint, she was tossing her copper curls, smiling readily, and even reaching across the table occasionally to touch his hand. She was a different girl. Toby was also on his second pint, sipping judiciously. He could feel his head spinning but not from the alcohol.

They had the saloon bar of the White Hart to themselves, with only an occasional burst of masculine laughter from the public bar to disturb their conversation. An old gray-muzzled dog padded through from somewhere in the rear of the pub and settled down in front of the coal fire. The smell of wet dog mingled with the odor of tobacco smoke and stale beer but did not quite overpower the heady scent of Evening in Paris wafting from Carol's wrists and making Toby even more lightheaded.

Rain was still hurling itself at the leaded windows, along with an occasional distant burst of thunder. Each time the thunder rolled, the pub grew silent. Old habits die hard, Toby thought, and there was not a person in that pub who did not hear the thunder and think of the thump of distant bombs, and did not still wait for the air-raid siren to chill their blood.

Somehow the old inn with its smoke-darkened beams had withstood the six years of war and come through unscathed. He doubted that any of the people laughing and joking in the public bar would call themselves unscathed. He doubted that the girl across the table was truly unscathed by the theft of her youth.

He took advantage of the moment of silence that followed a great clap of thunder to approach the subject of Vera Chapman.

"Were you with Vera when she met her husband?"

Carol threw her hands up in the air and scowled at him. "Is that what you want to talk about? Is that why you asked me out?"

"No, of course not. Forget I even asked."

Carol's breezy happiness had vanished in a moment. "I should have known. I thought it was all too good to be true."

"What do you mean?"

"A handsome man walking into the shop and asking me out." Handsome! Toby had never, ever thought of himself as handsome.

"A professional man, with a career and a car," Carol continued. "Things like that don't happen to me."

"No," Toby protested. "It was nothing to do with the case, with Vera. It's nothing. We won't talk about it."

Carol took a long swallow of beer. "Oh yes we will. We'll talk about Vera. You obviously want to talk about Vera, so let's just talk about her. Yes, I was with her on the night she met her husband. It was her birthday, and so her mother let her go to the dance. We were supposed to stay together, but as soon as we arrived, she was out on the dance floor with Nick. I swear they only danced one dance before she followed him out the door. It was a cold, rainy night but she didn't care. I warned her."

"Warned her about what?"

"Warned her what they were like. Hands everywhere. We called it desert disease."

"Why?" Toby asked before he could stop himself.

Carol gave him a long-suffering look. "Really? You really don't know?"

"No."

"Desert disease," Carol repeated. "Wandering palms."

Toby looked at her for a moment. He felt a flush rising up from his collar and was glad that the White Hart kept its lights low and he and Carol were only able to see each other by the glow from the coal fire.

"You get it, don't you?" Carol asked.

"Yes, I get it. Of course I get it."

Carol hesitated for a moment. "I suppose I should tell you the whole truth, you being a solicitor."

"You don't have to tell me anything."

"But that's why you asked me out, isn't it?"

"No."

Carol ignored his protest. "I don't want to speak ill of her," she said, "because she was my friend. We had some good times together, but I know she'd made her mind up even before we went into the village hall. If it hadn't been Nick Malloy, it would have been someone else. She wanted an American."

"Are you sure?"

"Yes, I'm sure. We'd both turned seventeen and finished with school. We were waiting to be called up for war work and sent away somewhere. Vera didn't know if she'd get another chance at an American, so she had to do the best she could in the time she had." Carol hesitated. "None of us knew how much time we had," she added softly.

"So you think that the first night …"

"What difference does it make if it was the first night or the last night? She had more time than she expected. We weren't sent to a factory, we were sent as land girls to work on the Earl's estate. That fitted right into Vera's plans. She could still see her American and make sure she got pregnant by him, and if not him, then some other American."

She drained the glass and set it down on the table. "Vera always knew how to turn things to her own advantage."

She stared thoughtfully at the empty glass. Toby wondered whether it would be a good idea to buy a third pint. Carol's mood had swung from withdrawn to outgoing to bitter. He had no idea where another pint would take her.

"Was Vera's mother any help to you in whatever it is you're doing?" she asked.

"No," said Toby, "no help at all."

"I'm not surprised. She was only too ready to sell her daughter for a box of chocolates and a pound of tea. My mother would never have let me carry on like that."

"So you didn't—"

"No, I didn't, and I didn't need my mother to tell me not to. I had already made up my mind that I wasn't going to get caught out, not like Vera."

"You didn't want to go to America?"

"No. Why would I want to go to America?"

"Oh, well, you know, for a better life."

"That's what Vera wanted," Carol said. "The Yanks all said they had ranches in Texas, or penthouses in New York, or God only knows what in Hollywood, but they stood around gawping at us like a bunch of farm boys. She took a big risk. He could have been from anywhere."

Toby was suddenly acutely aware of the letter in his pocket and its promise of a new life in Africa.

"So you wouldn't take a risk and leave England?" he asked.

"Not a risk like that," Carol replied. She looked down at the table, her expression unreadable. "I would never trust a man I don't know."

She looked up and gave a quick shake of her head. "You should probably take me home now. I'm feeling a little lightheaded."

Toby looked at his own glass, not yet empty. Surely she wouldn't expect him to leave before he finished his drink.

"And I mean take me home; I don't mean anything else," Carol said sternly.

"Anything else?"

"Yes, you know what I mean. Nothing else. No coming in for coffee or anything like that."

Toby took a small sip of the beer and set the glass down again, wondering what had prompted Carol's sudden decision to go home. Perhaps she had misjudged her capacity to drink beer. There had been desperation in the way she had gulped her drinks, and there was another kind of desperation in the way she was now warning him that he couldn't expect any favors from her at the end of the evening.

"If I could ask you just one more question," he said. "Just one more?"

"Is it about Vera?"

"No."

"Ask away."

"Can you tell me about the bomb crater on the village green? I almost fell in it today. I think there's a story there."

Carol ran her hands through her hair, turning the curls into a wild copper halo. "Vera again."

"No, not Vera. I was asking you about the bomb. Why does that have anything to do with Vera?"

"Because she was the hero," Carol said.

She took a deep breath. "I'm sorry. I don't mean to sound so angry. I have no right to be angry. We would all be dead if it wasn't for Vera. She saved us all, but she could just as easily have got us all killed. They called her a hero, and I suppose she was, but she was just looking out for herself. That's what Vera always does. She always looks out for herself."

A burst of sound from the public bar stopped Toby from asking any more questions.

"Hey up," shouted a loud masculine voice. "What's the matter with you, Sam?"

The reply, as much of it as Toby could hear, was a string of slurred words.

Carol turned her head and looked toward the low opening that led to the public bar.

"Now what?" she said. "That's sounds like Sam Ruddle. He was the air-raid warden when it happened, but he's gardener at the Hall now. It's not like him to be making all that noise."

Another burst of shouting erupted from the bar. The old dog got up from its bed by the fire, shook off a fine spray of mud and dander, and walked stiffly toward the door.

Sam Ruddle, clad in an old overcoat and wellington boots, came to a stumbling halt in the doorway as the dog blearily stood his ground.

"Get out of my way," Sam shouted to the dog.

The barman was close behind. "Hey, don't you be touching my dog. What's the matter with you? Go on home."

"No." Sam was drunkenly stubborn. "There's someone in here I want to see. I saw his car outside."

Carol rose, pushed past the bewildered dog, and took hold of the old man's arm. "Mr. Ruddle, what's the matter?"

In the light filtering from the public bar, Toby could see the kindness in Carol's eyes and the compassion behind her question. His heart thumped uncomfortably in his chest. She was far from perfect; in fact, she was a complete puzzlement, but he wanted to know more about her. He wanted to spend the rest of his life getting to know her. He wanted to take her to Africa. Ridiculous, of course; she would never agree to go with him.

Carol looked up at the barman. "How much did you give him to drink?"

"Not me. I didn't give him anything. He's been drinking at home, that's what he's been doing."

Sam lifted a gnarled hand and gently removed Carol's hand from his arm.

"I'm all right."

"Mr. Ruddle—"

Sam was looking past Carol to where Toby sat like a statue, mulling over the fact that he seemed to be falling in love with a woman he had known for less than twenty-four hours.

"You're the solicitor, aren't you?"

"Yes."

Sam stumbled forward. "I want to talk to you. I want to tell you something. Saw your car outside. Want to tell you—"

The barman's voice was firm. "Not now, Sam. You don't need to be telling anybody anything."

Sam looked at him indignantly. "Yes, I do. I'm going to talk to the solicitor."

Toby stood up. "Perhaps you should sit down, Mr. Ruddle."

Sam pushed past the dog and collapsed into the chair that Carol had vacated. "I don't have to put up with her nonsense," he declared.

"I'm sure you don't," Toby agreed.

Sam sighed deeply and seemed to be gathering his very scattered thoughts.

Toby's eyes slid past the old man's face and fastened hungrily on Carol, who was now talking to the barman.

"Do you have any idea what's the matter?" she was saying.

Another man approached tentatively from the public bar. A farmer, Toby thought, looking at the man's muck-spattered boots and ancient tweed jacket.

The barman protested. "Hey, you can't come in here, not with those boots."

The farmer was insistent. "Just wanted to say as how I know what's up with him."

Carol turned her smile on the farmer, and Toby continued to fall in love. "What is it?"

"It's his Maisie."

In his bewildering state of newfound love, Toby had trouble interpreting. Maisie? What was a maisie?

"My granddaughter," Sam said, thumping his hand on the table and causing Carol's empty glass to fall onto the floor.

The barman approached Sam with the obvious intention of ejecting him for inappropriate behavior. Perhaps table thumping and glass spilling were acceptable in the public bar, but certainly not in the saloon bar, where ladies were allowed to drink and beer cost an additional sixpence.

Sam glared at the barman. "I've had a few drinks," he admitted, "just to settle me down. Just a few drinks, but I know what I'm doing. I know what I'm saying." He looked at Carol. "Fired her, she did. Fired my little Maisie and then she fired me."

"Lady Sylvia fired you?" Carol asked. "Why did she do that, Mr. Ruddle?"

"I put mud on her carpets," Sam replied. A brief smile lit up his face before anger and an underlying sorrow returned. "It don't matter about me. I don't need their rotten job. I don't care about His Lordship's rosebushes. Robbie Pearson will kill them in a month; all brawn and no brain."

Toby tried to follow the conversation as it veered from muddy carpets to the death of His Lordship's roses and then back to Sam's granddaughter.

"She called my Maisie a thief. She called her a slut."

"Language," said the barman. "I won't have no bad language in here."

Sam nodded his head. "Beg pardon. Sorry about that, but that's what she said."

"Who did?"

"Bloody Nell Pearson."

"Language," the barman protested again.

Sam ignored him. "No reference. Fired her without a reference, and Lady Sylvia going along with everything she said. What's Maisie going to do now with no reference?"

"So," Toby said, attempting to bring the situation into a legal framework where he could take control, "Mrs. Pearson at the Hall accused your granddaughter of being a thief."

"And a slut."

"Let's leave that aside for a moment," Toby suggested.

"She's no slut."

"Of course not, but let's first deal with the accusation that she's a thief. Would you like to take legal action? What would you like me to do?"

Sam thumped the table again. "I don't want you to do nothing. We take care of our own, that's what we do, and I'll take care of Nellie Pearson and Her Ladyship too if I have to. I want to talk to you about the baby."

"What baby?" Carol asked.

Sam laid a grimy finger alongside his nose. "That's the question, isn't it? What baby? What baby indeed? I know a thing or two."

The farmer laid a heavy hand on Sam's shoulder. "Now then, Sam, no need for loose talk."

Sam stumbled to his feet and confronted the farmer. "We don't have to let them get away with it. Times have changed, and they can't just be stealing babies away from honest folk. They can't just take some poor girl's baby."

The barman reached out and grabbed the collar of Sam's old raincoat. "That enough, Sam."

Sam appeared to lack the coordination necessary to shake himself free of the restraining hand. "I know things about Nellie Pearson," he declared. "If she's going to say things, then I'm going to say things, and we'll see who says the most."

The barman tightened his grip on Sam's overcoat. "Not in here, you won't."

Toby kept his tone mild and non-confrontational although his mind was racing. "I'd really like to talk to him, if you don't mind."

"Well, with all due respect, sir, I do mind," the barman replied. "I keep a peaceful house here, and this isn't peaceful. And I don't like the way he's talking about the people up at the Hall. The Earl holds the lease on my cottage, and I won't keep it if I allow loose talk in here."

Good heavens, Toby thought, no wonder the Communist Party is gaining ground. Apparently, the feudal system was still in place in Rose Hill.

Sam pulled himself free of the barman's grasp. "This is what I think of them up at the Hall," he declared. He spat magnificently onto the floor, and Carol moved quickly and efficiently out of his way.

"That's it," said the barman. "You're done, Sam. Come back when you're sober."

Before Toby could get in another word, the farmer and the barman had hustled Sam out of the saloon bar and into the rainy night.

Silence reigned except for the shifting of coals in the fireplace and the snuffling of the old dog as he settled down by the fire to resume his snooze.

Carol came back to the table. "Sorry about that."

"It's not your fault," Toby replied.

"You're staring at me. What's the matter? Do I have a smudge on my nose or something?"

"You have a perfect nose," Toby said before he could stop himself.

Carol smiled slightly. She seemed to have forgotten her previous anger. "Thank you. I'm not so sure about the freckles."

"They're lovely."

"And you are, I think, slightly inebriated."

"Certainly am," Toby agreed. "I'm a different person when I'm sober."

"You can't be very drunk on two beers."

"Oh, no." Toby wondered if he had offended her. "I didn't mean that I have to be drunk to appreciate your beauty, I just—"

Carol laid a hand on top of his. "That's enough, or you're going to get yourself into trouble. Anyway, you're not as drunk as poor old Mr. Ruddle. I do feel sorry for him. Little Maisie is the apple of his eye, and that Mrs. Pearson, well, she's a real spiteful old cow."

"I met her," Toby said, "when I went up to the Hall to see the Earl. Well, I wouldn't say I exactly met her, but she brought in the tea and scowled at me, if that counts as meeting. So I suppose the girl I saw was Maisie. She seemed to be a happy little thing."

"Oh, she is," Carol agreed, "and I don't think she's a thief, and she's most certainly not a … slut. She was probably listening at doors, but that's what all the servants do. I suppose the secrets of the aristocracy are far more interesting than the secrets of us everyday people."

"Would you ever listen?" Toby asked.

"What do you mean?"

"When you put through telephone calls."

"No, of course not."

Toby hesitated for a moment. Sam Ruddle had accused the people at the Hall of baby-stealing, and that was the exact opposite of what he had been told by Lady Sylvia. She was convinced that Vera Chapman had stolen her baby, but what if it was the other way around? What if Lady Sylvia was stealing Vera's baby?

He thought of Robert Alderton, dead on the office floor, and the file that had turned up in Lady Sylvia's possession but minus Alderton's notes. He felt his heart pounding as he realized the implications of what he was suggesting and the danger of saying it even to himself.

He would need solid evidence before he could go to Mr. Champion with such a wild accusation. He forced himself to calm down and think things through. If Maisie had heard something, then maybe Carol had also heard something. The post office was the center of the village. All phone calls came through the switchboard, all letters, parcels, postcards, and telegrams.

"Would you listen in or report something if you thought a crime was being committed?" Toby asked.

Carol shrugged her shoulders. "I suppose I would if the police asked me, not that they ever would. But—"

Toby was quick to interrupt before Carol could launch a digression. "What if I asked you?"

"Why would you do that?"

"If something illegal was going on, and—"

"What are you talking about?"

"Baby-stealing," Toby muttered under his breath.

"What?"

"Baby-stealing."

"No, no." Carol waved a dismissive hand. "That was just the drink talking. No one's stealing babies. Do you think we're stuck in the Middle Ages here, sacrificing babies at full moon?"

"Oh no, nothing like that, but there is something going on, and I need to get to the bottom of it."

"Not by turning me into an eavesdropper," Carol said, anger returning.

"Of course not," Toby said. "My mistake. I'll find Mr. Ruddle in the morning when he's sober and see what he's talking about."

Carol collected her coat from the back of the chair. "Speaking of being sober," she said, "I think it's time for me to go home. I've asked you once already."

"No, please don't go," Toby protested. "I didn't mean to offend you."

Carol smiled. "You haven't offended me. It's been an interesting evening."

"Could we do it again?"

"You mean, I haven't told you enough about Vera Chapman and her American husband?"

"I'm not interested in Vera Chapman."

"Oh, I think you are. I think you're very interested. I'll tell you what, Toby, if you tell me why you're so interested in Vera, I'll tell you whether I'll go out with you again."

Toby wrestled with his conscience, and his conscience won. "I can't. I'm sorry, but I really can't."

Carol buttoned her coat with quick, efficient movements. "Don't bother driving me home. I'll walk."

"No."

"I'll walk," she repeated.

Terry Chapman

Terry fought against the stranglehold of the bedclothes pinning him to his narrow bed. He was hot and feverish. His body ached. No surprise to that, every man in the hut was hot, feverish, and aching. Some of them had tropical ulcers, some had head injuries from the beating of their Japanese guards, some had malaria, and all of them had dysentery.

For a few minutes, as he finally kicked off the bedclothes, Terry experienced a return to reality. The memory of three years of imprisonment faded, and he knew where he was. The bedclothes were to protect him from the cool damp of his mother's cottage. The door was to keep strangers out, not to keep him in. The window curtains covered a small lattice window with no bars, and outside the window was the village of Rose Hill, not the hell of Burma. He was safe. He was home.

His stomach gurgled and his bowels cramped. He had left Burma, but Burma had not left him. Burma was in the scars on his back, the neuropathy in his feet, and most of all in the parasites that still infested his stomach and bowels. Now that his mind was restored to fragile reality, he recognized the need to go down the garden to the lavatory and the need to put on a coat and shoes. The noise in his head was not the noise of slave laborers sleeping the sleep of the exhausted, but simply the sound of rain lashing against the window. He was home.

He shuffled his feet, damaged by working barefoot, into hard leather shoes and shrugged on his father's overcoat. His father had been a big man, and the coat hung loosely on Terry's wasted frame. As he cracked the door open, he heard his mother stir in the bedroom next door.

"Terry?"

"It's all right, Mum."

"What are you doing?"

"Going down to the lav."

"I put a pot in your room."

"Not that, Mum. The other."

"Oh! Well, be careful. It's a wild night."

"I like it. I like the rain. I like feeling cold."

He heard his mother turn over in her creaking bed. "That prison camp has made you daft in the head."

"Go back to sleep."

Terry made his way down the narrow stairs to the kitchen and found the flashlight his mother kept by the back door. He turned the key in the lock and stepped out into the night.

Thunder rolled overhead with a quick flash of lightning. The noise would have been sufficient to confuse him, but the lightning added to the confusion. He was at the harbor in Singapore again, with explosions all around as the British Army destroyed docks, cranes, and warehouses, ahead of the approaching Japanese.

"We're going to surrender."

Word had spread through his squad as they laid charges and ducked flying debris.

"God help us all."

"We're going to surrender."

"They're killing the wounded."

"Japs don't take prisoners."

"Bleeding Churchill. Wants us to fight to the death."

"Unconditional surrender."

"Slave labor. We'll all be slaves."

Terry's bowels cramped again, and his mind was gone from the chaos on the docks. He was in the labor camp.

Latrine. Where was it? Had to get to the latrine. Couldn't be found out here. What was he doing out here? If anyone found him, he'd be three days in the hot box. Three days and as good as dead.

Panic overtook him. How had he managed to get out of the hut? He dropped the flashlight. How had he even managed to get a flashlight? Prisoners were not given flashlights.

He stumbled through a tangle of bushes and found himself in the open. The ground squelched beneath his feet. Monsoon season. He knew about the monsoon season; he had survived three monsoon seasons. Even rain that fell as though the heavens had been split wide open was no reason to stop work. The railway was all that mattered. The Japanese wanted a railway, and the prisoners would build it, if they lived long enough. Most of them would not.

Terry knew very little except that he was alive and somehow out of the hut and free of the guard towers and the wire fence. He shuffled forward through the clinging mud. Sheet lightning lit the trees around him, and he glimpsed a figure coming toward him through the rain. This was it. He would not go back. He would die here. Oh, please God, let them kill me. Don't let me go back.

CHAPTER SIX

Toby Whitby

The storm blew itself out in the early hours of the morning, and bright rain-washed sunshine smiled down on Toby as he drove to the office. His time in the office would be brief because he was confident that he had a good reason to return to Rose Hill; a reason that would satisfy Mr. Champion and even Miss Clark.

Old Mr. Ruddle had made an accusation of baby-stealing, and it would be Toby's duty to follow up the lead. Ruddle would be sober by now and ready to talk, and perhaps he might even shed some light on Alderton's murder. It was a lot to hope for, but obviously something was going on and, one way or another, Ruddle was involved.

He decided that he would drop by the office, explain the situation, pick up some petty cash so he could put fuel into the Morris, and then he would be off to Rose Hill.

As he had no idea where Mr. Ruddle lived, he would have to ask Carol, the post mistress, for an address. She couldn't turn him away. He had every right to ask her for information, and while he was asking, why shouldn't he ask her to lunch? The morning sunlight would surely have dispelled last night's gloom, and he wouldn't say a word about Vera Chapman; not a single word.

The tide was out and the ocean was as flat as a millpond, last night's storm no more than a memory. A pack of dogs snuffled their way along the tideline, nosing into the drying seaweed for stranded wildlife. Toby thought he would get himself a dog in Rhodesia, something large and fierce. Did Carol like dogs? She hadn't objected to the barman's smelly old retriever, so perhaps she did.

He was getting way ahead of himself. He hadn't even kissed her, let alone asked her if she wanted to go to Africa with him. She hadn't given him any real encouragement, but she had called him handsome, and she had admired him for having a car and a career. That was a good beginning. He was grinning as he entered the office.

"You're late, Mr. Whitby."

Edwin Champion himself was standing in the reception area. Without the framework of his massive desk and leather chair, the lawyer looked very small and frail. However, his dress was as formal as ever, his hair neatly combed, his little moustache trimmed, and his black tie, still in mourning for the King, neatly knotted.

"No, I—"

"One minute," said Champion. "Minutes count, young man."

"Yes, sir."

"You have work to do."

Toby's heart sank. Would there be time to go to Rose Hill? So far as Carol was concerned, he should strike while the iron was hot, or at least lukewarm. And what about Sam Ruddle?

"You're wanted at Southwold Hall," Anthea Clark said from her seat behind her typewriter. "She has someone for you to interview. A nurse; Irish I think, although that can't be helped."

"Two o'clock," said Champion.

Toby breathed a sigh of relief. Two o'clock; he would still have plenty of time. He followed Mr. Champion into his office without waiting to be invited. The old man looked up at him, his eyebrows raised in surprise.

"Did you want something?"

"Well, yes."

Toby waited while Champion creaked his way across the room and settled into his chair. "Get on with it."

"Last night, I heard a rumor in the village about baby-stealing."

"That's hardly a surprise. I imagine that the village gossips know everything that goes on at the Hall. I'm glad that you're listening, but I don't suppose they have anything new to say."

"Well," Toby insisted, "what I heard was something quite different. The speaker implied that it was Lady Sylvia or someone else at the Hall who was doing the baby-stealing."

"Ah."

Mr. Champion looked at Toby with faded gray eyes. Toby waited.

"There's a good deal at stake here," the lawyer said eventually. "If Lady Sylvia should die childless, the estate would go to another branch of the family tree, distant relatives who may not be interested in saving Southwold Hall."

"Really?"

"They're overseas," Champion explained. "Australia, the last resting place of the penniless gentry. The children would be third or fourth generation Australians now with no ties to England. They would have no understanding of the obligation placed on them by history."

"But they'd come back, wouldn't they, if they inherited a place like Southwold?"

"A wreck," said Champion. "Just because my eyes are old doesn't mean I can't see. We may have solved the problem of death duties for this generation, but it won't matter. Southwold is a ruin. I imagine the Australian relatives would be happy to relieve themselves of the burden. They'll sell the estate to a developer for whatever they can get; someone who can build houses to replace all those that Herr Hitler destroyed. Far better use of the land, really."

"But tradition, history—"

Champion eyed Toby wearily. "My dear young man, tradition and history don't put food on the table. I suggest that you look at this situation with a suitably jaundiced eye. The Earl and his daughter are passionate about their title and their lands, and one wonders to what length they would go to be sure that Southwold remains intact. I imagine that money from a rich American would be very helpful to them."

"So you're suggesting …?"

"I am suggesting, in light of this new information you have gathered, that you keep an open mind. I have not forgotten that Her Ladyship has asked if you are flexible. I find that question offensive."

"Oh, so do I."

"I would hope so." Mr. Champion gestured to the door. "I suggest you go to Rose Hill and meet this Irish nurse person and see what she has to say. Meantime I will ask Miss Clark to send yet another telegram to find out when we can expect Mr. Harrigan to arrive in person. You must try to complete your inquiries and come to your conclusion before he arrives and starts throwing his American money around. Money tends to make people lose their sense of perspective."

"I wouldn't do that, sir. I wouldn't lose my perspective."

Mr. Champion looked at him for a long moment, his pale face unreadable. Toby, not for the first time, wished that Mr. Champion would voice a straightforward opinion. Did Mr. Champion believe Lady Sylvia's story? Did he want Toby to believe it? What would he do if Toby told him his suspicions about Sam Ruddle, the missing baby, and Robert Alderton's death?

The legal affairs of the Blanchard family and the Southwold Estate provided the bread-and-butter income of Champion and Company. He had no right to accuse their most important client of being complicit in a murder; and he had no evidence, just a hunch.

Mr. Champion waved a dismissive hand, and Toby realized that now was not the time to speak. Later, perhaps, when he knew more. He backed out of the door and almost into Anthea Clark, who was poised on the threshold with her notebook in hand.

"He wants me to send a telegram," she said.

"How did you know?"

"I always know."

She pushed past Toby and into the room, closing the door behind her. He realized that he had not been allowed time to ask for money from petty cash. He dug around in his pockets and discovered a folded ten-shilling note. No need to ask for petty cash; ten shillings would be more than enough, and he would still have money to buy lunch for Carol, if she would agree to lunch.

He made his way back over the Downs toward Rose Hill. The little Morris purred along quietly, and the sun lent a stark beauty to the leafless trees. Overhead, seagulls wheeled and dipped as they returned from taking shelter inland. Much as he wanted to think about Lady Sylvia and the question of whether she had or had not given birth to a little girl, he found that he could only think about Carol Elliot and the spray of freckles across her nose.

He left the main highway and took the one-lane road into Rose Hill. Leafless hedges lined the road and blocked his view until he made the final turn alongside the parish church.

When the village green came into view, he braked abruptly. Yesterday the green had been deserted, but today it seemed that every inhabitant of Rose Hill was out on the green, along with a contingent of black police cars and an ambulance.

From what he could see, the crowd consisted only of adults, men in caps and women in headscarves, and they were gathered around the infamous bomb crater. With police cars blocking the road, he parked the Morris outside the White Hart and followed his curiosity into the crowd. He found Carol immediately, or maybe she found him. She had abandoned the post office and was standing at the back of the crowd, a green cotton scarf tied over her hair, and red curls escaping and falling across her eyes.

"Toby!"

She ran toward him. It was a scene that he might have dreamed up for himself except that she wasn't smiling and the light in her eyes was not joy but fear.

"What is it? What's going on?"

"Mr. Ruddle."

"Ruddle? I was going to ask you where he lives. I want to talk to him."

She shook her head. "Oh, Toby, someone attacked him. He's unconscious. They think he's going to die."

"Excuse me." A tall young policeman pushed past officiously. "Clear the way."

The ambulance men were behind the policeman, with a patient on a canvas stretcher. A hand and arm hung out from beneath the blanket. Water dripped from the sleeve of an old raincoat.

The crowd murmured angrily among themselves, and the murmuring crystalized into questions and comments.

"Are you going to arrest him?"

"He'll kill us all in our beds."

"He shouldn't be allowed out."

"Touched in the head."

"Shell shock, that's what it is."

And then one plaintive young voice rising above the others. "Is Grandad going to die?"

Toby pulled Carol aside. "What happened?"

"No one knows but everyone suspects. His son found him this morning on the green. Mr. Ruddle never went home last night, so Derek went looking for him this morning."

Toby watched as the ambulance attendants loaded the stretcher into the back of their vehicle. A man, a younger version of Sam Ruddle, stood helplessly beside them with Maisie, the maid from the Hall, grasping his hand.

"What do you mean by 'everyone suspects?' What do they suspect? Maybe he just fell. He was very drunk last night."

"No, the police are saying it wasn't a fall. Someone hit him on the head."

The words reverberated in Toby's head. Someone hit him on the head. Was it the same someone who hit Alderton on the head? "Why?"

He didn't realize that he had spoken aloud until Carol answered him. "If Terry Chapman did it, there wouldn't have to be a why. You've seen him yourself. He doesn't know what he's doing."

"Terry Chapman? Why would anyone think it's Terry Chapman?" Toby asked. "He's not violent. I watched him with his mother. He's quiet as a lamb, and he's terrified. I don't think he knows where he is. He seems to think he's back in Burma. I don't know what they did to him, but he's a broken man."

"The neighbors heard Mrs. Chapman calling for him in the middle of the night," Carol said. "He wasn't in his bed, and she was out in the garden, looking for him. He probably wandered out onto the green and came across Mr. Ruddle on his way home from the pub."

"So he wasn't in his bed. That doesn't mean he was out attacking people."

"Well, if it wasn't him, then who was it?" Carol asked with an edge to her voice. "We'll all sleep safer in our beds with him out of the way."

"No, that's not right," Toby protested. "You can't just say he's guilty, because you don't know who else might have done it. That's not fair, Carol."

Anger flashed in her eyes. "You don't have to live here and we do. It's not as if they'll put him in jail. They'll lock him up in a mental hospital. That's what they should have done in the beginning."

"Not much of a reward for all he's been through," Toby said.

"We've all been through a lot," Carol muttered.

Now she's angry with me, Toby thought. He wondered how to defuse the situation. Perhaps Carol was correct, and perhaps Terry Chapman belonged in a mental hospital, but that didn't mean he was the one who had cracked old Sam Ruddle over the head, and he certainly wasn't the one who killed Alderton.

He looked around at the villagers. If not Terry, then who and, more to the point, why? Sam had been drunk and angry last night and threatening revenge on the housekeeper at the Hall, or was he threatening revenge on Lady Sylvia? Baby-stealing. Did this come down to Sam's knowledge of baby-stealing? Did it come down to something Alderton had known and written in his notes?

He looked into Carol's agitated face. "Excuse me a minute." She still looked angry. "Are you leaving?"

"Just going to have a word with someone."

"I'll come with you."

Telling her to stay where she was could only lead to more bad feeling, so he said nothing as she walked beside him to the ambulance.

Sam's son had a comforting arm around his daughter. Maisie's face was streaked with tears. Her nose was running, and she bore little resemblance to the perky little teenager who had opened the door for him at the Hall. He looked at the way she leaned into the protection of her father's arm. It would not be enough; not if she knew something she shouldn't know.

"Mr. Ruddle?"

"Who are you?"

"I've seen him at the Hall," Maisie said. "He's a solicitor."

Toby extended his hand. "Toby Whitby."

The other man hesitated and then stuck out a large calloused hand. "Derek Ruddle, and this is my daughter, Maisie."

"Could I have a word with you in private?"

Derek looked doubtfully at his daughter, and Carol removed her hand from Toby's arm. He could feel her affront even in that small gesture.

"I don't need no private words with a solicitor, especially one from the Hall. You might have private words with them up there, but down here we don't have no secrets. Anything you want to say, you can say in front of Maisie and Miss Elliot, if she's a mind to listen."

Toby chose his words carefully. "I think you should send your daughter away for a little while, just until this is cleared up."

"It's cleared up. Terry Chapman, poor sod."

"I don't think so."

"Look," said Derek, "we all feel sorry for him. God knows he had a hard war, but he can't go around attacking people. Now, if you'll excuse me, I have to go to the hospital. My dad's unconscious, and no one knows if he'll wake up ever again. I don't have time to be talking to you."

Toby looked past Derek and caught Maisie's eye.

"Maisie," Toby said, "what happened at the Hall? Why were you dismissed? Why was your grandfather so upset?"

"That's our business," Derek snapped. "We'll take care of it ourselves."

"Your father wanted to talk to me last night," Toby said. "He wanted me to know about something that Maisie had overheard."

"He was so angry," Maisie said softly. "He stamped his feet and left mud on the carpet."

"I know. He told me about it last night. And he talked about a baby."

"She don't know nothing about babies," Derek said.

"It's alright, Dad," Maisie said in a small voice. "I told Grandad what I'd heard Mrs. Pearson say."

"Maisie!" Derek's voice contained a warning, but Maisie ignored him.

"Me and Grandad, we knew why you came to see Her Ladyship. It was about her baby, wasn't it? They think Vera Chapman stole her."

Toby heard Carol's sharp intake of breath, but he kept his eyes fixed on Maisie.

"I heard them talking yesterday," she said, "Her Ladyship and Mrs. Pearson, and Her Ladyship asked how much it was going to cost to get the nurse to say what needed to be said."

"What nurse?" Carol asked.

Toby stayed silent. He already knew the answer to Carol's question. He had a two o'clock appointment to meet a nurse, and this was the nurse he was to meet.

"I wasn't listening at keyholes," said Maisie. "I was doing the dusting, but they didn't know I was there. I was sort of hidden by a curtain."

Derek frowned at his daughter. "Maisie!"

"Perks of the peasantry," Maisie replied. "That's what Grandad calls it." She took a deep breath and choked back tears. "Mrs. Pearson went over to the desk by the window to get the checkbook for Her Ladyship, and that's when she saw me. Her Ladyship was really angry and Mrs. Pearson slapped my face, and they were screaming at me like a couple of tea kettles. Then Mrs. Pearson said I was trying to steal money from the desk, but I wasn't. I wouldn't. I was just listening. What's wrong with listening?"

Toby looked at Derek. "Mr. Ruddle, you shouldn't leave Maisie on her own. If you're going to the hospital, you should take her with you."

Derek shook his head. "The hospital's no place for a child. I wouldn't make her suffer like that, watching her old grandad die."

"He's not going to die," Maisie insisted.

Derek took his daughter's hands in his own. "We don't know, love. It's bad. That Terry Chapman hit him really hard. It did things to his brain, that's what the ambulance men said. He might not wake up again. You should stay here with your mum."

With a cough and a splutter of badly tuned plugs, the engine of the ambulance rattled into life. A policeman laid a heavy hand on Derek's shoulder.

"Are you going with him?"

"Aye," said Derek.

The crowd stirred again. Now they were all looking across the green, where two police officers were confronting Mrs. Chapman at the front door of her cottage.

"This is going to be ugly," Toby said. "You don't want Maisie to see this."

Mrs. Chapman's voice rose above the sound of the ambulance in a long protesting shriek.

Derek nodded in reluctant agreement and took his daughter's hand. "Come on, love, we'll go with Grandad. Your mum can fetch you later."

By the time the ambulance door had closed, the two police officers were crossing the green, with Terry Chapman supported between them. He was a stick figure with his head down, eyes fixed on the ground in front of him. Mrs. Chapman followed behind clutching at her son's clothing.

"He was in the lav," she screamed. "He was down the garden in the lav. You leave him alone. Leave him alone."

Terry turned his head and looked at his mother, and then his shoulders drooped and he allowed the police to lead him away. Toby could hardly imagine the man's pain. From what little he knew of the prisoners who worked the Burma Death Railway, he was sure Terry thought that being dragged between guards was just the prelude to brutal punishment. Weak and shell-shocked, he would think himself back in Burma, and the watching crowd would become Japanese soldiers or half-starved fellow prisoners.

Terry's feet scraped a path through the mud as the police hurried him toward the waiting car. Mrs. Chapman stood alone, her face buried in a handkerchief.

"This is awful," Carol said softly.

"Yes, it is," he agreed.

"Do you really think this has something to do with Vera?"

"I don't know."

"He talked about baby-stealing. Does someone think Vera stole a baby? Is that why you're here?"

"I can't talk about it."

"All right then," said Carol, "you keep quiet and I'll talk about it. I want to show you something. I wasn't totally honest with you when I said I hadn't heard from Vera. Actually I had a letter from Vera. I didn't think you needed to know, but now I don't know what to think."

CHAPTER SEVEN

Carol pulled Toby into the cluttered interior of the village store and flipped the sign on the door.

"I'm closing early for lunch," she declared as she shot home two bolts. "I don't want them all in here gossiping. Come on into the back."

Toby followed her through an interior door and into a cozy sitting room where a banked coal fire sent out a steady heat.

"Is this where you live?" he asked.

"Yes, it's all mine. It goes with the shop."

"Do you live on your own?"

She nodded her head. "My mother died in '46, and I took over the shop and the post office. I thought I might have … someone … but it was a long time ago, and it couldn't be, so I'm alone."

Toby longed to get up and examine the framed photos on the mantelpiece. Someone? What kind of someone? Would there be a photo of a man in uniform? He resisted the urge; none of his business. Just being with her in the warm little room was sufficient intimacy for the time being.

Carol left the room and came back carrying an airmail envelope. "This is it," she said. "I can't show it all to you, because some of it's kind of personal."

"There is no legal requirement for you to show me the letter," Toby assured her.

Carol looked alarmed. "Why would there be a legal requirement?"

"I can't tell you."

She frowned. "There you go again, keeping secrets. Look, just read what she says, and you'll know that everything you've heard about baby-stealing is nonsense. Vera didn't steal a baby. She could be really selfish and annoying, but she would never do a thing like that. She has her own little girl, why would she take one from someone else? Her life hasn't turned out the way she expected it would, but she loves her baby. Everything she did was for that little girl."

Carol handed him the envelope. Toby sank uninvited into an armchair, and she leaned across him to turn on a table lamp. He pulled the sheets of flimsy paper from the striped envelope and started to read.

…didn't tell them I was coming. Didn't even tell them he had married me. His grandmother, a horrible old woman called Barbree (and I have no idea how to spell it, but that's what it sounds like), says that he was engaged to someone called Darlene, so he can't be married to me.

He met me in New York, and I asked him how long it would take to get to California, and he just laughed. He said we weren't going to California, that he lived in West Virginia.

Toby rested his eyes for a moment. Vera's handwriting was little more than a scrawl, as if she was writing in a hurry, just dashing words down on the paper in a rush of emotion.

"When did she send this to you?" he asked.

"Five years ago. I haven't heard a word since."

Toby refocused.

It's a horrible place, coal dust and dirt. They're all miners, and when they're not at the coal mine, they're out shooting rabbits and things. I don't even recognize some of the animals they bring home and expect us to eat. Barbree guts them and skins them in the kitchen and hangs up the fur. It smells awful. His mother is quite nice but his father is always angry, and he has two little brothers who just keep staring at me and saying they don't understand me. Well, I'll be damned if I'm going to start talking like them just so they can understand me.

Don't worry, I'm not going to try to come home. I know I can't do that. I've made my bed and I'll have to lie in it. The one good thing is that Nick loves Anita. She has him wrapped around her little finger. She's two now and starting to talk. I'm going to make sure she has an English accent and doesn't sound like all of the rest of the Malloys. Horrible old Barbree keeps saying that Anita isn't Nick's child, but Nick just tells her it's none of her business and of course Anita is his child. I haven't even written to my mother. I don't want her to know how…

"Do you want a cup of tea?"

He looked up. Carol was standing in the kitchen doorway.

"Yes, that would be lovely."

It was all lovely; the cozy room, the Closed sign on the door, the glowing fire, and Carol making tea in the kitchen. The only unlovely thing was the content of Vera's letter.

While Carol bustled around the kitchen, Toby studied the young bride's letter. It was apparent that Carol had only given him a couple of pages of what might have been a very long epistle. Toby had formed a mental picture of Vera as a free and easy young woman, selfish, impetuous, headstrong, and full of fun. The woman who had written this sad letter sounded disappointed but determined. She didn't sound like someone who would give up her child to strangers.

Carol bustled in with a tea tray.

"I'm surprised she said that she doesn't want to come home," Toby said.

"She can't," Carol said firmly.

"Are you sure?"

Carol concentrated on pouring the tea. "She doesn't have the money, and there's no reason for her to expect anyone to help her. No one in her family has any money, and I know what they'd say if she asked. They'd say exactly what she said, that she made her own bed and now she has to lie in it."

She took the letter from Toby's hand. "I just wanted you to see that the baby is fine and there is absolutely no possibility that she belongs to anyone other than Vera and her husband. She says how much Nick loves her."

"Maybe he does," Toby agreed, "but I can't imagine why he didn't tell his family that he had a wife and a child."

"No, neither can I," said Carol. "I thought he really cared for her. He's a big disappointment."

"I suppose he promised her the moon," said Toby.

"He promised her a home in California, and a swimming pool and orange trees and no more worries," Carol confirmed. "I haven't told anyone else about where she is or what it's like. I can't see any reason to let the whole village know about his lies. Better that they think she's living the high life in California."

"Did you tell her mother?"

"No, not even her mother. Mrs. Chapman has had enough to deal with, and now this business with Terry attacking Mr. Ruddle."

"I don't think he did," Toby protested.

"Can you think of anyone else who would do such a thing?"

Toby shook his head. That was the problem. He was convinced that Terry was not the perpetrator, but the idea of Lady Sylvia sneaking around banging people on the head was ridiculous.

Carol tucked the letter back into the envelope. Toby wondered how many pages the young bride had written and hoped that he would never be forced to ask Carol to show him the rest of the letter. The fact that Nick Malloy had taken a liking to the child hardly proved that he was the father. He couldn't help wondering what else Vera had said and why Carol wouldn't let him read the other pages.

Carol extended a heaping sugar bowl. "Sugar?"

"No, really, I can't use your sugar ration."

"There are certain perks attached to running a shop," Carol said. "Don't worry, it's not black market."

He knew she was trying to distract him. He appreciated her effort and smiled as she put two heaping teaspoons into his teacup. He paused, savoring the sweetness, but he couldn't abandon the subject entirely.

"Carol?"

"Yes?"

"Are you sure that the baby she took to America was hers?"

Now she was angry. "Of course I am. Who else's would it be? That's a ridiculous question. The baby was the whole reason he married her and why she could go to America."

Toby said nothing. Mr. Champion had taught him the wisdom of silence.

He watched the play of light across Carol's face as she set the teacup back into the saucer. Her mouth was set in a stubborn line. "It was her baby. She was pregnant, she gave birth, she took the baby to America."

"Were you actually there?"

"When she gave birth?"

"Yes."

"No, of course not. She went to a clinic. Why do you need to know?"

"Did you ever see the baby?"

Carol set her teacup back onto the tray. Her face was flushed. "Why are you asking?"

"I can't tell you."

"Then I can't answer you. Obviously, something is going on. First Mr. Ruddle talks about baby-stealing, then you start asking me questions about whether or not I actually saw Vera's baby, and now you say things about legal requirements. Well, I'm not going to tell you anything more until you tell me what this is all about."

Their eyes locked, and Toby knew that she would not back away from her ultimatum. He broke the gaze and looked at his watch. He was due at the Hall in thirty minutes to meet the nurse who had delivered the baby and who was being paid to give answers. He thought about the telegram from the wealthy Harrigan grandfather who would soon be arriving along with the disputed child. How was that going to be kept a secret, especially if Lady Sylvia named the child as her heir?

"Do you know anything about Lady Sylvia marrying an American?" he asked.

Carol laughed derisively. "What American?"

"An American officer. She married him in 1944."

Carol shook her head. "No, that's not possible. Even if she got married in London, we would have known. Mrs. Pearson would have said something. She was always boasting about how close she was to Lady Sylvia. I certainly didn't hear anything about it, and I've never seen any sign of an American husband. Haven't even seen any letters from America coming through the post office."

"You wouldn't," said Toby. "Apparently, he died in the Normandy invasion."

"Well," said Carol, "there were American officers in the village, and they used to go up to the Hall to dine every now and then. We all thought the Earl invited them because they'd bring him extra rations. The Earl was rationed just like we were. There were a couple of nice-looking young officers." She paused thoughtfully and then shook her head. "We would have known. No one keeps secrets in a place like this."

"And you were working as a land girl on the Earl's estate the whole time," Toby confirmed, "so you would have seen for yourself."

"No, not the whole time. Just before the Americans left for Normandy, we were sent to a farm in Billingshurst."

"So it could be true about Lady Sylvia marrying an American," Toby persisted.

Carol shook her head vehemently. "No, it's really not possible. Billingshurst isn't that far away and news travels. I would have heard about it from someone. What gives you the idea she married an American, and if he's dead, why does it even matter?"

Toby took a deep breath. The image of Robert Alderton's battered body floated before his eyes. Where were Alderton's notes? How had Lady Sylvia known already that Alderton was dead? Why did the Earl have Alderton's file? Mr. Champion had urged secrecy, but secrecy was getting him nowhere. The secret behind the child's birth could only be found in this village, where Sam Ruddle had kept a careful eye on the comings and goings of the American soldiers. Sam Ruddle was in no position to answer questions, but Carol was.

Toby set his foot on the slippery slope of flexibility.

"Can you keep a secret?"

Carol rolled her eyes. "Yes, I suppose so."

"No, I need your word."

Carol patted the empty space on the sofa. "I give you my word. Come and sit here."

Toby sank down beside her. The sofa was small, and he felt the warmth of her shoulder against his, and the pressure of her thigh.

He looked at his watch again. Time was racing by. She was silent for once, looking at him with inquisitive brown eyes and waiting for him to speak. The feeling was intoxicating. Instead of his usual stumbling small talk, he had something to say. He could talk to this girl, really talk. He could be very flexible.

When it came out, he was surprised by how little he really had to say. He could not mention Alderton's murder, and all that remained took little time to tell. Lady Sylvia claimed that she had married Jack Harrigan, an American officer, and that Vera Chapman had stolen the baby that resulted from the marriage and taken it to America.

Carol could hardly contain an impatience that verged on anger. "No, no, no. Vera came home with the baby. We all saw her. The vicar christened her. It was Vera's baby. The Earl came to the christening."

"Then why did Sam Ruddle talk about baby-stealing," said Toby, "and why has he been attacked?"

"Terry Chapman—"

"That's too easy. It's obvious that the whole village wants Terry Chapman to be guilty; less work for the police, less problems for the village. Even his mother won't really be sorry to see him go. I'm telling you, I saw Terry, and he's not violent. He wouldn't have done it."

Carol snatched the teacup from Toby's hand. "Well, it's more likely than some crazy story about Lady Sylvia marrying an American and Vera stealing her baby. I wouldn't have shown you Vera's letter if I thought you were going to twist it around like that."

The teacup trembled on its saucer. Toby could see that she was shaking with emotion.

"You're on their side, aren't you? How much are they paying you to tell lies about Vera?"

"No," Toby protested. "No one is paying me to tell lies. I'm just trying to get to the truth."

"Truth!" said Carol. "I'll tell you the truth. Vera's baby is nothing to do with Lady Sylvia. I was there. I saw her at the christening. The Earl came and Her Ladyship came with him. She wouldn't even touch the baby; didn't even want to look at it? What kind of mother would refuse to even hold her baby? Go and ask the vicar if you don't believe me."

Toby rose to his feet.

"Please, Carol, I—"

"Times are changing," Carol said defiantly. "People like the Earl can't just take whatever they want anymore."

She turned her back on him and walked away. "I'd like you to leave," she said over her shoulder.

CHAPTER EIGHT

Dennis Blanchard, Earl of Southwold

The Earl surfaced from a drugged sleep. The new pills relieved the pain in his chest, but there was a price to pay for the relief. With every pill he took, his mind grew more confused. He had only brief moments of absolute lucidity, and this was one of them. He searched among the pill bottles on his bedside table. He didn't need more pills, he needed a cigarette. No cigarette case. No cigarettes. Someone had confiscated them.

What was the point? he asked himself as he swung his frail legs out of the bed. Did Sylvia really think that his cancer would just disappear if he stopped smoking? He was not personally convinced that his cancer had even been caused by smoking, but if Sylvia wanted to blame the cigarettes, that was her problem, not his. Everyone agreed he was going to die, and there was nothing to be done about it. If the doctors had been unable to cure the King, they certainly weren't going to cure a mere earl. It was just a matter of time, and in the time remaining, he intended to smoke as many cigarettes as he damn well wanted.

He slid his feet into worn leather slippers and wrapped a Chinese silk robe around his shoulders. The air in his bedchamber was distinctly chilly. Mrs. Pearson believed that fresh air was the cure for most ills, and so the windows had been flung open first thing in the morning and would remain open come rain or shine until late at night. The small coal fire smoldering in the grate did nothing to alleviate the chill.

He shuffled outside into the corridor, where the air was marginally warmer. The rule about open windows applied only to bedrooms and bathrooms, not to corridors and reception rooms.

He made his way to the top of the stairs. It was more than two weeks since he had been downstairs, and that time, he had been helped down the stairs by old Ruddle the gardener. It was the thought of Ruddle that was now prompting him to set one trembling foot after another as he descended the oak staircase. Old Ruddle was a smoker, and old Ruddle kept his cigarettes in the tool cupboard by the back door. This was a secret shared only by the Earl and his gardener as an alliance against the two women, Nell Pearson and Lady Sylvia. They'd be Woodbines or something even worse, the Earl thought, but they were cigarettes, and the craving was definitely on him.

He arrived at the foot of the stairs and clung to the newel post, desperately suppressing the urge to cough. At last, when the pain in his chest was under control, he shuffled across the wide expanse of hallway in the general direction of the kitchen and tradesman's entrance.

"Daddy!"

Oh no, she was going to make him go back to bed and take another pill. He would not allow it to happen; not this time.

"Daddy?"

Sylvia, looking heartbreakingly like her mother, in a green woolen dress and pearls, was staring at him from the doorway of the library.

"Hello, dear."

"What are you doing down here?"

"I believe that is my own business," said Dennis.

"But—"

"I am feeling better," Dennis improvised, "and I have come downstairs to see you."

"Really?"

"Yes."

"But—"

"I shall take tea in the library."

"Mrs. Pearson can bring it up to your room."

"I shall take tea in the library," Dennis repeated.

"But we have visitors."

Good, Dennis thought, maybe one of them will have a cigarette.

"You're not dressed, Daddy."

Dennis rewrapped his silk robe and knotted the belt. "Are we entertaining royalty?"

"No, of course not. It's just Mr. Whitby, the solicitor."

"Then I am sufficiently dressed," Dennis declared as he walked ahead of his daughter into the library. He suspected that, despite his best efforts, he was actually tottering like an old man, but he kept his head high and his shoulders square.

A tall bespectacled young man leaped to his feet as the Earl entered. He wore a dark suit, rather ill-fitting and certainly not the product of a quality tailor. His brown hair curled in uncontrolled profusion, with curls actually touching the collar of his white shirt, and his tie was not from any school that the Earl could recognize. But, he thought, the young man had an honest face, and behind the thick spectacles, his eyes brimmed with intelligence.

"Your Lordship."

"Mr. Whitby," said the Earl.

He studied the other occupants of the room. Nell Pearson rose rapidly from a chair by the fire. Since when had the housekeeper been allowed to sit by the fire? Sylvia was fond of the woman but surely not that fond. The other occupant of the room was a red-faced woman whose sturdy body occupied most of the sofa. She made some small effort to rise before giving up the challenge and sinking back against the cushions.

"Nurse Tierney," said Sylvia.

"I don't need another damned nurse!"

"No, not for you; Nurse Tierney is here to talk to Mr. Whitby."

"And why should she want to do that?"

"Daddy, you don't have to trouble yourself with all of this. Why don't you let Mrs. Pearson bring a tray to your room?"

"It looks as though Mrs. Pearson is rather too comfortable to be carrying tea trays," Dennis said acerbically.

He made his way past his daughter and, with a triumphant smile, sat down in the chair formerly occupied by the housekeeper.

"So, what is this about?" he asked. "Why do we have a solicitor, a nurse, and a housekeeper assembled in my library?"

"Nurse Tierney is here to explain to Mr. Whitby about what happened to Celeste."

"Celeste who?"

Sylvia raised her penciled brows and fixed Dennis with a look of long-suffering patience. "My daughter, your granddaughter, Celeste Harrigan."

He tried to clear his muddled thoughts. How could he have forgotten about this whole business of a stolen child and a secret marriage? He looked around the room. Whitby was a lawyer. Sylvia would want him to be careful.

"I'm the one," said Nurse Tierney in a very matter of fact tone.

"The one what?"

"The one that made the mistake."

"Well," said Dennis, "everyone seems to be on remarkably good terms, considering this woman stole my granddaughter."

"I didn't steal anything," said Nurse Tierney truculently. "I'm not after coming here to hear myself accused of stealing."

Irish, thought Dennis, and straight out of the bog.

"Mrs. Tierney was a nurse at the clinic where I gave birth," said Sylvia. "Really, Daddy, you don't have to bother yourself with this."

Yes, I do, Dennis thought. Some twist of fate had placed the future of Southwold in the hands of the stout Irishwoman. If Sylvia had taken the trouble to bring her here, presumably from Ireland, then she must have something important to say. Perhaps everything would be all right after all.

"Let's hear what she has to say," Dennis said. "Sit down, Sylvia, and you too, Mr. Whitby."

He took perverse pleasure in excluding the housekeeper from his invitation to be seated. Mrs. Pearson sniffed and took up a post behind Sylvia's chair.

The solicitor was flicking through pages in a small notebook as if reminding himself of where they all were when the Earl had interrupted them.

"So, Nurse Tierney," the solicitor said, "you were not the person who delivered the baby."

"No." Nurse Tierney's lip curled in annoyance. "That was for the nuns, foreign women, French, I think. All they wanted from the Irish girls was cleaning and sweeping and bed pans."

"But you are a nurse?" asked Whitby.

"No, not exactly. But they were pleased enough to have our help. They didn't want to do all the skivvying themselves."

"And was the clinic very busy that night, the night when Lady Sylvia's baby was born?"

"Sure and I don't know, I wasn't there."

"But—"

"Nurse Tierney," said Mrs. Pearson, "you told me you were—"

"It was the next night," Sylvia interrupted. "Celeste was already a day old. The registrar had come and registered the birth. I already told you, Mr. Whitby, that the birth had been registered."

The solicitor nodded. "Yes, you did."

Dennis leaned forward. "Mr. Whitby."

"Yes, sir."

"Do you have any cigarettes?"

"Daddy!"

"Only Woodbines," said Whitby, feeling in the pocket of his jacket and retrieving a crumpled package.

"Daddy!" Sylvia exclaimed again.

Dennis removed two cigarettes from the package, placing one in his top pocket and the other between his lips. The solicitor produced a packet of matches and lit the Earl's cigarette with a hand that trembled slightly.

Nervous, Dennis thought. Not used to this kind of pressure.

"Daddy, you shouldn't," Sylvia protested.

"I think I should." Dennis drew deeply on the cigarette; terrible tobacco, low quality, harsh smoke, but better than nothing. He met his daughter's troubled gaze. "If I smoke, I don't talk. You don't want me pestering the nurse with my questions, do you? You want her to keep the facts straight."

"It was the next night," said Nurse Tierney. "That's when it happened. I'm sure no one can blame me for the mistake. Sure and it was a terrible thing."

"Flying bombs," said Sylvia.

The words dropped into the room and created their own sphere of silence. Dennis looked around the room and saw memory written on each face.

September 1944
Toby Whitby

The evening sun was low on the horizon when Toby left his digs for the long walk to Whitehall. With little to amuse him in his cramped room, he preferred to stretch his legs and walk to the Home Office instead of waiting for the notoriously unreliable buses.

Whitehall was now working around the clock as the allied armies pushed toward Berlin. Toby was on the evening shift, and his office work would be followed by five hours of patrolling with the fire watch on the roof of the building.

His landlady's house was the only home still standing on the northern side of Montague Road, although it had not escaped without damage. The chimney no longer functioned and tiles were missing from the roof, but Mrs. Larimor herself was indomitable. Wearing a pair of her husband's trousers and with her hair tied up in an old headscarf, she was digging industriously in the front-garden vegetable bed.

"Back to work already?" she asked, taking a break from her labors and leaning on the garden fork.

"Hitler doesn't give us any days off," Toby said.

"No, he don't," she agreed. "Well, you be careful. He's still chucking stuff at us."

"No more bombers," said Toby.

Mrs. Larimor wiped her hand across her forehead and left a muddy trail across her face. "I'd rather have a bomber than those blooming flying doodlebugs," she said. "That's spite, pure spite. He ain't gonna win, not now, but he won't give up. Evil, that's what they are, pure evil. Nasty noisy little things, and no one knows where they're going to land. South coast, Cornwall, Midlands, he don't care. Just wants to kill people. Not even pretending he's aiming them at anyone. He don't care who he hits."

She looked past Toby and down the street, where her four children were playing Germans and Americans in the ruins of the neighboring houses.

"I let them be evacuated," she said, "when they was bombing London. Broke my heart to see them go, but it kept them safe. Then the Ministry says we can bring them back, and look what happens, blooming doodlebugs landing anywhere they please."

"You shouldn't blame yourself," Toby said. "I don't think the V-1s are aimed at London. They're just aimed across the Channel, and when they run out of fuel, they land and explode. It wouldn't really matter where your children were. They're as safe here as they would be anywhere else. They're with you and that's important."

"Where are your parents, Mr. Whitby?"

"My mother's in Scotland," said Toby. "She went up at the beginning of the war. My father died when I was a boy."

Mrs. Larimor smiled. "You're still a boy, Mr. Whitby. I know you're doing important work and all, but you're still no more than a lad. They're all boys; all the soldiers, just boys."

Toby looked up as Mrs. Larimor's oldest son jumped from a pile of rubble to land on his brother.

"The game's up, German swine," he shouted, in a passable American accent.

"I'm not a German," responded his prisoner. "Why do I have to be a German?"

Toby shook his head. "Don't worry, Mrs. Larimor, the war will be long over by the time they're old enough to fight."

"I should blooming well hope so," the landlady agreed. "You be careful out there, Mr. Whitby."

"You too, Mrs. Larimor."

Toby closed the gate behind him and set off westward into the setting sun. The children raced ahead of him, two boys and two girls, dashing through the abandoned gardens of their long-vanished neighbors. Apparently, they were no longer Germans and Americans; now they were Battle of Britain pilots, with arms spread as they swooped down on their imaginary enemies.

Toby wished he could have given Mrs. Larimor a little more comfort. He would like to have said that the menace was over, but rumor in the War Office was that Hitler had something even nastier than the V-1 doodlebug up his sleeve. Rumor said that there would be a V-2, something even more deadly.

Toby sighed. He was exhausted. Everyone was exhausted. This new weapon of Hitler's was not as deadly as the Blitz, but it was unpredictable. Without a pilot, and with only the most rudimentary of guidance systems and no particular target in mind, the V-1 could be launched anytime, night or day, and wherever it fell, it exploded. The sirens were now blasting in the daylight. No sooner had the all clear sounded than the guns would start up again and the alert siren would be wailing its message again and the ack-ack guns would return to action.

Slowly but surely, what fear Toby had of the missiles was being replaced by a weary fatalism, and he was no longer diving for cover when the sirens started. He would watch the sky and listen for the sound of the V-1's engines buzzing and howling overhead. So long as the engine was running, he was in no danger. Danger was in the silence, in the moment when the missile ran out of fuel and tipped its nose downward.

As if in response to his thoughts, Toby heard an alert siren from somewhere nearby. The children barely glanced upward and continued their aerial warfare among the ruins. He looked back and saw Mrs. Larimor looking up into the sky. Her mouth was moving. She was calling her children, but they couldn't hear her above the sound of the guns mounted on the roof of the police station. No, Toby thought, not just the sound of guns, the droning sound of a V-1 coming toward them out of the sunset.

He looked back at Mrs. Larimor. She had abandoned her work and was racing down the road toward him. He had thought of her as old, or at least middle-aged, but as she sprinted toward him, she ran like a young girl, head thrown back, arms pumping.

They'll be all right, he thought. It's going to pass right over us. Someone will get it, but not us. And then he thought, my God, how much of this can we stand? How long can the mothers live like this? He was too war weary to care about the German missiles, but Mrs. Larimor, poor soul, still had a mother's instinct.

"Number 23," Mrs. Larimor shouted. "The Morrison. Number 23."

The children had stopped playing and turned toward the sound of their mother's voice, and reality hit Toby. The children could hear their mother. The doodlebug was silent. It had run out of fuel. Its nose cone with one thousand kilos of explosive was tilted down toward the ground on a long dive into wanton destruction.

As he hesitated, Mrs. Larimor flew past him.

"Number 23."

The children seemed to know what she meant. Her arms were reaching to gather them in and guide them through the gaping front door of the neighboring ruined house. Toby started to run. He glimpsed something inside, something green; a Morrison shelter, still intact.

They dove together through the doorway, Mrs. Larimor shoving the children ahead of her into the space under the reinforced table. Toby was hot on her heels, and he didn't hesitate for even a moment to take hold of her trouser-clad backside and heave her into the space alongside her children. When the doodlebug exploded, only his head and shoulders were under cover, but the children were safe.

The Library at Southwold
March 1952

Toby leaned down and scratched his right leg. The deep cut had been stitched in haste and left a jagged scar, his one and only visible war wound.

"You should get a medal for what you done," Mrs. Larimor had said.

"We should all get a medal," Toby had replied, "just for living through this."

He brought his mind back to the present and looked around the room. Each face held its own memory of the V-1 raids. Time had passed, but time had not healed.

"Horrible," said Nurse Tierney. "Evil, horrible."

"Hmm," said the Earl with a challenging note in his voice, "I thought you Irish were in favor of Hitler."

"I'm from Ulster," Nurse Tierney replied, "and even if I wasn't, even if I was from Dublin itself and never spoke a word of English, I would still call it evil. What it did to those babies …"

Toby hated to probe the wound, but he knew Edwin Champion would demand a full reckoning of the nurse's story. "Did it land on the ward?"

"God, no. I wouldn't be here to tell the tale if it had landed on the ward. It landed on the chapel, but it brought down the nursery wall, and them that wasn't crushed in the fall was burned up in the fire."

"Good God," said the Earl, taking a long drag on his cigarette. "Do we have to go over this? Can't we just leave it that some of the babies died?"

"And some of the nuns," Sylvia added.

"Perhaps you could tell me in your own words," Toby said.

The nurse gave him a hard look. Toby was puzzled by her. He could hear compassion in her voice when she spoke of the babies killed by the bomb, but when her eyes darted to the housekeeper, she seemed to be issuing a challenge.

"Shall I be after telling it all?" she asked, looking to Mrs. Pearson.

The housekeeper retained her rigid stance behind Lady Sylvia's chair. "Of course. That's why we brought you here."

"In your own words," Toby repeated.

"It wasn't a real hospital," said Nurse Tierney, "just a converted convent, papist, of course. The walls was that thick we didn't hear it coming over. We heard the alert, but what difference did that make? If we were going to run and hide every time we heard the alert, those babies would be staying inside their mothers' wombs forever, poor little mites. Besides, you know how it was; they usually went right over us on their way to somewhere more important. I suppose it didn't have enough fuel, and that's why it fell on us."

"Maybe it came from farther away," the Earl said. He was staring fixedly at the nurse, his forgotten cigarette accumulating a long column of ash.

"What does it matter where it came from?" said Nurse Tierney, who seemed to be unimpressed by the Earl's exalted position.

"Doesn't matter at all," the Earl agreed.

"The babies was mostly in the nursery," Nurse Tierney said. "It was a fancy kind of place where the mothers wanted their peace and quiet. Didn't want the babies lying in with them, so we had to take them away and just bring them for the feeding."

Toby made a note in his notebook. Babies were brought in for feeding; maybe it was important, maybe not. Better to write it down.

"We had gathered up the babies from the twelve o'clock feeding," said Nurse Tierney. "Most of them were in the nursery, and just the last few left with the mothers. Some mothers take longer than others to get the hang of the feeding, you know. I went back to get the last three. We was in a hurry. Our shift was ending and we wanted to be finished with the babies. None of us was nuns with nothing to do but pray. We had places to go, and I wasn't afraid to tell those mothers that I didn't have all day to wait while they fussed around. Everyone else was ready to leave, so I went back and got the last three. I could carry them three at a time. The mothers didn't like it, but I wasn't there to please the mothers, I was there because that's where the recruiter said I had to be. I was Irish, so all I was good for was skivvying."

Nurse Tierney might well be from Northern Ireland and officially British, Toby thought, but she was still Irish, and her soul carried a thousand years of resentment. He could only imagine how unpleasant it would be for a new mother to give her baby into Nurse Tierney's uncaring hands. He wondered why she was being so carefully referred to as "Nurse" Tierney when quite obviously she had not been a nurse.

"I had three babies in my arms," Nurse Tierney continued. "The explosion blew me off my feet. I was lying on the floor, still holding the babies."

A puzzled expression crossed her face. "It's funny, you know, you'd think I'd want to be saving myself, but I had those babies, and I don't know why, but I didn't give a thought for myself. I had to look after those babies."

"Very commendable," said the Earl.

Nurse Tierney didn't seem to notice the Earl's caustic tone. "It was a terrible thing, Your Lordship. Fire, flames, smoke, and the screaming."

For a moment the library was wrapped in silence. Toby held his pen poised above the paper, but he had nothing to write. They had all lived through the war years. They had all seen terrible things. Their quiet, orderly peacetime lives had been turned upside down. Of the people in the room, only the Earl had seen service in World War I. Perhaps he had been prepared for the violence and the way the brain protects itself by not visualizing, not filling in the details, but Toby could not stop himself from filling in the details.

Choking smoke, rafters crashing down in a shower of sparks, walls collapsing on helpless babies imprisoned in their little wood cribs. Nuns with hands reaching out to protect their charges, and the infants breathing in acrid smoke until all breathing ceased. His mind tried to soften the blow. He wanted to believe that several gasping but painless breaths were all that was needed to return the infants to their home in heaven.

And in the ward, where the walls had withstood the blast, the surviving mothers screaming for their children. Beds overturned, women pinned down under collapsing ceilings, and one Irishwoman with three babies in her arms.

The Earl looked at his daughter. She was pale but composed.

"I didn't know what was happening. I had given Celeste to the nurse to be taken back to the nursery, and I was just lying there in the bed. I heard the explosion, and then I suppose something fell on my head and knocked me out. I don't remember anything."

"Sounds like a blessing to me," said her father.

"No, Daddy. If I had been conscious, I would never have let anyone take my baby. I would have recognized her, I know I would. But when I came round, the Red Cross worker told me all the babies were dead. She never said anything about three of the babies still being alive. I thought Celeste was in the nursery with the other babies. I saw where they'd been, and it was just a pile of burning ruins. How could I find her in there? I had to believe what I was told."

Toby dutifully wrote down his client's words. The words were easy to write, but the emotion was hard to convey. Something in the way Lady Sylvia spoke seemed forced and unreal. When she had first spoken to him of finding her daughter, she had been almost without emotion, and even now the emotion she was displaying seemed shallow. On the other hand, the Earl was white-faced, and his hands shook as he reached for another cigarette, and Nurse Tierney was trembling on the edge of tears. Toby was certain that the air in the room was full of false words and false emotions, but Nurse Tierney's memory was not false. She had been there.

"I was just lying there on the floor," said Nurse Tierney, "with the babies in my arms, still wrapped up tight in their blankets."

"Because of rationing, we each had to bring our own blankets," said Lady Sylvia, as if the information was very important. "We had our own blankets and our own baby clothes. Every blanket was different."

"A woman came at me out of the smoke," Nurse Tierney continued.

"I thought maybe she was a rescue worker. There were all kinds of people by then, moving around everywhere, trying to get the women out. She took the baby."

"All the babies?" Toby asked.

"No." Nurse Tierney's tone indicated sorely tried patience. "Not all the babies, just the one. She said it was her baby. Said she recognized the blanket. She was crying, and I think she was wearing a dressing gown, but it could have been a coat. I don't know. I didn't recognize her, but she seemed really sure it was her baby, and I just wanted to get up off the floor and give the babies to someone who would look after them."

"Did you see her again?" Toby asked. "Was she outside when the smoke cleared?"

The nurse shook her head. "They was taking the women away as fast as they could. Didn't want them to stay there looking at the ruins, I suppose, and the other walls were going to be collapsing at any minute. Sure, it wasn't safe for anyone to be there."

"But what about the other babies?" Toby persisted.

"I gave them to the Red Cross worker. Boys, both of them."

"And the third one was a girl?"

"I didn't look."

"It was Celeste," Lady Sylvia insisted.

Toby hesitated, testing the tension in the air. The Irishwoman's description of the burning nursery had been brief but terrible, and he was sure that mere words could not convey the horror of the event she had witnessed.

The Earl, puffing on his second cigarette, was still trembling. Mrs. Pearson stood ramrod straight, eyes downcast, her face unreadable. Lady Sylvia had not lost her composure and was looking at him inquiringly. After a moment of silence, the Irishwoman crossed her arms across her ample bosom and settled back on the sofa with an air of completion. She had a story to tell and she had told it.

"Nurse Tierney," Toby said eventually, "can you tell me why it has taken you so long to tell your story?"

She leaned forward aggressively. "What do you mean? "

"It's been six years."

"Sure and I didn't know anyone was looking for that baby. Do you think I've spent the last six years wondering if I'd given her to the right woman? She said it was her baby and I gave it to her, and no one to tell me any different. You might as well ask Her Ladyship there why it has taken six years to ask about it?"

Indeed I might, Toby thought, but, preferring not to upset Mr. Champion's illustrious client, he rephrased his question. "If you could just tell me why you have come forward now …"

"Come forward? Come forward? You make it sound like I've committed a crime."

"No, no, of course not. I wasn't suggesting any such thing."

Lady Sylvia rose gracefully to her feet. "Mr. Whitby, I can assure you that there has been no suggestion of wrongdoing by Nurse Tierney. You have to understand that I was firmly convinced that my daughter had died in the explosion. I had no reason to think that she might still be alive until Nurse Tierney contacted me."

"Ah," said Toby, "so it was Nurse Tierney who initiated the contact."

"And what if I did?" asked the nurse.

"I was just wondering how that happened."

The Earl rose slowly to his feet. "I think I'll go back upstairs," he said. "Not feeling too good."

Mrs. Pearson was beside him in a moment. "Shall I help you, sir?"

"No, I don't need any of your damned help."

The Earl shuffled past Toby and then paused. "Don't ask any more questions, young man. It's insulting. We don't like to be insulted. If my daughter says the baby was hers, it was hers."

Toby stood up, opened his mouth to protest, and then thought better of it.

"Daddy," Lady Sylvia protested, "we don't need to talk like that. We're perfectly happy to provide Mr. Whitby with all the evidence he needs."

"Poppycock," said the Earl. "No need to provide him with anything. Just get on with it, young Whitby. Just get the child here and make everything legal. That's what you're being paid to do."

"Really, Daddy—"

The Earl glared imperiously at Toby. "No more poking around. Just get on with it and no more questions. If you keep this up, I will have to talk to your employer. Work is hard to come by these days, and I'm sure you would like to keep your position."

Toby remained standing as the Earl tottered away into the darkness of the hallway.

"So sorry," said Lady Sylvia as soon as her father was out of sight. "My father is somewhat feudal in his outlook."

"You're making a mystery where there is none," Mrs. Pearson said firmly. "It's a simple thing. It was the blanket. The Southwold crest was on the blanket, and Nurse Tierney happened to remember."

"So I told them," said Nurse Tierney. "Better late than never."

Toby looked at the three women and they looked back at him, their faces blank and innocent. He was quite certain that no matter how many questions he asked, he would get no more information from them today. He felt a deep-seated resentment at their assumption that he could be fooled by such flimsy evidence or bullied by the Earl with such obvious threats. He had no doubt that there was a kernel of truth in the Irishwoman's story. Her emotions had been real. Somewhere, at some time, she had witnessed the destruction of a nursery full of babies. As for the rest of the story …

He closed his notebook and slipped his pen into his pocket. He was unsure what he should do next. He was surrounded by liars, but one lie was more important than all the others. Only one question could and should be answered. Who was the mother of the child? Was it Lady Sylvia or Vera Chapman? It was a problem worthy of King Solomon, but unlike Solomon he could hardly suggest that the baby should be split in half.

Mrs. Pearson resumed her seat by the fire with an air of triumph, and it was Lady Sylvia who rose to show him out.

Nurse Tierney remained firmly in her seat. Toby reached into his pocket and produced one of his business cards.

"If you think of anything else," he said, holding it out to the Irishwoman.

"I won't."

"Just in case."

"I won't," she repeated, but she took the card and dropped it into her pocket.

"This way, Mr. Whitby," said Lady Sylvia.

Dennis Blanchard, Earl of Southwold

The Earl shuffled back to his bedroom, cursing the fact that he had already smoked both of young Mr. Whitby's cigarettes.

He paused at the top of the stairs, overcome by a paroxysm of coughing. When he was finally able to draw a gasping breath, he heard his daughter in the hall downstairs.

"So, you will be in touch, Mr. Whitby?"

"Yes, of course."

"We really have no time to waste."

"I understand."

The front door opened and closed, and then Dennis heard his daughter's footsteps on the stairs.

"Daddy."

He moved as fast as his trembling legs would carry him and was seated on the side of his bed by the time his daughter burst through the bedroom door.

"What's the matter, Sylvia?"

His daughter's face was pale and taut with suppressed anger. "You shouldn't have talked to him like that."

"Really?"

With as much dignity as he could muster, Dennis slid back under the bedclothes. The coughing fit had left him breathless. Needing a moment to restore authority to his voice, he allowed his daughter to berate him.

"We need Mr. Whitby on our side. You can't just talk to him like a peasant, and you really shouldn't have threatened to lose him his job. Times have changed, Daddy."

Dennis managed to make a disapproving grunt, which his daughter ignored.

"You should have let Nurse Tierney explain."

"Explain!" Dennis's voice was slowly returning. "Explain? What kind of explanation did you expect from Nurse Tierney, not that she's even a nurse, just a glorified orderly.

"The shield on the blanket."

"Poppycock. Is that all you have? Mr. Whitby is not going to be satisfied with that. My only intention, my dear, was to get him out of the room and give you time to come up with something better."

"We didn't need anything better."

"That young man is not a fool. If he had gone on asking questions, that stupid Irishwoman would have told him that she wasn't the one who found you, you were the ones who found her. How much are you paying her for her cock and bull story?"

"It's not a cock and bull story."

"Well, it certainly sounds like one. And how are you going to explain the fact that you kept silent for six years and said nothing to your husband's family? Mr. Harrigan will want to know."

"I didn't want to upset them. Their son was dead and I believed his child was dead, so why say anything? They had enough grief."

"I hope he believes you."

"He'll believe me. He wants to believe me."

"Yes, I suppose he does."

"Of course he does. He's overjoyed."

"I worry about young Vera," said Dennis. "She was a remarkable girl, and taking her baby away is—"

Sylvia glared at him in cold determination. "Do you want the estate to go to the Australians?"

Dennis sank back against his pillows. "I'm tired, Sylvia."

"Of course you are, Daddy. Don't worry about anything. It's all under control. Why don't you just stay in bed? You don't have to talk to Mr. Whitby again."

"I'll have to talk to Harrigan."

"Not if you're not well enough. Let's cross that bridge when we come to it."

She straightened his blankets and dropped a kiss on the top of his head. He closed his eyes wearily. He heard the creak as she closed the heavy oak door.

He pulled the blanket up closer to his chin. He should have asked Sylvia to close the window. He knew he was close to the grave, but that damned Pearson woman and her open windows would have him in there well ahead of schedule.

He thought ruefully about his own death and wondered if he would even be missed. What use was an Earl in these new modern times? He didn't even know how to talk to people. Sylvia complained that he had not treated that young solicitor with sufficient respect. How was he supposed to treat him? He was one of the new breed, educated at a grammar school, no doubt, and raised to think of himself as the equal of any man. With his law degree and his cheap suit and his determined quest for truth, he was probably more relevant in the new postwar society than an Earl who could read Homer in Greek and had once led a cavalry charge.

He had to think back to the war years to find the last time he had been of any use to anyone.

February 1944

The cellar at Southwold had been crudely converted into a bomb shelter with the addition of corrugated iron sheets nailed to the ceiling. The Earl had lobbied for a separate Anderson shelter for the staff, but even that modest request had been denied him. They were required to shelter democratically, family and staff together.

Sylvia was home for the weekend, taking time off from the comfortable office job her father had managed to obtain for her in London. Dennis thought it somewhat ironic that she should escape the bombing in London only to sit through an air raid at home in the Sussex countryside, not that anywhere was safe from the Luftwaffe. Something would have to be done. The Americans encamped on Rose Hill Common would have to do something. They couldn't just sit there forever. They had come to fight, so let them fight.

At last the all clear echoed across the village green, its sound seeping in faintly through the doorway held open by Robbie, Mrs. Pearson's slow-witted nephew. He was too slow-witted to go to war and too slow-witted to stand away from the open door.

"It's over," Sylvia declared. "You'd better go and look, Daddy."

"Yes, I should," Dennis agreed. "Let's see what damage Adolf has done this time. Do you want to come with me and show yourself around?"

"The caring lady of the manor? No, thank you."

"Your mother would have."

"Well, my mother is not here and I'm going back to bed."

Dennis had requisitioned the gamekeeper's bicycle early in the war, and he had formed the habit of riding out after every bombing raid just to reassure the people that he had survived. The King and Queen visited the suffering people of London as often as they could, and he liked to think that he was made in the same mold. Noblesse oblige.

The moon was playing hide-and-seek among scattered clouds, but the night was bright enough for him to see where he was going, and he knew better than to use the headlight attached to the handlebars.

He was crossing the green when the girl came out of nowhere. She appeared to simply rise out of the ground in front of him, waving her arms and shouting.

He applied the bicycle's rusty brakes and came to a juddering halt as she flung herself toward him.

"There's a bomb," she shouted.

"A bomb?"

"Yes, a bloody great bomb."

The moon came out from behind the clouds and illuminated her face. She was not someone that he recognized, but she was a pretty girl bearing a faint resemblance to his own daughter. The resemblance did not surprise him. In ages past, the Earls of Southwold had sown their wild oats very close to home.

"Are you an air-raid warden?" the girl asked.

"No," he said. "I'm the Earl."

She seemed unimpressed by that piece of information. "I need to find whoever is in charge."

"I'm the Earl," he repeated. "I'm in charge."

This time the information seemed to sink in. "Oh, all right. Well, Your Lordship, there's a bomb."

"Where?"

She pointed behind her to the place where she had seemed to rise out of the ground. "There, across the steps."

"Steps?"

Now she was annoyed. "The air-raid shelter; that's the air-raid shelter and it's full of people, and they can't get out."

"Were you down there?" Dennis asked.

"Yes, I was, but—"

"You got out." Dennis thought his statement was not unreasonable.

"I slid past it. I didn't touch it."

"You slid past it?" Dennis repeated. "You slid past it! Good God, girl, it could have blown up in your face."

"Well, it didn't."

"Any slight touch," Dennis scolded, "could set it off."

"I know, I know." The girl was impatient with him. "It could go up any

minute and everyone's in there. My mum's in there. What are we going to do?"

"Where's the air-raid warden?"

"He's in there with everyone else."

"Ah," said Dennis.

The girl repeated her question. "What are we going to do?"

Dennis gathered his scattered wits. He had been bred to take command. From the playing fields of Eton to the trenches of the Great War, command and the unquestioned obedience of the lower classes were all that he knew. He took charge.

March 1952

People said that Vera had saved the day, but Dennis, lying in his bed with the cold winter wind blowing across his face, knew that he was the one who had saved the day. Vera Chapman had helped, of course, but he, the Earl, had saved the day. Nonetheless, he felt bad about taking her baby, if it was her baby.

Someone has to do the right thing, he thought sleepily. He didn't have the strength or the willpower, but Whitby was young and strong and intelligent.

The heavy oak door creaked. He opened his eyes.

"What are you doing up here?" he asked. "You're not allowed up here."

CHAPTER NINE

Toby drove slowly away from the Hall. What he should do was to go back to Brighton and write a report of his interview with Nurse Tierney, but what he wanted to do was to go back to the village store and make a groveling apology to Carol. He wanted her to smile at him.

No, he couldn't do it. His first duty was to his employer. He approached the wrought iron gates, willing himself to go straight out onto the Brighton road. He found his way blocked by the very person he wanted to see. Carol, in a camelhair coat, her hair tucked up under a headscarf and her face set in an expression of grim determination, stepped out from beside the gate and held up an arresting hand.

He brought the car to a halt, and she opened the passenger door and dropped into the seat beside him.

"We're going to the church," she said.

"What?"

"Church." She pointed with a gloved hand, and he saw the church spire looming above the naked trees about a half mile away.

"Why?"

"To see the vicar."

Toby seemed incapable of expressing more than one word at a time. "Why?"

"So that you'll believe me."

"I do."

"No, you don't." She still sounded irritated but not as angry as before. "But if you won't believe me, perhaps you'll believe the vicar."

"It's not a question of not believing you," Toby said, glancing sideways at her as he pulled out onto the road. "I'm gathering evidence, and, well, you don't really have any firsthand evidence. You didn't see Vera give birth, so—"

"Did anyone see Lady Sylvia give birth?"

"I've just been talking to a nurse who was there," Toby replied.

"She saw it?"

"No, not exactly."

"Of course not, because it didn't happen. Turn right here."

She directed him into a narrow road that took him across the back of the village green and into a small parking area beside the white stone parish church. A faded sign proclaimed that the church was dedicated to St. James, and the vicar was Rodney Farley-Reed.

"He's waiting for us," said Carol. "I told him we needed to talk to him."

"Did you tell him why?"

"Of course I did. I had to stop him from jumping to conclusions. He thought I was bringing my young man to see him so we could set a wedding date."

Toby felt himself blushing, and saw the ghost of a smile cross Carol's face.

"Not really," she said. "He knows me better than that. He knows I don't have a young man."

"Don't you?"

"No, I don't."

Toby opened the car door and welcomed the rush of cold air on his flushed cheeks. Carol was out of the passenger door before he had time to run round and open it for her. He hoped she knew that he had intended to act the gentleman even if she had not given him the opportunity.

They found Farley-Reed in the church vestry, where he was pawing through a box of ragged choir robes.

"It'll be Easter before you know it," he declared, "and these robes aren't fit to be worn. The way new clothes are rationed, you'd think we were still at war. We'll have to make do with the choir wearing their street clothes."

"You're welcome to my clothing ration," Carol offered. "I don't need new clothes. I never go anywhere glamorous."

Toby wanted to interrupt with an invitation to dinner at the Ritz or tea at the Savoy, but he couldn't do it; not in front of the vicar. "Your turn will come," said Farley-Reed. "Don't give up yet." He was an old man, Toby thought. He was not as old as Mr. Champion, but he was quite definitely on the wrong side of seventy and maybe nearer to eighty. His shock of white hair stood up like a halo around his head, and his stooped shoulders, encased in a rusted-brown cassock, gave him the appearance of an eccentric scholar rather than a kindly country parson.

"This is Mr. Whitby," Carol said.

The vicar extended a gnarled, arthritic hand, and Toby shook it as gently as he could, fearing that he might injure the old man.

"He wants to ask you about the christening when you baptized Vera Chapman's baby."

"Vera Malloy," the vicar corrected. "I married her to that young American. It was all legal and aboveboard, although he didn't seem very enthusiastic. But he was wounded, you know, so I don't expect he was feeling very chipper."

"And she was, you know, well …" Toby hesitated.

"Pregnant?" Farley-Reed asked.

"Yes."

"Yes, she was and quite noticeably so. But that's the way it is sometimes. Better late than never, that's what I say. I married them in March and baptized the baby in May."

"And was the husband there?" asked Toby.

The vicar shook his head. "He was on his way to Berlin with Eisenhower. Young Vera was fortunate to get him back for the wedding. If he hadn't been wounded, she might never have seen him again."

"Really?" said Toby. "Are you saying he didn't want to marry her?"

The vicar smiled. "I've seen many a reluctant bridegroom in my day. I know when a young fellow feels like he's been trapped."

"She didn't trap him," Carol protested.

The vicar looked down his long nose at Carol. "He was trapped all right. Millie Chapman had been to the Earl, and the Earl had got onto the poor fellow's CO, and as soon as the lad was out of the hospital, he was in my church reciting his wedding vows. White as a sheet, he was. He could hardly get his vows out. Vera was loud and clear, but I thought the poor boy was going to choke on the words."

"Mr. Whitby wants to know about the baptism," Carol said.

"All legal and aboveboard," the vicar confirmed. "I can show you the record."

"Perhaps you could just tell me."

May 1945Rodney Farley-Reed

Rodney Farley-Reed removed the lid from the font and poured in a small amount of water, only one baby to baptize today. The afternoon was fine and sunny, allowing for the church doors to be left open and for a shaft of light to illuminate the ancient font standing just inside the entrance. Sounds and smells of summer drifted in through the doorway. A lawn mower rattled in the distance, and the first roses of summer sent their perfume into the clear air.

The vicar cleared his throat and addressed the small gathering. "We are here to mark the beginning of this child's life as a Christian. The font stands beside the door to symbolize her first entrance into the church. Later she will be confirmed at the communion rail, and later still she will come to the altar to be married."

He looked at the young mother holding her child awkwardly and fussing with the skimpy baptismal gown.

"Everything in due season," he said.

Mildred Chapman's harsh laugh broke the respectful silence. "Due season. Fat lot she knows about due season."

"Shut up, Mum."

Although he wanted the whole ceremony over and done with as soon as possible, Farley-Reed looked at his watch. "Should we wait?" he asked.

"He said he'd come," Mrs. Chapman replied. "It would be very rude to start without him."

The baby squalled loudly.

"Mum," Vera said, "can we just get this done? We don't have to wait for the Earl. I don't suppose he's coming anyway. Why should he?"

"I don't know," Mrs. Chapman hissed at her daughter. "You tell me. I don't know what you've been up to."

"I haven't been up to anything."

"That's what you say."

Before the vicar could admonish the ladies for their unseemly squabbling, Vera's uncle, Joe, short and stubby and encased in an ancient tweed suit, stepped forward to restore the peace. "Now then, let's not get ourselves upset. What's done is done, and Vera's married her soldier boy. Leave it alone, Mildred. She saved a lot of lives in that bomb shelter. No reason the Earl shouldn't be grateful."

To the vicar's relief, a shadow darkened the doorway, and the Earl himself stepped inside with Lady Sylvia beside him. He could not help noticing that the beam of sunlight caught their shadows and cast them across the ancient font. The Earl and his daughter were bathed in golden light, while the villagers were cast into darkness.

Mrs. Chapman adjusted the battered silk flowers on her hat and bobbed a curtsey. Vera jiggled the crying baby.

Farley-Reed straightened his stole and stepped up to the font. "Shall we begin?" he asked.

This time the small congregation was in agreement. His Lordship had arrived. They would begin. He took the squalling infant from her mother and held her at arm's length. The godparents recited the chosen names. He applied water from the font as he had done so many times before, as he had done for Vera herself and for Carol Elliot, the only one of Vera's friends who had seen fit to attend the ceremony. He offered the appropriate prayer and waited for the low murmurs of amen. The baby continued to cry until Mrs. Chapman took the child from him and jiggled it so energetically that the infant had no breath left for screaming.

The congratulations that Vera received from Mrs. Chapman's brother and his wife, the new godparents, seemed grudging and halfhearted. Carol was the only one who appeared to be at ease with the situation, giving her friend a warm hug and kissing the baby on the top of its downy head. The Earl placed something into Vera's hand. From the size and the crinkling sound it made, the vicar judged it to be a five-pound note, a generous gift indeed.

As Vera and Lady Sylvia stood momentarily side by side, Farley-Reed noted their resemblance to each other; the same dark hair, the same tall, lean figure, the same pale complexion. Rose Hill was filled with Southwold by-blows from the days when the aristocracy exercised the droit de seigneur, but the resemblance was not normally so strong. He looked at Vera's stolid mother. No, she was not the one who had given Vera her aristocratic looks, and the father, well, he was long gone.

Mrs. Chapman bobbed another curtsey and held the baby out to Lady Sylvia. "Would you like to hold the baby?"

Her Ladyship looked as though she had been offered a snake.

"God, no," she exclaimed, holding up both hands as if to defend herself against the very possibility.

The vicar took in the hurt expression on Vera's face. So much for noblesse oblige, he thought.

Carol stepped in hurriedly to save her friend from embarrassment. "I'll hold her."

Mrs. Chapman handed the baby into Carol's keeping, although the twitch of her lips made it clear that the village girl was a poor substitute for the Earl's daughter.

The Earl patted Vera on the shoulder. "Well done. Jolly good show. Off to America, I hear?"

"California," said Vera.

"Yes, well, good show," the Earl repeated. "Jolly good show. Come along, Sylvia."

The two aristocrats made a hasty exit. Mrs. Chapman retrieved her granddaughter from Carol's arms.

"Thank you for coming."

The vicar took Mrs. Chapman's tone of voice as a dismissal.

"Do you want to come back to the house?" Vera asked. "We don't have much, but—"

"My daughter's supply of jam and tea ran out when her husband ran off."

"He didn't run off, Mum. He returned to duty. He couldn't stay any longer

after his wounds healed."

"Wounds," sniffed Mrs. Chapman. "A couple of scratches. Still, if he hadn't been injured, he wouldn't have come back here to marry you, so I suppose we should be grateful for small mercies. At least you were married before the baby was born."

"I don't think I can stay," Carol said.

"What about you, Vicar?" Mrs. Chapman sounded as though the invitation was being dragged from her by force.

Farley-Reed could not imagine spending any more time with Mrs. Chapman. "No, thank you. I wouldn't want you to use up your rations. You have a baby to feed now."

"Not me," said Mrs. Chapman. Her gaze flicked to her daughter. "That's her responsibility now, her and the American army. Let them feed her, that's what I say."

"They will," said Vera truculently.

Farley-Reed watched as the christening party, consisting of Vera, her mother, and her uncle and aunt, walked out into sunshine. Carol lingered for a moment.

The vicar smiled. No doubt she was allowing time for Mrs. Chapman and her sour disposition to be well on their way, and who could blame her for that?

March 1952
Toby Whitby

Toby felt foolish. The vicar had told him nothing that Carol couldn't tell him herself. Vera had been pregnant at her wedding. She had given birth and the baby had been baptized. Lady Sylvia had attended the baptism and shown absolutely no interest in the child. The Earl had given Vera a five-pound note. The vicar had offered to show him the baptismal record. Unlike the records of Lady Sylvia's child, this record of Vera's child still existed.

The phone on the desk was ringing. It had been ringing for some time, but the vicar had so far ignored it.

"Would you excuse me?" Farley-Reed asked, indicating the jangling instrument.

"Oh, of course."

Toby touched Carol's arm and led her out of the vestry and into the vaulted church.

"Satisfied?" Carol asked, her voice echoing among the dusty timbers.

"I'm sorry."

"And so you should be."

"There's just one thing."

"What?"

Toby hesitated. She would know soon enough. The whole village would know soon enough, but he thought he should be the one to break the news to her.

"What?" she asked again.

"The Earl, or maybe it was Lady Sylvia, employed an agent to look for Vera."

"They'll never find her," Carol said. "Everyone thinks she went to California. No one is going to look in West Virginia. You didn't tell anyone, did you?"

"No," Toby said, "of course I didn't, but Lady Sylvia's father-in-law is not the kind of man who will give up easily."

"America's a big country," Carol replied, "and even if he does find her, she's never going to let the baby go."

As Toby hesitated on the verge of telling Carol the truth, the vicar came out of the vestry, hurrying as fast as his arthritic bones would allow.

"Mr. Whitby, you're needed at the Hall."

"It can wait," Toby snapped, still looking at Carol.

"No, it can't. They're asking for you to come now. We'll go up together. We can take your car."

"I'm talking to Miss Elliot," Toby protested.

The vicar looked away and called into the gloom of the sanctuary. "Tom, where are you? Tom?"

"He seems very upset," Carol said. "I had no idea he could raise his voice like that."

"Tom," the vicar called again, even more urgently.

A voice called out from the gloom of a side chapel. "What do you want, Vicar?"

"The bell. Toll the bell."

"What? Now?"

The voice was coming closer. A solid shape was emerging from the shadows.

"How many times?"

"Let me think. Sixty-eight. No, sixty-nine."

"Sixty-nine? Who died?"

"The Earl," said the vicar. "Toll the death bell sixty-nine times, once for every year of his life."

Toby forgot about Carol. He forgot about Mr. Harrigan and Vera, and even the child who was already on her way across the Atlantic. The Earl was dead. An hour ago he had been sitting in the library, begging for cigarettes, and now he was dead, and he, Toby Whitby, was being called to the Hall.

He would have to phone Mr. Champion and see if he could even be allowed to handle the matter himself or if Mr. Champion would be required, but first he should act to protect the Earl's will. Suppose he had changed it at the last minute. Suppose a new will lay hidden beneath the Earl's bedcovers. He knew he was being overly dramatic, but as the great bell began to toll and the vicar hurried beside him, his cassock flapping in the wind, he felt the sudden weight of his responsibilities.

"Toby." Carol reached out to stop him.

"Not now. I have to go."

CHAPTER TEN

Harry Harrigan

"Why is she crying? Can't you keep her quiet?"

Blanche Harrigan looked down at the little girl in the red velvet Valentine dress, and the girl looked back with a tearstained face and renewed sobs.

"She's just like her daddy," said Blanche fondly. "Jack used to cry."

"Not when I was around," said Harry. He bent down and looked the child in the face. "Be quiet, Celeste."

The girl's sobs became a shriek of defiance. "I'm not Celeste. I'm Anita and I want to go home."

"You are home," said Blanche. "This is where your mommy lives."

"No, she don't."

Blanche corrected her automatically. "Doesn't."

"She's a little savage," Harry Harrigan said between clenched teeth. "You'd better keep her quiet while we go through Customs and Immigration. I'm not having her tell them that her name is Anita Malloy."

"She's understandably confused," Blanche said mildly.

"Well un-confuse her."

Harry turned his broad back on grandmother and child and reached into his pocket for their documents.

Behind them the bulk of the Queen Elizabeth was nestled up against its berth, held steady by massive mooring ropes. A carpeted gangplank led to the First Class Customs and Immigration Hall. Harry left Blanche to deal with the child, proceeded down the gangway, and pushed his way into the line of disembarking passengers.

The Customs Hall was the first new and fully functional building he had seen since the Queen Elizabeth had come within sight of the devastated British Isles early in the morning. When the Isle of Wight had loomed out of the morning fog, the jagged rocks of the Needles guarding the approach to Southampton, he had been relieved that the voyage was over. He was impatient to meet the woman who claimed to be the mother of Jack's child.

Blanche had been naively excited, with no thought of the difficulties that could be ahead as they entered Britain with a child of disputed parentage. Even the child had been momentarily overawed watching the waves break against dark rocks, but she had soon resumed her whining and crying for her mother.

Harry had stood on the deck regarding the war-damaged approaches to Southampton harbor with a jaundiced eye.

"We took quite a battering," said a mournful-looking Englishman standing beside him.

"You sure did," said Harry. "About time you fixed it up."

The Englishman gave him a thin smile. "I'm afraid you American chappies have taken all our money. Lend lease, you know. Not much left for repairing the war damage. Wait until you see London. Were you there at all before the war?"

"No, never been. My son was here."

"Oh, is he with you?"

"No, he's dead. We took all your money and you took all our sons."

"Oh, sorry," said the Englishman. "I didn't mean it quite like that."

"Sure you did," said Harry.

He stomped away from the rail and back to his cabin, where his wife was attempting to get the little girl dressed in a concoction of red velvet and white lace ruffles.

"We should have brought a nursemaid," he said.

Blanche looked up, red-faced and frustrated.

"I thought she'd take to us."

"Well, you thought wrong. Little hellion."

February 1952
Beaver Creek Hollow, West Virginia
"God, what a dump."

Larry Dunbar threw the Studebaker around yet another steep curve and looked at his employer out of the corner of his eye. "You never been in West Virginia before?"

Harry Harrigan barked his disapproval. "No, thank God; made my money in Chicago. Let's get this over and done with. Get the kid and get out. Where is this goddam place?"

Dunbar brought the big car to a halt and pointed through the windshield at the valley below them. "Down there."

Harry looked down into the narrow valley. A light snow was blowing across the treeless hillside, but even as the snow settled, it was blanketed in black dust from the coal smoke belching from the chimney pots below. A polluted stream, red with rust, ran alongside the narrow road. On the far side of the stream, a string of coal carriers shunted along the railway tracks, the steam from the locomotive making its own contribution to the layer of smog hovering over the valley.

"She lives here?" Harry exclaimed.

"Yup," said Dunbar. "Blue house down there."

"What blue house?"

Dunbar pointed again. "It's blue, under all the dirt."

"Could have fooled me. So what are we waiting for? Let's go get her and get out of here. You're sure it's her?"

"Yes, sir. It's her. Father was Nick Malloy, who served with Bradley's division, stationed in Rose Hill, England, wounded in Normandy, and word is her mother was a war bride, name of Vera."

"Was?"

Dunbar pointed up onto the hillside where the coal conveyor snaked its rickety way among the rocks.

"Nick Malloy was killed in a mining accident last year, and the mother, well, she went missing not long ago. Rumor is she went to Pittsburgh to earn some money, but no one knows for sure. They won't give you any trouble about taking the kid, Mr. Harrigan. They don't want her. The great-grandmother is pretty much convinced that she's not Nick Malloy's child."

"So no complications?" asked Harry.

"None at all."

"Okay." He looked down at the squalid mining camp. "She's a lucky kid, going from all this to being a highborn English lady."

"And the granddaughter of a millionaire," Dunbar added.

Down in the valley, the air was even more polluted than it had been on the hillside. Dunbar turned on the windshield wipers and quickly turned them off again, as they did no more than smear damp coal dust across the windshield. The headlights of the Studebaker barely pierced the enshrouding smog. They passed along the ramshackle main street, jounced across the railway tracks, and started to climb a rutted road on the opposite side of the valley.

With his head partway out of the window, Harry identified the Malloy homestead. From close up he could see that the paint peeling from the weathered boards had indeed once been blue, just as the picket fence around the tiny front yard had once been white.

Dunbar brought the car to a halt. The big car blocked the road, but Harry could not imagine that any other cars would be passing by. No doubt the road went from nowhere to nowhere; from one rat-infested coal camp to another; from one hopeless community to the next. There was no road here that would take residents to New York or Chicago, only, perhaps, to the coal-fogged city of Pittsburgh, where they would still feel at home.

"Do they know we're coming?" Harry asked.

"I wrote," said Dunbar. He pointed down into the valley where a US flag fluttered outside a small cinder block building. "They have a post office."

As they climbed from the car, Harry saw that the front door of the ramshackle house had been opened. A woman stood framed in the doorway with a child at her side.

"That's the great-grandmother," Dunbar said.

Harry's eyes were focused on the child. Could this possibly be his grandchild? He wanted to believe. His heart was pounding with hope, as it had been pounding ever since he had received the first communication from England. Jack had been everything for him, his golden boy, destined for a bright future in Harry's increasingly successful business. Blanche had cried when Jack had told her that he had enlisted in the army, and Harry had responded with anger.

"You don't have to go. We can get you an exemption."

"I don't want an exemption. I'm going."

Less than a year later, two officers, solemn-faced and rigidly upright, had brought the news. Blanche had fainted. Harry had unleashed a torrent of curses, but nothing had made any difference. Not until now.

Dunbar pushed open the rickety gate and motioned Harry through. He fixed his eyes on the child, smudge-faced, her hair hanging in rat tails, her dress no defense against the chill wind. Anger welled up in Harry's chest. Was this how they treated Jack's child? How dare they?

The old woman looked at him with shrewd brown eyes, pinpoints of light in a weathered face.

"You want her?"

He tried not to sound too eager. Negotiations would take place, and he needed to be in a good position. But, really, how much could they possibly want? This was a place where they would be lucky to see a five-dollar bill, and he had a stack of them in his pocket. It was just a question of how many.

"Barbree," said Dunbar, "this is Mr. Harrigan."

"Does he want her?" The old woman's voice crackled with impatience.

"I want to look at her," Harry said.

"You'd better come in."

They stepped inside, and Barbree Malloy led them through a cluttered hallway to a lean-to kitchen at the rear of the house. Onions hung from the rafters, along with rabbit pelts and the hide of some larger animal. Light filtered in from a dirt-streaked window above the chipped kitchen sink. Harry looked at the little girl, hoping to see Jack's features beneath the dirt.

"Are you sure this is her?" he asked.

"This is her," Dunbar confirmed.

"I knew she wasn't our'n," the old woman declared.

"Her father was Nick Malloy," said Dunbar.

"No, he weren't," said Barbree. "That little English tramp said he were, but he weren't."

"Do you think that the Englishwoman was her mother?" Harry asked.

The old woman looked at him for a long moment with a thoughtful expression on her weather-beaten face. "Could be," she said at last, "but maybe not. Who can say?"

"We hoped that you could say."

Barbree sniffed. "I wasn't there. I didn't see her born, but even if that little tramp is her mother, I know Nick ain't her father. She don't look nothing like our Nick. Cuckoo in the nest, that's what I think."

"And where is your grandson now?" Harry asked. "Perhaps if we could speak to him …?"

"Dead," said Barbree. "A year agone, up at the coal tipple. Him and four others. Crushed."

"My daddy was crushed," the little girl said unexpectedly and with very little feeling.

"He weren't your daddy," said Barbree, giving the girl's shoulder a rough shake.

"Hey," said Harry.

"He weren't," the old woman repeated.

"Are you sure this is the right Malloy?" Harry asked. "There could be more than one."

"No," said Dunbar, "this is him. He was at Rose Hill in 1944, married a village girl called Vera Chapman, and brought her here in 1946."

"This ain't our Nick's child," Barbree declared. "Look at her, don't look nothing like him. That's what I said, right from the beginning. She didn't fool me."

Harry fixed the old woman with a stern stare. "Tell me about the Englishwoman. What makes you think that she might not be the mother? I don't want you to say something just because you think it's what I want to hear."

"I don't care what you want to hear," Barbree snapped. "You ask me if she's the mother of this brat, and all I can say is that she ain't much of a mother; she don't care for her like a real mother. A real mother wouldn't go and leave her child behind."

"Where has she gone?"

Barbree shrugged her shoulders. "Dunno."

"When did she go?"

"Right after Mr. Dunbar there sent us the first letter. Like as not she knew the game was up, so she took herself off; gone to Pittsburgh most like."

Barbree looked slyly up at the battered kitchen clock hanging above the kitchen range. "You want her or not? Make up your mind."

"Are you in a hurry?" Harry asked.

"Don't got all day to waste," Barbree replied. She turned away and lifted the carcass of a dead animal from its resting place on the floor. She laid the unfortunate creature on the kitchen table. Harry's stomach lurched as he realized that her victim was a possum.

"I have supper to make," Barbree declared. "If you don't want her, then I'll send her to the orphan home in Wheeling. We don't want her here."

She picked up a hatchet and lopped off the possum's head with one practiced blow. "Make up your mind."

"Perhaps we should go to Pittsburgh and find Miss Chapman," said Dunbar. "Should we do that, Barbree?"

Barbree's eyes slid sideways. "You're welcome to try. Pittsburgh's a big place. She could be anywhere. And who's to say she's even in Pittsburgh? Could be gone somewhere else by now. Could have changed her name."

Harry looked at the old woman, her blood-covered hands pulling entrails from the possum.

"Does the child have a coat? It's cold outside?"

"You can wrap her in that one," said Barbree, pointing to a tweed coat hanging on a peg. "It belongs to the Englishwoman, fancy thing, fancy label."

Harry felt a cold chill creeping along his spine.

"She went to Pittsburgh without her coat?"

"Seem so," Barbree agreed.

Harry patted the little girl's tangled hair. "We're not going to find her, Dunbar."

"We can try."

"No, we're not going to find her. No one's going to find her."

"So what shall we do?"

Harry thought of Blanche, waiting back in Chicago, her heart full of hope. He pulled a handful of five-dollar bills from his pocket.

"We'll take her."

March 1952

Harry shuffled forward into the brightly illuminated Customs Hall, where porters were delivering cartloads of expensive luggage to be claimed by their smartly dressed owners.

Blanche moved in beside him. Her face, normally serene and smooth under a layer of makeup, was smudged with stress, and her tightly curled blond hair fell far short of its normal perfection.

"We should have brought a nursemaid," Harry said, as he had said every day since they began their journey to England.

"I wanted to get to know her."

"So now that you know her, what do you think?"

Blanche smiled fondly down at the child. "She reminds me of Jack. He had a temper."

"He sure did," Harry agreed.

Blanche's sudden smile made her look ten years younger and hardly old enough to be a grandmother. "We're so lucky, Harry. When Jack died, I thought we'd lost everything, but now we have Celeste. It's like a miracle."

"I still wonder why it took six years for Jack's wife to ask for our help."

Blanche patted his arm. "When you see her, you can ask her. Not long now."

The child took advantage of Blanche's momentary distraction to release herself from her grandmother's grip. She darted away into the crowd, a flash of red vanishing and reappearing among a sea of dark suits and fur coats.

"Oh my God," Blanche screamed. "Go after her, Harry."

Harry was a big man, broad shouldered with large meaty hands that had made him a sought-after college ball player, and he was quick on his feet. There had been a time in Harry Harrigan's early life, before the college scholarships, when fleet-footedness had been a distinct asset. He took off after the child, elbowing the other passengers aside, and caught up with her just as she was about to run out of the Customs Hall and back toward the ship.

"Let me go. I ain't going with you. I want to go home."

Harry winced at the piercing West Virginia accent and the voice pitched at a level that could be heard in her home valley above the clanking of the coal trains and the screeching of mine whistles.

"Celeste."

"Anita."

He shook her, none too gently. "Celeste," he repeated. "Your name is Celeste Harrigan and you are my granddaughter."

"I ain't. I ain't Celeste Hurricane."

"Harrigan."

"I ain't her. I ain't, I ain't. I want my mother."

"Well, she doesn't want you," Harry said harshly. "You're going to get a new mother, so stop your squawking and get back over there with your grandmother."

"You gonna hit me?" the little girl challenged. "Go on, hit me. I don't care."

Harry looked down at the defiant face, trying to find a trace of his son in the angry features. It wasn't in the dark eyes, but perhaps it was in the tilt of her nose and the strawberry-blond curls that Jack had inherited from his mother and passed on to this unexpected child. News of her existence had come as a blessed relief, a miracle that had sent Blanche rushing to the Church of the Sacred Heart to light a dozen candles. So she was an uncouth, unschooled, foulmouthed little brat; it didn't matter. Her mother, Lady Sylvia Blanchard, would take care of all that.

He tucked the child under his arm and carried her squirming body back to Blanche. He smiled happily at the immigration officer and handed over three passports, two of which were genuine and one of which had been created by Inky Feinstein of Elk Grove. The immigration officer glanced at them, stamped them with a large rubber stamp, and welcomed them to Britain.

Harry set the child back on her feet.

"Where do we go now?" Blanche asked. "Should we take a taxi? How far is it to London?"

"Not London," said Harry, "Southwold. They're sending a car. I plan to get straight down to business. There'll be legal formalities. I may have to spread some money around."

Disapproval showed on Blanche's face. Harry knew that his wife's conscience was more tender than his own.

"You want this to happen, don't you?" he asked sharply.

"Yes, of course, but—"

"Then let me do it my way. Trust me, Blanche, I know what to do. You worry about the kid and I'll worry about the legalities."

They stepped out of the Customs Hall, and a porter followed dutifully behind with a cartload of luggage. Harry looked up at the gray sky, where dark clouds scudded in the wind. The air was filled with the sound of seagulls calling as they circled above the oily waters of the harbor.

The buildings around the Queen Elizabeth's dock seemed to have been recently repaired, but beyond lay the skeletal remains of a once busy harbor. Looking across the water, he saw a flotilla of battered naval vessels, warships, frigates, even a submarine. Beyond the harbor a line of hills broke the gloomy horizon. A cold wind ruffled the fur on Blanche's mink coat and played with the hem of the little girl's dress. Harry turned up his coat collar.

"Someone from the solicitor's office is meeting us," Harry said.

He looked along the line of waiting vehicles, where passengers were already climbing into taxicabs. A tall bespectacled young man approached diffidently.

"Mr. Harrigan?"

"Yeah, I'm Harrigan."

The young man removed his hat. "Toby Whitby from Champion and Company."

"Good, good. Hope you brought a truck. My wife doesn't travel light."

The young man seemed bemused.

"A truck," Harry repeated impatiently. He gestured to the porter with the luggage.

"Oh." The young man thought for a moment. "We'll need an estate car."

"Do you have one?"

"No, not with me."

Harry concluded that the young man was not giving the problem his full attention. He was staring at the little girl who was, even now, pulling impatiently against Blanche's restraining hand.

Well, Harry thought, it was understandable. This child had been the subject of much correspondence, and here she was. Not surprising at all that the young lawyer should stare at her instead of addressing the problem of transport. Not surprising, but not acceptable.

"Well?" Harry barked.

Whitby tore his worried gaze away from the child. "I'll take care of it. I'll arrange for an appropriate vehicle. In the meantime, the Countess has sent her personal car for you. If you would like to come this way ..." He gestured along the line of waiting vehicles, where a massive black car with a crest on the door stood out from the line of taxicabs and smaller proletarian vehicles.

As they approached, a liveried chauffer sprang from the interior to hold the door open for them.

Blanche lifted a worried face to Harry. "The luggage? All my things? My jewelry?"

"Don't worry about it."

Blanche lowered her voice. "Everyone looks so poor, Harry. Are you sure they won't steal—?"

Her question was interrupted by an eruption of energy from the child they called Celeste.

"I wanna go home. I want my mom."

Blanche took a firmer grip of the child's hand. "Not now, Celeste."

"I ain't Celeste."

Harry looked back at the Customs Hall. He was worried that someone would hear the shrieking child's declaration that she was not who her passport said she was.

"Just get her in the car," he ordered.

He followed his wife into the cavernous interior of the car and was assaulted by an odor of old leather, gasoline, and stale cigarette smoke. He looked back to see the solicitor giving instructions to the porter. His wife's red leather train case was on the top of the pile of luggage.

"Bring the red one," he ordered.

When the train case had been placed safely into Blanche's hands, and the solicitor had taken a seat inside, the car pulled away from the curb and moved smoothly into the line of traffic leaving the docks. The vehicle was obviously old but it rode smoothly, the engine purring so softly that it could hardly be heard.

"I want one of these," Harry declared. "What is it?"

"A Bentley," said their escort.

"I'll have to get me one."

Blanche opened the train case and produced a handful of wrapped candy. She gave one to the child. The young man looked on in surprise. Rationing, Harry thought. They still have rationing. When's the last time he saw a piece of candy? He hesitated over the idea of offering to share the child's candy and then thought better of it. The man on deck, the one who had suggested that the United States had bankrupted Britain, had made it clear that he and his money might be a mixed blessing. Offering children's candy to the dignified young lawyer might not be a good way to start.

"What was your name again?"

"Whitby, Toby Whitby."

"Mind if I call you Toby?"

The lawyer looked surprised. "No, I suppose not."

"I'm Harry, and this is—"

"Oh no, I couldn't do that. Mr. Champion would never agree to that, Mr. Harrigan. We have to retain a certain amount of formality."

"When in Rome," Blanche muttered under her breath.

"So," said Harry, "what's the story, Whitby? What do we do now?"

"I'm escorting you to Southwold Hall," said Whitby. "The Countess is very anxious to meet you and to see her … daughter."

Harry noticed the hesitation. Not for the first time, he wondered if everything was on the up-and-up. Blanche wanted it to be the case and he wanted what Blanche wanted, but he had no intention of putting aside his naturally suspicious nature. He had not made his fortune by being naive and credulous. He looked at the little girl who was huddled in the corner, sucking on candy. She had Jack's hair and coloring, but what about those dark eyes? He would reserve judgement until he had seen Lady Sylvia herself.

"Shall we meet the Earl?" Blanche asked. "I understood he was not well, but perhaps seeing his granddaughter will lift his spirits. I know it's done wonders for me."

She smiled at the sulking child, and Harry felt a twinge of guilt. Blanche was so certain that this child was Jack's legacy, and therefore, Jack's life had not been without purpose. How could he disappoint her?

Whitby cleared his throat. "Unfortunately," he said, "the Earl has succumbed to his illness."

"Succumbed?"

"Died."

The word was flat and unambiguous. They had all seen so much death in the past ten years, Harry thought, that euphemisms had become pointless. Death was death, whether at the hands of an enemy soldier or in the debris of a bombing raid or just in the inevitable progress of an illness. The Earl was dead, just as Jack was dead; a word that left no room for misunderstanding.

"So what happens now?" Harry asked.

"Perhaps we shouldn't intrude," Blanche suggested. "We could go to a hotel. I'm sure they won't want us in the house while they make the arrangements."

"Oh, no, Mrs. Harrigan," said Whitby. "It wasn't unexpected. Well, not totally unexpected. The Earl had been ill for some time. We have retained copies of his major documents, and everything is in order. The Earl had already gifted most of the estate to his daughter in order to avoid death duties. Legally speaking, there is little to do. The title has passed automatically to Lady Sylvia. She has become the Countess of Southwold."

Whitby looked at the little girl, still sucking on her candy and glaring around with the feral eyes of a trapped animal.

"That little girl is now Lady Celeste Blanchard and next in line to become the Countess. She'll probably have a seat at the coronation next year."

"Oh my," said Blanche. "Imagine that. It all sounds very grand,"

"Maybe so," Harry agreed, "but titles and invitations to coronations won't get you far without money, and there's no money, is there, Mr. Whitby?"

"I'm not free to divulge details of the estate," Whitby said stiffly.

"Of course not," Harry agreed, "but I don't need you to tell me. I have my own ways of finding things out, so let me tell you. There is no money."

"Really, Harry," said Blanche, "I don't think this is the time to talk about that. I don't suppose they've even had a funeral yet."

"Tomorrow," said Whitby.

"We'll have to get Celeste a black dress," said Blanche.

Harry looked out at their surroundings. They were passing through a dreary townscape of boarded-up buildings.

"Do you even have any shops?" he asked.

"Yes, we have shops," Whitby replied with a bitter edge to his voice, "but we also have rationing. You won't be able to buy any clothes, not legally."

"Oh dear," said Blanche.

Harry smiled. "It's just a question of money."

"I'm sure it is," said Whitby, in a tone that seemed not quite neutral.

The big car carried them away from the docks and purred quietly through a landscape of rolling hills while rain lashed at the windows. The little girl grew quiet, her eyelids drooping. Eventually she laid her head in Blanche's lap and went to sleep.

Harry looked at the serene expression on his wife's face. She was, at long last, content. The death of her only child had left her stunned. For six years she had been nothing but a walking shadow, unable to find any meaning in life. He had bottled up his own grief and expended his energies on growing his business, although the fortune he amassed gave him no pleasure. The news from England jolted them out of their separate mourning and brought them together again. Jack had married. Jack had a child. Harry threw every resource he possessed into finding the child and rejoiced in seeing Blanche come alive again.

Blanche's hand rested on the child's head, smoothing the curls. Harry tried to think of Jack as a child before his first haircut and the taming of his hair. Had the curls been the same? Blanche was convinced, but Harry was uncertain, and Jack's eyes had been gray, while this child's eyes were deep, dark brown. Harry would withhold judgment until he had seen the mother.

And, he asked himself, what if it's all false? What if she looks nothing like the English aristocrat and not very much like Jack, what will you do then? Will you walk away? Will you deprive Blanche of her new hope?

He closed his eyes, lulled by the comfort of the leather seats and the sound of the rain against the windows. When he opened them again, the car was turning into a driveway marked by stone pillars and wrought iron gates.

"The Southwold crest," said the young lawyer, pointing to the emblem on the open gates. "This is Southwold Hall."

Celeste stirred in her grandmother's lap.

"We're here, dear," said Blanche.

Harry peered through the window as the house emerged from the curtain of rain. "Good God," he said.

Blanche turned from the window, her eyes bright. "Oh, Harry, it's beautiful."

Harry stared at the great house. The facade was white stone, with arched windows that would not have been out of place in a cathedral. At each corner of the building, graceful turrets reached up into the mist. The red-tiled roof was ornamented with more than half a dozen chimneys. The driveway, lined with dark skeletal trees, swooped in a graceful curve to bring them alongside a massive front door, standing open to welcome them.

Blanche pulled Celeste onto her lap and pointed through the window.

"This is your mommy's house."

"Is she here?" the child asked hopefully. "Is my mommy here?"

"Yes," said Blanche. "Of course she is. She's waiting to see you."

Harry caught the young lawyer's eye. It was obvious that Mr. Whitby was thinking exactly what Harry was thinking. Any minute now there would be an explosion of tears.

Harry took another look at the house. "It's going to cost a fortune," he said.

"Then we'll spend a fortune," Blanche replied.

CHAPTER ELEVEN

Toby could hear the child sobbing as Harry Harrigan carried her up the grand staircase, with Blanche Harrigan patting the child's head and making soothing noises. The child lifted her tearstained face and fixed her eyes on Toby as if pleading for help. For the second time that day, he felt a flash of recognition; something in the eyes and the shape of her nose.

Mrs. Pearson and Lady Sylvia trailed up the stairs behind the Harrigans. Mrs. Pearson's expression was grim, and Lady Sylvia had not ceased to glower since the moment Celeste had rejected her attempts at mother-child bonding.

"That didn't go well," Toby said.

"What else did Lady Sylvia expect?" asked Mr. Champion from his seat beside the fire in the Earl's study.

"The child really thought she was going to see her mother," Toby said. "I mean, she thought she would see Vera Chapman."

"There must be some resemblance between Lady Sylvia and Vera Chapman," said Champion. "The child was fooled for a moment."

"A very brief moment."

"Yes, very brief indeed," Champion agreed. "Come in and close the door."

Toby closed the heavy oak door and took a seat across from his employer. "I'm glad to see you here, sir. Are you feeling better?"

"No, not in the least, but duty calls. It's the least I can do for the Earl. He was a good man in his own way; a product of his age. I know that everything is changing and you young people are running the world now, but the Earl and I understood each other. It was appropriate for me to be here for the reading of the will."

"Any surprises?" Toby asked.

"No, none. A few bequests to loyal servants and nothing for Mrs. Pearson. The Earl did not care for her."

Toby maintained his silence, keeping his opinion to himself.

"Something for old Ruddle. We shall have to look into whether that bequest can go to his son if Mr. Ruddle doesn't recover."

"Have we heard anything from the hospital?"

"He's still unconscious. If he dies, I'm afraid it will be a murder charge for Terry Chapman."

"I don't think it was him, sir. I met him and he didn't strike me as dangerous. Very confused, but not dangerous."

"Shell shock," said Champion. "I saw it myself in the Great War. The mind can only take so much, and then it snaps."

"He was afraid of his own shadow," Toby argued. "I can't imagine him attacking someone."

"Hmm." Champion was silent for a moment, his tired eyes assessing Toby. "The Earl should not have died," he said eventually.

"He was very ill."

"I am very ill," Mr. Champion countered, "but I am not ready to die, and neither was Lord Dennis."

"But cancer …"

"Yes, I know, I know. The King died of cancer, and so you will say that if the King could not be cured, then the Earl could not be cured. I agree with you in principle, Whitby, but I am convinced that the Earl's time had not yet arrived. We had spoken on the telephone and he was planning to make some changes."

"To his will?"

"I believe so. Of course, he could not change the fact that he had gifted his estate to his daughter. That was done some years ago and could not be undone. But there were other matters causing him concern. I imagine he had discussed them with Alderton. No doubt Alderton had made a note."

Toby leaned forward. He had to ask. "Do you think that Mr. Alderton was killed by someone who wanted those notes?"

Champion's eyes flashed. "Of course I do, don't you?"

"I didn't like to say."

Champion nodded. "Quite right! We must leave the police to deal with the matter. We are still the legal representatives of the Blanchard family. It is not appropriate for us to tell them of our speculations."

"So you think it was one of them?" Toby asked.

"I can see no other possibility."

Champion sat back in his chair and stared up at the ceiling. Toby hesitated. Without Alderton's notes, no one would ever know what had passed between Alderton and the Earl. Toby could do nothing about that, but there were other secrets that needed to be brought into the light of day, and they had become Toby's responsibility. All he needed was permission to ruffle a few aristocratic feathers.

"What would you like me to do, sir?"

"Do? What would I like you to do?" The old man sighed. "I don't know, Mr. Whitby. I am troubled by this situation. Mr. Harrigan seems a decent enough man, for an American, and I can see that Mrs. Harrigan dotes on that child. Their lives have been marked by tragedy, and I have no wish to spoil their obvious joy in this child, but can we really believe this story? Mrs. Harrigan insisted that the child resembles her son, but I have to say that she bears very little resemblance to Lady Sylvia. We have no evidence of the marriage beyond the word of Lady Sylvia and some records that may or may not be forged."

Toby thought of the child, whose temper tantrum only accentuated her terror in being dragged away from all that was familiar. The little girl was more than a piece in a legal puzzle, and her future hung in the balance.

"That poor child is alone now," Toby reminded him. "Nick Malloy died in a mining accident, and Mr. Harrigan suspects that Vera Chapman is dead or, at the very least, she has disappeared. What will happen to the child if we challenge her identity?"

"The lack of any other plan does not change essential truth.""No, sir."

"If she is truly Vera Chapman's child, then we should take her to her grandmother, Mildred Chapman."

"Oh, no." The words flew out of Toby's mouth before he could stop them. He couldn't imagine what would happen if he tried to place the tempestuous little girl into Mildred Chapman's sullen keeping.

"Are there no tests that can be performed?" Champion asked. "I am not au fait with modern technology. Is there no way to test the child's parentage?"

Toby shook his head. "There is no exact science, sir. We can match her blood type against that of her supposed parents, but it is nothing definitive. Through blood typing, it is possible to say that someone is not the father or even mother of a child, but it cannot prove the reverse. Blood typing can only show that the blood types are compatible or incompatible, leaving millions of possibilities of people who have the same type of blood. The U.S. Army has a record of the blood type of Malloy and Jack Harrigan."

"And has this test been performed?"

"According to Mr. Harrigan, it has."

"Do we believe him? I am under the impression he wants to make his wife happy."

"He showed me the test results. It is quite possible for either of the men to be the father."

"And what about the mother?"

"That's a test that is not usually necessary."

"Well, in this case it is necessary. Have the tests been performed?"

"I don't think we can test Vera Chapman; she is either missing or dead."

"Then we shall test Lady Sylvia."

Toby shuddered at the idea of asking the new Countess to submit to a test. "Surely that request should come from Mr. Harrigan."

"No, it should come from us, Mr. Whitby. We have a duty beyond that of Mr. Harrigan. Make the request."

"Yes, sir. Should I do it now?"

Mr. Champion leaned back wearily in his chair. "Not today. We all have enough to contend with today. It will keep for a few days. Wait until after the funeral."

"Yes, sir."

Mr. Champion reached into the breast pocket of his old-fashioned morning coat. "Miss Clark has received a message for you, Mr. Whitby."

He handed Toby a page torn from a message pad.

"She has been unable to reach you at your flat, and you have not been in the office—"

"I was in Southampton, sir."

"That's what I told her. I am afraid that Miss Clark does not approve of you, Mr. Whitby."

A little pop of anger fizzed through Toby's brain. Was it really up to Anthea Clark to approve or disapprove? Miss Clark was the secretary, and he was the solicitor. Since when did he answer to Miss Clark? Perhaps he should tell Mr. Champion that the prim and proper Anthea Clark was a devotee of women's romantic fiction. The angry words and temptation to ruin Miss Clark's reputation died unspoken as he looked at the message slip.

"Detective Sergeant Slater?"

"I'm afraid so."

"Perhaps he has found out something about Mr. Alderton."

"If that were the case, I would hope he would share it with me. However, it is you he wishes to see. Perhaps you have been careless with your motor car."

Toby continued to stare at the card. Slater wasn't interested in motor cars and traffic violations.

"Did he say anything to Miss Clark?"

"Only that he wanted to speak to you urgently."

"Just me?"

"Yes, just you."

"But why?"

Mr. Champion had grown impatient. "Don't ask me, ask him. There's a telephone in the hall and I suggest you use it."

Edwin Champion

Edwin watched his young employee leave the room. He felt a certain fondness for the young Whitby. He was intelligent but not overbearing, scrupulously polite but not in any way servile. Given the chance, he would have made a fine officer. Surely the army could have found some way to put him into uniform and spare him the embarrassment of being in civvies while the rest of the world was in battle dress.

Behind the thick-rimmed glasses, Whitby's gray eyes were honest and his gaze unflinching. The boy could go far. He amended the thought with a little shake of his head. Unfortunately, the boy was already going far. If office gossip as reported by Miss Clark was to be believed, Toby Whitby would soon be on his way to Rhodesia.

Edwin looked around at the late Earl's study. How many estate managers, foremen, and gamekeepers had stood in this room, cap in hand, waiting for orders from their master? Had any of them raised their eyes from the carpet and looked around at the moth-eaten curtains, the worm-infested paneling, or the cracked windows? Did they know that their world was crumbling around them? Did they even care? Mr. Whitby had the right idea. Move on while he could. Make a fresh start away from the weight of tradition and the habit of servility.

But here was Mr. Harry Harrigan of Chicago, ready and willing to throw his millions of dollars into shoring up Southwold's outdated lifestyle. And Mrs. Blanche Harrigan, a sweet-faced, uncomplicated woman, beaming in delight at the idea of her son's child receiving an invitation to the coronation of the Queen of England. Not a thought in her head beyond finding a dress for the little girl to wear for the Earl's funeral.

Edwin wished that he could share in Mrs. Harrigan's certainty, but it was no longer up to him. It was up to young Whitby to ferret out the truth. Edwin would keep his doubts and his memories to himself, and he would wait and see what Whitby made of the situation.

He rose shakily from the chair and walked over to the window. He looked out across the winter landscape of abandoned fields and lowering clouds. His thoughts returned to a day that now seemed long ago; a day when the sky was blue, and hope was rising.

August 1944

"Champion. Glad you could come."

The Earl's handshake was strong.

"Take a seat. Take a seat."

Edwin lowered himself gratefully into a chair beside the Earl's massive desk.

"Tea?" asked the Earl. "I can get that awful Pearson woman to bring us

some."

Edwin hesitated. His arthritic knees were paining him, and he'd had a tedious journey on the train up from Brighton in the heat of the summer day. The thought of tea and a few minutes of rest was very inviting. However, rationing had changed the very fabric of social commerce. Tea should be offered, of course, but these days it was polite to refuse.

The Earl read his hesitation.

"American teabags," he said. "You know we had the Yanks here for months. We had visits from the officer class, not bad chappies really, and always ready with a pound of tea and a packet of fags. I built up my own stockpile. I'll ring the bell."

"Thank you."

The Earl rang the bell and occupied himself for a few moments in straightening the papers on his desk. When he was satisfied with the state of the desktop, he looked up again.

"We're going to win," he said.

Edwin considered the statement and acknowledged the hope welling in his heart.

"I think so."

"Our boys will be in Berlin by Christmas," said the Earl. "Have to admit that the Americans are putting up a bloody good show; couldn't have done it without them. Couldn't have taken the beaches at Normandy on our own."

"No, we couldn't," Edwin agreed.

He looked round as the door to the study opened and Mrs. Pearson entered. The housekeeper was, as always, dressed in gray with her hair pinned into a neat uncompromising bun.

"You rang?"

"Tea," said the Earl.

Mrs. Pearson's mouth set in a line of sour disapproval.

"Sir, we don't—"

"The American tea, woman. Serve the American tea, and some of those American biscuits."

He gave Edwin a wry grin. "Cookies, that's what they call them. Infantile name but they taste good. Get on with it, Pearson."

Mrs. Pearson spun on her heel and left the room.

"I hate to impose," Edwin muttered.

"No imposition. She has ideas above her station. Sylvia seems to be very attached to her, but I can't stand the woman."

"Perhaps Mrs. Pearson could be sent away to do war work," Edwin

suggested. "It's compulsory for single women, and I understand that the title of Mrs. is purely an honorific for a housekeeper. I've lost most of my office staff. The men have been called up, and the young women have been taken by the Land Army. There's not a shorthand typist to be found anywhere in Brighton."

"Pearson's too old, and the Women's Voluntary Service has not asked her to volunteer. She's not popular in the village."

"Unfortunate."

"I can put up with her a little longer. It's all coming to an end, you know. We will have to change our ways if we are to survive. That's why I asked you to come. I've been thinking about the future, now that we can be certain that we have a future."

Edwin waited.

"A couple of years ago, I would have said there was no future for us. Don't look like that, Champion, you know what I mean. It all looked pretty hopeless. If you'd asked me in '42 what the future would hold, I would have said that we'd be under German rule by now. Some jackbooted Nazi would be master of this house, and we'd all be shouting 'Heil Hitler.'"

"No," Edwin protested.

"Hitler should have invaded while he had the chance," said the Earl, "but he didn't, and now he's on the run. I've been thinking about the future of Southwold. Of course, my daughter will inherit."

"Of course."

"But the estate taxes will ruin her. I want to make everything over to her now, get it out of the way so there will be no death duties. That's legal, isn't it?"

"Perfectly legal. It's a common practice these days. Do you want her to have the title also?" Edwin asked.

"Certainly not. I'll never give up the title. She'll have to wait until I'm dead, but she should have everything else."

The Earl rose from his desk and moved across the room to look out of the window. Edwin pulled himself to his feet, his knees creaking in protest, and went to join his client.

Southwold Hall was perched on a clifftop high above the waters of Rose Bay, but the Earl's study looked out on the landward side. Edwin's heart lifted at the sight of the Earl's cultivated fields ripe with grain. Food for a hungry nation.

"Tolly Oliver," said the Earl with a sigh.

Edwin waited.

"Lord Livet's oldest."

Edwin continued to wait.

"Gone," said the Earl. "His father heard last week. When it's an enlisted

man, they send a telegram, but when it's an officer, they arrive in person. Not that it makes any difference. Personally, I'd rather have a telegram. Let's you do your grieving in peace, you know. Wouldn't want to stand there with a stiff upper lip while a couple of junior officers tell me that my son has bought it. No, I wouldn't want that."

Edwin, not for the first time, felt the blessing of being childless, and the possible grief he had been spared.

"I was going to marry Sylvia to him," the Earl continued. "They both knew. We'd been planning it practically from the cradle. The Olivers have a good estate in Scotland, fine trout stream and some good shooting. The Olivers have money."

Edwin waited while the Earl reached into his pocket for a handkerchief. He blew his nose hard and straightened his shoulders.

"I don't know how Sylvia will take the news," he said when he had regained his composure. "I hope she doesn't do anything foolish. She has to understand the importance of finding the right husband."

"I'm sure she does," said Edwin soothingly.

The Earl offered him a worried frown. "With all these Americans around, one can't be too careful."

Edwin looked out across the sunlit countryside. The sky was a bright, clear blue ornamented with puffy white clouds blown in by the breeze from the ocean. A patient horse pulled a wagon across the field, and workers forked hay up and over the high sides. The timeless scene pulled at Edwin's heart, reminding him of how much was at stake. They had come close to losing everything, and the war was not yet over.

"She could join the land girls," Edwin suggested. The Earl's daughter had grown up on the Southwold Estate; she would know more about farming than the current crop of young women being sent from the cities to the countryside to work on the farms. "She won't meet many Americans working on a farm."

The Earl gestured toward the bucolic scene outside the window. "Do you know whose working my fields?" he asked.

Edwin looked again, seeing men in brown uniforms. He turned a questioning look on the Earl.

"Prisoners of war?' he asked.

"German," said the Earl.

Edwin stared at the brown-coated figures. Yes, of course. The trickle of German prisoners brought into Britain after the North Africa campaign had recently become a flood. The Allied army, moving through Europe, was sending thousands of captives back to Britain. Edwin had been spared the sight of them in

Brighton because no one thought it a good idea to have German prisoners anywhere near the beach defenses, but he knew they existed. He knew that housing and feeding them had become a problem.

"You allow them in your fields?" he asked in surprise.

"Don't have any choice," the Earl replied. "We have to get the hay in, and they're all we can get. They send them down from the Billingshurst camp. I was hoping for Italians. Peasants, you know, good Italian peasants, but instead we got Germans."

Edwin shivered at the idea of a squad of German soldiers let loose across the Sussex countryside. He stepped away from the window but the Earl called him back.

"Look at that," he said. "That's the sort of thing I have to put up with."

The workers had laid down their pitchforks and turned as one to watch an old estate car bouncing across the field toward them.

"Lunch," said the Earl. "They get the same rations as our own troops."

"Really?"

"Geneva Convention."

"I see."

Two young women in the green uniform of land girls exited the estate car. The prisoners gathered around.

"Oh dear," said Edwin. "That seems very unwise with our boys away at the front and the Americans gone from the village."

"Couldn't agree more," said the Earl. "I'm keeping Sylvia well away from here. No sense in asking for trouble."

"I see what you mean, but surely your daughter—"

"You never know what foolishness might occur in wartime," the Earl replied. He walked away from the window and seated himself at his desk.

"Come here, Champion, I want to show you something."

Edwin stood behind the Earl and watched as the Earl's long aristocratic fingers moved across the ornate scrollwork of the desktop. "It's here, right here. You press the center of this scroll and … voila!"

With a faint mechanical click, a drawer slid out from its hiding place among the tracery at the base of the desk. The Earl leaned down and pulled out a bundle of papers wrapped in waxed paper and tied with a faded red ribbon.

"What is it?" Edwin asked, impressed by the apparent age of the package.

"Documents that could change the future of Southwold."

Edwin held out an eager hand, but the Earl returned the documents to their hiding place.

"Not now. You will know if they're needed."

"I don't understand."

"But you will. My daughter is the last of my line. If she dies without issue, these documents may prove important. All I ask is that you remember that they exist." The Earl rose and clapped Edwin on the back rather too heartily. "Sylvia doesn't know about this. Let's hope she never has to find out."

He slid the drawer back into its hiding place and studied Edwin's face. Their eyes met, and Edwin saw a deep sadness hidden behind the Earl's determined expression.

"I didn't know how to raise a girl. If she'd been a boy, I would have sent her to Eton, but she's not a boy, and after Lilian died, I'm afraid I let things slide. She's not …"

His voice trailed away.

Edwin waited.

The Earl shook his head. "When the time comes, Champion, I'm relying on you to do the right thing."

The Earl's eyes flicked toward the desk. "Do I have your word?"

"Of course."

"Good. Now let's go and see if the Germans have left us anything to eat."

March 1952

Edwin's thoughts traveled round and around in weary circles. The Earl, gone now, his body awaiting burial; the war, over, but leaving behind a trail of destruction and weariness; the Americans, returned to their own factories and farms, taking their war brides with them; Blanche Harrigan, filled with hope; Harry Harrigan, with money to burn; the new Countess of Southwold, cool, distant, and sharp-tongued.

Sending Toby Whitby to cope with her that first time had been an act of cowardice. With Alderton dead, he should have gone himself, but he had not wanted to face the Earl. He had wanted someone fresh and unbiased to consider Lady Sylvia's claims. Well, matters were coming to a head. The Earl was dead, and the child was here. Decisions would have to be made.

Toby Whitby came quietly into the room, closing the door carefully behind him.

"Well?"

"Troubling news, sir."

"I assume we are not talking of your motor car."

"No, we are not."

"Do you wish to tell me?"

Toby dropped down into a chair. His face was pale and anxious. He seemed to be groping for words. "I had some cards printed. Business cards."

"Yes, I know. I authorized the expense. Surely the police are not involved in the printing of business cards."

"No, of course not."

Another hesitation, interrupted only by a small crash and a shower of sparks as the coals in the fireplace caved in on themselves, sending a welcome wave of warmth.

"The police have recovered a body, washed in by the tide and snagged on some barbed wire."

"They should have cleared the beaches by now," said Edwin, knowing he was speaking of an irrelevancy. The shingle beaches of the south coast were still littered with anti-tank traps, coils of rusted wire, and all manner of improvised defenses left over from the time when the German Army was amassing across the Channel.

"If she hadn't been caught on the wire, no one would ever have found her," said Toby. "She'd have been washed away."

"She?"

"Yes, a woman who had my business card in her pocket. Apparently the card withstood the seawater very well."

"We use only the best printing establishments."

"Yes, sir."

Edwin waited impatiently. Whitby seemed lost in his own thoughts.

"Well, who was she?"

"The police don't know. They want me to look at her to see if I can identify her."

"And you don't want to look?" Edwin sighed in exasperation. "We've all seen our share of dead bodies, Mr. Whitby. Surely you can take a look."

Whitby leaned forward in the chair. "I don't need to. I know who she is."

"Then tell them."

"If I tell them, I might have to tell them everything, and Slater will connect it all to Alderton's murder."

Edwin thought of the red file folder, the missing notes, and the documents impossible to refute, and equally impossible to verify. The war had been an excuse for many things, but the war was over. The rule of law had to be restored. Lawyers could no longer be flexible, and aristocrats could no longer live protected lives.

"Volunteer nothing, but answer all questions truthfully." "I'm not sure I know the truth."

Whitby's eyes were shielded by his thick spectacle lenses, but Champion could see conflict and denial written plain across his face. He fixed his young employee with a steady gaze.

"You know the truth."

Whitby shifted his gaze, and Edwin wondered if Whitby knew another truth; something he had not yet mentioned. Well, let him keep that to himself for the time being. Not all thoughts should be given voice.

"I'm relying on you, Mr. Whitby. Go now. No need to attend the funeral. I will represent the firm."

He watched as Whitby went quietly out of the room, and he listened to the opening and closing of the front door. The short winter day was drawing to a close, and the room was lit only by the dim glow of the coals.

When the time comes, Champion, I'm relying on you to do the right thing.

He had given the Earl his word, and surely the time had come. He went to the Earl's desk and turned on the lamp. He ran his fingers along the scrollwork and found the trigger. The hidden drawer slid open.

CHAPTER TWELVE

Brighton Mortuary

Toby looked down at the bloated face as Slater flicked the sheet aside. It was five days since he had seen her alive in the drawing room at Southwold. The intervening days had been busy ones for him, but for Nurse Tierney, they had not been kind.

"Her name's Tierney."

"First name?"

"I don't know."

"Where does she come from?"

"Ireland, I think. Northern Ireland."

"And why does she have your business card?"

"Ah."

Toby's hesitation had not been intended to try the patience of Detective Sergeant Slater, but the man had a short fuse and was already suspicious of every word that came from Toby's mouth. Who could blame him when he had another dead body on his hands and Toby's card in her pocket?

"Was she your client?" Slater asked impatiently, gesturing with his remaining hand to the cold, damp figure on the table.

"No, not exactly."

"And you don't know her first name. Do you know her address?"

"No. All I know is that she was a nurse. Well, not really a nurse, more of an orderly."

"When is the last time you saw her?"

Toby hesitated. He could tell Slater the when but not the where.

"I saw her five days ago."

"Do you want to tell me anything else?"

Toby considered his instructions from Mr. Champion. Don't volunteer information but answer truthfully. What was the truth? The only truth he knew of the woman on the slab was that she spoke with an Irish accent. He had no proof of anything else, not even her name.

"No, I don't know anything else," he said.

"Irish you say?"

"Yes, definitely Irish."

Slater reached forward and inserted his left hand under Nurse Tierney's head. Toby saw movement in Slater's right shoulder as though he still could not overcome his body's instinct to move the nonexistent right arm. He moved clumsily, lifting and turning the dead woman's head. The hair that had been tucked under a hat for her interview at Southwold was now revealed as a clumsy mass of drowned gray curls.

"Can you state for the record that this woman presented herself to you as a Miss or Mrs. Tierney, that she claimed to be a nurse or an orderly, and appeared to be Irish?"

"Yes."

Slater replaced the sheet.

"Normally I wouldn't take a blind bit of notice of something like this. I could easily put it down as death by drowning resulting from a fall from the cliff. I would even assume that she was drunk at the time."

"Why?"

Slater looked at Toby with raised eyebrows. "You say she was Irish, so we can assume she was drunk; drunkards, all of them."

"You can't say that," Toby protested.

Slater gave him an icy smile that matched the temperature of the mortuary. "It would be easier all around if I did say that, don't you think?"

Without waiting for Toby's reply, he pulled the woman's limp arm from under the sheet and looked at the multiple gashes and scrapes.

"Dragged along the seabed by the tide," he said. "All kinds of stuff lying on the bottom these days, barbed wire, tank traps, not to mention rocks. My guess is that she entered the water, unwillingly, from the cliff path at Saltdean and the tide brought her down here. If she hadn't been tangled in the wire, she would have gone out with the next tide and never been seen again."

He tucked the corpse's arm back under the sheet. "We're busy people. One war is over and another is beginning. They're calling it the Cold War; let's hope it stays that way. We're on the lookout for Soviet spies and we're still rounding up Nazis. Normally I wouldn't go to much trouble over a drunken old woman falling off a cliff, but this one is not as simple as it looks, is it?"

Toby stared down at the shrouded body. "I don't know what you mean."

"I'll spare you another look at the damage," Slater said, "and I'll just tell you that Miss Tierney here received a heavy blow on her head, and it was not caused by anything she encountered underwater."

He made a movement with his right shoulder and then groped in his pocket with his left hand. Toby felt a pang of sympathy. The missing hand was Slater's constant companion; his brain had not accepted the truth.

Slater looked down at his notes. "Robert Alderton, Miss or Mrs. Tierney, and Sam Ruddle."

Toby gasped. Last he had heard, Sam Ruddle was still unconscious. Had he taken a turn for the worst?

"Is he dead?"

"No, not yet, but if he dies, we may not be charging Terry Chapman with murder. In light of this latest evidence, we may be looking at someone else."

"You're trying to connect these three things, Alderton, Ruddle, and Tierney?"

"I don't have to try very hard."

Slater fumbled the notebook back into his pocket.

"So, Mr. Whitby, let me ask you again. What is your connection to this woman?"

"She had evidence to give in a civil matter. I've told you everything I am able to tell you without breaching my client's need for confidentiality."

"And your client is?"

"I can't answer that."

Slater sighed. "Southwold." He shook his head. "No, you don't have to confirm it; it's written all over your face. Let me tell you, Mr. Whitby, I don't regard anyone as being above the law. Go ahead and claim client confidentiality, but it makes no difference to me. I have my eye on you."

He gestured with his head. "Go out that door. The desk clerk will have forms for you to sign to say you identified her as someone named Tierney. We'll take it from here."

Toby emerged from the mortuary and walked the narrow lane to the seafront. The office was just a short distance away, and he hoped that brisk wind blowing from the sea would clear his mind.

He made his way past the repaired Palace Pier, once again open for business, and no longer a potential landing ground for Hitler's invasion forces. The short winter day was drawing to a close, and lights winked on outlining the dome of the theatre perched precariously at the end of the pier. He tried to take his mind off Slater's veiled accusations by examining the posters that proclaimed the many entertainments on offer. He imagined inviting Carol to see a show; a musical was playing at the Palace Theatre. Would she like Ivor Novello? Would she go with him to see The Dancing Years?

He looked at his watch. Four o'clock. He would like to have stayed at the foot of the pier, dreaming about a date with Carol, but Mr. Champion would expect him to return to the office.

Anthea Clark rose from her desk as soon as he entered the door. "You have a visitor," she said disapprovingly, "an unpleasant woman in an unsuitable hat."

"Did she give her name?"

"She refused."

Toby tried to imagine how anyone could refuse Miss Clark. The visitor must indeed be formidable.

"Did she say what she wanted?"

"Only that she wanted to see you and she has information. She is in the waiting room. She's been there for over an hour. I gave her tea, although I did not use the best china. She does not appear to be the kind of woman who should be served on our best china."

Toby frowned. Miss Clark's social barometer was no doubt accurate, but if this woman, whoever she was, had information to give, perhaps she should be treated with more respect.

"I also gave her a biscuit," Miss Clark added.

Well, Toby thought, a biscuit was probably more important than the quality of the teacup.

He pushed open the door of the waiting room and was greeted by the sight of Vera Chapman's mother dressed in a black woolen coat and a bright yellow hat pulled down low over her forehead and topped with a cockade of red feathers. He had to agree with Miss Clark; the hat was indeed unsuitable, both for the time of year and also for the wearer, whose scowling face negated any possible levity suggested by the colorful headgear.

Mrs. Chapman rose from her seat. "I've been waiting since three o'clock," she said accusingly. "Shall we get on with this?"

"I'm sorry," said Toby. "Did we have an appointment?"

"No."

Toby wondered why he had apologized. He had no appointment with this woman. She could have waited all day and he still would not need to apologize.

"I have something for you; something you've been looking for," said Mrs. Chapman, patting her battered leather handbag. "You can have it for a price."

"Mrs. Chapman," Toby protested, "this is a law firm. We don't pay for information."

"It's not information; it's proof."

"Proof of what?"

"Proof my Vera had a baby. Proof that Nellie Pearson up at the Hall is lying through her teeth. That's what you want, isn't it? You wrote me letters, didn't you? You wanted proof."

"Yes, I did, but—"

"But nothing. You wanted proof, and I have proof. If I give it to you, what are you going to give me?"

Toby took a deep breath. "Mrs. Chapman, it would not be lawful for me to give you money."

Mrs. Chapman drew herself upright, and her face assumed an expression of outraged innocence.

"Money? Who said anything about money?"

"Well, you said—"

"I didn't say nothing about money. Did you hear one word about money pass my lips?"

Toby's anger was sharp and sudden. He knew it was anger that he should have directed at Detective Sergeant Slater and his accusation, but Slater was not standing in front of him, and Mrs. Chapman was. He stretched out his hand.

"Give it to me."

"No."

"Do you want me to call the police?"

"Police?"

Mrs. Chapman's voice rose to a protesting shriek, and Toby heard the door of the waiting room open behind him. He knew Miss Clark would be standing behind him disapprovingly, but he could not, and would not, take his eyes off Mrs. Chapman.

"Withholding evidence is a criminal offence, Mrs. Chapman."

"I ain't. This ain't a criminal—"

"Yes, it is," Toby persisted. "I suggest you give me whatever you have before you further incriminate yourself."

"Incriminate?" Mrs. Chapman's voice cracked as she repeated the word.

Toby heard Miss Clark speaking softly behind him. "Mr. Whitby, I don't think—"

"Not now," Toby snapped. He continued to glare at Mrs. Chapman. His extended hand remained steady. "Give it to me."

Mrs. Chapman fumbled her purse open and pulled out a folded paper.

"I don't want no money," she said softly, "I just want you to help my Terry."

She thrust the paper into Toby's hand and collapsed suddenly into a chair. Her face crumpled, and Toby saw her expression for what it was, not the greedy desire for money, but the despair of a woman who had suffered too much loss.

Toby glanced over his shoulder at Miss Clark. "Tea," he said, "and biscuits. The best china."

"I think so," Miss Clark agreed.

Toby desperately wanted to read the birth certificate, but he knew that this was not the time. He sat down next to Mrs. Chapman.

"How is Terry?"

"I don't know. They won't let me see him."

"Has he been charged?"

"No. I asked Constable Arkwright, and he said they won't charge him until they know whether Sam Ruddle is going to live or die. If he dies, then it's murder. He didn't do it, Mr. Whitby. He wouldn't do nothing like that."

"I agree with you."

She looked at him with surprise in her faded blue eyes.

"You don't think he did it?"

"I'm quite sure he didn't," Toby replied.

"Then who?"

"I don't know who, but I think I know why."

"Why?"

Toby looked down at the folded paper. "This is why."

"That's just a birth certificate," Mrs. Chapman said, "just to prove that my Vera had a baby. Vera had a passport for the baby when she left to go to America, so she didn't need the birth certificate no more. She threw it away in the dustbin, but I took it out. I knew I'd need it one day. I know what people are like, and I won't have Nellie Pearson saying that my Vera is lying. Vera didn't steal no baby and she married that American; it was all legal and aboveboard. I don't know why they want to say that it's Her Ladyship's baby. Why would they say a thing like that?"

"They have their reasons," Toby said.

He unfolded the certificate. The document was printed on heavy paper with a raised seal; an original, somewhat stained and faded along the fold lines, but an original. At long last he had something in his hands that was indisputable evidence of the birth of Anita Mary Malloy on April 15, 1945. Her mother was listed as Vera Chapman Malloy, and her father as Nicholas Joseph Malloy. The raised seal indicated that the birth was registered by the registrar of Dorking in Surrey.

"Dorking?" Toby said. "Not Brighton?"

"What?" said Mrs. Chapman.

"The baby's birth was registered in Dorking, not Brighton."

"Of course it was." Mrs. Chapman looked at Tony with a baffled expression. "Why would the baby be born in Brighton? Vera was with the Land Army in Billingshurst right up until the end. She wasn't nowhere near Brighton. Who says the baby was born in Brighton?"

Toby refrained from answering the question and continued to study the document. "It doesn't actually say where she was born. It doesn't give the name of a hospital."

"She wasn't born in a hospital."

Toby raised his eyebrows.

"You think every baby is born in a hospital?" Mrs. Chapman asked. "Babies come when they're ready. They don't wait for an ambulance; they just come."

"So Vera talked to you about this? She talked about the birth?"

Mildred Chapman's eyes slid sideways. "She didn't say much. Just said it was sudden. She didn't give me all the gory details. Not everyone wants to hear all the details. I've had my own babies; I didn't need her to tell me what it was like."

"So you don't know where …"

"On the farm, I suppose," Mrs. Chapman snapped, "just like one of the animals. Do you think I want to tell that to everyone? You have what you were asking for, so what are you going to do for my Terry?"

Toby wanted to reach over and pat the woman's hand. Unpleasant as she was, Mrs. Chapman had been given more than her fair share of grief, and the idea of Terry Chapman being charged with murder was more than any mother could be expected to bear.

Before he could make a gesture of sympathy, Miss Clark came quietly into the room, carrying a bone china teacup and a small plate of biscuits.

Toby rose. "I'll see what I can find out," he said, "and I'll visit your son myself."

"You do that," Mrs. Chapman said with a return of her usual belligerence. "And you tell those people up at the Hall that they're not getting their hands on my granddaughter." She took a sip of tea. "Don't you have no sugar?" she asked.

CHAPTER THIRTEEN

Beaver Creek Hollow West Virginia
Barbree Malloy

The Englishwoman came home just before midnight, dropped off by a hunter in an old pickup truck. Barbree, who was a light sleeper, hurried to the window as the pickup pulled away with a diminishing volley of backfire explosions.

The night was cold and clear under a brilliant moon, and Barbree watched the Englishwoman open the rusted gate and stumble up the steps, unsteady in her high-heeled shoes and dragging her suitcase. She was wrapped in Nick's old hunting coat, which explained why she had left her own fashionable coat behind her when she ran off to Pittsburgh.

Barbree shuffled into her slippers, threw a ragged patchwork quilt around her shoulders, and picked up her solitary candle. The house was cold, the only warmth coming from the banked coal stove in the kitchen and what little heat remained in the chimney. She was halfway down the stairs when the Englishwoman opened the door with a key that she should not have possessed.

"You don't belong here," Barbree said by way of greeting. She held up the candle so that it illuminated Vera Malloy's face and the wisps of breath from her decorated lips.

"Says who?" Vera asked.

"Tramp," Barbree whispered.

Vera pushed past her, heading upstairs.

Barbree was triumphant. "Not up there. You don't got no bed up there."

"What do you mean?"

The irritating English accent was as strong as it had been the day Nick so reluctantly brought her home. There were those, of course, who thought it attractive. No doubt the driver of the pickup had thought so. She'd probably persuaded him to do all kinds of things just by using that silly little voice. He was probably a God-fearing family man led astray, just as Nick had been led astray.

"Why don't I have a bed?"

"You left. This ain't no boarding house where y'all can come and go anyways it pleases you. You left, and we don't want you back."

"I went to Pittsburgh. I told you where I was going. Someone had to earn some money."

"Oh yes," Barbree agreed, "someone had to earn some money, and you knew how, didn't you?"

"You evil-minded old witch," said Vera. "Where's my daughter?"

"Gone."

"Gone? You let her go out on a night like this. What's the matter with you? How long has she been gone?"

"I didn't let her go. Someone took her."

Vera raised her eyebrows. Even by the light of the single candle, Barbree could see that the eyebrows were no longer the way God had made them, thick and dark. They were little pencil lines on a plucked-bald forehead. What did she think she was, a movie star?

"What are you playing at, old woman? Who took my daughter? Whoever it was had better bring her back. Your son's not going to like this, Barbree. She's Nick's daughter, and his granddaughter. He loves her just as much as Nick did."

"She ain't Nick's daughter."

"Oh, don't start this again. She's Nick's daughter. We even went to Morgantown for the blood test. O positive blood group, that makes her Nick's daughter."

"I don't trust them doctors. I could tell by looking."

Vera looked away. "I'll sleep down here by the fire. In the morning you can go and get her from whoever took her."

"She's not coming back."

"Of course she is."

"No, she's not."

Barbree laughed softly, careful not to wake up the rest of the family exhausted from the day's hard work. Decent folk, folk who worked in the mine or tramped through the woods looking for game, went to bed at night, and slept the sleep of the righteous. Decent folk didn't run off to Pittsburgh and then return unexpectedly in the middle of the night. "We found out who her real father is."

The Englishwoman stepped back. "What do you mean? Nick was her father."

"No, he wasn't. Her father was Jack Harrigan."

Barbree had to admit that Nick's faithless bride made a good show of seeming surprised.

"Who?"

"Jack Harrigan, and you ain't even her mother."

Ah, now there was guilt mixed with the surprise.

"You're talking nonsense. Of course I'm her mother."

"That ain't what Mr. Harrigan says."

Vera set down her suitcase and grabbed Barbree's arm. She pulled her into the kitchen, where the moonlight streamed through the cracked windows.

"Look at me."

Barbree eyes slid away from the Englishwoman's fierce glare. Vera grabbed her by the chin and forced her to turn her head.

"Look at me." The words were an angry hiss. "What have you done with Anita?"

"She went with Mr. Harrigan. He's her grandfather."

"I thought you said he was her father."

"Not Jack Harrigan, Harry Harrigan. Jack Harrigan is dead, died over there in Europe."

Vera took a deep breath but her grip was as firm as ever. She forced Barbree to meet her gaze. "And this Harry Harrigan says that I'm not Anita's mother?"

"That's right. He says you stole her from her mother, and her mother is some English lady, some high-up."

"High-up?"

"Yeah, not someone like you pretending to be high up, someone really high up. A lady."

"Did he say her name?"

Barbree made another attempt to pull away, and Vera's fingers bit into her flesh.

"Did he say her name?"

"Sylvia something."

Vera's fingers released their grip.

"Sylvia? Lady Sylvia? "

Barbree stepped back, out of reach of the Englishwoman's grasping hands. The red lips were open in a gasp of surprise, the penciled eyebrows raised, and the blue eyes wide with shock.

"You stole her, that's what Mr. Harrigan said. You stole her so that Nick would marry you, and you brought her here so you could live off our family."

"Live off your family!" Vera kept her voice low, but her hiss was more menacing than any shout could have been. "You live no better than rats. If I'd had any idea that this was how Nick lived, I would never have come here. I've done my best, and God knows it was difficult, but I've done my best for all of you. I only went to Pittsburgh to earn money. I can't earn any money here. I can't work in the mine, but in Pittsburgh they have office buildings and steel mills, and they like my accent. They pay good money just for me to answer their phones. That's why I went. I've come back with enough money to connect the house to electricity and running water so Anita and I can live like human beings."

"We don't need your money."

"Oh, don't worry; you're not going to get any."

Barbree wrapped the blanket tightly around her shoulders and shuffled back toward the stairs.

"Wait."

Barbree turned to look at her grandson's widow. Vera's expression had changed from shocked to calculating. She was opening her purse and looking inside.

"I need information."

Barbree waited.

"I need to know more about this Mr. Harrigan."

"Oh, you'll never find him. He's taking her to England."

"Really?"

"Yes, really. I signed something that said she wasn't ours. He said that would be enough to get her some papers so he could take her away. They're gone. Left in a big car."

"When did they leave? How long ago?"

Barbree looked at Vera's open purse.

"Oh, for God's sake," said Vera, her hand dipping into the purse and creating rustling sounds.

"A week, maybe ten days."

"And he had a big car?"

Barbree locked her eyes on Vera's purse. "Mr. Harrigan's a rich man."

"Where does he live?"

"Why should I tell you?"

"So that I won't go to the police," Vera replied. "I'll bring charges of kidnapping, or maybe even worse. You sold my child, didn't you? Mr. Harrigan gave you money."

"No."

Vera's hand dipped into her purse and came out with a handful of paper money. "Listen to me, you evil old hag, we can do this the easy way, or the hard way. You can tell me everything you know about this rich man who has stolen my daughter, and I will pay you what I think is a fair price for the information. Alternatively I will start screaming bloody murder that my daughter has been sold by you to white slavers. People won't like that, not even in this benighted place. What do you want, Barbree? Do you want to do this quietly, or do you want the whole world to know?"

"Chicago," said Barbree.

Vera handed Barbree a couple of dollar bills.

"Is that all?" Barbree asked.

"Yes, that's all. I don't need anything else from you. You've told me what I need to know."

Barbree tucked the money into the sleeve of her flannel nightdress. The Englishwoman lowered herself into the rocking chair by the banked fire and eased her feet out of the high-heeled shoes.

"Are you leaving?" Barbree asked.

"Yes," said Vera, "I'm leaving. First thing in the morning."

She leaned forward, grasped the poker, and stirred the coals into glowing life.

"You're wasting coal."

Vera opened her purse and produced another dollar bill.

"Buy some more. Now go away and leave me alone. I have to think."

CHAPTER FOURTEEN

Sam Ruddle was unmoving on his hospital bed, but his eyelids fluttered as confused images flickered through his mind. He fought to hold on to at least one thought. He was at the bottom of a stinking trench on the Somme, buried alive in a blasted landscape of withered trees, barbed wire, and acres of mud where once there had been poppies. His feet, inside sodden boots, ached with raw discomfort. He was waiting for the order. Fix bayonets. Up the ladder.

Mercifully, the image left him, swept away by the image of another trench. No, not a trench, a bomb shelter. He was underground in the Rose Hill bomb shelter. His feet were dry, the memory of their stinking infection now nothing but a mass of scars and a limp he would carry his whole life. But he was underground with no ladder. No way to go over the top. Pale faces stared at him in the flickering light of the kerosene lantern. Mrs. Shenton knitting ferociously, Mrs. Elliot grasping her daughter's hand, Mrs. Rollins weeping quietly, and Mrs. Chapman staring at the door. Vera had been gone a long time. The bomb still lurked outside, and he felt that all eyes were on him. He could not resist a sneaking suspicion that Vera was not coming back. She had not found help. She had run away as fast as her long legs in their high-heeled shoes would carry her.

And then came the noise, not from the doorway, but from the back wall of the shelter where the ventilation pipe brought an occasional draft of fresh air. First a rattling on the pipe, and then a voice hollow and echoing.

"Mr. Ruddle. Sam Ruddle, can you hear me?"

Good God, it was the Earl! There was no mistaking the Earl's elegant drawl. Sam pushed past the women and lifted his face to the exposed end of the pipe.

"We're here, sir."

"Good man. Keep calm. I've brought the Americans."

Americans? Why Americans?

And then another voice, full of authority.

"Hi, Mr. Ruddle, this is Captain Harrigan."

Toby Whitby

The weekend crawled by at an agonizingly slow pace. Mr. Champion, according to his housekeeper, was away for the weekend, visiting his sister, whose health was even more precarious than his own. The promised visit to Terry Chapman in jail could not take place without advance arrangements, and such arrangements would take at least two working days. Most importantly, the registrar's office in Dorking would not open until 9:00 on Monday morning.

Much as he would like to, he decided that he should not go back to Rose Hill and see Carol. His heart still fluttered at the thought of her. He still imagined how it would be if she would agree to go with him to Rhodesia, but he couldn't bring himself to visit her. He had questions that he was not ready to ask, or maybe he didn't want to hear the answers.

Carol was Vera's friend. They had been close. They had been in the Land Army together, posted to the same farm for at least some of the time. Why had Carol said nothing about Vera giving birth in Dorking; in a completely different county? He'd given her every opportunity to tell him what she knew, but she had said nothing and left him to continue his wild goose chase looking for proof of a birth in Brighton. Perhaps she didn't know about Dorking. Perhaps she had been moved to a different farm long before the baby was born and knew nothing about the birth.

On Monday morning he drove north across the Downs as the winter sun was rising in a cold blue sky. February would soon give way to March, and the promise of spring was in the noisy cloud of seagulls following a farm tractor as it ploughed a hillside field. The gulls dipped and whirled, screeching in triumph as the plough turned the rich earth, exposing hibernating insects. He topped a rise in the Downs and saw the town of Dorking nestled into a protective fold and bustling with traffic. Before long he was enmeshed in a traffic jam, crawling along behind a string of lorries and looking for a place to park.

The registrar's office was an ocean of quiet after the chaos of the crowded streets. It would be peaceful like this in Africa, he told himself. How much traffic could there be in Bulawayo? He would have a driver to ferry him along the dusty roads and someone to bring him a cup of tea when he arrived in his office. And Carol would be … He reined in his wandering thoughts; for once, the daydream was not giving him any pleasure.

The registrar's waiting room was wood paneled with a frosted glass door leading into the office of the registrar himself. The office staff moved at the pace of all civil servants, polite and unhurried.

Having made it clear that he, himself, was not a new father and did not wish to register a birth, he was at last admitted into the inner sanctum.

The registrar, a cheery little man with a round face and a bald head that appeared to have been newly polished to a fresh shine, flipped the heavy pages of the register.

"Here it is," he said at length. "Birth took place at Smallfield Farm, attended by Doctor …" He hesitated, staring through reading glasses as round as his face. "I don't recognize the name." He turned the ledger so that Toby could read the notations. "That's a puzzler. What name do you make it out to be?"

Toby, also peering through spectacles, studied the elegant calligraphy. "Smethers? Could it be Smethers?"

"Smethers," the registrar repeated. "I don't know any Doctor Smethers."

Suddenly the little man slapped his own forehead so hard that the reading glasses jiggled down to the end of his nose. He pushed them back impatiently. "Smethers. Yes, of course. I heard about this."

He looked at Toby, and it seemed that his bald head actually glowed. "I wasn't here in the war," he said. "You know how it was. We all had to do our bit. Signal Corps. Saw a spot of action in Normandy."

Toby knew that he was expected to respond with his own war credentials, but for once, he felt no guilt and no need to explain himself. He was far too anxious to find out what was so special about the birth of Anita Mary Malloy and the involvement of Dr. Smethers.

"What did you hear?" Toby asked impatiently.

"Smethers isn't a doctor," said the registrar. "Or at least, not a doctor in the way you would think of a doctor. He's a vet."

"A vet?"

"A veterinary surgeon; you know, dogs, cats, cows, that sort of thing."

"This child was delivered by a veterinary surgeon?"

The registrar smiled. "That's what happened. The mother was a land girl, and from what I understand, she never told the farmer about being in the family way. Came as a surprise to everyone."

Toby tried to make sense of what he was hearing. Vera Chapman, who had announced her pregnancy to the world in order to force a marriage to the baby's father, had returned to the farm and said nothing to the farmer. Why?

"Would I be able to speak to Dr. Smethers?" Toby asked. "Do you know where he is?"

The registrar bounced out enthusiastically from behind his desk. "I'll ask the young ladies in the office," he said. "They'll know more than I do. I think one of them has a dog or a cat or something like that. Don't have any pets myself. Just wait here. I'll find out for you."

Toby waited impatiently while the registrar trotted across the hall and through a frosted glass door marked "Typing Pool." He was back within moments.

"I was wrong about dogs and cats," he said.

"He's not a vet."

"Oh yes, he's a vet. I was wrong about the girl in the office. She has a parrot. Could have sworn it was a dog or a cat. Fluff, I'm sure she said its name was Fluff; never heard of a parrot called Fluff. They're not even fluffy, are they?"

Toby suppressed an urge to shake the information out of the little man. "The vet?"

"Yes, yes. Mostly cows and pigs, but he's retired now."

"So where do I find him?"

The registrar smiled, his cheeks glowing as red as his bald head. "Mr. Whitby, this is your lucky day."

It doesn't feel lucky, Toby thought.

"Agricultural Advisory Committee," the registrar said. "They're meeting today and Dr. Smethers is on the Committee. I sent one of the young ladies to fetch him out of his meeting."

"Well, thank you."

"Happy to do it. I rather wanted to hear the story myself. Can't imagine such a thing. Big difference between delivering a baby and delivering a calf."

"Yes, I suppose there is," Toby agreed. He had never seen the birth of a calf, and most certainly had never seen the birth of a baby, so he had only the haziest notion of what would transpire in either case. He felt himself blushing as he tried to form a mental picture. When he was a child, his cat had given birth to kittens. His mother, of course, had hurried him from the room as soon as the process had begun.

He tried to force the flush from his cheeks by taking several steadying breaths. He would do better in Africa. It would be different there. Women gave birth in the fields; that's what he'd heard. Gave birth in the fields like it was nothing at all and went right back to work. It was ridiculous that he was more than thirty years old and he knew nothing about the processes of life. He had seen death, but he had never seen birth. He knew how babies were made, but he had never made one. He had never even seen a naked woman, except for a brief glimpse at a cabaret show in London, interrupted by an air raid. The memory did nothing to calm him.

He was relieved when the door opened to admit a gray-haired man with the stooping shoulders of a man who had once been tall but was now the victim of age and infirmity.

"Smethers," said the man.

"Toby Whitby."

"So, why do you want to know about the birth up at Smallfields?"

"Some questions have been raised," Toby said.

The vet picked up the ledger and looked at the entry. "What kind of questions?"

"I can't really say. My clients are entitled to their privacy."

"No privacy giving birth in a barn," said Smethers. "Don't know why the poor girl left it so late. She shouldn't have been on the farm at all. It was just her luck that I was there to take care of a sick cow, or I don't know what would have happened."

"Was anyone else with you?"

Smethers smiled. "The farmer disappeared the minute he realized what was happening. No place for a man, you know. I can't say I was all that comfortable myself. It's one thing to put your hand up a cow's backside and quite another when it's a young woman."

Oh God, Toby thought, how much is he going to tell me?

"She should have been in a hospital," Smethers continued. "From what I heard, her husband was an American. They would have looked after her. There was absolutely no need for her to be working on the farm."

"So it was just you and her?" Toby asked. He wasn't sure why he was asking the question. Smethers had already told him enough that he could have no doubt that the woman was Vera Chapman.

"Her friend was there," Smethers replied. "I don't think she wanted to be but I needed someone, and she was the only other woman."

Her friend, Toby thought. Did he mean Carol? Had Carol actually been present?

A smile lit up the veterinarian's weather-beaten face. He stabbed a finger at the entry in the ledger. "Anita. That's my wife's name. The mother wanted to give the little girl my wife's name. Good thing it wasn't a boy."

"Why?"

"Cardrew," said Smethers. "My first name is Cardrew. No little kiddie should be given a name like Cardrew. But they seemed pleased enough with Anita."

"And no one else was there?" Toby asked, still feeling that something was missing. There was something here that he didn't know.

"No," said Smethers. "No one else. Isn't my word good enough for you? You won't be able to ask the POWs, not now."

"What POWs?"

"The ones that were working on the farm; half a dozen of them, all Germans. One of them spoke good English. He's the one who came and fetched me from the cowshed. No idea what his name was and you'd never find him now. Gone back to Germany, I should think. No one wanted them to stay over here."

Smethers set the ledger back down on the desk.

"There's no problem here, Mr. Whitby. I don't know who you are representing or what they might be saying, but I can assure you that Vera

Chapman Malloy gave birth to a healthy baby girl. I delivered the child, and I signed the birth certificate. Now, if that's all you need to know, I have to get back to my committee meeting. Hoof and mouth disease. We're in for a hard time, as if times are not already hard enough."

Toby extended his hand. "Thank you, doctor. Sorry to have troubled you."

"No trouble at all."

He opened the door, and then turned back. "Have you seen the child, little Anita?"

"I have. I saw her this week."

"How is she? No ill effects from being born in a barn and delivered by a vet?"

"None that I could see."

"Did she inherit her mother's red hair?"

Toby stared at the veterinarian. Gears began to slip and grind and then fall into a new place, the correct place. A new truth emerged, one that would mean the destruction of all his dreams.

London Airport, Croydon
Vera Malloy

The BOAC Stratocruiser completed its descent from the cloudless blue sky, bounced a couple of times on the runway, and rolled to a halt in front of the terminal building.

Vera Chapman Malloy gathered her possessions together and stashed them in the elegant overnight case she had purchased in New York with Harry Harrigan's money. A uniformed stewardess helped her into her coat and thanked her for flying BOAC. The main door was open. Steps had been rolled out from the terminal. She paused in the doorway and breathed deeply. Even here the air carried the tang of salt; wispy traces of ozone to remind her that she was home again. Six years ago she had vowed never to return, but here she was. From the top of the steps, she could see the car park and make out the distinctive shape of the black Bentley that had been sent from Southwold Hall.

In the terminal building, she presented her passport and waited while it was stamped. As she turned from the counter, a uniformed chauffeur approached her. His face was only vaguely familiar. She had half hoped that the chauffeur would be someone she had known from school, someone who would be impressed by the change in her fortunes.

"Mrs. Malloy?"

"Yes."

"I'm to take you to Southwold."

"Of course."

The chauffeur looked her up and down. She remembered him now.

He was older, and he walked with a limp, but he was Price, the old Earl's chauffeur restored to his prewar position. Vera looked down at her luggage. She could call a porter, or she could establish her ascendancy over the chauffeur.

"Bring my luggage," she said.

She followed the chauffeur, threading a path through the throng of passengers and out into the chilly morning. Her new high-heeled shoes, also purchased in New York, made for slow progress, and by the time she reached the Bentley, the chauffeur was well ahead of her. He deposited the luggage on the ground and opened the passenger door with a flourish.

"Southwold Hall."

Vera chose to treat the chauffeur's remark as a question rather than an instruction.

"Not yet," she said. "I have to go somewhere first. There's someone I need to talk to."

CHAPTER FIFTEEN

Sam Ruddle opened his eyes, saw the white room and the bright light, and closed them again. Was he dead? Was this heaven? Was the brightness the light of the angels surrounding the heavenly throne? His mind raced through memories of hymns he had sung as a child. God on his throne, cherubim and seraphim, a crystal sea, saints without number casting down their crowns. Had he arrived? Was he on the shore of the heavenly sea?

He kept his eyes closed and reached out with his hands to explore his surroundings. He was lying on a bed. That didn't seem right. There had been nothing about beds in his Sunday school classes, and nothing about cool sheets tucked in so tightly that he could hardly move or a soft pillow cradling his head. Compared to the trench he had inhabited on the Somme, this was indeed heaven; anywhere warm and dry was heaven.

If this was heaven, then he'd soon be seeing some old comrades; the ones who had not made it back to Blighty; the ones whose bones rested somewhere in the poppy fields of Flanders. Well, there would be a rousing reunion when he saw them again. He wondered if God would allow them to drink beer. If God would …

His mind began to clear, and he pushed his foolish thoughts of heaven aside. Obviously, he wasn't there yet. He was in a bed in a brightly lit room. Hospital! He was in a hospital.

An excited voice pierced the tangled web in his mind.

"His eyes opened. Dad, he opened his eyes."

A man spoke, his voice filled with sadness. "No, he didn't, love. His eyes have been moving around, but he hasn't opened them. Don't get your hopes up, love."

I did open my eyes, Sam thought, and by golly, I'm going to open them again. He blinked again and then forced his eyelids to stay open.

"Grandad."

He stared into a familiar face. Brown hair surrounding pixie features, a turned-up nose, hazel eyes brimming with tears, an open mouth revealing a gap-toothed smile.

"Maisie."

"Grandad."

She was beside him on the bed, her arms around his neck, her tears falling on his face. Her fingers clung to him as someone tried to remove her. He lifted his arms to hold onto her, but he had no strength. His arms felt like rubber, and his hands tingled. Pins and needles, he thought, because I haven't moved them. How long since I moved? How long have I been here?

"Maisie, go and fetch the nurse."

Sam knew that voice, the accent so similar to his own. He looked up at his son, who was prying Maisie away from him and sending her to the door of the little white room."

"I thought I was dead," Sam said.

"So did we," his son replied. "You've been out for days."

"Out?"

"Unconscious."

"For days?"

"Yes, Dad. Do you know what happened?"

Sam found that he had regained at least some control of his right hand. A sudden sharp memory made him lift his hand to his head. His fingers located a mass of bandages. "What's this?" he asked.

"You were hit on the head," Derek said. "He almost killed you. It was almost murder, Dad."

Force of habit made Sam reach up again to scratch his head as he tried to sort out his thoughts. Derek took hold of his father's wrist and pulled it away. His hand was rough and calloused from hard labor.

"Leave it alone, Dad."

"Where am I?"

"Cottage hospital. Do you remember anything? The police will want to know for sure. You were at the White Hart."

"I don't drink at the White Hart," Sam protested.

"You weren't drinking there," Derek said. "Seems you'd had a few at home and you went down there looking for that young solicitor that's been calling at the Hall."

Sam furrowed his brow. "Why would I do that?"

"Because of Maisie. Because Mrs. Pearson sacked her, no references, no nothing. You wanted to tell the solicitor something."

"What did I want to tell him?"

"I don't know." Derek sounded irritated. "All I know is that you were three sheets to the wind and making threats about the Earl."

"I wouldn't," Sam protested. "I wouldn't make threats about the

Earl."

"Well, whatever it was," Derek interrupted impatiently, "it doesn't matter now. The Earl's dead."

"Dead?"

"You've been unconscious for a long time, Dad. More than a week. All sorts of things have been happening. Don't worry about it now. I can tell you all about it later. All we need now is for you to tell the police about Terry Chapman."

Sam remembered a book he'd read when he was a child. A girl had fallen down a rabbit hole, or maybe through a looking glass, or maybe both. He wasn't sure of the details, but he remembered her confusion as the world changed around her, and nothing made sense. Talking animals, a disappearing cat, a white rabbit. All nonsense. Everything was nonsense. He felt as though he had become that poor bewildered child.

"Why do I have to talk to the police about Terry Chapman?"

"He hit you, Dad. He almost killed you."

"Terry Chapman, Millie Chapman's son?"

"Yes, that's the one."

"Shell shock."

"That's what they're saying," Derek agreed. "Maybe he'll be declared insane. That's not up to us. You just have to tell them what he did, and they'll put him away so he'll never do it again."

"It was raining," Sam said.

"That's right."

"I got thrown out of the White Hart?"

"Yes, you did, Dad. But don't mind about that now."

"Raining?"

"Yes."

Sam groped around in his mind and located the hazy memory of stumbling across the soggy village green while thunder crashed overhead and lightning crackled across the sky.

"Did you see him, Dad?" Derek asked. "Did you talk to him?"

"Yes." Sam had a firm hold on the memory now. "He was out there in his pajamas, poor bugger. Terrified, he was. I know how he felt. It comes back, you know, and it's like you're there again."

"I know, Dad. I had my own war."

"Not like his," Sam snapped, "and not like mine. He was crouched on the ground, hands over his head. Thought I was a Jap guard. Thought I'd come to kill him, or worse."

"So he hit you?"

"No, you don't understand." Sam's bewilderment gave way to annoyance. "He didn't hit me any more than he would have hit a Jap. He was terrified. I got him to his feet, talked to him a bit, and pointed the way home. He came around. He knew where he was."

"Then why did he attack you?"

"He didn't."

"Someone did."

Sam reached up and touched the bandage around his head. Reluctantly he drew the memory from its hiding place.

"A woman."

"A woman hit you?"

"I heard someone behind me. I turned around to see who it was, and it was a woman. She ran at me. She had something, a stick or something like that. I think she was trying to creep up on me from behind, but I turned around."

He put his hand to the swelling on his forehead, just above his right eye. He winced. "She hit me from the front," he said.

"And the back," Derek added. "You have a big bruise on the back of your head."

Sam levered himself upright in the bed. His head was swimming but he was determined to be heard. "It wasn't Terry Chapman."

"Then who was it?"

Sam struggled to find the memory. Lightning crackled across the village green. The cottages seemed to sink into the ground, water streaming from their thatched roofs. The church spire reached up as if daring the lightning to strike the metal cross. The white hart displayed its antlers against the red background of the inn sign. A woman in a headscarf raised her arms and ran toward him.

"I don't know," said Sam, "but it wasn't Terry Chapman."

Toby Whitby

"Red hair," Toby said. "The mother had red hair?"

Dr. Smethers smiled at the memory. "A real redhead," he confirmed.

"What about her friend?"

"What do you mean?"

"The friend who was with her. What did she look like?"

Smethers gave Toby a look of long-suffering patience. "I wasn't looking at her friend. I've delivered hundreds of four-legged creatures, you get used to seeing ears and snouts, or a couple of legs if it's a breach, and if it all goes wrong, well, it's just a farm animal, just a question of buying a new one. This was different. I had a human life in my hands, two lives really, because the mother was struggling. I didn't have time to look at her friend." He clasped his hands together as if giving himself a congratulatory handshake. "I was just glad it came right in the end."

"So you can't tell me anything about the friend?"

"Dark hair. That's all I can tell you. Now, if you'll excuse me, I have to get back to my meeting."

Toby's thoughts were racing. He was no longer in the comforting surroundings of the registrar's office with daylight streaming through the tall windows. He was in a barn lit only by the light of a kerosene lantern, where three people crouched on the floor. He imagined Dr. Smethers in overalls, called in from attending a sick animal. He saw two women, one a shadowy figure with dark hair and the other a familiar figure; red curls, a spray of freckles across her nose, her brown eyes wide with pain.

Somewhere in the distance, a telephone jangled, and then he felt a touch on his arm.

"Mr. Whitby."

Why? Why had she given her name as Vera Malloy? Why?

"Mr. Whitby."

Was Carol the mother of Anita Malloy?

"Telephone, Mr. Whitby."

The registrar's touch on his arm pulled Toby back into the present.

"You have a telephone call from your office."

Toby stared uncomprehendingly at the telephone receiver in the registrar's hand and the long cord stretched from the desk.

"For me?"

"Yes, it's a Miss Clark, from your office. She said that she knew you were coming here this morning."

Red hair and freckles.

"Mr. Whitby." The registrar was becoming impatient. "I would be obliged if you would answer your telephone call."

"Oh, yes, of course."

Toby held the receiver to his ear, and Miss Clark's authoritarian tones jerked him closer to the present reality.

"You are needed at Southwold Hall, Mr. Whitby."

"I'm sorry, what did you say?"

"You are needed at Southwold Hall. You should go there at once. Apparently, Vera Malloy is here, and they wish you to draw up a document regarding the parentage of the child."

Toby gathered his scattered wits and settled on the only thing he could state with certainty. "Vera Malloy can't be here. They've only just contacted her. She won't be here for a week or more."

Miss Clark allowed a note of awe to creep into her voice. "She came in an aeroplane. She has landed at London airport and is on her way to Southwold Hall. I have informed Mr. Champion."

"An aeroplane," Toby repeated.

"Yes," said Miss Clark. "Mr. Harrigan would like to have this matter settled immediately. He doesn't like to be kept waiting, so I suggest that you do not keep him waiting."

Toby heard his own voice coming from somewhere far away. "I have to do something else first. I have to …"

"Mr. Whitby, is something the matter? Has something happened?"

Toby remembered the romance magazines on Miss Clark's desk, and her unexpected kindness to Vera's mother. He would have to trust her.

"I need you to help me, Miss Clark."

"Yes?"

"I think I know who the child's mother is, but I need time to prove it. I need you to say that you were unable to find me."

"But I have found you."

"Please, Miss Clark, this is really important."

Miss Clark's voice dropped to a whisper. "What have you found, Mr. Whitby?"

"A web of lies," said Toby softly. "Everyone is lying, Miss Clark. Everyone! I need time to find out why."

"Very well, I will say that you could not be reached."

"Thank you."

Miss Clark's whisper was still conspiratorial. "Where are you going?"

"To find the real mother," Toby replied, and he replaced the receiver before Miss Clark could ask any more questions.

Vera Malloy

The chauffeur-driven Bentley glided to a halt outside the village post office. Vera sat quietly for a moment taking in the familiar surroundings. The scene was blessedly peaceful after the six years she had spent amid the noise and stench of the Beaver Creek Coal Camp. A leaden sky hung low over the village, but the air was clean and clear. She recognized an ancient orderliness to the grouping of the cottages around the village green, the way the parish church set itself slightly aside from daily life, and the way the White Hart Inn sat squarely at the center of the village. She had not known that she was homesick. She had not knowingly missed the quiet rhythms of village life amid the chaos of the coal camp. Of course, when she had left, the village had been reeling under the effects of war, and only now was it at peace.

She turned her head to catch a glimpse of her mother's cottage huddled behind an unkempt hedge. Only the chimney was clearly visible, sending a faint wisp of smoke into the morning air. She had no wish to see her mother or to sit in the dreary parlor with its memories of her dead father and her missing brother.

She pushed all thoughts of homesickness aside as mere sentimentality that would soon pass. Get in and get out, she told herself. Sign the papers, take the money, and leave. She would live in a city, maybe London, maybe New York, but she would never again live in this village, and she would never again set foot in West Virginia.

One small piece of business stood between her and her dreams. Surely it would not take long. Carol was the only person in a position to object, but how could she?

She stepped out of the Bentley and opened the door of the village shop, setting the alarm bell jangling. Nothing new here; the shelves were better stocked than they had been during the war, but nothing else had changed. She made her way through the cluttered space toward the grill at the back of the store. Why did everything seem so small and cramped? Even the ramshackle Malloy house had offered more space and light than any house in Rose Hill, although every room in Barbree's house had been too cold in the winter and too hot in the summer, and coal dust had settled in a fine layer over all of the sparse furnishings.

"Hello, can I help you?"

Carol stepped out from behind a stack of tin cans. Baked beans, Vera thought irrelevantly. In Beaver Creek baked beans came from a sack in the corner and long hours on the stove. Vera doubted that Barbree Malloy even possessed a can opener.

"Can I help you?"

Vera turned to face her friend. She heard Carol's sharp intake of breath, and then the stack of beans fell to the floor with a crash as Carol flung her arms out in surprise.

The cans of beans rolled noisily across the uneven wooden floor, drowning out Vera's carefully prepared Americanized greeting. "Hi, long time no see." She had thought this might make Carol laugh, but it would also let her know that Vera was not the girl she used to be. She was older, stronger, tougher, and she no longer needed an American soldier to help her find her place in the world.

The cans rolled to a standstill, and Vera tried to repeat her greeting.

"Hi—"

"You!"

"Hi, Carol."

"Where's Anita?"

Even in the dim light of the shop, Vera could see anger written across her friend's face. Time to talk some sense into her.

"She's at Southwold Hall with Lady Sylvia, her new mother."

"New mother!" Carol was almost spitting in anger. "Lady Sylvia is not her mother. You are."

Vera felt the power that came from staying calm while her opponent, and Carol was most definitely her opponent, gave way to emotion.

"As you and I both know," Vera said softly, "I am not her mother."

"You promised."

"I promised to take care of her, and that's what I've done."

"She's supposed to be with you."

Vera stepped carefully across the litter of tin cans and took hold of Carol's arm. "She's at Southwold Hall being taken care of by her millionaire grandmother."

Carol shook off Vera's hand. "Why did you let her go? Why did you let them take her?"

"I was in no position to stop them."

"What do you mean?"

"I wasn't there. I was away. I had to earn money. I had to keep bread on the table. Your daughter needed food and clothes."

Carol took a deep breath. Vera waited. Soon the anger would dissipate. Soon she would see reason.

"So now you've come to take her back?" Carol asked. "She must be completely lost without you."

Vera caught Carol's arm and felt relieved when Carol stayed where she was, not pulling away.

"Think," Vera whispered. "Think carefully. Why would I want to take her back?"

"Because you're her mother." Carol raised a hand to silence her before Vera could say, yet again, that she was not Anita's mother. "You're the only mother she knows. She must be terrified."

Vera smiled. "I doubt if she's terrified. She's probably hopping mad. Anita doesn't scare easily."

She thought for a moment about the little girl she had claimed as a daughter. Anita was a wild and difficult child given to temper tantrums when things didn't go her way. In summer she roamed barefoot and unrestricted along the mountainside, and in winter she whined and fretted at being confined to the house.

Nick had loved the child, but after Nick's death Vera had found little to love in her, and no need to keep up the pretense of being a dutiful daughter-in-law. She knew, without any sense of guilt or shame, that sooner or later she would have abandoned Anita to the care of Nick's family, but she had not imagined that the chance would come so soon, or be so advantageous to both of them.

"I want to see her," Carol said.

Vera remained calm. "I don't think that's a good idea. If you and Anita were seen together, people might talk. They might find a resemblance."

Carol drew in a quick breath. "Does she look like me?"

"A little, but she was spared your ginger hair. She's more blond than red."

"Like her father," Carol whispered. "I want to see her."

Vera kept her hold on Carol's arm and kept her voice low. "Are you sure? We can go up to the Hall if you really want to. We can tell the truth, the whole truth?"

Carol's eyes widened.

"The whole truth," Vera repeated. "It doesn't really matter to me, because Nick is dead, so no one will care that I lied to him, but what about you? Do you want the truth to come out? The war's over, but people have long memories, and if people find out who Anita's real father was, well …"

"You have to take her back to America."

"Really? Do you think she'd be better off in America? Didn't you get my letter, the one where I told you that West Virginia isn't exactly California?"

"But it must be better than here. It's better than her being, well, you know …"

Vera provided the word. "Illegitimate."

"Yes."

"But is it better than being the future Countess of Southwold?"

Vera allowed the silence to lengthen. Carol bent over and began to pick up the cans of beans.

"I don't understand," she said. "Why is Lady Sylvia trying to claim her?"

Vera picked up a can and added it to the pile. "I don't know. Honestly, I don't know. She can't have any idea that Anita is your baby, so she must have some reason for wanting a baby of mine. Anita's the right age for a war baby, but there are plenty of orphans already in England. Why does she want to claim my baby? Why did she have detectives looking all around America for a baby she thought was mine? I don't know."

Carol stood thoughtfully with a can in each hand. "Do you think she was even married to that American officer?"

"Jack Harrigan," Vera said.

"Yes. Wasn't he the officer who dug us out of the bomb shelter?"

Vera picked up another can, glad to be keeping Carol calm and focused on the task of retrieving the cans. "So that's the connection," she said. "I didn't remember his name. Harrigan. Yes, you're right. I met him. The Earl invited me and my mum to tea after the bomb incident, and a couple of the Americans were there. It was the Earl's way of saying thank you."

March 1944
Southwold Hall

Vera's mother looked disapprovingly at her daughter. "You should have worn a hat."

"Your hat's big enough for both of us," Vera said, scowling disapprovingly at her mother's yellow headgear with its ornamental red feather.

Mrs. Chapman looked anxiously at her wristwatch. "We shouldn't be early, that would be rude, but we shouldn't be more than two minutes late." She stared at the watch for a couple of seconds and then nodded her head, the red feather swaying jauntily as she did so. "All right, we can go now."

As her mother turned to go along the path that led around to the back of the Hall, Vera marched up the front steps and stood with her hand on the bell pull.

"Vera, what are you doing? We can't go in the front door. We have to go round the back, to the kitchen."

"I'm not going in the back door," Vera declared. "The Earl invited us to tea. We're guests just like any other guests."

"Don't ring that bell," Mrs. Chapman ordered, hurrying up the steps behind her. "Don't you dare ring that bell."

Vera ignored her mother and pulled the metal bell pull. For a moment she was able to hear the clanging of the bell as it echoed somewhere inside the mysterious inner reaches of Southwold Hall, but then the sound was drowned by the roar of an engine as a motor vehicle ground its way up the gravel driveway and skidded to a halt at the bottom of the steps.

Vera turned to look at the three American officers who leaped energetically from the jeep. They stood for a moment and gave instructions to the driver.

"That's him," Mrs. Chapman whispered to Vera.

"Who?"

"The tall one with the blond hair. He's the one who was in charge. He's the one who dug us out. Don't you recognize him?"

Vera kept silent. Of course she didn't recognize him. By the time the Earl had returned from his bicycle ride to the American camp, she had been on the other side of the village; far away from the unexploded bomb.

The Earl had made a rapid decision that the only way to rescue the villagers trapped in the bomb shelter was to bring in the Americans.

"Our own chaps will never get here in time," he said. "We're very thin on the ground these days, and the Americans are just sitting there doing nothing. I'll ride over there and see if they have a bomb-disposal chap." He snorted disapprovingly. "They seem to have everything else. You wait here, young lady, and I'll be back in before you know it."

She watched him wobble away on the rusty old bicycle. As soon as he was out of sight, she turned her back on the bomb that still glinted menacingly in the starlight, and hurried to put distance between herself and the obvious danger.

She had watched the rescue from the safe vantage point of the church porch. The squad of American soldiers had been nothing but shadowy figures and silhouettes in the headlights of their jeeps. They had shovels and spades and pickaxes and a kind of cheerful, reckless daring conveyed in the laughter and banter that were carried to her on the night wind.

"They dug us all out," Mrs. Chapman said, "and that bomb could have gone off at any minute."

"I know," Vera replied. "You really don't have to tell me again."

The Americans, with the Earl urging and encouraging them, had widened the ventilation shaft at the rear of the shelter. Vera had watched as the villagers emerged one by one. She had seen an American soldier kneel on the ground to receive a baby into his arms. She had been proud of the Americans that night, watching them in action made her even more determined to become a war bride. She wanted to make a life in the country and the culture that had bred these daring young men. She wanted her child to grow up in such a country.

Already her life was changing. She was a guest of the Earl. She would be admitted through the front door. It was the beginning of a new life.

The Americans bounded up the front steps to greet them. "Hi, ma'am. Hello, miss."

They removed their caps and smoothed their hair as the front door of the Hall swung open, and Mrs. Pearson greeted the party with her usual glare of disapproval.

"We should have gone to the back door," Mrs. Chapman whispered.

"No, we shouldn't," Vera insisted.

The officers stood aside, and one of them made a sweeping gesture toward the front entrance. "After you, miss."

Mrs. Pearson gave way grudgingly and indicated that they should go ahead of her into the drawing room, where a fire roared in the hearth. A silver tea service on an ornate tea trolley glinted in the firelight. Another trolley held platters of sandwiches and cakes.

"Quite a spread," Vera whispered to her mother.

"Not really," Mrs. Chapman replied. "Heaven only knows what's in those sandwiches, and it's only the second-best china."

"How would you know that?" Vera asked.

"Before the war, when the Countess was alive, they used to have big parties here, and they'd bring village girls in to help in the kitchen. I've seen the best china, and this isn't it."

The Earl's voice boomed out as he rose from a chair by the fire. "Welcome, welcome. So glad you could come." He shook hands with the Americans and then turned to Vera. "And here is our heroine."

He smiled at Vera and looked sideways at Mrs. Chapman. Vera felt renewed embarrassment at her mother's choice of headgear.

"And this is your mother?"

Mrs. Chapman bobbed a curtsey and remained silent. The Earl stared at Mrs. Chapman's hat and seemed to be groping for words. At last he looked away, and a smile lit up his face as a woman appeared in the doorway. "Ah, there you are."

"Yes, I'm sorry to keep you waiting."

Vera turned to look at the young woman as she came to stand at her father's side. She was tall and slim with long dark hair held away from her face by two side combs. Diamonds glinted at her throat and on her fingers.

Mrs. Chapman poked a sharp elbow into her daughter's ribs. "Don't stare."

"But, Mum—"

"Don't stare."

Vera ignored her mother and continued to stare. She knew what her own face looked like, she'd spent time enough examining it in her bedroom mirror, but she'd never seen her own features on someone else's face.

"Mum ..."

"We don't talk about it. We'll never talk about it, and she won't even notice."

Her mother was wrong. The Earl's daughter noticed. Her stare was hard and cold, and Vera felt a momentary guilt at having had the temerity to be born with the same face as the other woman.

March 1952

Vera was aware that time was passing and she was expected at Southwold Hall. She picked up the last errant can of beans, returned it to the display shelf, and turned to face Carol. "So," she asked, "are you going to say anything?"

"I want to see her."

Vera ignored the request. "If you do nothing and say nothing, your daughter will become the Countess of Southwold and the heir to Mr. Harrigan's millions. Why would you want to spoil that? What kind of mother are you?"

"I want to see her," Carol repeated stubbornly.

"You abandoned her."

"I still want to see her."

"If you say anything, I'll deny it."

"I can prove it."

"No, you can't."

"The birth certificate ..."

"Says that Vera Malloy is her mother, and I'm Vera Malloy."

Carol was silent for a long time. "I want to see her." Her voice was plaintive. "I won't say anything."

Vera crossed to the door and looked out at the village green. The Southwold Bentley remained at the curb. The chauffeur was relaxing in the front seat and smoking a cigarette.

Vera made a concession. "I'll say you're an old friend, and you won't say anything at all."

"All right."

"Come on, then. We can go together."

She opened the door, allowing a gust of cold wind to ruffle the stack of newspapers. Carol pulled on a coat and took a bunch of keys from a hook beside the door.

"Better put up your Closed sign," Vera said, "someone's coming."

A dark green car had come to a halt on the opposite side of the road. Vera watched as a tall young man with brown hair and horn-rimmed glasses climbed out of the driver's seat.

Carol looked up, the Closed sign still in her hand.

"I'll go out the back," she said abruptly.

"Why? What? Who is he?"

"Someone I don't want to see," Carol said breathlessly. She thrust the sign into Vera's hand. "Tell him I'm not here."

CHAPTER SIXTEEN

Toby rattled angrily at the locked door of the village shop. Closed. Why would the store be closed at this time of day? The store doubled as a post office, and surely it was illegal for a post office to be closed during business hours. What if someone wanted to send a telegram? He rattled the door again and his anger gave way to concern. Had something happened to Carol? She lived alone behind the shop, and she could be sick, or she could have been attacked. Someone could have broken in to steal from the cash register. Another thought sent shivers down his spine. Alderton, Tierney, Sam Ruddle; they had all been attacked.

"Mr. Whitby, excuse me, Mr. Whitby."

A uniformed chauffeur was leaning his head out of the window of the Southwold Bentley. Toby recognized Price, the driver who had driven him to Southampton to meet Mr. and Mrs. Harrigan.

He shook his head to clear his brain. Somehow he had walked right past the Bentley in his rush to find Carol and ask her what on earth was going on. Was she the redheaded woman who had given birth in a stable in Dorking? Was she the mother of the child that Vera Malloy had taken to America?

"They're closed, Mr. Whitby."

Toby walked toward the Bentley. "Why?"

Price turned his head to consult the passenger in the back seat. "Illness in the family," he said with finality, and wound up the window.

The Bentley pulled away from the curb. Toby caught a quick glimpse of a shadowy figure in the back seat before the car gathered speed, leaving him alone in front of the locked door.

He raked his hands through his hair in frustration. He had asked Miss Clark to give him some time, and she had agreed, but how much time did he really have? How long before someone came to find him, or before Mr.

Champion discovered that his protégé was dragging his feet, disobeying instructions, and becoming personally involved?

He turned back to his car. Where should he go now? He was expected at the Hall, where he would prepare a sworn statement for Vera Chapman Malloy. She would swear that she had been given the wrong child at the clinic in Brighton, and Lady Sylvia would swear that the deceased Nurse Tierney had admitted the error. In the ensuing legalities, Anita Malloy would become Celeste Harrigan, daughter of the Countess of Southwold and heir to the Harrigan millions. Everyone would be happy, and all he had to do was keep quiet.

He jangled his keys angrily in his pocket. He thought about Mrs. Chapman and her anguished insistence that Vera had given birth to Nick Malloy's child. She had brought the birth certificate to him as final proof, but it had proved nothing and raised even more doubts. He opened the car door and dropped into the driver's seat, the keys ready in his hand. Where was he going? He had no idea.

He slipped the car into gear and glanced into his rearview mirror. He waited while a large black car drew closer and then passed him by. A Wolseley; a police car. He put the gear lever back into neutral and watched the police car as it turned into the narrow lane in front of Mrs. Chapman's cottage. A heavyset man in a rumpled raincoat emerged. As the man trudged up the path to the front door, he saw that the right sleeve of the raincoat dangled forlorn and empty. Detective Sergeant Slater.

Toby pulled on the handbrake and climbed out of his car. For better or worse, he had agreed to help Terry Chapman, even if it meant running afoul of Slater. Terry was his client, and he had the right to ask questions on Terry's behalf.

He was relieved at finding a momentary sense of purpose and an enemy he could identify. He would put all the other questions on hold and throw himself into defending Vera's brother.

He locked the door of his car and made his way across the sodden grass of the village green. By the time he reached the sagging garden gate, Slater had already entered the cottage, leaving the gate open behind him. The front door also stood open, and he heard voices from inside. Slater's voice was slow and measured, and Mrs. Chapman was responding with high-pitched excitement. Obviously, something had happened. Had Sam Ruddle recovered consciousness, or had he died?

As he approached the front door, he saw Mrs. Chapman on the threshold. She was struggling into a raincoat. Slater was a dark shape behind her.

"I'm here to help you, Mrs. Chapman," Toby said reassuringly. "You don't have to say anything to the police. Let me deal with this."

"Deal with what?" Mrs. Chapman snapped. "You don't have to deal with anything."

"I agreed to help you. We made an arrangement."

Mrs. Chapman was busy knotting a headscarf under her chin. "Don't need your arrangement."

"It would be best to let me take care of things," Toby insisted.

"Nothing to take care of. They're letting him go. No thanks to you."

Toby stepped back. "Letting him go?"

"Yes, letting him go. Sergeant Slater is taking me to the jail. He's going to be released into my care."

"Well, that's very good," Toby said. "Have you arranged bail, or what have you done?"

Slater pushed past Mrs. Chapman. "What are you doing here, Mr. Whitby?"

"Terry Chapman is my client."

"Is he really?" Slater paused as if trying to find a place in his mind to file the information. "Terry Chapman is your client," he repeated.

"Yes, he is. Has bail been set?"

Slater shook his head. "No bail. He's a free man. He didn't do it."

The words were out of Toby's mouth before he could stop himself. "How do you know?"

"Ha!" Mrs. Chapman darted forward and poked an accusing finger into Toby's chest. "You didn't believe me, did you? You were pretending to help me so I would tell you what I knew, but all the time you were thinking he was the one what done it. Well, he wasn't."

Slater raised his eyebrows inquiringly. "What did Mrs. Chapman tell you?"

Mrs. Chapman was fairly dancing with impatience. "It don't matter. It were something else; something to do with my Vera. Can we go now?"

Toby blocked the path. "I would like to know what has happened to change your mind about my client."

"The victim, Mr. Sam Ruddle, has recovered consciousness," Slater said. "He's not clear on everything that happened to him, but he is very clear that his attacker was a woman."

Mrs. Chapman pushed past Toby, almost running down the garden path toward the waiting police car.

Slater stood in the doorway. "Aren't you going to lock the front door?"

"What?"

Mrs. Chapman turned back, and in that unguarded moment, Toby saw pure joy on her face. He thought that it had been many years since Vera's mother had felt joy. Her husband was dead, her daughter had disappeared into America, and her son was a broken man, but for this moment at least, she was able to find joy.

Mrs. Chapman pushed back past him, gestured to Slater to get out of her way, and closed the front door with a definitive slam. As she came back past Toby, she looked up at him, her lips pursed defiantly. "I'll want that paper back. You know the one. I want it back. You've not done anything to earn it."

"Mrs. Chapman," Toby said, "that paper doesn't prove what you think it proves. I went to Dorking and talked to the registrar, and—"

Mrs. Chapman poked his chest again. "Stop talking nonsense and get out of my way."

Slater eyed Toby speculatively. "I'll need you to come down to the station and answer a few questions about—"

"About what?" Toby snapped. "Terry Chapman is my client. I will not answer questions about him, and I will not permit you to ask questions unless I am present. Is that clear?"

Slater grinned. "Oh yes, crystal clear."

He followed Mrs. Chapman out through the gate and into the waiting car.

Within moments Toby was alone again on the deserted village green, with even more questions demanding answers, and an uncomfortable feeling in the pit of his stomach. The attack on Sam Ruddle had not been the random act of a shell-shocked soldier; it had been a deliberate attempt by an unknown woman to silence him. Sam Ruddle knew something. In fact, Sam Ruddle had told everyone in the pub that he knew something.

Toby thought back to his first meeting with Lady Sylvia, now the Countess of Southwold. She had told him a deceptively simple story, a marriage to an American officer, a baby taken by mistake in the chaos of war, records gone astray but replaced with certified copies. Seated in the ancestral hall, with the tacit approval of the Earl and the unswerving loyalty of Mrs. Pearson, Lady Sylvia had built up a solid wall of evidence.

Toby slipped his hand into the inside pocket of his suit coat and felt the stiff paper of the birth certificate. This was the loose brick that was going to bring down the entire wall. Lady Sylvia, the late Nurse Tierney, and Vera Malloy had all been willing to testify that little Anita had been born in Brighton, but the birth certificate said otherwise, and the birth certificate was in his hands.

Toby thought of Lady Sylvia's aristocratic confidence. She was the Countess, and therefore, she must be believed. Robert Alderton had investigated her claim and taken notes, and now his file was in Lady Sylvia's hands, and Robert Alderton and his notes were history. Nurse Tierney knew too much and she had been bludgeoned from a cliff. The Earl had sounded skeptical of Nurse Tierney's story. In his own clumsy way, he had even threatened Toby with the loss of his job if he asked any more questions, but the Earl was gone now. His death had been expected, but not so soon. Sam Ruddle had spoken like a garrulous old fool, but the story he told was not to Lady Sylvia's liking. The fact that he was not dead was just a matter of luck.

The Harrigans were here now. Mr. Harrigan was assessing the property and was ready to part with large sums of money. Vera had actually come by plane and had arrived far sooner than anyone would expect. Someone was in a hurry. Someone was becoming desperate.

Carol! Fear clutched at the pit of his stomach. Carol represented the greatest threat. Other people might suspect, but Carol knew. He thought about the Southwold Bentley parked outside the village shop. He remembered the shadowy figure in the rear seat, the Closed sign on the door, the chauffeur telling him that there was illness in the family. Carol had no family.

Toby took a deep breath. Lady Sylvia's carefully constructed wall of lies was collapsing around her, but he knew she would never back away. She would never change her story. She was the Countess. The world must arrange itself to please her, and anyone who stood in her way would not stand for long.

He looked back at the village shop, the door locked and bolted. Perhaps Carol was inside. She had not hesitated to close the shop when she wanted to show him Vera's letter. He should try again. He should go around to the back of the shop. He should find the back door.

He stepped out into the road and jumped back at the blaring of a car horn. The Bentley nosed its way out from the alley behind the shop and passed him by with a swish of tires and the hum of a well-tuned engine. He stared into the window, trying to get a glimpse of the interior. This time he saw the shadowy outlines of two passengers before the Bentley gathered speed and disappeared around the corner behind the parish church.

Harry Harrigan

Harry Harrigan prowled the cavernous cellars of Southwold Hall, examining the medieval stonework on which the ancient building rested. Jeremy Clowes, the local stonemason he had hired to make a preliminary survey, shone his flashlight at the ceiling.

"Now, this here," he said, "is the bomb shelter."

Harry had his own flashlight and was shining it on the bulging stone walls. He gave a disbelieving groan. "Bomb shelter? How can this be a bomb shelter? Look at it. Why would anyone think they'd be safe in here."

"They reinforced the ceiling."

Harry kicked at a brick pillar. "Did they reinforce this?"

Clowes shrugged his broad shoulders. "The family didn't want to use the village shelter."

"Ridiculous," Harry muttered. "Are you telling me they'd rather die in here on their own than be safe in the village shelter with the peasants?"

"That's the aristocracy for you," said Clowes.

Harry continued his survey of the cellars with a growing sense of admiration for the medieval craftsmen who had constructed the foundation of Southwold Hall. Surely they had only the most primitive of tools to work with and nothing but candlelight to illuminate the workspace, but somehow they had filled the space with graceful arches and meticulous stonework. Their work had lasted for five hundred years, but it was showing signs of wear. In fact, if he were honest with himself, he would have to say it was showing signs of total collapse.

"Doesn't look too good," Harry said.

Clowes grunted dismissively. "Needs a little work."

"More than a little," Harry argued. "It's a disaster waiting to happen. I don't think that anyone should even be living here."

The stonemason ran his hand along one of the pillars. "Look at the work here, sir. You won't see work like that these days. You won't see that in America. We value our history, sir. We like to hold on to things."

"I know, I know. I wasn't suggesting you abandon the place. I was just suggesting that the family should move out while the work is done."

A wide grin split the stonemason's face. "So you're going to do the work?"

Harry clapped Clowes on the shoulder. "Of course I am."

He stared up at the ancient brickwork forming an arch above their heads. He had no idea how the arch had even been constructed. He had seen nothing like that in Chicago. A little bubble of excitement rose from some unexpected place in his soul. He had never been a man who valued beauty above practicality, but this old building was speaking to him. Five hundred years of history was crying out to be preserved, and he, Harry Harrigan, could answer the cry. The money he had accumulated through years of hard work and hard dealing in the rough and tumble of Chicago politics would pay to preserve this place for Jack's child.

He breathed in the cool, damp air perfumed with the dust of ages and a whiff of sea air. This was Celeste's inheritance, and so it was Jack's inheritance. He no longer had his son, but Jack had not left them empty-handed. Blanche had a grandchild to love and fuss over, and he, Harry, would have this house. He cared little for the rooms upstairs with their dusty colonial furnishings and cracked windows, not to mention their appalling drains, but down here was true workmanship. Down here was where he would start. Here was where Harry Harrigan would make his mark in history.

He wasn't able to put his feelings into words, but he suspected that there was no need. The building had already worked its magic on Clowes.

"We can't replace the brickwork," Clowes said, "but we could leave it where it is and reinforce it with steel beams, if we can get the steel."

Harry looked up at the rickety wooden steps and the narrow doorway into the main house. "Let me worry about getting the steel, you worry about how we get the beams down the stairs without pulling down the walls."

"Easy, sir. You can bring them along the tunnel."

"Tunnel?"

"Smugglers tunnel," said Clowes. "Over here, sir."

Smugglers tunnel! Harry followed Clowes, ducking his head as they passed from the stonework cellar into what appeared to be a natural cave.

"What is this?"

Clowes laughed. "The old lords weren't as law-abiding as they are today. When Southwold was just a manor house, before all the new additions and fancy rooms, the Earls of Southwold used to turn their hands to a bit of smuggling. They'd offload the goods into small boats and bring them in through the caves."

Clowes' flashlight picked up a rounded opening in the wall of the cave, with a greater darkness beyond. "Want me to show you?"

Harry hesitated. "You want me to go through there? Is it safe?"

Clowes consulted his watch. "Should be safe for another hour or so."

"I don't understand. Either it's safe or it's not safe. How can it be safe for an hour?"

"It's low tide now, sir. You could walk right out of here and all the way along the beach to the harbor, if you wanted. High tide's a different story. When the tide's up, you can float a boat right into the cave. That's how we'll bring in the steel beam, just the way the smugglers did it. They'd bring a boat in at high tide, offload the goods, and be back at sea on the ebb tide before the revenuers could catch them."

An image flashed into Harry's mind in black and white, just as he'd seen it at the movie theatre. Errol Flynn, sword in hand, white teeth gleaming in a devil-may-care grin, and a band of swashbuckling pirates rowing their small boats on the rising tide into the shelter of the cave. He had no idea what might be in the barrels and bundles offloaded into the cellars of Southwold, but he could imagine the Lord of the Manor opening the cellar doors, a candle in one hand, a purse of gold in the other. He couldn't wait to tell Blanche.

"When is the last time anyone brought a boat in here?" he asked.

Clowes stepped back from the entrance and scratched his head. "I don't rightly know. I haven't been here since I was a kid. We used to come in from the beach, of course, not from the house. Don't suppose the Earl even knew we were there. We stayed in the cellar. We never went up into the side tunnels."

"What side tunnels?"

"Secret passages," Clowes said. "The house is riddled with secret doors and passages. I've heard tell that every bedroom has a hidden door."

"You suggesting some hanky-panky in the bedrooms?" Harry asked. He'd heard stories about what the aristocracy used to get up to.

Clowes grinned. "There may have been some hanky-panky before the war, when the Earl used to have people coming for house parties, but that's not why the passages were built. The Blanchards were royalists, and they made the passages as a way to escape or to hide people from Cromwell's men. We had some hard times here in the civil war."

Harry dismissed the English Civil War as something he would have to learn about later. All he needed to know now was that the great house itself stood on a shaky foundation of ancient brickwork, manmade tunnels, and natural caves.

He shone his flashlight into the darkness. "I don't like the idea of seawater running under the foundations; might be safer to seal it up."

Clowes was shocked. "It's our history, sir."

"It's my money," Harry responded.

"Harry." Blanche's voice floated down to him from far away. "Harry, are you down there?"

Harry turned to Clowes. "We'll talk about it another time. I'm needed upstairs."

"You'd have to get planning permission to do anything," Clowes said. "They won't like you sealing it up."

"We'll cross that bridge when we come to it," Harry replied.

He was already walking away from Clowes and the mysterious darkness of the tunnel. If Blanche was calling him, it meant only one thing, Vera Malloy had arrived, and the question of Celeste's identity could be settled once and for all.

"Should I stay here and take measurements?" Clowes asked.

"Yes, yes, take some measurements," Harry agreed. "Work out how many steel beams. We'll need to start work as soon as we can get the steel."

Blanche was halfway down the rickety wooden steps with a worried expression on her face.

"Is she here?" Harry asked.

"Oh yes, she's here."

"Have you talked to her?"

"No, not yet."

Harry climbed up the steps to meet her. "Is the solicitor here?"

"No."

"Damn. He's supposed to be here. I want this over and done with. Where the hell is he, and what are you looking so worried about?"

"Everything," Blanche said plaintively.

"It's going to be okay," Harry said reassuringly. "It's all going to work out. It's just a question of money, Blanche. It's always a question of money and we have plenty of money, so stop worrying. I'm going to get this place fixed up, and it'll be like our second home. Wait until you tell the gals in your bridge club that you'll be spending summers in your English mansion."

"It's not ours," Blanche protested.

"It's as good as ours. Believe me, if I put the money in, I expect a return."

He patted Blanche's arm and shone the flashlight around the cavernous cellar. "Look at that. Look at the workmanship, and there's even a smugglers' tunnel. Everything's going to be fine, and you can get to work decorating the house."

"No, Harry, I won't be decorating the house."

Harry looked back over his shoulder. Clowes was packing up his tools. He would be within earshot in just a few moments.

"What are you talking about?" Harry hissed.

"There's something else."

"What?"

Blanche tugged on his arm, pulling him farther up the steps and speaking in a low voice. "I was looking out of the window, waiting for the car to come. I wanted to see that woman, the one who stole Celeste. I saw the car come up the driveway, and there were two women inside. The car went around to the back, so I ran across the upstairs hall and looked out of that little window outside the bathroom. I saw them getting out of the car."

"So?"

"One of them was really smartly dressed. Tall, dark hair, looked a lot like Lady Sylvia."

"Smartly dressed on my money," Harry muttered.

"And the other one …" Blanche paused with an agonized expression on her face. "The other one …"

"What about the other one?"

"When she got out of the car, she looked up for a moment and I saw her clearly. I saw her face. Harry, I recognized her face."

"I don't know what you mean. How could you recognize her? You don't know anyone here."

Blanche's response was spoken very quietly. "I know Celeste."

Harry stared into his wife's face. He knew what it had cost her to say what she had just said. He knew how much happiness she was about to throw away. It took him a moment to frame an appropriate question, and in the end all he could say was, "Are you sure?"

She shook her head. "No, I'm not sure. It was just a glimpse. Something about the eyes or the mouth."

Harry glanced behind him. Clowes was taking a last look around.

"Where is she now?" he asked

"Celeste?"

"No, the woman you saw."

"I don't know. I ran down the stairs and tried to find her. Mrs. Pearson was at the front door with the other woman, Vera Malloy, I suppose. There was no one else. But I know what I saw, Harry."

Harry nudged Blanche up the last few steps, with Clowes following close behind. He set Blanche's problem aside while he completed his arrangements with the stonemason and wished him a cheerful goodnight.

At last they were alone. He tried to keep the frustration from his voice. "Let me get this clear," he said. "Vera Malloy arrived with another woman, and you think the other woman is really Celeste's mother, not Lady Sylvia?"

"I'm not saying that.

"Yes, you are."

Blanche's voice seemed to catch in her throat. "There was a strong resemblance, and she had reddish hair."

"So did Jack."

"No, Harry, Jack's hair was gold."

"Red. Gold. What difference does it make? You've been telling me the kid has Jack's hair."

"I thought she did."

"And now you think she doesn't?"

Blanche took a deep breath. "Don't bully me, Harry. Don't you dare get angry with me. I'm just trying to tell you what I saw. Do you think this is easy for me?"

"What about me?" Harry blustered. "I'm about to invest millions into this pile of stones, and now you're telling me it's nothing to do with me, that Celeste isn't Jack's child."

Tears trickled down Blanche's cheeks. "I don't know," she hissed. "I'm telling you that I don't know, but I am beginning to doubt."

"Why didn't you say something before?"

"I didn't know anything. It's just happened, Harry. I saw that woman getting out of the car, and all I could think of was that she looked like Celeste. You have to admit that Celeste doesn't look a whole lot like Lady Sylvia."

"What about the other woman, Vera Malloy?"

"That's another strange thing. Vera and Lady Sylvia look so alike that they could be sisters."

"This is pure baloney," Harry said. "Why the hell have I come all the way to this cockamamie country if this kid isn't our granddaughter?"

"You had her checked out," Blanche said in an accusing tone. "You had the detectives checking everything, and Lady Sylvia has the marriage certificate and the birth certificate. What were we supposed to believe? And that nice Mr. Whitby—"

"Where the hell is that nice Mr. Whitby?"

"No one seems to know. Mrs. Pearson says she's going to call the office in Brighton."

"And that's another thing," Harry said. "Why does this Pearson woman seem to be so involved? What's her stake in this?"

Harry knew that Blanche could only answer his question with more questions of her own. He also knew that he had no right to be angry with his wife. She didn't need his anger, she needed his assurance that he would get to the bottom of the situation. She needed him to tell her not to give up yet. He would find the mysterious new arrival. He would take a good look at her face and the color of her hair and make up his own mind.

CHAPTER SEVENTEEN

Toby drove in through the wrought iron gates of the Southwold estate. He was late for his appointment, and he had not even prepared the documents for Vera Malloy to sign. He knew that he would never prepare them. Perhaps someone else would do it, but it would not be someone from Champion and Company, not if he told Edwin Champion what he knew.

Flexible? No, he had no intention of being flexible.

This time he was not going to knock at the front door and confront Mrs. Pearson's disapproval. He was not going to talk to Lady Sylvia. He was not even going to seek out the mysterious Vera Malloy. He was going to find Carol. He had seen two people in the back of the Bentley, and he was convinced that one of them was Carol.

He assumed that the Bentley would be garaged somewhere behind the house, probably in the old stable yard. He took the winding driveway around to the back of the house and came to a halt in the cobbled enclosure in front of the converted stables. A muscular young man, short, squat, and slack-faced was washing the Bentley with a bucket and sponge while Price, the chauffeur, lounged on a seat by the back door. He saw no sign of the passengers.

Price rose from his seat and stepped forward to lean in through the car window.

"Mr. Whitby, what are you doing back here? You can park out front, sir, if you have an appointment."

Toby pushed the car door open and the chauffeur stepped back.

"You should use the front door, sir. No need to go through the tradesman's entrance."

"I'm not going inside," Toby said. "I want to talk to you."

"Me, sir?"

"Yes, you. When I saw you in the village, you said the post office was closed because of illness in Miss Elliot's family."

"Yes, that's what I said."

"And who told you to say that?"

"I don't understand."

Toby surprised himself and the chauffeur by squaring his shoulders, thrusting out his arm, and grabbing the front of the chauffeur's tunic.

"You understand perfectly well. Who told you to say there was an illness in the family? She doesn't have any family. You're a local man. You know she doesn't have any family."

Price attempted to remove Toby's hand, but Toby held fast. "Who told you?"

"My passenger."

"Your passenger?"

"Yes."

"And who was your passenger?"

"I'm not at liberty—"

Toby tightened his grip. "Who?"

"Vera Chapman, that was. I was told I was meeting a Mrs. Malloy from America; took me a minute or two to recognize her."

"You met her at the airport?"

"Came over by plane," Price said, "and very full of herself, if I may say so."

Toby could feel indignation radiating from the older man. He had not been happy at being asked to pick up a local girl, and Vera had done nothing to make the situation any easier for him. For the moment at least, he was on Toby's side.

He released his hold on Price's tunic and waited while the chauffeur smoothed out the wrinkles. "Why did Vera go into the village?" he asked. "Why didn't she come straight here?"

"I don't know, sir."

"She must have said something. What did she say?"

"She said to take her to the village shop."

"Did she say why?"

"No."

"So you took her to the shop and she went inside?"

The chauffeur dropped his gaze and stared uncomfortably down at the cobble stones.

"Did she go inside?"

"I can't rightly say."

"Yes, you can." Toby wanted to make another attempt at grabbing the chauffeur and forcing an answer from him, but he managed to restrain himself.

"Did she go inside?"

Price shrugged his shoulders. "Yes, she went inside. I suppose she had to buy something."

"So the shop was open and she went inside?"

"Yes, that's right."

"And when she came out, it was suddenly closed."

Price said nothing.

"So," Toby continued, "your passenger then told you to tell me that the shop was closed because of illness in the family."

"Yes, that's right."

"And didn't that strike you as strange?"

"It was none of my business, sir."

"Who was your second passenger, the one you picked up after the shop was so suddenly closed?"

"I didn't have a second passenger."

"Yes, you did. I saw her with my own eyes."

"You're mistaken, sir. I only had Vera, Mrs. Malloy."

"You're lying. Why are you lying?"

Price looked up for a moment and stared into Toby's eyes. "You shouldn't ask so many questions. Employment's not easy to come by, not for chauffeurs, not even for solicitors."

Toby recalled that this was the second time he had been threatened with the loss of his job. First the Earl had made the threat, and now the chauffeur, although Price was probably more concerned with his own employment. The Earl's remark had been a definite threat, but the chauffeur's was more of a friendly warning.

"You've been told not to talk to me, haven't you?" Toby asked.

Price glanced around the stable yard. The boy was still washing the car and paying no attention to them. "She went inside the house."

"Who did?"

"Carol Elliot. She went inside the house with Mrs. Pearson."

They both stepped back as the back door opened with a bang, and Mrs. Pearson herself hurried across the yard.

"What are you doing out here, Mr. Whitby? You're late, and why didn't you come to the front door?"

That's a new approach, Toby thought. Last time she had looked distinctly displeased at his temerity in ringing the front-door bell; now she wanted him to go to the front door, or maybe she just didn't want him to go to the back door and talk to Price.

She gave him no opportunity to speak. "You'd better go inside. Wait for me in the kitchen and I'll show you in." She waved him away like a disobedient child and turned her attention to the chauffeur. "Why are you still here? You were supposed to go back to the village."

"You told me to wait for, you know, her ..."

"Yes, you were to take her back to the village."

"She hasn't come."

Mrs. Pearson stared suspiciously at the chauffeur. Toby knew she wanted to say more, but she couldn't, not in front of Toby.

"Maybe she walked," said Price.

Mrs. Pearson sniffed. "Maybe she did. Take the car to the petrol station. You can look for her on the way. Hurry up."

The chauffeur hesitated a moment longer, his eyes fixed on Toby, and an expression of helplessness on his face. Toby gave him a barely perceptible nod of the head to let him know he understood. Carol had been here. The chauffeur was supposed to make sure she was returned to the village, but Carol had other plans.

Mrs. Pearson poked Toby's arm with a commanding finger. "Come inside. Do you have the papers?"

"I have some papers," Toby replied evasively.

Mrs. Pearson pushed the back door open and stepped into the vast kitchen. Toby was too worried about Carol to take in more than a faint impression of blackened pots and pans hanging from ceiling racks, white-tiled walls, and a dingy linoleum floor. Beyond the kitchen a door stood open revealing a wood-paneled butler's pantry, and beyond that he had an impression of sunlight shining through stained-glass windows and reflecting on the polished surface of a long dining table.

"What do you mean by 'some' papers?" Mrs. Pearson demanded.

"I have some papers that will be of interest to Mr. and Mrs. Harrigan."

Mrs. Pearson stepped in front of him, her angular figure barring his way, a scowl on her pale face. Anger flashed at him from her dark eyes, and Toby saw a sudden resemblance to Lady Sylvia. In repose their faces were quite different, but in anger he could see similarities.

The housekeeper's tone had lost any trace of subservience. "Vera Chapman is here. Did you bring the papers for her to sign?"

Toby looked down at her. She was shorter than him by at least a head. Perhaps she had managed to intimidate Price, but she was not going to intimidate him.

"I want to see Mr. Harrigan alone."

"Why?"

"I don't think that's any of your business, Mrs. Pearson."

Mrs. Pearson bit back a response as the back door opened and admitted the boy with the bucket.

"Is it time for tea, Aunt Nell?"

"Not now, Robbie."

"But I've finished washing the car. You said I could have tea when I finish washing the car."

"Later, Robbie. Not now."

Robbie set the bucket down and pulled a cigarette stub from behind his ear. Mrs. Pearson glared at him. "Not in here, Robbie."

The boy nodded agreeably and shambled toward the back door. "I'll be outside if you need me."

"Don't go far away."

"I won't."

Mrs. Pearson turned back to face Toby. Her quick anger seemed to have dissipated, replaced with an expression that Toby could only interpret as cunning. But what could she do? She was the housekeeper. He was the solicitor. He had the birth certificate from Dorking and he had the upper hand. He thought about the wall of lies that had been built up around the birth of the disputed child, and how the wall was now crumbling.

The Earl was dead, Nurse Tierney was dead, Ruddle was very nearly dead, but whoever was behind this couldn't kill everybody. Safety for everyone, and especially for Carol, lay in getting the birth certificate out into the open. Safety lay in letting Harry Harrigan know that the little girl from West Virginia was not his grandchild. The sooner he went home and took his millions with him, the sooner everyone else would be safe, because there would be nothing to gain by perpetuating the lie.

But what about Carol, he wondered. Where was she?

"You want to see Mr. Harrigan," the housekeeper repeated.

"Yes, I do."

"Alone?"

"Yes."

Again the sour expression and the cunning glance. "You can wait in the conservatory. I'll fetch him for you."

Toby started toward the butler's pantry and the daylight he could glimpse, presumably from the windows in the dining room.

Mrs. Pearson diverted him. "This way."

They left the kitchen through a side door and along a narrow passage with a single door at the end.

"You can go through here and into the conservatory. I'll see if I can find Mr. Harrigan."

Toby twisted the knob but the door was locked. He turned around. The housekeeper was no longer in sight.

"Mrs. Pearson, it's locked."

Her voice came to him from the kitchen. "I know. I'm bringing the key."

She was beside him in a moment, handing him a large brass key. He turned back to the door and inserted the key. The door opened onto darkness and a sense of a deep underground space.

He took a step back. His thoughts came fast and furious. Nurse Tierney, pushed off the cliff, Sam Ruddle, struck over the head by a woman. A woman! He heard a rush of sound behind him. Before he could turn and face his attacker, a blow landed on the back of his head and he was swallowed up by darkness.

Carol Elliot

Mrs. Pearson stomped her feet as she escorted Carol up the uncarpeted back stairs. Every step upward, every click of Mrs. Pearson's sturdy shoes was a rebuke. Even the set of the housekeeper's shoulders radiated disapproval.

The nursery occupied the bedroom wing of the house, just one flight of steps below the attic and the servants' rooms, and two flights of stairs above the drawing room. Mrs. Pearson opened a green baize door and, with obvious reluctance, ushered Carol onto the long hallway where wide doorways gave access to the family and guest bedrooms.

"Be careful," Mrs. Pearson said over her shoulder, "and don't touch anything."

Carol allowed herself a secret smile. Mrs. Pearson didn't know it, but Carol had been here before. On that occasion, her sandals had been damp from the sea, and she had left footprints on the carpet. No doubt some poor maid had been sent with a bucket and brush to clean the floor and to wonder who had been wandering the hallways of Southwold Hall.

August 1939

The fear of undeclared war that gripped England was reflected in the pall of rain and wind that had lashed the coast and driven everyone indoors to listen to their radios. A terrible foreboding draped Rose Hill like a black cloud. People spoke in hushed whispers, young boys and old men drilled with wooden rifles, and women cut and dyed fabric to make blackout curtains. The news on the radio left no room for doubt. Hitler was moving across Europe; Britain must defend itself. War was inevitable.

Warning signs appeared along the clifftops. The beach was to be closed. All civilian access would be restricted.

The last day of beach access coincided with the first time the sun had appeared in months.

"Better take a last look at the beach," Carol's mother said. "They'll be moving in the tank traps and the barbed wire any day now. Go on down there and have some fun while you can."

And so they went, Carol, Judy Pryke, Mike Shenton, who would die in Tripoli, and Cyril Evans, who would never come back from Normandy.

It was Mike who suggested going into the caves at low tide, but it was Cyril who carried the torch and ventured into the long-abandoned tunnel that brought them to the foot of a long flight of stone steps.

The four of them looked at each other, their eyes glittering in the torchlight. Generations of children had known that the steps existed and that they constituted a secret entrance into Southwold Hall, but no one had dared to climb the steps to see what wonders lay beyond.

Now, on the brink of war, Carol and her friends discovered a new kind of daring. Hitler's jack-booted, goose-stepping army was on its way, and boys only a few years older than Mike and Cyril's fifteen years had already been conscripted. Life had taken on a frightening impermanence, so why not risk what no previous generations had risked? Why not be the fearsome foursome who finally discovered the secret passageways of Southwold?

They hesitated at the foot of the stairs.

"We can't stay long," Cyril warned. "We've only got about an hour each side of low tide."

Fear kept them giggling and shushing each other as they climbed the damp stone steps. The steps gave way to a wooden staircase dusty with disuse. The climb seemed interminable. Carol was overwhelmed at the size of Southwold Hall.

The narrow passageway at the top of the stairs was studded with doors. Judy squeaked in alarm as Mike tried each of the door handles in turn until he came to an unlocked door.

The door screeched on its hinges, and the four of them clung together, hardly daring to breathe. No one came in response to the alarm, and so they crept in through the doorway.

Carol had expected they would be in a bedroom, perhaps a room with a four-poster bed and velvet drapes. This room was even more interesting than a bedroom; this was a child's nursery. She breathed a sigh of relief; the Earl of Southwold had only one child, and she was far too old for this room. She would not be interested in the dusty old rocking horse, and she would not fit in the little bed with its shabby covers and neglected pillows.

They crept through the nursery and out into the main hallway, where they were overwhelmed by the height of the ceilings, the magnificence of the paneling, and the brilliant colors of the carpet. Footsteps on the stairs brought their exploration to an end. They darted back into the nursery and huddled together, waiting for the footsteps to pass.

Carol looked down at their feet and the damp stains they were leaving on the floor. Had they left similar stains in the hallway? Would someone follow their footprints and find them?

The secret door had swung shut in their absence, and they held their collective breath as Mike groped along the wall to find the concealed door. As last he located the door handle, cunningly disguised by the faded paint of a mural and painted to resemble the center of a red rose.

March 1952

Mrs. Pearson disturbed Carol's memory by beckoning her forward. "You can look through here, and be quick about it."

A window was set in the nursery door, presumably so that a nursemaid or nanny could check quietly on a sleeping child, or a wealthy parent with a few minutes to spare could look admiringly at their progeny without the trouble of making conversation.

Mrs. Pearson barely glanced through the window before withdrawing. Carol was not sure she would be able to control her emotions, but she had to look. She had not seen her child since she was three months old. Could she bear to see what she had given up? The sight of her child almost took her breath away. Anita was asleep, but Carol could see the tracks of tears on the flushed face, and the rumpled bedclothes attested to the fact that the child had tossed and turned before finally giving in to exhaustion.

Carol studied her child's face. The golden curls held a hint of red, but the color was tempered by the father's input. Gunther's hair had been white blond. Anita's eyes were closed. Were they blue like Gunther's or brown like Carol's? Staring at the sleeping face and seeing Gunther's features so clearly reproduced, Carol wondered how Vera intended to get away with convincing Jack's American parents that Anita was, in fact, their grandchild. She knew of the resemblance between Vera and Lady Sylvia; everyone knew of that resemblance, but, not surprisingly, she could see nothing of Vera in this child. She could see only glimpses of herself and glimpses of the prisoner of war who had sworn his love and lied with every breath.

Mrs. Pearson pulled her away from the window. "You've seen her, so now you can go."

"No," Carol protested. "I'm not leaving her. This isn't right."

She felt a hand on her arm and turned to find Vera beside her. Vera looked at Mrs. Pearson. "You can wait for us downstairs."

She saw the twist of the housekeeper's mouth at the idea of taking orders from Vera, but Vera kept her gaze steady, and eventually Mrs. Pearson turned and left them alone.

"Carol." Vera's voice was calm and cold. "If you say anything to anyone, I swear I will tell the whole world the truth, and then what will become of your kid? Do you think anyone in this village is going to want a kid whose father was a Nazi?"

Shame and humiliation forced Carol's protest. "Not a Nazi, just a soldier."

"If I say he was a Nazi, then he was a Nazi."

Carol looked at Vera's cold determined face and tried to find a trace of the girl that Vera had once been. She thought of the little girl in the nursery. Could Vera really be as heartless as she now appeared?

"Aren't you going to miss her? You've been her mum for six years."

Vera shook her head. "She's my ticket out of Beaver Creek."

"But—"

"She's also a little devil. Frankly, Lady Sylvia is welcome to her. She'll ship her off to boarding school and that'll straighten her out."

Carol could feel tears pricking behind her eyes. She thought she would have the consolation of seeing Anita from time to time, watching her play in the school playground, maybe even serving her in the shop.

"No, don't send her away to school. I was hoping I would see her sometimes."

Vera shook her head. "Be glad that you won't. Do you want people to notice that she looks like you? That would be unfortunate for both of you, wouldn't it? It would be the end of her life as the heir to Southwold. You wouldn't want that, would you? In fact, it would probably be best if you left the village. I'm sure you can find another post office to run somewhere far away. It would be so sad for Anita if people find out that she's not an aristocrat and that her father's a Nazi."

"Not a Nazi," Carol protested.

Vera shrugged her shoulders. "It's up to you. If you keep quiet, none of this will come out. Leave now and don't let anyone see you. The Blanchard's lawyer is an old coot with one foot in the grave, and he won't notice anything, but there's a younger lawyer who has been asking questions. You should definitely steer clear of him."

At the thought of Toby Whitby, Carol's heart skipped a beat. She had grown accustomed to the feeling. The leaping of her heart had little to do with fear of Toby as a lawyer, and a great deal to do with the sparkle in his gray eyes, his curling brown hair, and his air of quiet strength. She struggled to stay calm. Nothing could come of these feelings. She had lied to Toby from the first day she had met him. The only way to stop lying was to make sure she would never see him again.

If she took Anita away …

The thought lodged itself in her mind and would not be budged. Vera led her down the back stairs and pointed to the door that would take her outside.

"Price will drive you back to the village," she said. She laughed softly. "You should have seen his face when he discovered I was the one arriving by plane. I thought he was going to refuse to carry my luggage, but he did it in the end. People will do anything if you offer them enough money, or if they think they're going to lose their job."

Carol stood by the back door and looked at the woman who used to be her friend. "When did you become so hard?"

Vera's face twisted. "When I found that Nick was nothing but a lie."

Carol turned and blinked her tears away. Lies! So many lies; and Nick had not been the only one that was lying.

She heard Vera's footsteps receding down the long corridor toward the main rooms of the house, the rooms where she, Carol, would not be welcome. Anita would be welcome in those rooms. She would be called Celeste and be heir to the fortune of a man who was not her father, and the title of a woman who was not her mother.

Carol thought of the child, who had so obviously cried herself to sleep. Vera had called her a little devil. Lady Sylvia would send her to boarding school. When would she know the love of a mother?

Carol's mind was made up; one way or another, she was going to take her child out of this house, and she knew how to do it. No one would see them leave and no one would know where they went.

Vera Malloy

Vera was alone in the drawing room, sipping tea from a chipped cup with a gold rim and the Southwold crest emblazoned on one side. Obviously, she had risen in importance since the last time she had taken tea at Southwold Hall. This time she was being given the best china, a dubious honor, considering that it was in such poor condition. They really need the Harrigan millions, she thought. Her thought was not clouded by any sense of shame. Anita, or Celeste as she would now be called, would be heir to all of this, and Harry Harrigan would preserve the estate for her and fund her for the rest of her life. Nothing to feel guilty about!

She looked at her watch, the one that she had purchased in New York with Harry Harrigan's money. Three o'clock and still no sign of the lawyer, or the Harrigans. She had hoped to catch the four o'clock train and be in London by nightfall. She had no wish to spend the night in the village, or run the danger of encountering her mother. God, that would be a scene! Her mother would never be fobbed off with some story about Vera being in Brighton and taking the wrong baby by mistake, but there would be nothing she could do about it once Vera was gone.

Shame would keep her quiet so long as Vera was nowhere in sight. She would never understand that Vera, in her own mind, had actually done a good thing. She'd helped out a friend in trouble and helped herself into the bargain, and now it was all coming right. She just didn't want to hear what her mother had to say about it.

She took another sip of tea from the chipped cup.

"Mrs. Malloy."

Vera looked up and saw Blanche Harrigan hovering in the doorway. Vera gave her a casual American greeting. "Hi."

"Can I talk to you?"

"Sure. Do you want a cup of tea?"

"All right."

Blanche perched on the edge of an armchair while Vera poured tea into another of Southwold's prize porcelain teacups. This one was not chipped, just slightly cracked.

"Milk?"

"No, thank you."

Vera handed over the teacup. "There's no lemon," she said. "I guess they're still not importing lemons."

"I suppose not."

Silence settled into the room. Vera waited. Blanche sipped nervously and glanced up at Vera with red-rimmed eyes. She had been crying. Vera had no intention of asking why.

Eventually Blanche managed a few words. "I wanted to talk to you about the young woman who came with you."

Damn! She had seen Carol. Well, no use denying it. If the woman had seen her, there was no point in saying that Carol had not been there.

"Just someone from the village," Vera said.

"I thought …" Blanche took another nervous sip of tea. "I thought …"

Thought what? Thought she looked like Anita? Thought that Anita looked like Carol? Thought that the whole idea of Anita being the child of Lady Sylvia and the deceased Jack Harrigan was a ridiculous charade?

Blanche placed the cup and saucer carefully on a side table and drew in a shuddering breath. "I thought that she looked like Celeste."

Celeste? Oh, yes, Anita's new name.

"Really?"

"Yes, I really did. I thought there was a strong resemblance."

Vera sensed a hint of iron behind Blanche's softly spoken words. Her mind was racing. This had to be settled here and now. No time to consult Lady Sylvia or Mrs. Pearson. This was up to Vera. She fell back on the rumors she had heard so often, on the many times a child had been said to resemble one of the old Earls, on the fact that she herself had the same build and coloring as the Countess, and she laughed.

"So you noticed?"

"Yes, I did."

Vera laughed again. "That's the way it is in a little village like Rose Hill. The old Earls used to sow their wild oats pretty close to home."

"I don't understand."

"The woman you saw, my friend Carol, she probably has the same grandfather or great grandfather as Lady Sylvia. I'm sure I do. We all do. We all look the same."

"No," said Blanche. "You don't look the same. I mean, I can see a resemblance between you and Lady Sylvia, but this other woman … no, I don't see it."

"It looks different in every generation," Vera said airily, "but the reason is the same. You're probably being confused by Carol's red hair, but we've had redheaded Earls in the past."

Blanche continued to look doubtful.

Vera pasted an anguished expression onto her face. "Mrs. Harrigan, I made a terrible mistake in taking Lady Sylvia's baby, your little granddaughter, but it was a genuine mistake. You've never been bombed, have you?"

"No, of course not. We weren't bombed."

"Then you really wouldn't understand. The bomb landed on the nursery. It was terrible. I expect Lady Sylvia already told you."

"She didn't say very much about it."

"I'm sure it's as painful for her as it is for me. She spent all these years grieving and thinking that her child had died, and I thought my child had survived. I thought Anita was mine." Vera leaned forward and grasped Blanche's hands. "Mrs. Harrigan, it's my turn now to grieve for the child I lost. Please don't make it harder by suggesting that we are all … all …"

"All what?"

"All lying."

"Oh, I wasn't."

"I think you were."

Vera looked at her watch again. She really had to get out of here. Sign the papers, take the money, and run. Minutes ticked by with Blanche Harrigan perched on the edge of her chair, apparently afraid to speak for fear of further offending Vera but also unwilling to leave.

As the clock on mantelshelf chimed the quarter hour, Lady Sylvia made her entrance into the room, checking the time on the clock against the time on her own wristwatch.

"I don't understand what's happened to Mr. Whitby," she announced.

As always, Mrs. Pearson was close behind. "He's late."

Lady Sylvia shook her elegantly coiffured head. "No, he's here somewhere. His car is in the stable yard."

"Perhaps he left it here and went somewhere else on foot."

Lady Sylvia deposited herself in an armchair and indicated that Mrs. Pearson should pour tea.

"Why would he do that? Why would he leave his car here?"

"I have no idea," Mrs. Pearson replied. "He's a very unreliable young man."

"Are you sure he's not somewhere in the house?"

"I'm quite sure."

Lady Sylvia accepted a teacup with only a tiny chip along the rim. "Mrs. Pearson, would you ring Mr. Champion and have him come out in person? You can send Price in the Bentley to fetch him. We can't wait any longer. Mrs. Malloy wants to be in London this evening."

Yes, I do, Vera thought, and you want it just as much as I do.

Harry Harrigan strode into the room and brought with him an air of masculine determination. He reminded Vera of the way the Malloy men had looked as they made ready to go hunting.

Harrigan looked at his wife. "Did you ask her?"

"It's all right, Harry."

"Did you ask her?"

"I didn't need to. She explained about the bombing and how dreadful it was."

"We're not talking about the bombing. What about the red hair?"

"Who has red hair?" Lady Sylvia asked.

"Your daughter does," Harry snapped.

"I wouldn't say it's red," Lady Sylvia argued. "It's gold, like Jack's."

"It's red like the woman my wife saw this afternoon."

Lady Sylvia looked up at her housekeeper. "Go and ring Mr. Champion, and make sure he comes immediately."

"Yes, Your Ladyship."

"Immediately."

Vera leaned back in her chair. "I explained to Mrs. Harrigan that the old Earls had a terrible habit of making free with the village maidens. We all have the same face, don't we? Just look at how alike we are, Your Ladyship. It's not surprising, is it, that someone else in the village would have some slight resemblance?"

"No," said Her Ladyship. "Not surprising at all."

Harry surveyed the tea trolley with its small plate of tea sandwiches. He looked at Lady Sylvia. "What's in these?"

"Cucumber."

"What else?"

"Nothing else."

"Cucumber and nothing else? No wonder we had to help you win your war. You can't grow soldiers on cucumber sandwiches."

He placed a handful of sandwiches on a tea plate and sat down next to his wife. He patted her hand. "So, you believe this story about a redheaded Earl sleeping his way around the village?"

"I do."

"Okay. Enough said. Let's get on with it. What are we waiting for?"

CHAPTER EIGHTEEN

Edwin rose slowly to his feet and looked down at the papers spread across his desk. Even in the bright light of his desk lamp, the writing was difficult to read. Some of the documents were more than a hundred and fifty years old, and the ink had faded with the passage of time.

He had before him the record of five generations of a family. Edward Blanchard, Earl of Southwold, had been the first to scrawl his name across the parchment and seal it with the Blanchard signet ring. Four more Earls had followed him in a direct line of descent and had added their own signature and made their own decision to say nothing. Although the documents had been hidden, they had not been abandoned. They showed signs of frequent folding and unfolding. Candlewax had been spilled by shaking hands. Wine had spotted the records of births and deaths. Insects had tracked across the pages and left behind their tiny desiccated bodies.

Edwin opened his office door. As he had expected, Miss Clark was still at her desk. The short winter day was drawing to a close, with dusk gathering outside the windows, but Miss Clark would not leave until he left. She would not leave while she thought that he might need her. He drew a deep breath. He needed her. He couldn't do this alone.

"Miss Clark, would you come into my office?"

She reached for her notebook.

"No need to bring your book. You won't be taking dictation. I want you to look at something."

She nodded her head and adjusted her reading glasses. When she rose from her desk, he saw that her gray skirt was wrinkled from long hours of sitting, and she winced as she straightened her back. She was growing old just as he was growing old. He would have to do something to let her know that he appreciated her fidelity; perhaps an addendum to his will.

Miss Clark followed him into the office and stopped abruptly at the sight of his desktop covered in old documents.

"What are these?"

"What are they indeed?" said Edwin. "Let me tell you what they are."

"Very well."

Edwin picked up the first document. "This is a family tree of the Blanchard family. Here we have Earl Rodney, born in 1780, married to Countess Elizabeth, and the father of five children, Michael 1812, Richard 1814, Mary 1815, Godfrey 1821, Sarah 1824. Michael, as the first born, inherits the title, Richard joins the army, Mary dies in infancy, Godfrey takes a colonial position in Australia, and Sarah marries Norman Newell.

Miss Clark traced the names with her index finger. Her hands, Edwin noticed, were knotted with arthritis, her fingernails square and unpolished.

"So Michael inherits the title," she said. "Richard appears not to have married, and presumably, it is Godfrey's heirs from Australia who stand to inherit the estate if it is not passed to the disputed child."

"Yes, exactly," said Edwin. "But things are not as they appear."

He searched among the papers and found another document, a handwritten letter from General Sir William Tregorran, addressed to Sir Rodney Blanchard, Earl of Southwold, informing him of the death in combat of Captain Richard Blanchard on May 15, 1835 in Accra, Gold Coast. He handed the document to Miss Clark.

"So that's why Richard never married," she said.

"One would assume so," Edwin agreed. "Therefore, one would assume that Richard would no longer be a consideration."

Miss Clark again cocked her head sideways inquisitively. "Obviously, there is more to this than meets the eye."

"Very much more," said Edwin. He slid another paper across the desk and into the light of the desk lamp. "This is a certificate of marriage dated July 12, 1834. It would appear that Richard married Lydia Chapman, spinster of the parish of Rose Hill."

Miss Clark adjusted her glasses and scrutinized the document. "Two witnesses," she said, "and neither one a member of the Blanchard family." She looked up, an expression of intense interest on her face. "A secret wedding?"

"Yes," said Edwin, "that would be my supposition. A village girl perhaps?"

"A secret love match," said Miss Clark breathlessly. "Perhaps it was discovered, and that was why he was sent away, forced to join the army." She consulted the family tree. "He was born in 1814, so in 1834 he was only twenty years old. Twenty-one when he died. How sad!"

She looked down at the document in her hand. "But why is this here? Someone in the family must have known about the wedding. Someone kept this marriage certificate. Why keep it all these years?"

Edwin sat back in his chair. "Let me tell you what I think, Miss Clark. I'm not in the habit of reading romantic stories such as one finds in women's magazines, so I will leave the details to your imagination."

Miss Clark blushed and protested faintly that she had no interest in the frivolities of women's magazines. Edwin ignored the protest.

"I believe that Lydia came to the Blanchards and told them that she had married their son and was expecting his child. I am quite sure they rejected her. Lydia went quietly away and gave birth to a son. Michael inherited the title, Godfrey went to Australia, and Richard's branch of the family tree came to an end, or so people were led to believe."

"But the family kept the marriage certificate," said Miss Clark.

"That's not all they did." He pushed another paper toward her. "They kept a record of Lydia's children. This is Lydia's family tree. These are the descendants of Lydia and Richard's legitimate child."

Miss Clark reached out to take the paper. Edwin held it back for a brief moment. He thought of the day that the Earl had opened the secret drawer in his desk and revealed the little cache of documents.

I'm relying on you to do the right thing.

He had given his word. The time had come. The lies could not continue.

Miss Clark dropped the paper and turned toward the office door.

"Someone is outside."

He knew that she was remembering what he was remembering. Scattered papers, a pool of blood, and Alderton dead on the floor. He gathered the papers together. Where could he hide them? His heart was pounding.

Sam Ruddle

Sam tried to catch hold of the memory. His brain had been playing tricks on him. No wonder really, considering the way that woman had attacked him. What woman? He couldn't bring the picture into focus. He was looking through a mist; no, it was rain. She had come at him through a curtain of rain. He lifted a hand and felt the bandages on his head. A blow to the back of the head, that's what the police said. How did she do that? She hadn't been behind him. No, she was in front of him.

He groaned. He would have to talk to that London policeman again. She hadn't hit him. She couldn't have. There had been someone else behind him. Why? Why had anyone hit him? Baby-stealing! He'd tried to talk to the young solicitor about baby-stealing. He wanted to tell him it was all lies, and he knew it for a fact because …

Because what? How could he be so sure?

He struggled against the headache and the fractured images, and found the memory he was seeking.

June 1944

He was shocked to see that the girl was defying wartime regulations by standing at the edge of the cliff. He paused to catch his breath and adjust the armband he wore on the sleeve of his Ministry of Defence–issued raincoat. Having assured himself that his badge of authority was prominently displayed, he limped onward in the teeth of a cold wind, toward the place where the tall white cliffs stood against the onslaught of the battering waves of the English Channel, and the armies of Adolf Hitler.

He squinted into the fading twilight, hardly able to believe what he was seeing. For a moment he thought it was Vera Chapman from the village; it would be just like her to disobey regulations. As he drew closer, he realized that it was not Vera. This girl had longer hair and was wearing a good quality coat. No one in the village had a coat like that.

Well, if it wasn't Vera, it had to be the other young woman. Everyone knew there was a strong resemblance, but no one commented on it. That's just the way it was with the aristocracy. Vera Chapman's parents were village folk; had been for generations. The Earls of Southwold had been sowing their wild oats in Rose Hill for centuries, and sometimes the evidence presented itself in the face of a new generation. He could not imagine that the Earl's daughter was signaling to the German Army just thirty miles away on the French coast, but rules were rules.

She had her back to him and was staring out to sea, with the wind tugging at her hair.

"Excuse me, Your Ladyship."

The wind grabbed at Sam's words and whipped them away. He took another couple of steps and stood beside her.

"Your Ladyship."

She spoke without turning her head. "Where are they going?"

"Who are you talking about?"

She reached out and pulled him forward to the edge of the cliff.
Sam looked down and saw more ships than he could have ever imagined still existed. This was not the time to ask where they had come from or how they had been concealed. This was it. The day they had been waiting for.

He should have realized that this was about to happen. The Americans had been confined to barracks for the last few weeks with rain and storms lashing the coast, and nothing but rumors to explain their absence.

Late that afternoon, as the sky cleared, he had felt the ground shaking as truck after truck pulled out of the barracks and headed for the harbor. He should have known. He should not have been surprised.

"Where are they going?" the girl asked again.

Sam could think of only one answer. "France."

"France," she repeated forlornly.

"Don't breathe a word of this," Sam warned. "You're not supposed to be out here."

Lady Sylvia turned to face him, and Sam was surprised to see that she had tears streaming down her face.

"All of them?"

"Yes, I'm sure it's all of them; the Yanks, the Canadians, our own boys, all of them."

"Will the Americans come back?" Vera asked.

Was that all she could find to say? Momentous events were unfolding before them. The invasion of Europe had begun, and the soldiers who had waited idly in their barracks were finally on the move. Would the Americans come back? He didn't know and he didn't care. By the time the sun came up in the morning, these ships would be somewhere off the French coast, and these troops would be going ashore.

Lady Sylvia scrubbed at her eyes with the back of her sleeve. The wind was not causing these tears; these were tears of anguish, or maybe anger. Her face twisted. Yes, she was angry.

"He didn't tell me," she said.

"It was a secret. I'm sure your father—"

"Not my father." Her lip curled contemptuously. "My father is nothing in this war. No one tells him anything."

"Who do you mean?"

He had to ask. If someone had been passing secret information to her, he would have to tell the authorities.

"I thought he would know. Captains know things, don't they?"

"An American captain?" Sam asked. Perhaps there was nothing to report. If the captain was on one of those ships, he was no longer Sam's concern.

"Captain Jack Harrigan," Sylvia said.

Sam kept quiet. Let her talk. Let her tell him if he was American.

"I'm not like those village girls throwing themselves at Americans," Sylvia said. "I told him, if he wanted a date with me, he'd have to take me to the Savoy."

She scrubbed at her eyes again, wiping away her tears. "Well, that's not going to happen now, is it? They won't be coming back, will they?"

"No," said Sam. "God willing, they'll push on through France to liberate Paris, and then on to Berlin, and then it will all be over."

He didn't at that moment want to think of his own war and the possibility that the whole great Allied army might be stalled somewhere in the French countryside. It would be unpatriotic to dwell on the trenches and the war of thirty years before. Not now, not when the ships were already at sea.

So Lady Sylvia had been hoping for tea at the Savoy with an American officer. He could not share in her disappointment.

"Come away from the cliff," he said. "Rules are rules."

Lady Sylvia sniffed and turned away from him, taking the path toward the turrets and mullioned windows of Southwold Hall.

Sam stood alone at the edge of the cliff. With the wind from the south, the village would awake to the thunder of the German eighty-pounders on the French coast. In the past the guns had been a reminder that Europe was held captive. Tomorrow the Allies would be returning fire. Tomorrow, God willing, was the beginning of the end. He pulled himself upright and raised his right hand in a salute. Despite his aching back, he held the salute until the armada had been swallowed up by the darkness.

March 1952

"Mr. Ruddle."

The soft voice of a nurse pulled him away from his memory but not before he had it firmly in his grasp. Now he knew for certain that Her Ladyship had not married Captain Harrigan. It was all a lie. He had been trying to tell that young lawyer, but the barman had stopped him, and then he'd been attacked. Someone had tried to kill him, and a woman had been there; a woman who knew that he knew the truth. Could it have been Lady Sylvia herself? Had she remembered what she had told him as they watched the invasion fleet?

The nurse interrupted his troubled thoughts. "Mr. Ruddle, there's someone to see you."

"Who is it?"

"It's a policeman."

The policeman was already looming in the doorway. It was the one-armed detective. Sam thought he was an unpleasant fellow, probably still angry over the loss of his limb, but he would have to do.

"Mr. Ruddle, I have some questions for you."

"And I have answers," Sam replied, "but not now. There's hanky-panky going on up at Southwold Hall, and you had better take care of it before some poor little girl is stolen away from her mother, and more people are killed."

The policeman sat wearily in the chair next to Sam's bed. "Tell me about it, Mr. Ruddle."

Sam waved an impatient hand. "Don't be sitting there like you ain't got nothing else to do. We have to go up to the Hall, you and me together. She didn't marry no American and I know it. Now help me get dressed."

"Mr. Ruddle, does this have anything to do with what happened to you?"

"Of course it does. Why else would I be talking to you? He didn't even take her to the Savoy. It's a pack of lies."

Sam climbed out of bed. His legs were shaky but he managed to stay upright.

"Where are my clothes? What's happened to my clothes?"

"Mr. Ruddle, if you could just explain—"

"I ain't got no time for explaining. I'll tell you everything on the way. I know things, and there are those that don't want me to say what I know. They want me dead, so I think I'll stick by you. I'll be safer that way."

Sam hobbled to the door and called out for a nurse. His voice echoed down the marble corridor. "Where are my clothes?"

Sam stepped back into the room.

"D-Day," he said. "I saw her on the cliff."

"Saw who?"

Sam was momentarily speechless. The cliff! He had seen it from the cliff. He beat at his own bandaged head. He was a fool; a stupid old fool.

He put a hand on the detective's shoulder and shook him slightly to get his attention. "Get on to the navy."

The detective pulled away from Sam's grasp and glared at him. "What are you talking about?"

"A mine," Sam said. "I saw a mine."

"On D-Day?"

"No," Sam croaked. "Not D-Day. Now! I'm talking about now. Before I got hit on the head, I was coming to phone the police. It's a mine. I could see it clear as day, rolling around in the waves."

"What kind of mine?" Slater asked.

Sam spread his arms impatiently. "What kind of mine do you think? There's only one kind that goes floating about at sea and blowing things up." He made a circle with his arms. "Big round thing with metal spikes."

"German?"

"I don't know," Sam snapped. "It don't matter, do it? German or British, it's just waiting to hit something and explode. The way it was going, I wouldn't be surprised if it came ashore at Rose Bay or got carried into the caves. That would make a fine mess, wouldn't it? Probably blow off a great chunk of cliff."

The detective seemed indecisive, but perhaps he hadn't been an air-raid warden. Sam knew what to do.

"Get onto the navy. They'll take care of it. They'll blow it up at sea where it won't do no harm, if they get there in time."

He pictured the mine rolling in on the tide and riding on the crest of a wave that would fling it into one of the caves along the shore. He thought of the cave that ran under the foundations of Southwold Hall. He wouldn't care if the whole place blew up.

CHAPTER NINETEEN

Harry cast an impatient eye over the lawyer and his secretary who had finally arrived to complete the paperwork that would give Blanche the granddaughter she so desperately wanted. The old lawyer looked to be on his last legs, and the gray-haired secretary hovering behind him seemed to be in only marginally better shape.

"Such a shock," the secretary muttered as she conducted the old man to a seat by the fire.

Mrs. Pearson looked at the secretary with a sour expression. "I don't see—"

Lady Sylvia stepped in front of Mrs. Pearson. "I'm so sorry, Miss Clark, we certainly didn't mean to startle you. We should have rung first before we sent the chauffeur."

The housekeeper gave a spirited defense. "We did ring and no one answered."

Miss Clark was not easily mollified. "Mr. Champion is naturally nervous after Mr. Alderton was murdered in his own office. I would have expected you to be more considerate."

Harry pricked up his ears. Murdered! Who had been murdered? Why were this old coot and his aged secretary talking about a murder?

Lady Sylvia's shocked expression was a second late in assembling itself. "I was not aware that Mr. Alderton's death was being called murder."

"What else would you call it when the man is battered around the head and his files are stolen?"

Files? What files? Harry's mind was alive with suspicion, but before he would ask any question of his own, the old lawyer put his hand on Miss Clark's arm.

"Not now, Miss Clark."

The secretary retreated and took a seat on an upright chair. "If you say so, Mr. Champion."

The old man cleared his throat and looked around the room, letting his gaze rest on each person in turn. His eyes were weary and bloodshot, but his faded gaze seemed to make an intelligent assessment of each person.

"Where is Mr. Whitby?" he asked.

Lady Sylvia sounded irritated. "Mr. Whitby is not here. We have been waiting for him and he has failed to appear. I assume you will require an explanation from him when next you see him, and we will require an apology for our wasted time. In the meantime, we would like to get on with the matter in hand. Mrs. Malloy would like to return to London tonight."

Harry, well accustomed to boardroom politicking, recognized Lady Sylvia's attempt at changing the balance of power with a frontal assault.

Mr. Champion's head lifted slightly as he met Lady Sylvia's haughty stare. "Mr. Whitby's car is outside."

Lady Sylvia hesitated. "I don't think so."

Harry admired the old man's thin-lipped smile. "It is not like Mr. Whitby to be late, and so I had your chauffeur drive us to the back of the Hall, where I saw Mr. Whitby's Morris Oxford with my own eyes."

Lady Sylvia's gaze flicked over to the housekeeper. If he had not been in a hurry to get the papers signed and thus cement his claim on the child, Harry would have enjoyed watching the contest of wills. He thought that the lawyer and the Countess were quite evenly matched when it came to keeping a cool head in a difficult situation. However, time was racing by, and the old man looked as though he could die at any moment. It was time to cut to the chase.

He rose from the embrace of a shabby armchair designed for a much smaller man; new furniture would be first on his shopping list. He nudged Lady Sylvia aside.

"Let's get on with this. Someone get this gentleman a pen and paper. Mrs. Malloy can write what she needs to write. The lawyer can witness it, and it will all be done. That's the way we do things in America."

Mr. Champion gave Harry the benefit of a cool stare. "This isn't America."

Harry loved his wife, and his wife wanted to believe that the little girl in the nursery upstairs was Jack's child. His frustration with the old lawyer reached boiling point. How long had he been hanging around in the shabby parlor, eating cucumber sandwiches and waiting for a simple signature on a piece of paper? He'd spent a fortune already getting the Malloy woman onto an airplane; he was going to spend another fortune propping up the moldering ruin of Southwold Hall; and what did it matter where the young lawyer had gone? The old one was here.

He reached into his pocket and took out his checkbook. "What do you want? You want overtime?"

The secretary gasped. "We do not require your money."

"Well, you must be the only people who don't," Harry snapped. "Everyone else here is happy to see my checkbook."

The secretary's response was drowned out by a cacophony from the front hall. Nothing could be heard above the thunderous knocking on the front door and the clanging of the doorbell.

The housekeeper stood openmouthed for a moment before remembering that it was her job to open the door. She hurried away. The noise came to an abrupt halt to be replaced by the sound of urgent masculine voices.

Harry stood with his checkbook in his hand until he heard Blanche speaking softly beside him. "Put it away, dear. These people don't want your money."

"The hell they don't," Harry retorted.

Three men followed Mrs. Pearson into the room. Two were policemen, and Harry took note of their helmets and their silver buttons. They looked like extras from the British movies that were making their way to America. They didn't even have guns. The other man was muffled in a dark overcoat with insignia on the shoulders. He had taken off his cap and carried it under his arm. Firelight glinted on the gold anchor embroidered on his cap badge, and the heavy application of gold braid.

"It's the navy and the police," Mrs. Pearson said, somewhat unnecessarily.

Lady Sylvia turned to face the newcomers. "What do you want?"

The naval officer inclined his head. "Good evening, Your Ladyship. Sorry to disturb you, but we have orders to evacuate this building. You are all to leave immediately."

Lady Sylvia's voice was cold as ice. "We will do no such thing. May I remind you that the war is over and no one is subject to evacuation orders? Southwold Hall is not available for your use."

"Of course not."

Harry sensed that the naval officer, with his upper-class voice and elevated rank, considered himself Lady Sylvia's equal. Perhaps that was why he had been given this task, but why on earth was the old building being evacuated?

"Your employee, Mr. Sam Ruddle—"

Lady Sylvia interrupted immediately. "He is not my employee."

The officer ignored her interruption. "Mr. Ruddle reported that he had seen a mine."

Harry's head was spinning. A mine! What kind of mine? A gold mine? A coal mine? A land mine? He looked around the room. Apparently, he and Blanche were the only people who attached no fear to the sighting of this mine.

"It's German," the officer continued.

"What's German?" Harry asked. "What the hell's going on?"

The naval officer turned to him. He could almost see the gears grinding in the man's aristocratic head. An American! He doesn't know. He doesn't understand.

"It's a German sea mine," he said patiently. "We still find them. They were anchored to the seabed, but now they break loose. It will explode as soon as it hits a solid object. Mr. Ruddle reported it this afternoon when he regained consciousness."

Harry thought that he heard a sigh of relief from Mr. Champion, but he kept his attention on the officer. "So where is this mine? How big is it? How much damage will it do?"

One of the policemen spoke up. "It's a five-hundred-pounder. You don't want to be around when that goes up."

"I don't intend to be," Harry replied. "Where is it now?"

"Well," said the officer, "I would say that it's just below this house."

He raised a hand to silence Harry's questions and the exclamations of surprise from Lady Sylvia and her housekeeper.

"We spotted it from the air just before sunset. With the tide coming in and the current the way it is, we think it will be carried onto the shore. It won't be so bad if it hits the beach, although it might blow a chunk out of the cliff, but, as the Countess knows, the smugglers' caves come right under this house."

Harry thought of the old cellars, the crumbling foundations, and Clowes showing him the dark mouth of the cave. No wonder the police were here to evacuate the house. If the tide brought that mine into the cave, nothing would be left of Southwold Hall.

Lady Sylvia abandoned all signs of dignified restraint and turned her panicked attention to Mrs. Pearson.

"Hurry up! Fetch my jewels and the deed box and my fur coats. I suppose you should also bring Daddy's medals."

Mrs. Pearson nodded, turned on her heel, and left the room.

Mr. Champion struggled to his feet. "How long do we have?"

The officer looked at his watch. "High tide in an hour, but it could come in before high tide."

The old gentleman turned and offered his arm to his secretary. "Come along, Anthea. We must go at once."

The secretary took his arm. Their slow exit was interrupted by Lady Sylvia and Vera Malloy pushing past them. Harry turned to Blanche.

"You want me to get your jewels?"

Blanche shook her head. "No, of course not. Let's go!"

They had reached the front hallway when Blanche stopped abruptly.

"Harry!"

"Keep going."

"No, I won't. What about Celeste? No one has gone to fetch Celeste. Mrs. Malloy didn't mention her and neither did Her Ladyship. No one cares what happens to that child."

"No one except you," Harry said. "I'll get her."

He passed Mrs. Pearson on the stair. She carried a leather jewel case, and a heavyset young man followed behind her with an armful of fur coats. They both shoved past him without speaking.

Harry sprinted along the wide hallway that led to the nursery where the child was housed. He tried not to think about the mine. He knew what it would look like; Germany had not hesitated to anchor mines off the coast of the United States. He had seen the propaganda films. The mine would be round and massive and covered in spikes. The tips of the spikes would contain the detonators. All that would be required for the detonators to do their work was a glancing contact with a solid object.

He flung open the nursery door. He had become accustomed to Celeste and her strong-willed protests, but he would take no nonsense this time. If he had to carry her over his shoulder, so be it. He would do whatever it took to rescue her. She was just a child. He thought of Lady Sylvia making her rapid exit along with her box of jewels, and Vera Malloy, who had hustled past him on her way out of the door. He was quite certain now that neither of these women had given birth to the little girl.

He flicked a switch by the door. Light flooded the room. Her bed was rumpled, and the pillows had been thrown to the floor, but the child was not there.

He abandoned the name that Lady Sylvia had insisted on calling the child. She was not Celeste Blanchard, and she was not Anita Malloy, but he thought she would probably prefer to answer to Anita.

"Anita!"

He kept his voice calm. Perhaps she was hiding in a closet.

"Anita, you have to come with me."

No response.

"Anita, come with me now. I'm going to take you home."

It was a lie. The child had no home.

He opened the wardrobe, searched under the bed, and looked behind the drapes, all the while picturing the massive spiked mine drifting with the tide.

"Harry."

He turned to see Blanche standing in the doorway.

"Have you found her?"

"No, she's not here. I don't know where to look."

Blanche stepped into the room. Her face was twisted with emotion. "It's all lies," she said. "It's like losing Jack all over again."

"I know."

"But she's just a little girl. None of this is her fault."

Harry spread his hands in an unusual gesture of helplessness. "I don't know where to look. This house is enormous. It's like a rabbit warren."

Blanche moved with measured calm. Harry knew that the emotional storm would soon break, but for the time being, she was keeping it at bay. He watched as his wife opened the closet and examined the dresses arrayed on padded hangers.

She nodded her head and turned back to Harry. "No hat, no coat, no outdoor shoes. She's gone outside. Maybe Mr. Whitby has her. Perhaps that explains why he can't be found. She's not here, Harry, I'm sure of it. "

Harry grasped his wife's arm. "We need to leave."

Carol Elliot

The flashlight Carol had stolen from the kitchen shone a dim light on the walls of the tunnel. At last they had reached the bottom of the stairs.

She was not sure how much time had passed since she had roused Anita from a deep sleep. The child should have been terrified to take the hand of a complete stranger and follow her into a labyrinth of crumbling tunnels, but Anita had not complained. From the moment she had set eyes on Carol and agreed to put on her coat and hat, their journey had been taken on an aura of inevitability where few words were needed. She had even smiled as Carol showed here the latch of the secret door, still hidden at the center of a painted rose.

Carol knew that this was not the time to claim to be the child's mother. Maybe there would never be a time. Nonetheless, she thrilled as the little hand tightened its grasp on hers.

"I'm sorry for all the things that have happened to you. I won't let them happen again."

Finally they were close to the cave. She could smell the salt air and hear the sound of waves grinding on gravel. The mouth of the tunnel widened, and the darkness gave way to a hint of light. Carol, who had explored the cliffs and beaches in the days before the war, knew they were emerging into the smugglers' cave. At low tide they would be able to make their way along the beach and around the headland to Rose Hill harbor. After that, who could say?

Unless Vera and Lady Sylvia were both willing to admit to their lies, no one would know that Carol was the true mother, and no one would know that she had Anita. Harry Harrigan would look for the child in many places, but he would never be told of Carol's existence. Eventually he and the police would have to conclude that Anita had run out onto the cliff path and fallen to her death. Carol shuddered at the thought but welcomed it anyway. She could slip into her house and retrieve the money she had saved, and then she would take Anita away. Where would they go? What did it matter?

She spared a regretful thought for Toby Whitby. He would have been able to help her, but how could she ask him when her every word to him had been a lie?

The light increased as they approached the mouth of the tunnel. Moonlight, Carol thought. They would no longer need the failing flashlight. She took a tight grasp on Anita's hand and led her out of the tunnel and into the cave. After a few steps, she realized that the tide was high and still rising. Unless they were willing to swim, they would be trapped here until the tide receded.

The cave was filled with the sound of waves grinding on pebbles and inexorably obliterating the last sliver of beach, but she could hear another sound. Someone was pounding and shouting.

Pounding on what?

The sound was coming from within another tunnel. She hesitated. Was someone else down here? Why were they pounding? Still clasping Anita's hand, she made her away along the rocks, following the sound of a man's voice.

"Hey, open the door. Hey!"

She knew the voice, and her heart skipped a beat. What on earth was Toby Whitby doing down here? Why was he shouting?

The tunnel was short and wide, the entrance outlined in ancient brickwork. The light was brighter here with the moon sending its rays through the entrance and directly into the tunnel. After a few steps, they found themselves among brick columns, and she realized that they were now in the cellar of Southwold Hall.

She looked down at Anita. "We can't stay here. We have to go back. We can't let anyone see us."

She was turning to go when Toby's voice reached her in an urgent shout. "Carol?"

She turned back. Toby was balanced at the top of a flight of rickety wooden stairs in front of a sturdy oak door. His face was veiled in shadow, but she could hear fear and urgency in his voice as he called her name.

"No, Carol, not that way. Don't go that way."

What could she say? How would she ever explain? Perhaps he had not yet noticed Anita. She turned away.

His voice stopped her.

"I know everything and it doesn't matter."

She couldn't look at him. How could he possibly know?

"I went to Dorking and met a veterinary surgeon."

Carol grasped Anita's hand as the familiar shame overwhelmed her.

April 1945

She had been milking when the pains started. She pressed her face against the cow's warm belly to muffle her screams, but Vera heard her.

"What's the matter?"

"I think it's started."

Vera pushed aside her own milking stool and came to stand beside Carol.

"It's not due yet."

Carol gasped as another wave of pain overtook her. The cow, a brown and white Jersey, turned its face toward her. Carol imagined sympathy in the soft brown eyes.

She felt the painful grip of Vera's hand on her shoulder and heard the impatience in her voice.

"Not here. We have to go up to the bedroom. You can't do it here; everyone will know."

Carol staggered to her feet, knocking over the three-legged stool. The milk bucket tipped, and she watched the warm creamy milk spilling across the toes of her boots.

What a shame, she thought. Someone, somewhere, would go without their milk ration today.

With Vera tugging urgently at her arm, she took a step forward and looked down in horror as a gush of blood turned the milk pink.

Another wave of pain grabbed at her. Panic and horror overcame her self-control, and she screamed, making no attempt to muffle the sound.

Vera pulled at her again. "Shut up!"

It was too late. A man in brown overalls stood in the doorway of the barn.

She heard Vera's protest. "It's nothing. Stomach ache."

The man shook his head. "That's no stomach ache."

Vera's grip tightened on her arm. "Your name is Vera. Remember. You're Vera Malloy."

March 1952

Toby's voice brought her back to reality. "I'm glad you found your daughter."

"She's not …" Carol's protest faltered. What was the point of denying it? He knew everything.

Toby turned his attention to the door. "We have to get out of here. I've smashed the lock but …"

"We could go out onto the rocks," Carol said. "I can carry Anita, and when the tide turns—"

Toby's voice was quiet and carefully measured. "You can't go that way, and we can't stay here."

"Why not?"

"It's coming in on the tide," Toby said, gesturing toward the mouth of the cave.

Carol followed his gesture and grew cold with fear. She pulled Anita toward the foot of the stairs. Every warning she had received as a child of war played in her mind. She had never seen one before but she knew what it was. It was mine, as playful as a giant beach ball as it danced on the cresting waves, with moonlight glinting on its metal spikes.

Toby turned from the door with a hopeless gesture. "I've broken the lock but it still won't open. Someone's barred it from the other side."

"But they must know you're in here."

"Oh yes," said Toby. "They know. God damn them, they know!"

He set his shoulder to the door and shoved. Beneath him the staircase shook, and its ancient timbers groaned in protest.

Carol looked back at the mine. It was in the mouth of the cave now, rolling with the incoming tide.

Behind her she heard a sharp crack, and she turned to see the wooden staircase collapsing. Toby tumbled from the top step to the cellar floor in a shower of dust and splinters.

CHAPTER TWENTY

Elsie Shenton

It was like the Blitz all over again. Elsie Shenton tended the teapots in the village hall and watched the villagers straggling in.

She poured tea for Mrs. Rollins, and a glass of milk for the little boy. "When I heard that siren," she said, "I tell you, I almost took a turn."

Mrs. Rollins nodded her head. "They shouldn't have done that, but I suppose it was the only way to get our attention."

Elsie sniffed and looked at Mildred Chapman, skulking in a dark corner with her poor deranged son. "The police brought her in. I don't know why. She don't live anywhere near the cliff. Don't care how big the mine is, it's not going to blow up her house."

Mrs. Rollins leaned across the row of teacups and whispered conspiratorially. "Fancy the people from the Hall coming in here. You'd think they'd have somewhere more posh to go."

Elsie nodded her head. "It's the police. I don't know what's going on, but I can tell you that they're only here because the police brought them in, and very upset they are too. They didn't want no tea. That Pearson woman said they had brandy, for the shock."

"They're going to need it," said Mrs. Rollins, "when that big old pile of bricks blows up."

Teddy pulled on his mother's hand. "What pile of bricks?"

"Ooh," said Elsie, "little jugs have big ears, don't they?"

"What pile of bricks?" Teddy repeated.

"Southwold Hall," said Elsie with relish. She looked down at the boy. His rabbity face was alight with interest. "Things might be changing around here." She looked back at Mrs. Rollins. "I never had nothing against His Lordship, but I don't like that Pearson woman, not one little bit. And as for that nephew of hers ..."

Mrs. Rollins let her gaze rest on the party from Southwold Hall. They had commandeered the best chairs and set them beside the radiator that was struggling to heat the drafty old village hall.

"I don't like the look of that boy," Mrs. Rollins said. "I know he's Mrs. Pearson's nephew, but I don't think he's right in the head. He shouldn't be here."

Elsie examined the young man in question, taking in his vacant expression, heavy brows, and broad shoulders. "Nasty piece of work," she said.

"And who is the old man?" Mrs. Rollins asked.

Elsie was happy to turn her attention away from Robbie Pearson's glowering face, and look at the blanket-wrapped lawyer. "Well, that's Mr. Champion, the family solicitor from Brighton."

"He's not the lawyer I met," Mrs. Rollins argued. "I met a young man, very nice, very polite, and quite good-looking. He was asking questions around the village about Vera Chapman."

"Yes, yes," said Elsie impatiently, "I know about him, but he's not here. The posh-looking old man is the Earl's old lawyer, and the woman with the gray hair is his secretary. Nice woman, came and got herself a cup of tea and thanked me very politely."

"I don't know why anyone would be interested in Vera Chapman, not after all this time," Mrs. Rollins remarked.

Elsie would have been happy to give her opinion of Vera Chapman, but her attention was suddenly taken by Mrs. Evans. Really, it was like being in the bomb shelter again.

"She's brought that cat of hers," Elsie said. "You'd think it would be dead by now. Well, she can't bring it in here."

She set down the teapot and prepared to deal with Annie Evans and her aged cat. Before she could speak, the door opened admitting a blast of cold air, a one-armed man in a brown raincoat, and Sam Ruddle.

"Well, look at that," Elsie said. "Sam Ruddle up and about, and us thinking he was going to die."

She tried to catch Sam's eye. He looked like he could use a nice strong cup of tea, and the man in the raincoat didn't look much better.

The two men ignored her as they approached the huddled group around the radiator. The policeman who had been standing guard saluted the man in the raincoat. So he was an officer in plain clothes. A detective! The officer did not return the salute. Of course not, Elsie thought, how could he when he didn't have a right arm?

Something was happening. Chairs were being pushed back. Faces were flushed. The one-armed man seemed to be taking charge.

Elsie poured a cup of tea and, careless of rationing, stirred in three teaspoons of sugar.

"I'm just going to take this to Sam," she said.

She stepped out from behind the counter and came face to face with Mrs. Evans. The cat offered her a toothless grin.

Mrs. Evans preempted Elsie's complaint. "Vera Chapman," she said.

"What about her?"

"She's been seen."

"What do you mean?"

"She's here in the village. Jim Price chauffeured her here from London Airport. She came from America in a plane."

The teacup wobbled in Elsie's hand. "I don't believe you."

"Believe what you like," Mrs. Evans said, "but it's the truth. Jim was very put out, I can tell you. Said she behaved like a real little madam, making him carry her luggage and parading around in American clothes."

"So where is she now?" Elsie asked.

"He said he took her to the Hall; her and Carol Elliot. He was supposed to take Vera to the station, but no one can find her."

Elsie looked at the huddled figures of Millie and Terry Chapman. "Does Millie Chapman know that Vera's here?"

Mrs. Evans sniffed. "Not according to Jim. He said that Vera didn't want to go anywhere near her mother's house. All she wanted was to go to the Hall."

"She always was selfish."

"She saved us from the bomb," Mrs. Evans said.

"Saved herself more like."

Mrs. Evans nodded her head in agreement.

"Now," said Elsie, "about that cat—"

Mrs. Evans deflected the comment with another titbit of information. "That nice young lawyer has disappeared. His car is still at the Hall but he's nowhere to be found."

Elsie considered the possibility that Mrs. Evans was concocting her stories out of thin air.

"Who told you that?"

"Jim Price. He was there all the time, and he drove them over here when the police came to tell them to leave."

Mrs. Evans leaned forward. "If that young lawyer's still somewhere at the Hall, and that mine is coming with the tide, well …"

Elsie hesitated. It was really beneath her dignity to ask, but it seemed that Mrs. Evans had tapped into a rich vein of information from the usually taciturn chauffeur. She fixed her eyes on the cat and waited for the information to come to her.

Mrs. Evans adjusted her grip on the cat. "There's a little girl and two Americans."

"Oh, yes?"

"Jim picked them up in Southampton and brought them to the Hall."

Elsie looked at the group of people that Jim Price had brought over from the Hall. Lady Sylvia was still sitting in dignified silence, with Mrs.

Pearson standing behind her. The old lawyer was on his feet, supported by his secretary. A large red-faced man stood face to face with the detective, while a pale woman with blond hair that had surely come from a bottle wept softly and held the man's arm.

"Where's the little girl?" Elsie asked.

Mrs. Evans made her way past Elsie and stood expectantly at the counter. "That's what they all want to know," she said. "Now, are you going to pour me some tea, or do I have to do it myself?'

Toby Whitby

His head was pounding and his vision was clouded with dust. He lay on his back for a moment, assessing the damage and searching for the sharp pain of broken bones. No, nothing was broken. He was bruised but he should be able to stand.

Instinctively he groped through the dust and debris for his glasses. Nothing. A face swam into view, and he could discern a cloud of copper-colored hair and the smudged outlines of a worried face.

"Toby, are you all right?"

"Yes, I think so. My glasses …"

"Can you stand?"

Didn't she understand? He needed his glasses. Without his glasses he could do nothing.

"My glasses. Can you see them?"

"They're all broke, mister." A child's voice, worried and impatient.

"Let me have them."

He felt the pressure against the palm of his hand and had a moment of blessed relief as he found both earpieces intact. He settled the glasses on the bridge of his nose. He sat up and viewed the cellar through cracked lenses. His eyes went immediately to the short tunnel. His vision was far from perfect, but he could see enough to know that the mine was still dancing at the mouth of the cave.

He staggered to his feet. His first instinct was to look upward at the barred door in the hope that he could make another assault.

Carol was beside him, holding his arm. "There's no way up," she said. "I tried."

"When?"

"While you were unconscious."

"How long was I out?"

"Not long."

"How long?" he asked insistently.

She sounded impatient. "A couple of minutes. Does it matter?"

He shook his head and drew in a sharp breath at the renewed pounding. "Not long enough for the tide to turn."

"No," said Carol. "I've been watching. It's still coming in. Do you think we should go back the way I came?"

"Back to the top of the house?" he asked.

"Yes."

"If the mine blows up in here, the house will collapse on you. You won't stand a chance."

Carol tugged on his arm and turned him so that he was looking directly at her.

"Do you have a better idea? If you do, I would love to hear it, and if you don't, please stop frightening Anita. She's scared enough without you talking about the house falling on top of her."

Toby glanced sideways and saw the fuzzy outline of the little girl. He adjusted his glasses, trying to find a way to bring the world into better focus. Moving them down his nose seemed to give the best result.

He could see Carol clearly now and read the fear on her face. She had given him her solution. Now it was up to him to come up with something better.

He grasped at one last hope. He spoke softly to the child, trying to keep the tension out of his voice. "Can you swim?"

He readjusted his broken glasses, and the child's face came into focus. Her eyes were wide with fright.

"I ain't never been swimming. I don't know how to swim."

Of course she couldn't swim. She'd grown up in some Appalachian mountain hollow, far from the sea and far from public swimming pools and private swimming lessons.

It had been, at best, a faint hope, and now he had to put that hope aside. He was left with only one solution. It was terrifying, but it was the only thing he could think of.

"Did you think we could swim past it?" Carol asked.

He shook his head. "No, not really. It was just a wild idea, but don't worry about it. I have another idea."

"What?"

"If I can hold that thing still until the tide turns …"

"How?"

"If I could get a rope around it and anchor it somehow and stop it from coming in, it will go back out when the tide turns.

She shook her head. "You can't do that. It will blow up if you even touch it."

"No, it won't. That's what they used to tell us in the war because they didn't want anyone to go anywhere near a mine, but actually there is a way to handle it."

"I don't believe you. You're just saying that because—"

"Because what?"

"Because you want to sound brave."

No, he thought, I am saying it because I love you. He knew he wasn't brave; in fact, he was terrified.

"It's not as dangerous as you think," he said. "The detonators are in the tips of the spikes. If you don't touch the tips, it won't blow."

"I still don't understand," Carol said. "How are you going to stop it from coming in?"

The plan was still forming in Toby's mind. It was ridiculous; impossible, but it would buy her some time.

He squared his shoulders. "We need rope. Shine that light of yours around and see if you can find some. The smugglers used to come in here, or so I'm told; there has to be rope."

"Are you going to put a rope around it?" Carol asked.

"I'm going to try. I'll hold it until the tide turns, and that will give you time to go back the way you came and be well clear of the house in case anything happens."

"I'd rather stay here with you and we can leave together."

He let his eyes rest on Anita. "Don't worry about me; worry about her. You owe her that much."

He could see the hurt in her eyes. She had taken his remark as an accusation. She was a mother who had abandoned her child once, would she do it again? Now was not the time to apologize. He would apologize another time, if he was granted another time.

"Are y'all looking for rope?" Anita asked, her accent grating on Toby's ears.

"Yes, we are."

Anita pointed. "There's some over there."

Toby was ready to swear that the child could see in the dark as she led them unerringly to several coils of rope hanging against the wall.

Toby fingered the harsh hemp braids. The rope was old and dusty and maybe not strong enough, but it would have to do. He took off his jacket and looped the coils over his shoulder.

For a moment he was just as much a hero as anyone who had worn a uniform. For a moment he was what he had always dreamed of being.

He took hold of Carol's shoulders and pulled her to him until her face was in clear focus. "How long will it take you to go back the way you came?"

She stared into his eyes. "There's a tunnel and then stone steps, and then a wooden staircase. It goes all the way to the top of the house, and then we'd have to go down the front steps and out the front door."

Toby held her gaze as he made a rapid calculation and rejected any thought of going with her. She would need more time than the mine would allow her. She would need all the time he could give her.

He saw the flicker of understanding in her eyes. She knew as well as he did that he had little hope of coming out of the cave alive.

Her voice was soft and hesitant. "I have to tell you …"

"You don't have to tell me anything."

"Yes, I do. I'm sorry that I lied to you. I didn't know what to do. I didn't think you'd understand the truth. Her father is—"

"I know who her father is," Toby said, "and it makes no difference."

"Really?"

He drew her into his arms. "I love you," he whispered. "I don't care about the past. I love you, and I will love her."

He wanted the kiss to last for a lifetime, but who could say how long a life could last? If the war had taught him anything, it had taught him that life was fleeting, and this moment with Carol in his arms, and her lips warm and tender, could be all that he would ever have.

He released her and walked slowly toward the water. "Go quickly. You'll be safe if you go now."

His words were more than just words. His words were a vow. The mine would not explode until Carol had time to escape. He would hold it until the tide turned. If he had to explode the mine and himself with it, Carol and her child were going to be safe.

He watched her turn away and walk back into the tunnel. He slipped off his shoes and stepped into the water.

Blanche Harrigan

Blanche watched through a veil of unshed tears as the village woman came toward them carrying two teacups.

The old man with the bandaged head took one of the cups with a nod of thanks. Blanche turned her head away as the woman thrust the second cup under her nose.

"I put sugar in it," the woman said. "To heck with rationing, I said to myself. You've had a nasty shock and you need strong sweet tea."

"No, no, take it away."

The woman frowned and offered the cup again. "It'll do you good."

"No, it won't."

The woman still did not move, and it occurred to Blanche that the tea was only an excuse. That woman, in her flowered apron and her hair still up in pin curls, wanted to know what was going on, and she was going to stand there until she found out.

The detective, Slater was his name, frowned at the village woman, but she stood her ground.

"I want to know what's going on," she said, looking directly at the detective.

"You've been told," Slater replied. "There's a German mine loose along this part of the coast. We're not sure where or if it will come ashore, but we've evacuated the houses that could be affected. Now, please, go back to making tea."

The woman settled her hands on her hips. "I will not."

The old man with the bandaged head chuckled and dug Mr. Slater in the ribs.

"You might as well tell her," he said. "You might as well tell everyone. Once Elsie Shenton gets her teeth into something, she don't ever let go."

"It's police business," Slater muttered.

"It's village business," Elsie retorted. "Sam's right. We want to know if we're all going to be murdered in our beds by the likes of Terry Chapman."

Her glance went to the woman in the corner who had her arms around a thin trembling man.

"Terry Chapman hasn't done anything," Slater said.

"Then why is he here?" Elsie asked.

Mrs. Chapman rose to her feet. "That's what I want to know. Why am I here? Why can't you leave us be?"

To Blanche's surprise, Miss Clark, the old lawyer's secretary, rose and put a comforting hand on Mrs. Chapman's arm. "I'm afraid you're here because your daughter is involved in something."

"My daughter is in America."

Elsie crowed with triumph. "No, she's not. She's here in this village, or leastways she was."

Mrs. Chapman's face crumpled, all pride and defiance gone. "She can't be. She's in America with my granddaughter."

Blanche felt a draft of cold air as the outer door of the hall opened and two people came in. She saw the distinctive outline of a policeman in a helmet, and beside him, Vera Malloy, upright and indignant.

"Vera!"

Blanche thought that Mrs. Chapman was going to faint, but the lawyer's secretary held her upright.

She heard a surprised choking sob from the dark corner of the room where Terry Chapman huddled, deep in his own fears.

Vera had been looking at her mother, her eyes wide and defiant, but now she saw her brother. Blanche saw the defiance give way to anguish. For the first time, she detected real emotion in Vera's face.

"Terry?"

He shambled forward.

"Oh, Terry, what happened to you?"

She held out her arms and he lurched into her embrace, resting his head on her shoulder.

Mrs. Chapman's voice was high and scolding. "What do you mean by coming here and not telling me? I had to hear it from someone else. What kind of daughter doesn't tell her mother that she's coming all the way from

America, and where is my granddaughter?"

Blanche bit her lip. Should she say it? Should she get this out in the open? She looked to Harry for affirmation. She saw him nod his head and saw admiration in his eyes. She would not be weak. She would not cling to a false hope.

"She's not your granddaughter."

A stifling silence blanketed the room. Blanche felt as though time was standing still. She saw the village woman staring, her eyes greedy for information. She saw anger overtaking compassion on Vera's face, and a flush of shame suffusing Mrs. Chapman's cheeks.

She looked at Lady Sylvia's confident smile. Lady Sylvia thought she was going to get away with it, but she wasn't. Blanche was not about to confirm Lady Sylvia's claim. That woman, with her aristocratic ways and her cold triumphant smile, had sullied Jack's memory. Jack would never have married a woman like her. Jack had been better than that.

Blanche kept her eyes on Lady Sylvia and watched the smile fade. "She's not your child. You were never married to my son."

"Ha!" The old man with the bandaged head emitted a triumphant snort and looked at the detective. "I told you. I knew it all along. Baby-stealing, that's what I said."

Blanche looked from one face to another. "Doesn't anyone care where she is now? I don't know who her father is, and I don't even know her real name, but I know that she's not here."

The door opened again. Blanche looked behind her and saw Mrs. Pearson slip out into the night.

Toby Whitby

The water was cold, but not cold enough to kill. By the time he was in up to his knees, he could feel the pull of the incoming tide resisting his efforts to move forward. He eyed the column of rock that stood just a few yards out from the mouth of the cave. Waves were breaking across its dark surface, and soon it would be swamped by the incoming tide. He would have to be quick.

He was not a man who routinely prayed, and even now his prayer was without words, but he was certain that it would take more than his own strength to do what needed to be done.

Pitting his muscles against the flow of the tide, he swam toward the mine. A breaking wave washed his glasses away and his vision blurred. The mine was now a heaving gray monstrosity at the very edge of his focus. He already knew where he was going, and he had no need to see with any greater clarity. Perhaps it was better not to see. He stopped swimming. He had no need to move toward the enemy, the enemy was coming toward him; and it was moving faster than he liked. Soon he would be out of time.

He imagined Carol climbing the stairs to the top of Southwold Hall. How fast could she climb with Anita beside her, and the flashlight flickering and almost useless? He had to give her whatever time he could.

The mine swam into his shortsighted focus with every detail visible. Its gray surface was scarred and scoured by its time in the ocean, and it bobbed and swayed in the waves, presenting its deadly spikes with every movement. He imagined it had only recently broken loose from its mooring on the seabed. It had waited eight, nine, maybe ten years for this encounter.

He trod water while he eased the coil of rope from his shoulders and found the loose end. He had to do it now before the mine drifted past, and if it exploded at his touch, at least it would not explode in the cellar beneath the house.

The wet rope was stiff and heavy in his hands. He watched as the mine rolled with a wave, and a spike came within reach of his arms. He would have only one chance. If the mine passed him now, it would be on the rocks before he could catch it.

He kicked with his legs and heaved himself out of the water. The rope settled around the base of the spike. Hardly daring to breathe, he lifted himself from the water again and caught hold of the adjacent spike. The two loops held and the mine was steady, no longer rolling but still moving with the tide.

He hung onto the rope, feeling as though he had a tiger by the tail, and swam awkwardly out toward the open ocean where a rocky spur still held itself above the high-tide mark. He knew he would never be able to hold the mine by himself, but if he could loop the rope around the rock, the tide would do the work for him. The mine would strain against the rope and be unable to reach the rocky shore.

All fear left him as he towed his terrible burden out to sea. The shame that had haunted him for years was finally banished. Whether he lived or died here in the cold water, he would finally have come face to face with the enemy. The war was over, but the threat remained. His weak eyesight that had kept him from combat was now his friend. His enemy was a gray blur behind him, and his destination was a black blur ahead, and nothing else was real. He welcomed the moment.

CHAPTER TWENTY ONE

Edwin sank back into his chair and looked at Vera. She would not meet his eyes. He could tell that she wanted to run. Hardly surprising, considering that she had been caught up in a tangle of lies, but she alone could give him the answer he needed. When he had the answer, he would tell them what he knew.

The village woman still waited to console Mrs. Harrigan, but he was certain that a cup of rapidly cooling tea would not be the answer to Mrs. Harrigan's grief. He felt nothing but sympathy for Jack Harrigan's mother. She had been offered hope and seen that same hope snatched away. He thought that she was a strong woman, stronger than anyone he knew; strong enough to face the truth and abandon false hope.

Slater had already dispatched someone to find Mrs. Pearson. Her nephew, Robbie, had made an attempt to follow her out into the night, but a nod from Slater had resulted in a reassuring click and a surprised grunt as the nephew found himself handcuffed to the radiator.

Edwin was willing to wait for the return of Mrs. Pearson. He wanted to see her face when he told her what he knew. Setting all other matters aside, he was affronted that she had tried to use Champion and Company to legalize her deceit.

First, however, he would like to know about the child, and he would really like to know what had happened to young Whitby. He settled his gaze on Vera Chapman.

"Why?" he asked.

Vera ignored him but not his question. She looked at her mother with the sullen eyes of a teenager. "I wanted to get to America. He wouldn't have married me unless I was pregnant."

Her mother looked at her with wide puzzled eyes. "You were

pregnant."

"No, I wasn't."

"But the baby, the christening, the birth certificate."

"What birth certificate?" Vera asked. "I got rid of the birth certificate."

Mrs. Chapman shook her head. "You got rid of it, but I kept it. I gave it to that young lawyer, Mr. Whitby."

Edwin sighed. There it was; almost the last piece of the puzzle. So where was Whitby?

Vera shrugged her shoulders. "When the baby was born, Carol told the doctor that her name was Vera Malloy."

"Carol?" Mrs. Chapman said. "Carol Elliot?"

"Yes. Anita's her daughter."

The teacup fell to the floor with a crash as the nosy village woman stood openmouthed.

"Carol Elliot," Mrs. Chapman whispered. She looked around at the other villagers, who all stood with their mouths agape.

"So who is the father?" Edwin asked.

Vera shrugged her shoulders. "Gunther something."

The news reverberated through the room, sending shockwaves of rattling spoons and slopping tea.

Edwin thought he detected a mixture of spite and sympathy in Vera's tone. "German prisoner of war; he was working on the farm at Billingshurst. Turns out he was married, and he didn't want anything to do with Carol having a baby."

Edwin felt truly sorry for the unknown Carol Elliot. Now she would have no choice but to claim her child, and he wondered if she would ever be able to show her face in the village again.

Mrs. Chapman was still staring at her daughter, and her right hand was twitching. Edwin thought that the mother was tempted to give her daughter a good slap. He could hardly blame her, but the poor woman only knew what was on the surface. She had no idea what lay behind this web of lies. Even Lady Sylvia, sitting stone-faced and emotionless, could not know the whole truth. Of the people in the room, only he and Miss Clark had seen the documents that had been hidden in the Earl's desk, but he was certain that other documents existed. The Earls of Southwold were not the only ones who had been keeping a record of births and deaths.

He heard the door open. He hoped it might be Whitby, but it was a police officer who was keeping a firm hold on Mrs. Pearson. Slater gestured with his left hand, and the officer pressed Mrs. Pearson into a seat.

The housekeeper glared around at the assembly. "I went to look for the little girl. No one else seems to be looking."

"You can leave the looking to us," Slater replied. He turned to Edwin. "I have the feeling that you know what's going on here."

Edwin nodded his head. "I understand most of it. There are still a few loose ends, but I can tell you who killed Mr. Alderton and Nurse Tierney, and who attacked Mr. Ruddle, and I can tell you why." He sighed. "I'm very worried about Mr. Whitby. There has been far too much violence already, and I would not like to think anything has happened to him. Is anyone looking for him?"

"I can't send anyone out to the house," Slater said, "and I've pulled them back from the cliffs. It's too risky. Until that mine comes ashore or the tide turns, he's on his own."

Edwin focused on Miss Clark's hands, clasped together so tightly that her knuckles were turning white. She was as worried as he was about young Whitby. He made a determined effort to suppress his fears and concentrate on telling what he knew.

He looked at Mrs. Pearson. "She didn't do it with her own hands, but she's just as guilty as her nephew."

He ignored the agitated jangle as Robbie Pearson strained against his handcuffs.

"Alderton was the first victim. It took a strong man to take him down, but Mrs. Pearson was the brains behind the brawn. It had to be done. Alderton was making inquiries among his friends in high society. It would not be long before he realized that there had never been a wedding between Lady Sylvia and an American officer.

"After that, things began to escalate. That's the way it is with lies. Mr. Ruddle was dropping hints that he knew something, and he had to be silenced. Fortunately for us, he didn't die, and when he recovered consciousness, he said he had been attacked by a woman. I think we should all be glad that he was able to make that statement and relieve Terry Chapman of any blame. It is quite obvious that this has nothing to do with that poor fellow. The evidence, which is written on Mr. Ruddle's unfortunate head, tells us that the blows came from behind him. My assumption is that Mrs. Pearson was in front of him and her nephew was behind him.

"As for the Irish nurse; I really cannot say, because I never met her, but it's no easy matter to push someone off a cliff. I think it would take a man's strength."

Edwin paused. He had no proof of what he was about to say, but he owed it to Dennis Blanchard to say it.

"I don't think it took much strength to kill the Earl. She could have done it herself, if she wanted to."

In the shocked silence that followed his statement, he heard a chair creak and saw Lady Sylvia lean forward so that her sleek black hair obscured her face. Did she know? Was she involved? That was for Slater to discover.

He let his gaze wander from the Countess to Terry Chapman. Terry's expression was shuttered, and his eyes roved nervously around the room. Edwin did not know if the mind behind the eyes was seeing a prison camp or if it saw the familiarity of home. He spent no time on asking himself meaningless questions. One day Terry Chapman's mind would return to his body, or perhaps it would not. It was not a question that needed to be answered at this moment.

Edwin looked at Miss Clark. Her knuckles were white with strain. "Anthea?"

She blushed and unclasped her hands. He had never before addressed her in such an informal matter, but she was more than his secretary now; she was his confidant.

"Yes, Mr. Champion?"

"Do you see the resemblance?"

She followed his gaze, looking first at Mrs. Pearson and then at Terry Chapman. She nodded her head, and he could see that she too was piecing the puzzle together.

He smiled his approval and received her tentative smile in return. This was really no smiling matter, but it was good to know that Anthea was there to back him up.

Edwin turned his attention to Mrs. Pearson. "What was your name before you married?"

She unclamped her lips and spat out her reply. "None of your business."

"Was it Chapman?" Edwin asked. "Were you, in fact, Nell Chapman?"

Terry's mother stepped forward in protest. "She's not a Chapman. I knew everyone in my husband's family. He wasn't a fly-by-night like that soldier Vera married. Walter was a village man. Everyone here knows who his family were, and that woman wasn't one of them. I don't know where she came from."

"She came from Norfolk, from another branch of the Chapman family; one that moved away before the Great War," Edwin said. "That's right, isn't it, Mrs. Pearson?"

"So what if it is?"

Edwin looked at Anthea. He had the documents with him, but he wasn't ready to produce them, not yet.

"July 12, 1834," Anthea said.

Mrs. Pearson's eyes flashed. "What about it?"

Edwin was assured now that he was on the right track. Mrs. Pearson knew. She knew the story just as well as he did, maybe even better.

"July 12, 1834," Anthea repeated, "Richard Blanchard, the second son of the Earl of Southwold, married Lydia Chapman in a secret ceremony."

Edwin tuned his ear to the sounds in the hall. Slater snorted impatiently. Terry Chapman murmured soothing words to himself, but his mother gasped and left him alone as she came forward to stand by Edwin's chair.

"What is this?" she asked. "What are you getting at?"

Anthea continued in unruffled confidence. "Because the Blanchard family would not acknowledge Richard's marriage, Lydia did not dare use their family name. She named her son John, John Chapman, and she lived with him in the village. Perhaps she was paid to keep quiet. I hope that money was involved. I hope that they allowed her to live comfortably."

"They gave her nothing," Mrs. Pearson said. "She had to raise her son in poverty."

Anthea leaned back in her chair. "So you know the story?" she asked.

"Of course I do," Mrs. Pearson snapped.

"Well, I don't," said Slater. "I don't know what any of this has to do with what's happening now." He looked from Mrs. Pearson to Anthea. "You women read too many magazines."

Edwin held up his hand for silence and gave Anthea a reassuring smile. "Now is not the time to discuss the merits of women's magazines. I am sure that, in their rightful place, at home by the fire, they are very informative."

Anthea blushed again. He hoped that his words would come as a gentle warning that she should not keep such magazines in her office.

"Lydia and her son were not forgotten," Edwin said. "The Blanchard family kept records."

"Why didn't they speak?" Mrs. Pearson asked. "Why didn't they acknowledge our claim on the estate?"

Lady Sylvia spoke for the first time. "Your claim," she hissed. "You have no claim."

"More claim than that brat you brought from America," Mrs. Pearson snarled. She glared at Vera. "You lied to us. You lied to everyone."

Vera smiled a cold tight smile. "Yes, I think we've established that I lied, but it was all in a good cause. Carol couldn't bring the illegitimate child of a Nazi into the village, but I could take her to America. I did what I had to do."

Slater held up a hand to command silence and attention. "Someone tell me what's going on here," he commanded. He looked at Edwin. "You tell me. You seem to know everything."

"It's a simple story," Edwin said, "when you boil it all down."

"Good," said Slater. "I'd like a simple story."

"Richard was the Earl's second son," Edwin said, "and he did what second sons normally do, he joined the army. He died in the Gold Coast. As no one was willing to acknowledge his marriage to Lydia Chapman, he was wiped from the family line of succession, supposedly dying without issue. His older brother, Michael, inherited, and the line continued until today, when the current Countess of Southwold finds herself without an heir. It is assumed that the estate and the title will be claimed by Godfrey's descendants in Australia, but they are not the rightful heirs. Godfrey was the third child. Richard's descendants have a better claim, but none of them will make a claim unless and until the current Countess dies childless. Everything that has happened here has happened in order to put one of Richard and Lydia's descendants into Southwold Hall."

"No!" Sylvia's voice echoed around the dusty room. "These are all lies."

"I have proof," Edwin said. "The Earl entrusted certain documents into my keeping."

"What documents?" Lady Sylvia asked. "Why didn't I know about them? Why didn't he tell me?"

Edwin could find no answer for her. Should he tell her that her father had not trusted her? No, not yet. He carried on speaking.

"Lady Sylvia is telling the truth. She knew nothing about the other branch of the family because Mrs. Pearson never revealed her true motives. Lady Sylvia's interest was purely financial and pertained only to maintaining her lifestyle. She was not interested in what would happen to the estate after her death."

He looked at the Countess. She had returned to her former calm.

"*Après moi le déluge*," Edwin said softly.

She acknowledged his comment with a cold smile. "I'm afraid the British have run out of money. We've given it all to the Americans."

Harry Harrigan rose from his seat, but his wife held him back.

"Let the man talk," she commanded. "Go on, Mr. Champion. We're all listening."

"Well," said Edwin, "I assume that Mrs. Pearson has been whispering in her employer's ear for several years and suggesting ways that the family fortunes could be improved. The Chapman family, Nell's relatives, have no money, and even if they can prove their claim, they will be unable to maintain the house. It was in everyone's interests to find someone with large amounts of money, and no such person could be found this side of the Atlantic. It was Mrs. Pearson who devised the plan that would bring in American money and solve all of their problems."

He looked at Mrs. Pearson. Her face betrayed nothing of the inner turmoil she was surely experiencing.

"It was a clever plan," he said with a nod of appreciation to her. "Almost perfect. The American money would return Southwold to its former glory and allow Lady Sylvia to live in style, and she would not even know that the baby she claimed as her own was one of John Chapman's descendants. Eventually the child would inherit the Southwold title, and the Chapman family would have what they have wanted for all these years, and some American money into the bargain. As an added bonus, Sylvia was already aware of the resemblance between herself and Vera. She was sure that the resemblance would carry down to Vera's daughter."

Edwin paused for a moment, taking in the stunned expressions of his audience.

"Fortunately, or unfortunately," he said, "none of this matters, because the child who was brought from America was not Vera's child."

He leaned back in his chair. He had told his story. He suspected that he had left some loose ends; it would be up to Slater to tease them out and see what was attached. Slater could surely find sufficient evidence to charge Mrs. Pearson and her nephew with murder. As for Lady Sylvia, her behavior had been cruel and entirely reprehensible, but he was not sure that it amounted to a crime; not if Vera had been a willing participant in the lie.

Slater's London voice interrupted his thoughts and brought him back to reality with an unwelcome jolt.

"So where's the child; and where's Whitby?"

Toby Whitby

How long had he been in the water? His feet and hands were numb, and he thought he might die of cold after all. He had looped the rope around the cone of rock in an attempt to relieve the strain on his arms. The tide was still rolling inward, with the mine straining against its tether, but the water was inching its way up the stone pillar, and waves were breaking across his shoulders as he clung to the rope.

How long had Carol been gone? How long would the rope hold? The moonlight allowed him to see the fuzzy outline of the rope as it passed around the boulder. He squinted to bring his eyes into focus. It was as he had suspected. The action of the mine, dancing at the end of its tether, was wearing at the rope. As he watched, several strands broke loose. He looked away, unable to maintain his focus. He was not about to let go; the rope burns on his hands meant nothing to him, but any minute now the decision would be taken from him. He turned to look at the dark expanse of ocean behind him. When the rope parted, when the decision was no longer his to make, what would he do? The tide was still coming in. He would have only a few seconds to get away, and the tide would be working against him.

A memory rushed at him from the back of his mind. A windy August day on the Welsh coast. He was a small boy, maybe nine or ten years old; those happy childhood years ran together in his memory. The sky was a bright blue, with the wind shredding the clouds into long streaks. The beach was crowded; August Bank Holiday, a day off for everyone. His mother held a towel up for him so that no one would see him struggling into his swimming trunks. Despite Mother's protests, his father had eschewed the towel and quickly stripped off his trousers and underpants. For a moment his father had been entirely naked. Mother had laughed in shock and hurried to hand him his trunks.

The screaming started just as Father was pulling up the trunks to cover his nakedness. People were gathered at edge of the water. The tide was receding, leaving the people standing on a patch of damp sand. A woman was screaming and pointing. Several men plunged into the waves.

Toby's mother rose to her feet and sheltered her eyes as she looked at the activity. Toby strained to see, but even then his eyesight had been poor. He had taken off his glasses when they reached the beach. They were in the picnic basket, swaddled in a towel to protect them from the sand.

"What's happening?" Toby asked.

His father placed a hand on his shoulder. "Someone's child has been swept out on the tide," he said. He shook his head in disapproval. "Why don't people keep an eye on their kiddies?"

"Is he going to drown?" Toby asked. His inability to see the details of the disaster set him at a mental remove from the action, and his question was more academic than emotional.

His father continued to stare out to sea. "Those men will bring him back," he said.

He squatted to bring his face on a level with Toby. "If this ever happens to you—"

"It won't," Toby promised. "I know how to swim."

"It's not a question of swimming," his father said. "It's all about keeping a cool head and not panicking. If you are ever caught in the tide, rising or falling, it doesn't matter, don't take it head on. Angle yourself across the current. You might end up a mile down the beach, but you won't drown."

He could still remember seeing his father's face drawn close enough to be in focus. He remembered the sudden serious tone that overtook the joy of his day on the beach. Angle yourself across the current.

He felt the rope go slack in his hands. This was it. The mine, freed of all restraint, rode the crest of a wave and became a gray blur. He dropped the rope and turned his face across the breaking waves.

Vera Malloy

The old lawyer was looking at her with prune-faced disapproval, and she could hear the murmurs of the villagers standing behind her with their teacups and prejudices. She felt their hostility like piercing darts in her back, but she had to ask. She had to know.

"So am I the heir?" she asked. "If my father was the heir to Southwold, the title passes to me, doesn't it?"

Her mother's slap came as a sudden stinging shock. She reeled back with the force of the blow and stared at her mother's red angry face.

She lifted her hand to shield herself from another attack. "What was that for?"

Her mother stood on tiptoe, her anger seeming to lift her from the ground and consume her.

"What was that for?" she screamed. "What do you think it's for? I have never been so ashamed in all of my life. Bad enough that you behaved like a common little tart, throwing yourself at a good-for-nothing soldier, but you lied, Vera. You lied to me. You lied to everyone."

Vera took a step backward and prepared to defend herself. "I didn't lie for my own sake. I did it for Carol. It was the best solution we had. I was a good friend to her. She needed me. What do you think would have happened if she'd come home with that baby?"

Vera's eyes scoured the onlookers. "What would you have done to Carol? The baby was half-Nazi; what would you have done about that?"

She stared at them until, one by one, they looked away; all except the lawyer and his mousy secretary. Even the American woman's expression softened slightly, but the lawyer was not swayed, and neither was Vera's mother.

"You made fraudulent statements to Mr. Harrigan," the old man said.

Her mother parroted him. "Fraud, Vera. That's a crime, and what about that little girl? All these years telling her you're her mother, and then suddenly you hand her over to a stranger. You're cold, Vera. Cold as ice."

Vera straightened her shoulders. None of this mattered. The future was getting brighter by the minute.

"Weren't you listening to what he said, Mum? Dad was the heir to the Southwold estate, and now I am. I'm going to be the Countess."

"No, you're not."

The voice was quiet and sad. She looked for the speaker and discovered her brother swaying slightly on his feet but looking directly at her.

"You're not the heir, Vera. I am."

Her heart skipped a beat as her new world of possibilities tumbled from its axis.

"But you won't have children …"

Terry gave her a look of infinite sadness. "Is that what you want for me, Vera? Do you hope I never recover? Do you think I'll never marry?"

Her mother's second slap knocked her backward, and she stumbled against the tea table, setting the cups rattling in their saucers.

Her mother's mouth was working, but she was, apparently, too angry to speak, and that, Vera thought, was a blessing in itself.

The old lawyer was creaking himself into an upright position. No doubt he was about to tell her how many crimes she had committed, but the one-armed detective was taking no notice of the lawyer. His head was cocked to one side, and he seemed to be listening for something.

Vera felt the floor tremble. The table that held the teacups gave up the ghost entirely and collapsed onto the floor. A window shattered and dust fell from the rafters.

The memory rushed at her; walls bulging, dust showering down on the cowering villagers. Not this time. She wasn't going to be trapped this time, not by falling bricks, and not by the accusing villagers.

She ignored the turmoil that broke out around her. Well, she thought, that's the end of Southwold Hall. Terry can have what's left. I don't want it.

She clasped her handbag, reassured by the amount of Harry Harrigan's money that was still in her possession. She left without saying goodbye.

CHAPTER TWENTY TWO

With her daughter's arms around her neck, Carol ran through the wrought iron gates while Southwold Hall rumbled and roared behind her. She felt its presence like a living thing; a monster reaching out to overwhelm her and bury her beneath its ancient masonry.

When she reached the road, she stopped to look behind her. One wall of the Hall was still standing, a silhouetted ruin with moonlight beaming through its shattered windows. As she watched, the wall seemed to lean backward. It held its shape for a moment before it tumbled over the cliff. The Hall was gone. Nothing remained, not even the ground on which it had stood. She was the last person who would ever run through the secret passageway, down the grand staircase, and out into the echoing front hall.

She set Anita on her feet and sagged to the ground, gasping for breath. Passing through the wrought iron gates and onto the road gave her an illusion of safety, as though the damage would somehow be limited to the Hall, and nothing else would be harmed.

Anita squatted beside her. "What happened to the man?"

Relief gave way to anguish. Toby had kept his promise. Somehow he had bought her enough time to reach safety, but what price had he paid? She could still feel his kiss and the strength of his arms as he held her. Somehow he had held the mine and given her time to escape. Had he given himself time to swim away? Were the strong arms that held her strong enough to swim against the tide?

"What happened to him?" Anita asked again.

Carol shook her head. "I don't know."

"Where's my mom?"

Carol's heart sank. How was she going to answer that question? Fortunately, Anita didn't need to have one question answered before she asked another. While Carol tried to regain her breath and form some kind of plan, Anita peppered her with questions.

"What happened to the big house? Why did it fall down? What's your name?"

Carol was lost for words. Anita didn't even know her name.

"I'm … I'm … You can call me Carol."

"Where are we going Miss Carol?"

Carol looked toward the distant lights of the village. She thought of the comfort of her home behind the post office. She would light a fire and make tea, or perhaps Anita didn't drink tea. She could give her lemonade. She could give her anything she wanted. She had a whole shop to choose from.

"I'm going to take you home with me," Carol said.

Anita stepped back as Carol moved to pick her up. "I can walk, Miss Carol."

Carol clasped her hand. "Of course you can."

Anita stopped after just a few steps. "Someone's coming."

The moonlight revealed a shadowy figure hurrying toward them, and Carol heard the clicking of high-heeled shoes. The figure was suddenly illuminated by the headlights of a car coming up from the village.

"Mommy!" Anita shouted as the figure was held for the moment in the beam of light.

Carol glimpsed a smart hairstyle, a formfitting coat, and a hand that held a large handbag, but the sight lasted no more than a moment before the figure stepped away from the light and vanished.

"Mommy!" Anita shouted again, tugging at Carol's restraining hand.

"No," said Carol, "that's not your mother."

"It is. It is. It is!"

Before Anita could work herself up into a full-blown tantrum, the approaching car turned its headlights toward them and drew Anita's attention. She went toward the light like a moth to a flame, and Carol, seeing that the vehicle was a police car, followed reluctantly.

She settled into the back seat and asked the driver to take her home. "The post office," she said.

He shook his head. "I can't do that, miss. I have to take everyone I find to the village hall. Is there anyone else with you?"

"No, just us."

"I thought I saw a woman on the road. We're looking for Vera Chapman."

Carol thought of the figure that had slipped away into the darkness; of the woman who had ignored a little girl calling out for her mother. Let her go. Let her follow whatever flawed star guided her. She would never again have a chance to harm Anita.

"I didn't see anyone. Why do we have to go to the village hall?"

"Detective Sergeant Slater is holding everyone there for their own safety."

"Everyone?"

"Seems like it." The driver laughed. "Lots of nosy village women."

Carol sighed. There would be no escape from this. If she entered the village hall with Anita at her side, everyone would know she was the mother. She tightened her arm around Anita's shoulders. For Anita's sake she hoped that they would never know everything. They would never know about Gunther.

She leaned forward and tapped the driver on the shoulder. "Is anyone searching for survivors?"

He twisted his head. "What do you mean by survivors?"

She told him about Toby, and before she had finished the telling, he was on the radio.

"Calling all cars. Calling all cars."

She looked out of the window and saw the moon go behind a cloud. She thought of the light vanishing from the ocean and Toby alone in the dark.

Toby Whitby

Toby heard the voice as if from a great distance.

"Wasn't sure I'd have any crab pots left. Still don't know. After I took a look at him, I knew he was in a bad way, and I'd best row back to the harbor." The slow speech and soft local accent made the finding of a half-drowned man sound like an everyday occurrence.

"I thought that the cliff falling like that would have done for my crabbing, but, well, you know how it is, we need the money, so it seemed it was worth a try. So I went out at dawn and found him floating on a big old tree branch. He's lucky the current had him and brought him around the headland, or he'd be halfway to France by now."

The owner of the voice coughed and spat and continued his story. "I had a hell of a time with him. He was holding that branch like his life depended on it."

"I expect it did. Has he said anything?"

Toby recognized the London accent of the second voice. Slater!

"Just mumbo-jumbo," said the crab fisherman. "He's a big lad. I had a time of it getting him into my boat, and then he just collapsed like all the wind had gone out of his sails. Don't know how long he'd been in the water."

"He went in just before the mine exploded," Slater said. "Someone should give him a medal, but I doubt they will."

Toby felt a hand on his shoulder. "Can you walk?"

It was time to open his eyes; time to face the truth. Had he bought enough time? Had Carol escaped from the Hall? He had no doubt about the Hall collapsing; masonry was falling all around him as he swam clear of the cave, angling across the pull of the tide, until he bumped into a floating branch. After that he had seen nothing; thought of nothing; felt nothing as he lost the use of his legs. If his hands had not been locked in frozen rigor around the branch, he would have been unable to hold it. By the time the old fisherman had pulled him from the water, amid a chorus of inventive curses and some strong words for how much Toby weighed, he had been unable to move a muscle to help him.

The hand squeezed his shoulder. "Can you walk?"

"I don't know."

"Give it a try." Slater's voice was not unkind. "I've an ambulance on the way. They'll bring a stretcher if you want, but it might be good if the young lady could see you walking. Might put a stop to the tears."

Toby opened his eyes to the fresh wash of dawn light. He lifted his head and saw the fuzzy outline of boats at anchor in the harbor, cliffs rising beyond, and an old man's face very close to his own.

The old man spoke under his breath. "Come on, lad, the policeman can't help, not with just one arm, and me, I'm out of puff from pulling you out of the water, so see if you can get your feet under you."

Toby made an effort; not because he cared about Slater's one-armed problem, and not because the old man was out of breath, but because he could see two figures on the beach. The morning sun turned her hair into a soft red corona around her barely discernible face, and it was mirrored in miniature on her daughter. For her, for them, he would do it.

He stepped out of the boat and felt the shingle beach beneath his bare feet. When did he lose his shoes and socks?

He could stand but he couldn't move forward. It didn't matter; she was coming to him. He waited and watched two faces come into focus; mirror images. Everyone would know now. The road ahead would be hard.

He buried his toes in the shingle to steady himself as he gathered them both into his arms.

THE END

I hope you enjoyed Air Raid. The next book in the series is Imposter. (See the next page).
I hope you enjoy that as well
Eileen

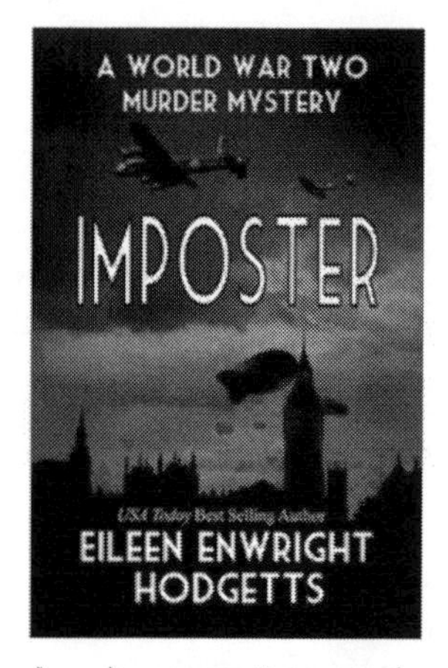

Imposter In the second book of the Toby Whitby series, Toby must look to the dark days of 1940 to find the true identity of the dead man with no hands.

England, 1952. A body washes up on Brighton beach and Lawyer Toby Whitby's secretary swears she nows the corpse's identity. One woman claims the man with no hands is the father of her child; another woman swears that he is her son.

Toby's search leads him from a child stolen by gypsies in the First World War, to a faded film star who lies for a living, to London gangsters, and on to a notorious member of the British Royal Family.

With danger and death at every turn, he faces his final battle for survival on board a sinking ship in the North Sea.

Can Toby find the truth? Is the man with no hands a hero or a traitor?

Imposter is another enthralling World War II mystery. If you like dark secrets, mysterious happenings at Buckingham Palace, and a sweet touch of last-chance romance, then you'll be delighted by Eileen Enwright Hodgetts' new tale of mystery and intrigue on the home-front.

Amazon USA Kindle Link

Audible Link

Air raid

Solicitor Toby Whitby's new client cannot remember his real name and calls himself Buddy. He was evacuated to Canada at the beginning of World War Two carrying luggage belonging to a boy named Edward Powley. When he returns twelve years later he discovers that Edward Powley is the name of another boy; a boy who did not go to Canada. When Buddy is accused of murdering his own mother and stowing away on the boat to Canada, Toby must discover what really happened on the night the ship sailed and Buddy's house was bombed by the Luftwaffe. As Toby digs into the past a new threat emerges and once again Toby finds himself at the center of a plot to prevent the Queen's coronation.

Amazon USA Kindle Link

Audible Link